ERIC

DEVOTED BROTHERS BOOK ONE

SIÂN UPTON

*For **The Committee.***
You were worth the wait, besties.

Contents

Chapter One

CARYS

Those. Jerks.

Carys had agreed to spending the week at this all-inclusive resort because her friends had not only insisted, but they had also paid her way. It was their "last hurrah" before she finished her master's degree. It was also the only spring break trip she had ever agreed to, and frankly, she was regretting it.

Because she was sitting alone at the bar, while some guy she might have changed diapers on in middle school tried to pick her up. *Eeew.* If there was going to be an age gap, she preferred an older man. One with enough facial hair to have a five o'clock shadow instead of residual hormone induced acne.

She was going to torture her friends when she found them until they felt the agony she herself was currently wallowing in.

What good was it getting sloshed in Cancun alone?

"There you are," a smooth voice said from behind her.

Carys's heart rate galloped away without her as his simple words wrapped around her like armor, racing down the beautiful sand and surf she and her friends had sunbathed on all day; just from the feel of the steady rhythm she could feel pressed against her back. A strong, toned chest radiating warmth up her spine and right into her cheeks, with an equally strong heart rate pounding into her backside like a drum. The immediate physical reaction to him was exhilarating—and a touch frightening.

"Sorry I'm late, sweetheart," he continued, laying a soft kiss on her exposed, sun kissed shoulder as his hands gently rubbed her biceps like he'd done it his whole life. Carys leaned back into him, too nervous—and twitterpated—to look back and make eye contact. Instead, she crossed one arm over her body to place her hand on top of his where it was currently branding her in the most delicious way.

Her voice came out breathy when she replied, "That's okay. I know you were tired after snorkeling earlier."

The guy beside her narrowed his eyes as he took in the solid wall of man behind her—he certainly *felt* solid—and the way he casually took ownership of her. "You could have just said you were taken," he mumbled as he grabbed his drink off the bar and slid off the stool next to her. "What a bitch."

"Hey," the stranger said low from behind her, the rich baritone of his voice sending goosebumps over her flesh and heat into her belly. "That's no way to talk to a lady. She doesn't owe you her time or an explanation. Learn to take a hint."

"Whatever, asshole. Bar is fresh out of crayons," he retorted, stomping away like an overgrown toddler.

"Crayons?" Carys said, momentarily dulling the heat her mystery man had infused through his touch. Although not as much as the feel of his hands slowly dropping down her arms until he released her. A cold shiver ran down her back as he put distance between them.

It was supposed to be hot in Mexico, yet she was suddenly freezing.

"It's probably the haircut," he said, moving around her to take the vacated stool. "My guess is Playboy over there has a Marine ROTC program at his third-rate university." His tone was playful, as was the smile he gifted her as he sat down. "I'm sorry I touched you without permission. He was laying it on thick, and you were clearly not interested. Seemed the easiest way to get him gone. I don't like guys like that."

"No, I appreciate it," Carys said. "My friends disappeared out on the dance floor, and he swooped right in. I guess I'm not very good at giving a solid brush off."

"It wasn't you, sweetheart. It was him."

"Oh. I figured it was something I did. Or didn't. Do, I mean. You know…to discourage him." Carys blushed profusely. She was almost twenty-five, but her dating had been minimal. She'd been focused on finishing school debt free, which meant constantly trolling for scholarship opportunities and working as much as possible. Talking to men wasn't her forte, especially sexy ones with jawlines that could cut glass.

"My name is Eric, by the way. And I'll leave as soon as you say the word." His tone was honest, his posture casual. She believed him. "I'd offer to shake your hand, but Playboy is over in the corner glaring darts my way with his frat squad."

Carys laughed, turning her head slowly toward the bar so she could see for herself in the mirror. He was right. Frat Boy Ken was in the corner with at least five other guys in similar cargo shorts and overly expensive flip flops, the collars on their Ralph Lauren polo shirts all popped, and sunglasses in various locations other than their faces so you could see how expensive they were. Probably all living off trust funds, given their designer duds.

And the way they had clearly spent hours achieving *just rolled out of bed after a good romp* hair.

Posers.

Not like Eric.

"Carys," she said softly as her eyes swung back to him. She knew her own face matched the amusement on his. His energy was infectious.

And his scent was heavenly.

Down, girl. It's the tequila talking.

"Hi, Carys."

"Hi, Eric."

"Would I be pushing my luck if I asked you to dance?"

She shook her head before tossing back the last of her margarita. The rocks clanked what seemed impossibly loud at the bottom when she slammed it down on the bar top harder than she'd meant to. It had been a long time since she'd danced with a man, and something told her this one was dangerous. He quirked a brow to match his grin. He was waiting for verbal consent, and she *genuinely* appreciated that.

"I'd love to dance," she finally said. "Soon as you explain the crayons comment."

Eric laughed, his chest heaving as he did. He wasn't impossibly bulky, like a body builder or anything. But he was obviously strong and valued fitness. The sound and sight of his joy made her ache. It felt good to make someone laugh, and he had such an authentic laugh too. Carys reminded herself this was a fun week away, not her forever.

Because *Forever* the movie—starring herself and Eric, soundtrack composed by her best friend and musical genius, Vinny—was previewing on the big screen in the back of her mind, and it looked like a winner. Two thumbs up. *And the Oscar goes to* worthy. An instant classic with international exposure. The film of the century…

"It's a bit crowded in here, but the patio area has more room to dance, and it's a little quieter," he said, cutting off her dreamy internal production right as she was choosing the color they would paint their home.

Wow. She really needed to date more, if a few margaritas and a chance encounter could ruin her like this.

"Yeah, I'd like that."

Eric slid off his stool and reached out his hand to her. Carys took it, noting how comforting his touch was. There was no way he would lose her in the crowd. Between his physical strength and size—he had to be at least six feet tall —and the firm way he held her hand, her nerves fell away.

Okay.

The girls ditched her at the bar.

But she was beginning to regret the trip a whole lot less now she was watching Eric's strong backside shift under his clothes as he cut through the crowd with her in tow. Carys shifted her eyes down. *What an ass. How do you even get an ass like that?*

"Enjoying the view?" he asked. Carys's eyes flew up. They'd reached the patio while she was ogling him and he'd turned to bring her to his side, catching her in the act. The easy going, slow smile transforming his face told her he didn't mind.

"It's very nice."

"Thank you."

"So."

"So," he repeated back as he gently pulled her in and started swaying with her. He'd been right about the thinner crowd, and the gentle breeze was refreshing too, after being pressed into the mob inside.

"The crayons?" she prompted.

"Right. Well, you know the kids in kindergarten you can't stop from eating paste, glue, *crayons?*" She nodded, and he continued. "It's basically that, an implication we aren't too bright, and therefore have the same juvenile need to do stupid things, regardless of being told not to. Like trying to gain nutrition from art supplies."

"We? *Are* you a Marine?"

His slow smile pulled a little higher, his eyes warm and hypnotic in the soft light provided by the strings of Edison bulbs crisscrossed above along the pergola they were dancing beneath. "You caught that, huh? Yes, I'm a Marine."

"Have you been in long?"

"About eight years."

"Do you like it?"

"No, I don't like it. I *love* it," he said, his tone full of pride. "I dreamed of being in the military as a boy, and almost joined the Army after high school. A surprise scholarship for swimming changed my course, and since I was already there, I visited with ROTC staff for all the branches available before deciding the Marines was the right fit for me. Best decision I ever made."

"Wow. I changed my major three times before I committed. I can't imagine knowing from childhood exactly what you want to be. I think I wanted to be an Operation champion as a kid. Get paid for playing my favorite board game, you remember?"

"The rubber band in the lower leg was always my downfall," he said. She laughed softly.

"The ankle bone is connected to the knee bone. It definitely took some finesse."

"And it didn't inspire you to become a doctor?" he asked earnestly.

"No, the cadaver lab in my high school anatomy class cured me of that notion. I passed out the second they pulled the sheet back!" She laughed at the recollection as embarrassment washed over her anew, looking over his shoulder as she did because seeing his reaction would be too much. "We didn't even have to cut it open. They borrowed it for a week after a nearby medical school was done doing all the...*stuff* to it." She shuddered at the memory.

"Sometimes we have to fail to find our way," he said.

Carys looked up into his eyes then, taking in more of his features. His skin was tanned olive, though it looked like it wasn't all from the Mexican sun. He was outside a lot, was her guess. His hair was a rich dark brown, with eyes to match. Eyes full of intelligence, perseverance, kindness, and beneath it all a touch of heat that thrilled her. She could date a guy like Eric.

Maybe this could be practice for when she got home.

"Yeah," she responded, a few beats later than was natural. Carys probably should feel awkward, but she didn't.

She was mesmerized.

"Slow!" a man said as he came up alongside them and clapped a hand on Eric's shoulder, effectively breaking off whatever was heating up between them. Eric blinked before turning his head toward the newcomer.

"What's up, Ruben?"

"I gotta go home, man. Carla called."

Eric scowled at his friend. "Why do you put up with her? She's just doing it for attention."

Ruben placed a hand over his heart with a smile which spoke more than words ever could. "I'm a man in love, Slow. She's my woman."

"Yeah, all right. When are you leaving?"

"Right now. I already called a cab. I made sure to cover my part of the bill for the week. And this," he added as he dug a hand into his pocket and yanked out a plastic card, "is the extra room key."

"You sure, Ruben? This whole R and R was your idea. Sucks you won't get to enjoy it."

"It's fine. Now introduce me to this lovely lady before I have to peace out," Ruben said, turning his full gaze on Carys and taking her completely by surprise.

Eric let out a sigh. "Ruben, this is Carys. Carys, this is Ruben, my idiot best friend and fellow Marine."

"Oh, I see," she said sagely. "He's the crayon eater."

Ruben's eyes widened in surprise a second before he busted out laughing. "I like you, Carys. Keep Slow out of trouble for me, okay?"

"Sure, if you tell me why you call him Slow." She smiled prettily at him.

"Because everything about his game is *slow.* My boy here takes ages to even approach a lady, much less agree to a date or an actual relationship. I've known him a decade, and he's never made it past the dating bit. Hell, even his smile is slow," Ruben teased, his jovial manner bringing a low laugh from Eric. "It's his well-earned nickname."

His smile *was* slow, Carys knew. It was sexy as hell too. You had to earn it, wait for it. It was *worth* the wait. Eric's smile was panty drenching.

"We can't all fall in and out of love like you, jackass," Eric said dryly. Ruben laughed again.

"Better to have loved and lost, man. But hey, I'm not losing this one. Carla's my future." Ruben spoke the last with conviction, his expression emulating his belief she was his forever.

One glance at Eric showed Carys he wasn't as convinced.

"It was lovely to meet you, Ruben."

"You too, Carys." His eyes moved back and forth between her and Eric for a moment, his face lit up like a kid who knew a secret and was debating on telling. "See you around."

Chapter Two

ERIC

Ruben disappeared back into the crowded bar, headed toward the front of the resort. It was just like Carla to take something he wanted from him, but Eric had known his best friend long enough to know he was the personification of the old phrase *we are all fools in love.* He wished Ruben could manage to be a fool over someone who deserved him.

"You're worried about him, aren't you?" Carys said, drawing Eric's eyes back to her.

"Yeah. I don't like his girl. I don't like most of his girls, but this one really has her hooks in deep," Eric said.

"That's unfortunate," she murmured softly.

Eric pulled her in more closely, craving the feel of her body pressed to his. He'd liked having her pressed to him when he first approached at the bar. He'd liked kissing her shoulder and staring down the walking talking pustule who couldn't read a woman if his life depended on it. The wave of bliss he'd felt when Carys agreed to dance with him had quickly morphed into heat.

He was attracted to her.

Eric wanted Carys in a way he'd never wanted any

woman in all his thirty years. She was pretty, sure. Light brown hair, freckles, hazel eyes, and the sweetest dimples when she smiled. More than that, she was natural. Past mascara, he wasn't sure she was wearing any other makeup. Carys had a classic, all-American sweetheart thing going for her, and it was doing crazy things to Eric.

Ruben wasn't lying about his track record with women. He'd had his heart stomped in high school and hadn't had a true girlfriend since. Eric dated. He had a few fellow Marines of the female persuasion over the years he would let off some steam with during long trips, but it was always an exclusive thing between them, not a romance. He didn't want to be like so many in his unit and come home with chlamydia—or worse.

Sometimes he understood the crayon jokes. A bunch of horny Marines could be stupid.

He'd rather move cautiously and live with the moniker "Slow" than spend all his free time dealing with relationship drama and messy breakups down range.

No, thanks.

"Are you hungry? Thirsty?" Eric asked after a few more songs. He held her firmly and danced close the whole time and couldn't have told you if the music had suited or been a faster tempo if he'd wanted to. He was too busy drinking in the way Carys felt and moved in his arms.

"Oh. Yes. I don't think I've eaten a whole meal since breakfast. I was on the beach sunbathing with my friends most of the day, and they wandered off this evening before we had dinner."

Eric didn't see any tan lines on her fully exposed shoulders. The mental image of her laying out on the beach topless had him leaning away from her enough to lead her toward a table with a view of the surf—and hoping she didn't notice or feel the growing bulge in his shorts along the way. He hadn't agreed to Mexico with Ruben so he could have a fling, damn it.

Besides, Carys wasn't *fling* material.

Carys was *wife* material.

Eric had another four-month trip into another sand box coming up, and no time to cultivate a relationship. He would have to settle for enjoying her company while he could.

"How long are you here for?" Eric asked after the server left with their drink orders.

"We got in yesterday, so six more days."

"No kidding. We leave the same day," he said. His signature slow smile took over his face.

"Well then. I can keep an eye on you like I promised your friend." She smiled brightly, both her dimples prominently on display.

"I thought you were on a girl's trip?" he teased.

Carys looked around with her wide hazel eyes, one hand over her brow as if to block the glare of the already set sun. Then she turned back to him with a shrug. "It seems my plans have changed—given I haven't seen either of them in hours."

She was joking. Eric appreciated she could do that. Carys seemed good at rolling with the punches, instead of getting worked up over an unexpected change in plans. Not a lot of women he'd met could do that. Especially not on vacation in a foreign country.

"Since it doesn't look like I'm going to be meeting them, will you tell me about your friends?" he asked.

"Sure. Well, I came here with my best friend and one of her friends. We all get along pretty well, so I didn't mind sharing Vinny."

"Vinny?"

"Her name is Lavender, but she usually goes by Vinny,"

Carys explained. "We grew up next door to each other. After she lost her mom, she would stay over with us a lot while her dad worked. He's a traveling musician. Vinny is now too. Sometimes they get to tour together."

"Sounds like they have a good bond," he said. Carys spoke of Vinny like she was the absolute best, her whole body animated as she spoke of her friend. Eric felt the same way about Ruben. "And your mutual friend?"

"Megan. She's a low key badass with a penchant for mischief and loves to travel. Megan has joined us before on smaller trips and outings, but she's more Vinny's friend. I like her though. She's easy to be around."

"But she's not close to you?"

"No, Vinny is my person. If you get to meet her, you'll understand. As long as I have her, I don't need the drama that sometimes comes when women get catty. I prefer to have a small friend group instead."

"I understand. Better to have enduring, strong relationships with those you let in. Keeps you safe." Even among his fellow Marines, you sometimes got a glory seeker who would plan out all sorts of ways to use you if you weren't careful.

"Exactly."

They chatted casually over dinner, glossing over anything too serious or personal.

Her favorite color was indigo, specifically. Not just any bluish purple tone.

Her favorite flower, daisies.

She preferred salty to sweet.

And somehow the most significant, Carys had one last term before she would graduate with her master's degree, with honors. Carys wasn't any freer than Eric. They both had lives and responsibilities to get back to come Saturday. She had some complex sounding project to complete in order to meet her goal, and he had the Big D to prepare for—deployment.

But they had the next six days.

After dinner, he thought about asking for another dance. One huge, adorable yawn was all it took for him to reconsider. "You look bushed, sweetheart. How about I walk you to your room?"

"Oh, God," she said, her cheeks pinking. "Sorry, I was trying *not* to yawn. I promise you aren't boring. It must be all the time we spent on the beach today."

"The sun can make you sleepy," he agreed. "Come on. I don't have to take you to your door if you don't want me to know your room number, but let me at least get you to the right floor, all right?"

"Yeah, okay. That would be nice, actually."

Eric got out of his seat. He took Carys's hand and pulled her to a stand beside him before protectively draping his arm over her shoulder, tucking her firmly to his side. "Let's go, Sleeping Beauty."

She laughed sleepily beside him as he guided her back into the bar area. Her arms came around his middle with what felt like familiarity right as frat boy looked up from where he was currently situated with his Hugo Boss model wannabes. Frat boy scowled. Eric pulled Carys in closer and tried not to let the way her hand was lazily caressing his stomach over his shirt go straight to his dick.

He couldn't fight the smug smile on his face though.

"It's down here," Carys said when the elevator opened on her floor.

"If it's all right with you, I'll hold the elevator until you're in," he said. She seemed fine with him knowing which room was hers, but she was also dead on her feet. It was better for him to keep his distance, before desire took over common decency.

"Okay," she said, stepping off the elevator. Carys hesitated, then turned to face him. "Will I see you tomorrow?"

"If you want to."

"I do."

"Breakfast?"

"I'm not too early a riser, but let's say eight. Will you pick me up at my door and meet my friends?"

"I can do both, sweetheart. Goodnight."

"Night," she said, a sleepy smile and finger wave adding to her charm.

Eric watched from the elevator door as Carys walked two doors down and pulled out her key. Soon as he heard the door click open, he leaned forward off the elevator door jam, ready to go to his own room soon as she disappeared inside.

He was not prepared for the quiet gasp he heard before her door gently closed again. Eric looked up to see a suddenly wide awake Carys staring at her closed door, slack jawed. Her shoulders started shaking.

With laughter. Carys was quivering with the effort to keep herself together.

"Everything okay?" he called out quietly, fully stepping into the hall and releasing the elevator. She turned to look at him, shock and humor evident where sleep had prevailed seconds ago.

"Megan!" she whisper shouted as she quickly moved back to him. She came to a stop close enough to grab his shirt and give him a jerky shake. "Megan is in there with a guy!"

Eric let out a low chuckle.

"Shit. I really want my toothbrush," she said.

"Do you think she saw you?"

"No way. He had her front pressed against the sliding glass door while he—"

Eric put a finger over her soft, pillowy lips. "Please don't finish that sentence."

Carys burst into a fit of exhausted giggles. "Oh my god!"

"Come on, sweetheart. Ruben always has housekeeping change his sheets daily. Why don't you take his bed?"

"Yeah?"

Eric shrugged. "You could go back to your room."

She bit her lip. "My toothbrush."

"We haven't touched the complimentary ones the resort provided in the mini bar." It would cost him eight bucks for the convenience, but Eric already knew he'd pay a whole lot more for a few extra minutes with Carys.

"Okay," she said, taking his hand.

Well, that was easy.

He led her in the opposite direction of her own room, down the hall and to the left, where the ocean facing rooms were. It made no difference to Eric, but Ruben liked to enjoy the finer things when they weren't deployed. Right now, he was grateful for the extra expense.

A dozen dirty fantasies ran through his head as he readied his key card, all featuring the woman holding his hand under the moon out on the balcony, the ocean breeze making her hair dance around her face as she gazed across the water. Preferably in something sexy. Or completely nude.

Eric discretely adjusted himself with his second hand as they came upon his door. He opened it quickly and stepped back so Carys could go in first. As if to torture him, she immediately walked over to the open balcony door and peered out.

"Oh, wow." She sighed.

Eric knew he'd need a cold shower before he could climb into his own bed alone, where he would likely dream of the goddess before him.

Chapter Three

CARYS

The sound of the surf slowly permeated her groggy mind. She must have left the window open. Carys burrowed down into her bed, determined to sleep a little longer. She took in a deep, relaxing breath—but it wasn't freshly laundered linens or even the ocean air she smelled. It was Eric. She didn't know how she knew; she just did. He didn't smell like a thing she could name. It was a combination of his aftershave, body wash, deodorant, and pure, male musk.

Her body warmed all over, her core throbbing greedily. How long had it been since she'd had sex? Hell, even with herself?

A long time. She felt a soft moan escape her lips unbidden. *Get ahold of yourself before you wake the girls.*

Still, the memory of Eric seemed wrapped around her, and despite pulling the blankets over her head, she couldn't escape him or the pent-up need burning through her elicited from the memory of his scent. She slowly moved a hand down into her panties, her breath hitching as her first two fingers grazed her clit.

Carys shuddered, holding back another moan. *Holy shit. I've never woken up this wet before.* Slowly, and with great deliberation, she swept her fingers down and back up over and over until there was enough slip where she needed it. She tried not to squirm overly much or breathe too heavily and give herself away as her fingers circled her nub.

The back of her eyelids showed a private highlight reel from last night. Eric coming to her rescue. Eric leading her around the dance floor. Eric's slow smile across the dinner table, and his impossibly deep voice. Carys bit the inside of her cheek hard enough for the metallic tang of blood to register, keeping herself silent as she soaked her own thighs with her release.

It took a minute. Maybe.

He wasn't even touching her, and he was already a stronger aphrodisiac than all her past partners put together.

Her body slowly relaxed and she removed her hand. Then she flitted back into dreamland.

————

Eric

She'd said his name.

As she came.

Carys gave herself a release on the bed beside him—while whispering his name like a sultry goddess—and then fell back asleep. Did she realize where she was? Or that he was awake?

He'd been struggling to sleep with her so close anyway, but now he knew he was definitely not sleeping tonight. The way his painfully hard dick was tenting the sheets was proof enough. He'd almost lost control hearing her soft little sounds from under the cover; watching her form in the early haze of dawn slowly undulating until she crested.

Fuck. Fuck. Fuck!

It was the hottest damn thing he'd ever seen, and he was positive she wasn't awake enough to know she was curled up in the same room as him, wearing one of his extra T-shirts since the strapless little number she'd been wearing last night wasn't suitable to sleep in. Eric couldn't keep Carys, but if he was going to keep any woman, he'd want it to be her. He watched her in silence as the sun rose, casting a warm glow across the room through the thin, gauze like curtains.

He'd left the balcony door open because the air felt so good last night, and he tended to sleep hot. But it was nothing compared to *her.* An hour or so passed, and still he watched her. When Carys's breathing lightened, he knew she would soon wake. Would she remember what she'd done?

Eric slipped into the bathroom, shutting the door behind him noiselessly. Then he turned on the shower and climbed in without waiting for it to fully heat up. The cold shower last night had done nothing to help. With the way his balls were threatening to fall off, Eric knew his only hope was the cheap travel sized lotion he'd grabbed off the counter on his way into the shower and some elbow grease.

He'd never hated his own hand so much.

No matter what he did, the lotion didn't smell like her. It certainly didn't feel as silky as he imagined she'd be if he ever got inside her. It was all wrong. Even as he replayed the sight and sound of her orgasming this morning in his mind, Eric was jerking desperately before his body got with the program.

"Jesus, sweetheart. What have you done to me?" he said quietly, followed by some strange noise that couldn't decide if it wanted to be a growl or a groan as he exploded, streaking the shower wall.

There was a release, but no real relief.

"I'm so fucked," he mumbled.

Eric shut off the shower, dried himself harshly, and yanked on the pair of workout shorts he'd had on while he *wasn't* sleeping last night. It was time to face the siren on the other side of the bathroom door.

He opened the door slowly, flicking off the light as he emerged. Eric's brows furrowed when he saw the second bed empty. Her summer dress was still draped across the back of the chair off to the right. Where was she?

"Carys?" he called out hesitantly. *What if she's hurt?* "Carys." This time he said it with more force, tamping down on his nerves so he didn't frighten her. "Sweetheart, where did you go?" By now he had checked both sides of her bed and his. It was a standard double room, albeit a spacious one.

The breeze made the curtain flutter, and he sighed with relief as he caught sight of her out on the balcony. Her toned legs were tan, glowing in what remained of the early morning light. His eyes traveled up to where his T-shirt clung to her curves. He walked across the room and out onto the small patio, stepping up close behind her.

He shouldn't. Eric knew he was already in too deep. Touching her when they were both barely clothed was trouble. He put his hands on her hips anyway, drawing her back from the rail slightly and into his chest.

"Good morning, sweetheart."

"Morning, Slow." She looked over her shoulder at him, her nose wrinkling. "Nope. Can't do it. Good morning, *Eric.*"

He slid his hands around her waist, hugging her as he laughed into the crown of her hair. Carys turned her body enough to relax into him further, her cheek pressed into his chest. "You don't like the name my brothers gave me?"

"I don't know. Does it still fit you? I mean, you brought me back to your room after only knowing me a few hours," she teased.

"To a second, empty bed you slept in all alone, in order to escape breaking up the love fest happening down the hall where all your stuff is." He meant to match her light tone, but it came out a little gruff, tinged with jealousy even he could hear.

She should have been in my bed. Her things should be here too.

"You okay?"

"Yeah," he lied, staring out at the view. "Why do you ask?"

"I thought I heard you on the phone right before I came out here. You sounded upset. But I also heard the shower running, so I guess that doesn't make sense. Why would you be on the phone in the shower?"

"No, I was just…talking to myself."

He could feel her smiling against his chest now. "You were upset with yourself?"

If only you knew, sweetheart.

"Just frustrated, I suppose."

"Because Ruben left." She said it like it was an obvious fact, and for some forsaken reason it bothered him. He hadn't wasted a second thought on his friend once he stepped out of sight last night. Carys occupied every one of his deliberations.

"No," he finally said. *Man up. You will regret it if you don't see where this goes. You're a damn Marine. Tell her.*

Carys turned fully in his arms, wrapping her arms around

his middle again like she had last night as they were leaving the bar downstairs. "No?"

"No. I was thinking of you. Ruben wasn't lying, sweetheart. I'm a slow mover. I'll let you call my mother if you need more than my word." She laughed, and some of the tension bled out of him. "I'm drawn toward you. I can't offer you more than the next five days, but my time is all yours until Saturday—if you'll have me. I'll be all yours."

"All mine," she murmured, looking up to meet his gaze. "I would like that. On one condition."

"Name it."

"No last names. No phone numbers. I don't think I could handle knowing you chose not to call me."

"That's not usually how I operate, sweetheart. Sounds a bit like lying to me." The idea more than bothered him, for reasons he didn't want to name. Never talk to her again? Could he do that?

"You haven't lied to me once. I can tell. You're a Marine, soon to leave on an extended trip abroad for work." *She even makes deployment sound good,* he thought. "You're about thirty, assuming you graduated at the typical age for a bachelors degree and factoring in your service time. I don't need to know your rank or unit or whatever its all called. To me, you're just Eric."

"Carys. I don't know."

"Please." Her whispered plea had its desired effect immediately. Eric pulled her in close again, resting his cheek on the top of her head and let out a heavy sigh.

"Can we renegotiate the phone number thing at the end?"

She shook her head against his body. "It will only distract us both. We have to part ways. There is no use pretending this can be more, and a phone number would be false hope."

She was right, damn it. He'd have to find another way. "Okay. If you're sure."

"I'm sure."

Fuck. Me. I'm not.

"Then let's get your things and head down to breakfast."

"My things?"

"Yeah, sweetheart. I'm moving you in."

She squeezed him tightly, nodding into his chest. "Okay."

Chapter Four

CARYS

She slipped into her room quietly. It was still early, and Carys wasn't sure if anyone was awake yet. A quick shower was a must before she tossed the few odds and ends she'd pulled out of her suitcase yesterday back in and took it with her to Eric's room.

Holy shit, I'm really doing this.

Shock aside, it felt right.

Carys turned the shower on and began stripping out of her dress. When she reached for her panties, her face caught fire. When she finally woke and remembered what had transpired, she'd been relieved Eric was in the shower. Her mind had raced, putting all the pieces in order on the timeline. Did he know she'd woken early and touched herself?

Of course she'd been wrapped in his smell, she was wearing Eric's shirt and sleeping in the same room. He was literally all around her. Last night had been a first on many fronts, including walking in on another couple getting it on, and agreeing to stay with a guy she'd just met.

Not a *guy* guy, either. A *man*. Frat boy last night had been just another guy. Eric was so much more. As she washed up, she thought about the muffled words she'd heard at his bath-room door as she was going to knock, call out a hasty good-bye, and skitter away before she had to face him. With a voice as low as his, it was hard to pick up precise words, but his tone conveyed quiet agony. She was pretty sure he'd said sweetheart—something he'd called her more than her actual name since he first approached her, so she knew the cadence of his voice when he said it—and it was followed by a sound she'd expect from a wounded animal.

Carys had stepped back from the door, lowering her raised fist back to her side. She wasn't as wild as Vinny, but even she knew what a man jerking off in the shower sounded like. So instead of running like the chicken she was, she'd gone out to the balcony and watched the last moments of sunrise. It was so quiet at that hour. A few random people were down on the private beach walking, but it was otherwise completely bare.

There was no music, no laughter. No sounds of glasses sloppily clinking together while the drunk fell deeper into their cups. The early morning calm gave her time and space to think.

Eric had been a gentleman. She knew being in the mili-tary didn't automatically make him "safe" for her. There were no guarantees a man wouldn't turn on you. She'd certainly seen it enough firsthand while trying to keep up with the bums Vinny tended to fall in and out of love with. Her gut told her Eric wasn't like that, and besides, she wasn't alone. Vinny and Megan were here.

Granted, Megan had taken over their room for her own carnal escapades and left Carys without access to her things or her bed last night. *At least not without it being extremely awkward. Don't mind me guys! I'm just gonna hit the hay here in the second bed. Pretend I'm not here.* Or worse, maybe they wouldn't have even noticed she'd gone to bed. She'd seen Megan get toasted enough times to know it was a possibility.

Eric had saved her from a heap of embarrassment last night. And from sleeping in a strapless sundress, which would have made this morning's short walk down the hall look like a full-on, rumpled walk of shame. If she was going to get knowing smirks from strangers, they should at least be justified, damn it.

Out of body parts to wash, she shut off the shower, toweled off, and quicky dressed in a soft halter top that made her curves look sculpted by Michelangelo himself, and a pair of cut off Levi's. Her freshly tanned legs made her smile. After six years of nothing but work and school, it felt good to get some sun.

Carys combed out her hair. The humidity made it do the beach wave thing with a dab of mouse and a shake of her head, and Carys liked the way it looked. A fresh coat of mascara, and she was content with her appearance. Once her toiletries were back in her travel bag, it was time to grab her suitcase.

Her path was blocked by Vinny, who was waiting on the other side of the bathroom door when she opened it. The look she gave Carys was enough to knock her right off her happy little cloud of anticipation. Only an idiot would argue with Vinny when she had murder in her eyes like she did right then.

Carys held up one finger, quietly scooted past her bestie to set her toiletries down on the dresser, then pulled Vinny back into the bathroom with her. She would have preferred a balcony, but their room didn't face the beach, and so only had a giant window with a guard rail. This would have to do.

"Where the hell were you?" Vinny whisper yelled as soon as the door latched behind them.

"*Me?* Vinny, I came back to Megan banging and didn't know what to do. I was exhausted, and neither of you exactly told me *your* plans," she said in a huff.

Vinny deflated a bit. "Sorry. That wasn't fair, and you're right. None of us got in the group message to check in. Which was dumb all the way around."

"You two ditched me at the bar, Vin. Some tool kept trying to drag me into a frat boy pow wow, and if it weren't for a stranger stepping in, I don't know if I would have been safe to come back alone. He was a grade A jackass, and you *jerks* left me to fend for myself. As I suspect I'm the only one who won't be flaunting hickeys at breakfast, I think you should cool it."

"I'm glad she stepped in."

"He."

"He, who?"

"His name is Eric."

"*Who is Eric?*" Vinny nearly squeaked in exasperation.

"The man who stepped in. We danced and had dinner. His roommate for the trip came and said goodbye while we were dancing; he had to leave early. So, when Eric walked me back and I opened the door to a *Good Girls Gone Wild* live demo, he offered the extra bed in his room."

"Carys. That sounds totally scripted."

"Where were you all night, Vinny?" Carys asked sweetly. Vinny narrowed her eyes.

"Fine, you've made your point. Although I wasn't in a strange man's *room.*"

"Fucking in the cabanas beachside isn't really all that different, Vin." Carys knew by the blush exploding over her friend's face she'd guessed correctly.

"Change of topic then," Vinny said. "What is the plan for today?"

Now it was Carys's turn to blush. "Ah, well…I'm going to take a page from your book, Vin. I'm taking my stuff down to Eric's room, and then we are going down to breakfast. Would you like to join us? I think you'll like him."

Vinny's mouth hung open, her violet eyes wider than Carys had ever seen—including when Vinny met her rock idol and got to jam with him. "I'm sorry, you're *what now?*"

"I'm having a fling with a hot Marine."

"Do you have condoms?"

Carys laughed. "If he doesn't, I'm sure we can get some."

Vinny shook her head. "No, they always sell the shitty ones at these resorts. I brought a whole bunch, just in case. What size is he? I'll hook you up."

"Vinny!"

"What?"

"I don't know what size he is," she hissed, "I slept on the second bed. *Alone.*"

"Geez. You really are a Pollyanna." Vinny rolled her eyes.

"Wait, you aren't mad at me?"

"No, why would I be? I drug you down here to have a good time before you stop killing yourself with school and work and switch to only killing yourself with work. You don't have any fun, Carys. You could tell me you were off getting your brains fucked out by one of the Fallen—Lucifer himself, even—and I'd still hand you the best of my rubber stash and send you on your way."

"You hang out with too many musicians, Vin. I think you need a career change."

Vinny laughed. "Not a chance. Music is my soul."

"I know, and it's the best part about you." Carys sighed. "I'm sorry I'm bailing on our girl's week."

"Don't be. You were the last to do so. I stumbled in from the beach at 3 AM, right as Megan's paramour was wobbling out with his shirt over his shoulder and his jeans still unzipped, *commando.* I did not need to know the carpet matches his drapes. Or that he's got a Jacob's ladder." She smirked, and Carys burst into giggles.

"Okay. Breakfast, then? If you hate him, I'll come back," Carys insisted.

"I won't hate him. You have better guydar than I do."

"That's because yours is set to *guydar* instead of *mandar.* Switch your settings and find a keeper, Vinny. You're worth it."

"Oh, I know I am," she said coyly. "But right now, I'm all for variety and fun. Love'm and leave'm. I'm a traveling musician, Carys. That isn't going to fly with a manly man who wants his woman home every night to *make love* missionary style."

"Not all men are like that, you know."

"And when the right one comes along, I'll be ready for him. Until then, get your ass out of *our* room and down to your own. You need this, even if you won't admit it."

Carys pulled her bestie in for a tight hug. They'd been through everything together, and despite having completely different ideals on what a good life meant on most fronts, Vinny was still her person. Now and forever.

"Thank you for this, Vin."

"Yeah, yeah. Let's get you laid."

Chapter Five

CARYS

With Vinny's blessing, Carys was more excited than she thought she'd be rolling her suitcase down the hall to Eric's door. He'd given her the extra key Ruben had handed over last night, and butterflies erupted in her stomach as she unlocked the door and pushed it open. He was sitting on the edge of his bed waiting. By the time she'd swung the door all the way open, he was there to hold it and take her suitcase from her.

"You were fast."

"You sound both surprised and relieved."

"I am." His beautiful slow smile appeared, prompting Carys to hustle inside and see where it would lead now things between them had changed. "Let's get you settled in."

"Sure," she said, hiding her disappointment. "Where is the luggage rack?"

Eric rolled the suitcase over to the second bed and lifted it like it weighed nothing, plopping in onto the mattress. "Right here," he said, turning toward the dresser across from the foot of the bed and opening the empty drawers.

"People don't use hotel dressers," she said. "Come on."

"I do," he said. "If I'm staying more than two nights, I empty my bags and make myself at home. I've lived out of a footlocker or duffel enough of my life to appreciate a dresser."

"I never thought of it that way," she said honestly. "Your job makes a lot of simple things feel like luxuries, doesn't it?"

"Sometimes, yeah."

Carys opened her suitcase and unpacked it into the dresser. Eric took her toiletries bag and set it in the bathroom for her, then stowed her suitcase in the closet next to his own once she was finished. He was right, it did feel different. More permanent. Like a trial run for something bigger.

Except this expires on Saturday, she reminded herself.

"Let's feed you," Eric said, taking her hand. "Will Vinny be joining us?"

"I believe so. If she didn't fall back asleep the moment I was out the door. She's used to long nights and sleeping in."

"I bet she'll make an exception for her best friend," he said as they walked down the hall toward the elevator.

Vinny was coming out of the other room as Eric pressed the call button. She saw their joined hands and smiled with satisfaction.

"Behave," Carys whispered in her ear as Vinny joined them.

"Would this be Megan or Vinny?" Eric asked.

Vinny held out her hand and said, "Hi, I'm Lavender. Most people call me Vinny. Nice to meet you, Eric."

He took her hand and must have nailed the shake because Vinny smirked. She appreciated a man with a solid handshake, firm but not bone crushing. She was always saying you could tell a lot about a man based on his handshake.

Carys had no idea what she was talking about, but if it

were true, she thought Vinny should shake a guy's hand before she hopped in bed with him. Might save them both a lot of trouble if she implemented it into her dating life as a sort of creep detector.

The bell dinged, and the doors to the elevator opened. Vinny went to the back corner, and Eric hit the ground floor button after they followed her in. They no sooner felt the shift of the box downward before Vinny tapped out a soft beat and hummed the melody of whatever song was stuck in her head.

"Change the World, Eric Clapton," Eric said.

"Astute. Very good."

"Did I just pass some sort of test?" Eric jested.

"Yes," Vinny and Carys said together.

"Vinny is a professional musician," Carys said. "And all-around music fanatic. She's got a great following on social media, especially her ArtBeat account."

"That's the one dedicated to all forms of creative expression, isn't it?" he asked Vinny.

"Yeah, I was one of the early sign ups when it first launched. By the time it was a household name, I already had half a million followers."

"Impressive," he said, his eyebrows rising. "What do you post?"

"Depends on the day. Once a week I post a video with my personal rendition of a song, old or new. Whatever I'm vibing with, really. I do *song in my head* posts, stuff about events I've performed. I don't keep a calendar of where to find me anymore because I had a few bad experiences that ended in restraining orders, but a day or two after I leave, I like to put up shout outs and pictures about the scene in the area, thank the crowd. That sort of thing. It's more about celebrating music and how it impacts my life than promotion," she gushed out. Carys giggled. She loved seeing Vinny's passion come out. "Sorry, that's probably TMI."

"I love music, but I'm no musician," Eric mused. "I don't mind at all."

The doors opened, and they stepped out.

Carys's insides were jumping all over. She could tell Vinny approved of Eric already, and even if this was only a fling, it meant a lot to her.

Breakfast was a blur of conversation and laughter. They kept everything light. Carys had told Vinny the conditions of their dalliance, and Vinny respectfully kept away from topics that would make things too personal, like where they were from. Eric joined them with a mimosa, and they toasted to chance encounters, forced vacations with friends who bail on you, and humor. At the end of it, Vinny hugged Carys, charismatically saluted Eric, and went on her way.

"I bet she's got an interesting story," Eric said as they watched her leave the dining area.

"Oh, she does. Like all musicians, it's fraught with loss, self-destruction, and rebirth. Vinny isn't afraid to feel. It's all part of the journey to her, a source of inspiration. I'm just glad she's smart enough not to fall into the ugly side of the business, where addicts are made and souls are lost."

"She's a little like Ruben in that way," he mused. "He barrels into things full tilt, convinced the possibilities are worth the pain of failure. Especially with women."

Carys laughed. "I hope Carla eventually proves herself worthwhile. He seems like he's on the level."

"He is. She's not. Ruben doesn't know I know, but he bought a ring for her."

Carys didn't say anything. Eric had made it clear he wanted better for his brother in arms, and it wasn't her place anyway.

They finished their drinks and headed back up to his room. *Our room.*

"What do you want to do today?" Eric asked her once they were inside.

"I don't know. There is a Mayan ruins trip tomorrow I signed up for, but I thought I was going to be at Vinny's mercy, so I didn't plan much for myself. Now I'm at your mercy. What do you have in mind?"

The heat in his eyes as he drank her in made Carys tingle all over. "I can think of a few things."

His low, rumbling words rolled right into her belly, crashing like a thunderstorm and causing a flash flood in her panties.

"Keep looking at me like that, sweetheart, and we won't be leaving this room."

Oh. God. Yes, please.

She walked over to him, hoping it looked sexy because her legs were trembling like a newborn colt. She hadn't packed fancy lace undergarments or padded bras to force her C cups up to her chin. What he saw was what he would get, and by the way he was admiring her, she could tell he was more than a little interested.

It gave her confidence.

"Sit down," she said softly. He obeyed, grabbing onto her hips and pulling her along as he took a step back and sat down on the end of the bed. His hands wandered up under her shirt, warm and gentle against her midriff. With a boldness she'd never possessed before, she straddled his lap as his hands continued to roam her body. "Kiss me, Eric."

His hands slowly moved up her body, taking her top with them. He paused for consent when he reached her bust, making eye contact. She nodded. Eric pulled her shirt up over her head and tossed it to the side, groaning in what sounded like approval when he saw she'd skipped a bra today. She pulled his shirt off too, desperate to feel his flesh pressed to hers.

Eric took her face in his hands and kissed her. It was slow and languorous, exploratory. His lips were softer than she'd thought they'd be, and she moaned in appreciation. Carys enjoyed the time he was taking in mapping her out with his own mouth, learning her before sweeping his tongue along her bottom lip and nipping it.

She opened her mouth and let him in, enamored with the way he began all over again, learning the feel of her tongue same as he had her lips. Without realizing it, she'd been grinding her hips against his erection. As amazing as his tongue felt caressing hers, she needed more. A desperate whimper escaped her throat as she ground down harder on his lap, with intention now.

Eric broke their kiss enough to speak. "Do you want it right now, sweetheart?"

She nodded her head and tried to kiss him again, but he still had her face in his hands, and he stopped her.

"Carys. I need you to say the words, sweetheart. There is no turning back once we go there." His voice emulated the same lust and need she felt.

"Yes, please," she murmured.

"Fuck, Carys. You and your *please.*" Eric kissed her hard, nipping at her bottom lip harder this time before pulling back. "You are going to be the death of me."

In response, Carys reached down and unbuttoned her pants. They'd already set all their ground rules while she was unpacking. All that was left was to give in to the pleasure. She nipped and sucked his bottom lip as she wiggled out of her shorts, taking her panties off with them.

"Eric. Please." She watched with awe and satisfaction as his restraint broke.

Eric leaned back, taking her naked body with him. Carys's hands were already undoing his pants. He rolled so her back was to the mattress, and she began shoving his pants down his thick, muscular thighs.

"Anything you want, sweetheart."

"I want your pants off," she said desperately. They'd gotten stuck around his knees, and she could no longer reach to push them lower. His chuckle reverberated in his chest, making her nipples ache beneath him. *He's so damn sexy.*

He kicked his pants off and settled between her legs, his shaft pressed against her folds. Eric let out a groan as he slid up and down her slit. Everything tingled. Carys's hips canted without her consent, catching his tip at her opening. He stopped.

"Please," she whimpered. "It's too much, Eric. So much sensation. I need you inside me."

His mouth sealed over hers, his tongue taking her mouth and distracting her as he pulled his hips away for a moment, driving her completely blind with desire. When he settled back against her, he didn't hesitate in giving her what she'd asked for. Eric's cock lined up with her soaking wet entrance and pushed inside.

Finally.

Carys met him, stroke for stroke, rotating and undulating her hips. He broke their kiss and sat up, locking eyes with her.

"I need to watch you come on my cock, sweetheart."

She nodded her consent through her delirium, continuing to watch his expression as his gaze wandered from where they were joined and back, to her face. He moved one of her legs from where she'd wrapped it around his middle up over his shoulder, slowing his pace enough to keep from breaking them apart completely. When he leaned into the new position, she let out a moan. He was deeper, and the angle targeted her G spot better. Carys arched her back and sunk her fingers into him wherever she could reach.

"Eric."

"Look at me, sweetheart. Let me see how beautiful you are when you come."

Maybe it was the way he said it, like he'd die if she didn't hold his eyes with her own. Maybe it was the genuine emotion she found within the warmth of his brown eyes. Or the way he made her feel like she was the only thing that mattered. Carys looked up at him and pleaded.

Every look, every touch was a silent *please,* until she heard her own voice begging as her walls tightened around him. Without losing pace, he shifted her second leg over his other shoulder and kept going. She lost it.

If he was deep before, it was skimming the surface compared to now. Carys exploded around him, her own pleasure amplified by the way he looked at her as she came. He made her feel like a goddess, *his* goddess.

"Please," she whispered again. He slammed into her a few more times before he stilled, his body shuddering above her as he found his own release. She rolled into him as he did, surprising them both when her walls tightened and she came again along with him.

"That damn *please,* sweetheart," he said as he collapsed onto one elbow, still inside her. "It's a weapon."

She smiled at him, suddenly feeling shy. No man had ever made her feel in control during sex before. It was both empowering and mystifying. "I promise only to use it for good."

He settled more onto his side, pulling her along so they wouldn't separate. "You are so much better than I imagined."

"You mean during your shower this morning," she said. Her eyes went wide, and she felt her face flush scarlet. He looked down on her with amusement.

"Figured me out, did you?" She buried her face in his chest, but he lifted her face back up by the chin and waited for her to look at him again before he spoke. "It's okay. I was awake most of the night, trying to keep myself in my own bed."

Oh, God. He knew.

"You were whimpering in your sleep, sweetheart. You said my name as you touched yourself. I'm only a man, Carys. Knowing you wanted me even subconsciously was making me crazy, but I would never make a move without your consent. The shower was supposed to help me remain a gentleman," he confessed.

"I'm glad it didn't work."

Chapter Six

CARYS

They spent most of their first day together in bed. Or in the room, at least. It was amazing how many places you could have sex if you put your mind to it. Eric watched Carys, gauging her reaction to every touch, sweet nothing, and position change. *Attentive* didn't quite seem to cover it, but it was the best she could do.

The more he drew her out, the more she wanted him. It was something she'd heard women talk about before, but she'd always bobbed her head along like she understood when she hadn't. Not until Eric. His touch was balm to her neglected heart. His words soothed the wounds left by former lovers.

Carys lost track of how many orgasms she had by the time the sun rose the following day. Eric had woken her at dawn, the curtains parted and the patio door open. The warmth of the new day blossomed before her as he rolled into her from behind, clutching her backside to his broad chest as he drew out her pleasure until she was begging for it.

Eric went on the hiking trip with Carys to the Mayan ruins. It was steep, and the height bothered her more than she thought it would, but Eric had kept her distracted from the drop as they scaled the temple. It was completely worth the view, and the way he told her he knew she'd make it all along, as if she hadn't begged to go back down a dozen times on the way up.

They walked on the beach, ate every meal together—sometimes joined by her friends—and when she kept eyeing an empty cabana one evening down on the sand, he pulled her inside, closed the thin curtains so she wouldn't feel as exposed, and told her to use the magic word.

Please.

It was the only word she needed around him.

Friday night, he asked again if she would reconsider phone numbers, but she shook her head, repeating the reasons it wasn't a good idea. "What about something else, then?"

"No last names, no numbers. You agreed."

"I'm an idiot for agreeing."

She laughed, but didn't give in. Didn't tell him she agreed but was too terrified the memory of their week together would be ruined when he stopped calling and texting. When he got busy or bored. He didn't seem the type, but why take unnecessary chances.

Carys had worked so hard on her degree, and she wasn't willing to entertain the heartache he could deliver—and the slip in focus it would create—in her regular, boring life. *Carys in Mexico* turned out to be Eric's Aphrodite, but *Carys at Home* was nothing special, and this was how she wanted him to remember her.

She thought he'd let it go, until she woke in the middle of the night to the sound of the door closing. Carys looked up so see Eric setting down some papers in one of his top drawers before crawling back into bed with her.

"Sorry, sweetheart. I didn't mean to wake you."

"It's okay. Where did you go?"

"Down to the front desk. I had a few questions and wanted to settle them while you were resting, so I wouldn't miss a moment with you before we leave in the morning."

He wasn't lying, but there was something not sitting right with his explanation. She thought about asking him, but the feel of his erection against her ass worked like a tonic on her mind. Instead of asking what he wasn't telling her, she whimpered into the darkness, *"Please."*

———

"COME HERE, sweetheart. I want to talk to you before my airport shuttle gets here."

Carys followed Eric across the empty bar to a tall table in the back corner, where they wouldn't be interrupted. She'd dropped her stuff with Megan and Vinny in the other room since their flight was later than his and they would be on a later shuttle. But Eric's things were all packed, his huge duffle a glaring reminder to her it was over.

He dropped it on the floor and pulled out the tall bar chair for her. She sat down, and he sat beside her. Taking up her hands in his on the table he looked her in the eyes and began to speak.

"I know you feel this, Carys. There is no way I'm alone here."

"No," she said softly, her voice choked with emotion. "You aren't alone, Eric."

He nodded. "No phone numbers, no last names. I'm a man of my word, sweetheart. But I also think I'll regret this the rest of my life if I leave it at that." He let out a shaky breath and squeezed her hands.

"You're scared, aren't you," she said, understanding him because she felt the same.

"Fucking terrified. But I took a chance asking for a week, and you said yes. So now I'm asking for another week."

"Eric—"

"Please, sweetheart."

Carys closed her mouth and nodded. She would hear him out. It was the least she could do, after all he'd given her.

"I know we both have to get back to reality," he continued. "And you're right, we both need to focus. Consider this a graduation gift if it makes you feel better."

He dropped one of her hands and reached down for a bag, pulling out a thick envelope. She watched as he slid it across the table toward her. "One week, sweetheart. If you don't show, I'll know you have moved on, and I will accept it. If you *do* show, I'll take it as consent to pursue a future with you."

Her breath hitched. "You...want that? With me?"

He nodded. "Yeah. I want that."

Carys took the envelope and opened it up. Inside was a wad of cash, and a folded up something or other. She took out the papers—no sense flashing that much cash even if they were alone—and unfolded it. "This is for five months from now."

"Yes."

"How did you..."

"I got lucky. Someone had canceled online right before I came down to the desk last night, so I took the only room available. I remember being tight for money in school, so the money is for the plane ticket. And if you don't come, spend it setting up your new life," he said quietly.

She stared at the reservation confirmation. "Your last name and information are blacked out."

"I promised," he said, gifting her one last slow smile before he got serious again. "I *will* be here, sweetheart. Shit happens down range, delays, crazy stuff. Check in without me, enjoy yourself. Meet at this spot," he said, knocking on the tabletop. "Dinner and dancing. We'll pick up where we left off."

"Okay," she said. Carys didn't have to think about it. She knew she would be sitting at this exact spot in five months, come hell or high water. She'd never wanted anything or anyone as much as she wanted to take a chance on Eric—not even her education.

He checked his watch and stood up. Carys moved to stand too, but he held out his hand to still her. "No," he said. "Let me leave you right here, so when I'm miserable as fuck overseas, I can imagine you here, waiting for me. Please."

The thought made her heart ache so deeply, she knew she'd cry if she spoke, so Carys nodded instead. Eric leaned in, taking her face in his warm palms and kissed her goodbye. It was sweet, filled with promises and a few tears she couldn't hold back.

Eric stepped back too early, watching her with sorrow filled eyes as he shouldered his bag and nodded.

"Take care of yourself, Eric. *Please.*"

"You know I can't say no when you ask nicely, sweetheart."

She watched as he slowly backed across the room, smiling reassuringly at her until he had no choice but to vanish from sight.

Carys finally let out the sob she'd been holding back.

———

"WOW."

"Yeah," Carys managed through her tears.

"Carys. He's in love with you," Vinny said.

"Don't be silly. He just wants to see me again," she insisted.

"No, babe. Guys who want to see you again shout back an *if you're ever in town again, look me up.* They do not book the honeymoon suite at an all-inclusive resort in advance."

"The *what?"* she cried.

"Check the booking sheet he gave you," Vinny said smugly. A little too smugly.

Carys yanked the paper out of her purse and looked again. "Oh my god. He said he got lucky. He said it was a cancelation, so he took it because it was the only room available."

"Well then someone else's shattered relationship is your gain," Vinny said.

"Please stow all personal belongings for takeoff," the flight attendant said through her too bright smile as she passed.

Carys quickly refolded the papers, crammed them back into her purse and shoved it under the seat. The strap was wrapped around her ankle because the thousand dollars cash Eric had given her was also in her purse. One grand. *Cash.* She had no idea how he got so much money together, unless he'd been planning for days and had been hitting the ATM every time she hit the bathroom to get around the daily withdrawal limits.

That's probably exactly what he did, she thought. *Eric must have been thinking about it from the moment I laid down stipulations on our time together.*

The plane began to taxi away from the gate as the flight attendants went through their safety spiel. Carys mostly tuned it out, her mind hyper focused in one direction. How was she going to wait five months to tell Eric he was crazy. That this was all crazy, and she was obviously as crazy as he is.

"You're really squirmy," Vinny said from beside her as the plane leveled off. "Are you okay?"

"Yeah, I'm fine. It's probably nerves or something. I'm just uncomfortable."

"Uncomfortable how?" Vinny asked. Carys leaned in and explained to her best friend. "Sounds like your amazing week in Mexico filled with daquiris and sex landed you with a UTI."

"A what?"

"I think you have a bladder infection," she elaborated. "No worries. It's common, especially after tons of hot sex," she said, a little too loudly. The grandpa next to Carys grinned over at her from the aisle seat. His seatmate—and from the looks of it, his wife—smacked him in the chest until he turned forward again. But he still smiled.

"Holy shit, Vin! Talk a little louder will you!"

"Sorry," she said, not looking sorry at all.

"Ugh."

Vinny leaned in, speaking at a blessedly appropriate volume this time. "Just go see County Health when you get back, like you do for your birth control. It's no big deal, Carys. Happens to the best of us."

Oh, goodie. Every person's favorite place. County health. Carys appreciated the free birth control, but she couldn't wait for a good paying job with benefits, so she could go see an actual doctor again. She'd aged out of her mother's insurance plan before graduating, and she missed her old practitioner.

Of course, if she went to Mexico in five months, she'd likely need a new doctor anyway. *When I go to Mexico in five months.* She thought about what Eric had said— *If you* do *show, I'll take it as consent to pursue a future with you*—and smiled for the first time since he'd slipped away.

Okay.

One last visit to County Health.

Chapter Seven

CARYS

She looked at the reservation confirmation page again, taking in the details that weren't blacked out. His first name popped out at her, along with the words Honeymoon Suite. If he didn't show, at least she'd have an extra-large, jetted tub to drown her sorrows in. Vinny thought Eric was in love with Carys, and the envelope full of cash along with the expensive suite certainly made the idea sound more possible. Still, she struggled to believe a man like Eric would want more with a simple woman like her.

Carys slowly read the paper over a second time before she began to fold it back up to put in the empty envelope—she had deposited the cash as soon as the bank had opened after her return—when a line at the bottom of the page caught her eye. The font was smaller than the rest, so she hadn't really read it before when she scanned the page. Now she wondered how she'd ever missed it.

A copy of this reservation has been emailed to Crayon-Lover@mailwarrior.net. *Please send all reservation inquiries to our customer service team through the portal link at the bottom of the confirmation message. Thank you!*

"Holy shit," she murmured. "He didn't black out his email address."

She had said no last names and no numbers. Had Eric left it there on purpose? Or had he missed it while he was taking the felt tip marker to her copy? He'd even photocopied the page he'd taken the marker to, so there was no chance she could decipher the printer ink through the marker on a light board. What were the chances a man that thorough *forgot* to cover up his email address?

Her fingers trembled as she ran them gingerly over the maybe on purpose contact point he'd failed to conceal. Her insides fluttered as a hopeful smile softly lifted her cheeks. She'd missed Eric so badly since he walked out of the bar, more than she'd understood was possible before he came into her life.

Does it matter if it was intentional? It's here, in black and white. There are so many things I wish I could tell him. So many questions that pop in my head when I should be paying attention in class, answers I'm desperate for him to provide. Do I even care, so long as I don't have to wait almost half a year to tell him our time together was life altering in all the right ways?

Carys reached across her bed to her night stand where her laptop sat. After unplugging the power cord, she hauled it back to her lap and flipped it open. The only thing that mattered to *her* was she no longer had to live with the self-inflicted regret of being cut off from *him*.

To: CrayonLover@mailwarrior.net
From: ByAnyOtherName@Eden.com
Subject: Please
Hello, Eric.
I hope you are taking care of yourself like you promised

me you would. Have you left yet? Wherever you are in the world, a piece of me has gone with you.

My classes are going well, but I find my mind drifting to white sandy beaches and a handsome Marine I dreamt up when I should be focused on the lectures. It feels too wonderful to have been real. Then I look at the paper you gave me again and I know that while you *are* a dream, you *aren't* a fantasy.

Please, Eric. Answer me.

Yours,

Carys

P.S. Your email was at the bottom of the reservation page. I hope you don't mind me using it.

There. Maybe he would answer her, maybe not. Maybe he couldn't wherever he was right now. But she'd reached out, which was more than he could do given her rules.

———

Eric

"Who is *By Any Other Name?*" Ruben asked, looking down at the new email notification on Eric's tablet screen.

"Who?"

"That's what I'm asking. Sounds like a woman," he said with a grin.

"Give me that," Eric said dryly, swiping the tablet from Ruben's hands soon as he'd lifted it from Eric's footlocker. "You aren't checking *my* email, Ruben."

"So it *is* a woman!"

"I don't know; I haven't opened it yet." If he wasn't so jet lagged, Eric might have taken a cheap shot at his best friend.

As it was, he was grateful he'd snagged the tablet before Ruben could unlock it and read the message aloud.

Because of course Ruben knew his password, no matter how many times Eric changed it. He never told Ruben it had changed, yet somehow the guy always knew exactly what it was.

New message from ByAnyOtherName@Eden.com
Subject: Please

Eric's heart started working overtime in his chest. It couldn't be *her,* but nobody else would know the impact that one little word had over him. *Please.*

"Take care of yourself, Eric. Please."

"You know I can't say no when you ask nicely, sweetheart."

The last words they spoke before he forced himself to leave her behind crashed into Eric in a blur of sound and light. He unlocked the screen, almost fumbling the device in his haste to open his email. It *was* Carys.

"Ffffuuuck." He stared at her brief missive in disbelief.

"That a good *fuck,* or more of an *oh, fuck* you got over there?" Ruben butt in, reminding Eric he wasn't alone.

"It's her. Ruben, it's *her.* I forgot to blank out my email address on the reservation and she sent me a message." Eric's voice carried his disbelief.

"Well, *yeah."* Ruben chuckled, like Carys emailing him was the most natural thing in the world. "Why are you surprised?'

"Why *aren't* you surprised? She said no contact."

"Not because she didn't want it," he pressed.

"Sure fooled me," Eric quipped back.

He read the message half a dozen times before hitting reply.

To: ByAnyOtherName@Eden.com
From: CrayonLover@mailwarrior.net
Re: Please

Hey, sweetheart.

You know I can't deny you anything when you say that word. Daydreaming is dangerous where I'm currently located, so I promise I'll keep my dreams of you to my sleeping hours and dedicate my waking hours to fulfilling your request. Not a second passes where I don't miss you.

You are my reward, Carys. My reason for making it home in one piece. I promise you, I'm highly motivated to keep my word.

Affectionately,

Eric

"You gonna tell me what she said or just keep on staring at the screen like a grinning idiot?" Ruben asked.

Eric tapped send and closed out his email. "I don't see how it's any of your business, Ruben."

"Come on, I share what Carla writes."

"Yeah, because you can't keep your trap shut," Eric managed to say before breaking into a deep belly laugh. "Not because I ride your ass about it."

Eric stretched out on his surplus bed like a king. He told Carys he wouldn't recklessly daydream and get himself hurt, but he wasn't on the clock right now. Eric closed his eyes and pictured the way Carys had looked in the mornings, with her hair splayed out all over the pillows and tickling his cheek. The way the sunrise made her glow like the goddess she is. By the time he conjured up the way her body perfectly fit against his, he was already on his way into an exceptionally erotic dream.

When he woke an hour later, Eric's first thought was to

check his email again before heading to the chow hall. Sure enough, Carys had responded to his email. Eric's cheeks hurt from smiling so wide as he opened up the thread.

To: CrayonLover@mailwarrior.net
From: ByAnyOtherName@Eden.com
Re: Please
Eric,

I'm so relieved. I thought you might be mad at me for reaching out, even though the no contact was my idea.

Your reward, huh? How flattering. Nobody has ever made me feel as seen as you do, Eric. You spoiled me, and now I'm again just another body, a nameless blur in the higher education hallways. Forgotten as soon as I leave my advisor's office or pass out of the lecture hall and into the hallway.

I think it's fair to say you are my reward too. I get to see you again as soon as this semester passes, and I want to be able to tell you I graduated without a single bump in the road —aside from missing you more than I ever dreamed I could miss anyone. Even Vinny, though I'll deny it to her face.

You have the strangest effect on me. I'm both highly motivated to finish strong and irrationally irritated I have to do it at all when I could be spending time with you. But that isn't real either, is it? Because you are away right now.

Please keep your promise.

Yours,
Carys

Again, Eric read her words over and over before beginning his reply.

To: ByAnyOtherName@Eden.com
From: CrayonLover@mailwarrior.net

Re: Please

Sweetheart,

How could you ever be a nameless anything? I'm sure you are misrepresenting yourself. The idea your peers and educators don't recognize how extraordinary you are is, frankly, ludicrous. Don't you know you light up the room everywhere you go? Even the Mexican sun couldn't outshine you.

I'll keep my promise, but I'm asking one of you too. Make time to have some fun your last term. It's so easy to bury yourself in schoolwork and forget to take time for yourself. Treat yourself to takeout once in a while. Go out to a coffee house just for the ambiance. Be around others like you for the fun of it, not only for a study session. You deserve to get the most out of these last moments of your education, sweetheart. Walk away without regrets.

Affectionately,

Eric

Chapter Eight

CARYS

"I can't believe you emailed him," Vinny gloated.

"I can't believe he emailed back. Immediately too. He's already deployed, Vin. I don't like it." Carys's heart squeezed with the thought. Just the idea of Eric being in danger upset her.

"He'll be okay, Carys. *You* on the other hand…"

"What about me?"

"You look pale. Are you feeling okay?"

"I feel fine," Carys answered with a shrug. "Just extra tired. With school and my final project, plus worrying about Eric's safety, it's been a lot to process since we got back."

"Admit it, worrying about Eric is your tipping point."

Carys blushed. "Yeah," she admitted softly. "I really like him, Vin. I mean—and I know this is completely insane but hear me out—he's everything I ever dreamed of. Every time he sends me a message, I can't believe he's real. The way he talks to me, Vinny."

"That's because you are more than a little smitten, my friend."

She was. Carys was obsessed with her email right now,

more so than she had ever been before. Every time she got a message notification, she immediately checked to see if it was from Eric. The disappointment she felt when it wasn't him was heavy.

"I've never met anyone like him," she finally said after a long pause. "He's just…I don't know, *perfect.* And his friend is great too. I hope you get to meet him someday."

"The one that skipped *Mexico* to hang out with a woman?"

"Yeah, Ruben."

Vinny didn't seem too impressed, but Carys wasn't going to ask why. She *was* pretty tired this evening, and getting Vinny riled up was not on her to do list whatsoever. The only thing she wanted to do was sleep and talk to Eric.

Carys got ready for bed after Vinny left her tiny apartment. Tomorrow was Saturday, and she needed to hit the research lab in the morning before it got crowded. After lunch was always a gamble, and she needed time on the library's server before she could write the next section of her dissertation.

Just as she was settling into bed, her phone chimed. She looked at the screen eagerly, bouncing in place on her mattress when she saw it was an email from Eric.

To: ByAnyOtherName@ Eden.com
From: CrayonLover@mailwarrior.net
Subject: Missing you
Sweetheart,

I'm going out today. I won't be able to talk to you for three to five days, depending on how long the job takes. It's just a small exercise, with minimal risk. The worst part about leaving is missing our conversations. Keep the emails coming. I'll read them all when I get back. Knowing there will be a piece of you waiting for me when I return will make it all worthwhile.

Affectionately,

Eric

Carys scrambled to reply, hoping her words would reach him before he left. She couldn't sleep unless she tried even though she was genuinely dog tired lately.

To: CrayonLover@mailwarrior.net
From: ByAnyOtherName@Eden.com
Re: Missing you

Eric,

That seems like an eternity to wait just to hear your voice. When I'm reading your messages I hear your voice in my head, saying your words to me like it's any other conversation instead of an email. You sound so soothing and kind when you speak.

I'm going to miss you, too. Keep your promise! Be safe. Be well.

Yours,

Carys

There. Now all she could do was hope he read it before he headed out. She reread the thread, a pang of worry over Eric being away from his main dwelling and out in an actual war zone was already coming on. He said it wasn't going to be too risky, but she couldn't help wondering if he said so because it was true or because he didn't want her to worry.

I am already worried.

Sometimes she would have vivid nightmares of Eric laid out in a hospital bed wrapped in bandages. Carys had stopped watching or reading anything featuring war in her rare spare time. It helped to avoid those stories, and the nightmares weren't as graphic.

But it didn't stop her from worrying about Eric.

Somehow, he'd managed to become a light keeping her going, her focal point when she was overwhelmed. Carys knew she would reread all their emails many times while he was gone—well, *gone* gone since he was technically already gone—and wait anxiously to hear back, to know he was safe and sound.

She wasn't foolish enough to believe he was totally safe at his main camp or whatever they called it. Putting up a fence didn't make you safe. Even on US soil, a fence could only deter those who wanted to do harm and had an opportunity. A person set on making problems wouldn't let something as benign as a fence stop them, no matter what was on the other side. Eric was in a place where nobody would care about their flimsy border. If the bad guys wanted him, all a fence did was slow them enough to buy a little time.

———

TO: **ByAnyOtherName@Eden.com**
   From: CrayonLover@mailwarrior.net
   Subject: Safe

I'm safe, sweetheart. I'm headed to the shower now to wash off the last four days. I can hardly stand how bad I smell, so believe me when I say, a convoy full of sweaty Marines four days without a shower is not a pleasant olfactory experience. I'll be reading all your messages as soon as I'm clean.

   Affectionately,
   Eric

To: CrayonLover@mailwarrior.net
From: ByAnyOtherName@Eden.com
Subject: Senioritis

Eric,

I just finished my very last midterms. I have loved my time in college, but there was a relief in knowing this was the last time I'll have to do this. I doubt I will pursue a doctorate, but time will tell. For now, I'm happy to plan out what comes next in my life.

How are finals only a few weeks away? And my dissertation. I've been working on it for so long it feels like it'll never be done. My advisor scheduled my presentation meeting today, so clearly it's just my mind playing tricks on me. I am, in fact, presenting the culmination of my education in five weeks to a panel of educators.

I wish it were over and done with.

I'm so ready for Mexico.

Yours,

Carys

P.S. Wish me luck. I'm finally going to confront my professor about the TA who hates me.

To: ByAnyOtherName@Eden.com
From: CrayonLover@mailwarrior.net
Subject: Ruben

Sweetheart,

I'm sorry to say, you won't be seeing Ruben again. He's been sneaking my tablet and reading your messages. I know you were looking forward to spending more time with him, and I regret disappointing you. There is a strong possibility he will be left behind.

Accidentally, of course.

To: CrayonLover@mailwarrior.net
From: ByAnyOtherName@Eden.com
Subject: Sweet Memories
Eric,

I've been obsessing over the way you made my body sing under your touch. How your tongue thrust into my depths, leaving me soaked and panting for you. Do you still carry my lace panties with you? You know, the ones I drenched while your mouth worshipped my breasts. God, I can't wait to feel your teeth marking me as yours again. I think I'm ready to try that thing you asked about with the toys. Do you want me to research the best lube for you? I don't want your ass hurting the next day.

I have a talent for researching, you know. You should see the naughty ideas I've been collecting for us. If you're a good boy, I'll let you pick your favorites.

To: ByAnyOtherName@Eden.com
From: CrayonLover@mailwarrior.net
Re: Sweet Memories
Sweetheart,

Well done. I didn't know Ruben *could* look pale. Great visuals. Serves him right for snooping in my damn messages. I haven't stopped laughing since he left our bunk.

For the record, I'd love to hear all your "naughty ideas." If I'm honest though, the thing I'm most looking forward to is waking with you in my arms and seeing your hair fanned out across the pillows. Your scent is addictive, and the softness of your skin is the only aphrodisiac I need.

How was your meeting? I can't believe that TA tried to fail you on the sly. I hope your professor saw through her and corrected your grades. Some people just can't be happy while others are thriving.

To: CrayonLover@mailwarrior.net
From: ByAnyOtherName@Eden.com
Subject: Long Weekend

Eric,

You were right. I was so focused on school, I wasn't living. Vinny agreed and took me away for a weekend. It was relaxing, but missing the charm of Mexico—namely, *you*. I'm back to class now, counting down the days until my last presentation.

And yes, I did go to a coffee shop just for the ambiance. Maybe this weekend I'll try living it up at a kegger on Frat Row.

Kidding!

Frat Boy Ken was enough for me to last a lifetime. How does that moment feel so long ago, but meeting you still feels like yesterday, given you saved me from the cargo shorts crew he crawled out of? He's an afterthought, a blip that justified and granted you permission to touch me for the first time.

I wish you were here, Eric. For so many reasons.

Yours,

Carys

Chapter Nine

ERIC

"Man, what did you do to Perez? She's been psycho since we got here."

Eric let out a sigh that ended with a groan. "I didn't continue with the arrangement we had the last time we were down range."

"Ooooh. She's horny," Ruben said. "That'll do it. Carla gets all riled up too."

The last thing Eric wanted to hear about was Carla. Or Perez, for that matter. The *only* woman he was willing to distract himself stupid with was Carys. Walking away from her had been a kind of torture the military did not train you for. He was out of his depths and scared shitless she wouldn't show at the appointed time, even with the constant flow of conversation they had kept over email.

Hell, the way things were going right now, *he* might not make it. Word of an extension hit almost as soon as his boots had on foreign soil, which was never a good sign. Somehow, he had to make it back to her. He knew no other way thanks to her first name only policy—well, no *legal* ways, at least. Her messages gave her email, not an actual name. Another dead end for tracking her down soon as he was stateside again.

"Earth to Slow!" Ruben shouted in his hear. Eric startled. "There you are my man. Get your head outta the sandy beaches of Mexico and back in the ones all around you. We gotta get moving. You wanna see your PYT again, you have to keep from getting blown the fuck up first."

"PYT?"

"Pretty young thing! Man, don't you listen to the Prince of Pop?" Ruben said, aghast.

Just to fuck with him, Eric said, "Right. I prefer the song 'When Doves Cry' though."

"That's *Prince,* not the *Prince of Pop*, man! What's wrong with you? Don't white boys in the burbs listen to Michael Jackson same as the rest of the free world?" Ruben's face went from straight up horror film extra to simply amused ala Chris Rock when he saw the slow smile creeping up Eric's face. "Man, fuck you."

They both let out a needed laugh.

So far, everything that could go wrong *had.* Whatever information had launched the hasty assembly of this mission seemed to be falling apart faster than Eric's lovesick brain. He'd heard from a guy at home station whose cousin worked a job in the know that, had the intel been solid, they'd be home by now. As it was, it looked like the branch whose sleuthing had landed them here had made a few speculations and passed them off as solid facts.

In other words, they were fucked. The Department of Defense doesn't appreciate wasted resources and had decided to find a purpose for Eric's unit anyway, since it was too late to call it off. By the time they'd confirmed an extension, it was also too late to apply for leave in route—permission to take transport stateside, then fly to wherever he wanted without reporting in first.

"What if she doesn't show, Ruben? I warned her things like this happen, but what if I'm not there the first day, and she leaves?" He'd asked his best friend this exact question at least a dozen times, and every time Ruben came back with the same answer.

"She'll be there."

"How do you know?"

Ruben turned his shoulders so he could better face Eric from where he was sitting next to him. "Because I saw it, man. The thing between you two is the same spark I grew up with, before Mom died. That kind of chemistry can't be faked, and it can't be extinguished."

It probably wasn't smart to turn to the most hopeless romantic he knew for assurance—especially given Ruben's own track record with love—but he was the only person who'd met Carys. As brief as it had been, it had happened. When Eric started thinking it was all a dream, he could count on Ruben to confirm she was real.

His American beauty, dimples and all.

"Fuck, I don't know how much longer I can stay out of range from Perez. She seemed pretty chill last time with the expectations, but now…she's malicious."

"Because you gave her a taste and then fell for someone else," Ruben said, smiling. "I think she thought good ole Slow would eventually warm up to her and break his own rules, if you know what I'm saying."

Eric shook his head. "I didn't make her promises, or hint something more would develop. Hell, the second we got home, the arrangement ended without issues. She wasn't like this until we left again."

"V12 overheard her talking with one of the other medics

he works with. Sounds like she thought she'd eventually hook you if she kept you between her sheets while away, get you to climb in her sheets back home too. Instead, you came back from a week in Mexico smitten, and she obviously didn't bring enough batteries to make it through a measly four-month out and back." Ruben smirked, his eyes full of mischief.

"A four-month which should have been closer to three," Eric said, his mind refocusing on Carys.

Ruben put a hand on his shoulder and squeezed reassuringly. "You'll make it, man. I'm telling you; I got a feeling about this one. She's the reason you've always moved so slow with women; so you wouldn't be caught up with the wrong lady when the right one came along."

Ro*mantic as fuck, Ruben.* But he knew what Eric needed to hear, and he was feeling a touch better. Enough to drive out with his head on straight.

"Thanks, Ruben."

———

ERIC SCRAWLED his signature over the last page with the clipboard midair, already half handed over to his superior. He practically threw it at the man's face once the pen was off the page.

"In a rush, Major?" he said coyly.

"Yup. Have I met your expectations, sir?" Eric asked.

"I'd really like to yank your chain, but I hear you have a mean left hook. You're excused. Enjoy your leave," he said lightly.

Thank fuck.

They'd gotten back too late the night before to do all the proper check in shit. Eric had come in early to get all his paperwork started ahead of time and had been waiting for the rest of leadership to arrive so he could get the hell out of there.

Last minute flights to Mexico weren't a sure thing—forget affordable—but he'd managed to snag a standby ticket, and the agent assured him he was first in line. He was already a day late leaving, but if the universe would cut him a little slack, he'd get in right on time for dinner and dancing.

Ruben was already waiting outside in his truck, engine purring and ready to hit the freeway. Eric was all but running once he came out into the sunshine, barreling toward the passenger door.

"Airport, ho!" Ruben said cheerily as Eric climbed in and closed the door behind him.

"No," he said as he clicked his seatbelt into place, looking into the back seat to make sure he'd remembered all his bags. "I need to make a quick stop at Gustav's."

"Gustav's?" Ruben said, not bothering to contain his mirth.

"Just get there," Eric said.

Ruben laughed. Twenty minutes later, he was still smiling as Eric hopped out of the truck. "Take your time, lover boy," he called out as the door closed on him.

If he wasn't in such a rush, Eric would knock his buddy down a few pegs. Ruben was constantly chasing down his forever, looking for the rare something he'd grown up with. The Holts had known a love so pure; you could feel it from down the block—even now his mother was gone. Ruben insisted he'd settle for nothing less than what his parents had demonstrated, but Eric didn't think it was as simple as that.

Eric moved slow for a reason. He knew he was out of his mind, jumping on a plane less than twenty-four hours after returning from an international assignment. It went against every one of his instincts, as far as relationships went. The thing was, Carys didn't set off any of his alarm bells. Nothing about her tickled those instincts into alarm mode.

On the contrary, they were unusually quiet with regards to her.

He was a complete hypocrite, and he knew it. Eric found it unnecessary to tell Ruben he thought he was an idealistic nut job where women were concerned. Now he was doing an extremely *Ruben* thing to do…chasing after a woman he'd spent six days with. A woman he'd already promised the moon if she took a chance on him and showed up.

Eric was in and out of the shop in under five minutes. Ruben had them barreling toward the airport in no time, while Eric twitched nervously in the passenger seat.

"Calm down, man. She'll be there," Ruben said seriously.

"No jokes?"

"You know I never joke around about love."

He didn't. Eric took in a deep breath and blew it out shakily. "I'm way out of my depths here, Ruben."

"We all are. But tell me this—and I want you to say the first thing that comes to mind, not some overthought bullshit you think is the right answer—does she feel like the real deal?"

"Yeah. Yes." Eric smiled. "She feels like my real everything."

"Then go get your lady, Slow." Ruben smiled then, a light laugh escaping. "Show the rest of us idiots how it's done."

"And we're back to jokes."

They pulled up at the departure drop off area an hour later. Eric reached behind him for his travel bag, But Ruben stayed him with a hand on his shoulder while he was turned facing him. "She's going to be there. You are going to be so besotted all over again, you'll almost forget to tell me when to expect you back. *Almost,* but I'm your best friend and you won't do that to me. So instead, you're going to send me a last minute text on when I need to come get you."

He pulled back his hand and Eric grasped his bag again, pulling it into the front seat. "Thanks, brother," he said, and Eric knew from the shine of love and pride in Ruben's eyes, the man knew he meant it as more than a comrade in arms.

"See you soon," he answered with a nod.

Eric got out of the truck and headed into the airport without looking back. Backward wasn't an option anymore. The only way was the one taking him to her.

Chapter Ten

CARYS

The first night had been agony. Carys had sat alone in the back corner table like Eric had asked her to, waiting. By the time midnight rolled around, even she had to admit he probably wasn't making it. Not yet anyway.

But soon. He'd booked them a seven-night stay. There was still time.

It didn't detract from the way her face heated when the staff gave her knowing eyes and trilled behind serving trays in Spanish to each other, their gazes still focused on her—the woman who checked into the honeymoon suite *alone*. It was hard to keep a stiff upper lip while she sat in the corner drinking by herself.

She knew she looked desperate, pathetic even. As soon as Eric arrived, it wouldn't matter. Let them stare. She wouldn't notice anything but *him* then.

The only person back home who had supported her returning was Vinny. She'd hoped her mother would understand, but those soap bubbles of optimism had been burst immediately. Carys had believed her mother a romantic—her *This is my Hallmark movie blanket* she used regardless of it being Christmas season or not certainly fit the notion—but her romanticism seemed to stop cold in its tracks the second it crossed out of the fictional realm and into reality. Not only had her mother been harsh, but she'd also been cruel. Carys had needed to call Vinny for a ride back to her old LA apartment, she'd been sobbing so hard.

It didn't matter her mother was trying to protect her. In the moment, she'd needed support to do what she must, what Carys knew was the *right* thing to do. Eric deserved to know how she felt about him and decide if he could accept her as she was. A lot had happened in five months, and she wasn't the same person now.

She would never be the person he'd asked to give them a chance ever again.

Sleeping alone in the embarrassingly large bed had been difficult last night too. Carys had ordered room service for both breakfast and lunch this morning, along with an assortment of snacks. She didn't feel like being seen around the resort alone. Instead, she'd stayed in her jammies all day, pretending Eric was off getting her an ice cream or something, and watching cheesy telenovelas. She didn't know Spanish, so she made up the dialogue for herself.

It was way more fun than turning on English subtitles. In her mind, the fighting lovers were devastated their pet chimpanzee had fallen in love with a boa constrictor and run off together. He yelled their "son" needed to man up and make his way in the world. She slapped him for allowing "that snake" into their lives in the first place.

Carys had giggled uncontrollably as the couple's fight came to its crescendo—basically, dramatic soft-core porn. Then she had burst into tears, because she wasn't supposed to be imagining scripts for foreign television. She was supposed to be curled up in bed with Eric, after he spent the night taking her to the heights the actress on the screen was supposedly reaching.

Television was stupid anyway.

She'd cried herself to sleep and woken up an hour later, her face still puffy and eyes red from the desperately needed emotional release. After a long shower, she'd styled her hair into the same beachy waves she had the first time she'd been there, applied a coat of mascara, and pulled out her favorite sundress. It was new and made her cleavage the focal point.

Vinny told her she needed to learn to embrace the "new Carys," and insisted this dress would help. It certainly didn't hurt. She smiled as she smoothed the soft fabric down her sides. It was sexy, something she generally didn't aspire to be, but for Eric she wanted to be more than sexy. This dress was for him, which was why she had a matching cardigan to wear with it until he arrived.

Carys met her own eyes in the mirror. *I am waiting on my literal dream man to walk through the door and apologize for keeping me waiting. He'll flirt, tell me he's thought of nothing and nobody else since we parted, and hold me close while we dance. He won't care I'm not who he left behind, because I am more than a good time to him.*

Pep talk over, she slipped on a pair of strappy flat sandals, squared her shoulders, raised her chin, and then headed out to her lonely corner table where she would be surrounded by lovers and those looking for lovers. On the bright side, Frat Boy Ken wasn't here, and nobody else had bothered her.

Small favors.

The waitress approached with a water and drink as Carys slid into her chair. She ordered the same appetizers as she had last night, knowing she was too nervous to do more than graze. A full meal would be wasted on her right now. Then she waited with as relaxed an air as she could manage.

Her food arrived, but she didn't touch it right away. She told herself it was because it was too hot and she didn't want to burn her tongue. By the time she gave up on the lie, everything was lukewarm at best. She ate it anyway.

Her hubris was fading fast. Carys had been wrong. She couldn't do this another night, much less another *five* of them. She needed Eric. Right now.

The hair on the back of her neck stood on end, a wave of goosebumps rippling down her arms. The air felt cooler, the music softer. The water she'd been sipping more refreshing.

"Sorry I'm late, sweetheart."

She closed her eyes, fighting off the tears threatening to transform her back into the blubbering mess she'd been earlier.

"Carys," he said, his warm hand taking hers across the tabletop. "I'm so sorry, sweetheart. Thank you for believing in me."

She opened her eyes, his warm brown gaze staring back at her with a mixture of concern and affection. "That's okay," she murmured. "I know how tired you get when you go snorkeling."

She watched as Eric's slow smile made it's first appearance in five long months. He was here. "If by snorkeling, you mean hopping from one international flight to another with barely enough time to shower in between, yeah sweetheart. I could really use a rest."

"Pull up a seat," she said shakily.

Eric set down his bag and slid into the chair next to hers, exactly as he had before he left, and reached over for her second hand. With both their hands clasped on the table, she finally felt like she could breathe again. He kissed the tops of her hands and then settled them back down, rubbing his thumbs over his kisses, like he was afraid they would fall off.

"We were delayed, but we made it."

"You told me it could happen," she reminded him.

"Knowing doesn't mean it was easy for you, or that you could trust it actually *did* happen."

"You told me you would be here, Eric. I had to try."

He took her in with his eyes, silently assessing her. "Are you okay? You seem different. Not bad different, just… different."

"I am different, but you're right. It isn't bad, it just *is.*"

"How was your last term? Did you finish your project in time to graduate?" She nodded. "I knew it," he said confidently. "You're smart, sweetheart."

Carys picked up her drink and found it empty. The waitress must have noticed too, because she was right there with a fresh one to swap out. Carys thanked her and took a sip. It wasn't her favorite, but it was better than nothing but plain water.

Without meeting his eyes, Carys began to speak. "Did you mean what you said before, about wanting to pursue more with me?" He squeezed her hands and her gaze shifted to where their hands were joined.

"Yes. It's all I've thought about since we met."

"What does that look like to you?"

"It depends on you, but ideally, we'll find you a job near me and we can date."

"Date?" It sounded good, but was it what she really wanted? "Is it expensive there? I mean, could we be roommates or something?"

"Roommates? Carys, you're more than a roommate to me."

"Right. I meant for starters; you know. I won't know anyone but you, and I don't even know where you live but—"

"Carys, look at me." When she hesitated he added, "Please."

How could she say no? He smiled softly when she conceded, his eyes so full of emotions she couldn't have sorted them if she tried. "I'm scared," she whispered.

"Me too." Eric reached down and dug something out of his bag one handed, holding eye contact the whole time. He must have known exactly where he'd put it because whatever *it* was didn't take long to find. He sat back up, his hand curled around something she couldn't see. "Are you afraid of *me, sweetheart?*"

"No," she answered without hesitation.

He slid his hand forward, back toward the one he'd released a minute ago. Then he turned it over, revealing a small, burgundy box. Carys's eyes moved back and forth between the box and his face. *Is that what I think it is?*

"Everything you need to know about my intentions is inside this box, Carys. It's yours. I don't want to frighten you anymore than you already are. What I am offering you is not going to be easy. You will be alone sometimes, but you'll be cherished too.

"I don't want to date you, but I will. For as long as it takes for you to be ready for the contents of this box, I will do everything I can to show you how much I want you in my life. I'm not *usually* an impulsive man, and I don't expect you to be an impulsive woman. I want you to know I've made up my mind on where I see us going if you give me a chance." Eric took her hand and placed it on top of the box, the velvety texture warm against her palm.

"Thank you." *It's now or never.* "I have to tell you something really important that might make you change your mind."

"I won't," he said firmly. "What do you need to tell me, sweetheart."

Oh god. "Uh…" Carys laughed nervously. "How much do you know about antibiotics?"

"Aside from they save lives, not a whole lot. Medicine isn't my area of expertise."

She took a deep breath and let her words out in one continuous, garbled mess. "I had to take antibiotics as soon as I got home because…well, all the…I had a bladder infection from the combination of our *activities* plus all the tequila, and everything seemed fine for a few weeks until I started feeling sick and did you know antibiotics make some other *equally important* medicines not work right? Because I hadn't really thought about it, I mean I *knew,* but it didn't really worry me until it *did,* and I was so afraid you'd hate me for it because I'm so *happy* it happened and I want you to be happy too but if you aren't, that's okay. I'll be okay. We'll…"

Erics eyes were still focused on her, but they'd glazed over a bit. She was talking too fast with nerves, messing this whole thing up. He had no clue what she was trying to tell him, but he was trying, damn it. She had to get to the point, and since words were clearly not her thing right now, she'd just have to show him.

Carys slid off the tall bar top chair she was perched on and took a step toward her dream man.

"We made a baby, Eric."

Chapter Eleven

ERIC

He was so busy admiring the way her body moved as she came to a stand—feeding his craving for what he'd been missing—it wasn't until his eyes reached her rounded stomach her words registered in his brain. *We made a baby, Eric.*

They'd made a baby.

My baby.

In her body.

"Carys," he whispered with awe. "You're so beautiful." He pulled her in closer, needing to touch her. "I'm so sorry, sweetheart."

"Oh," she said, trying to pull back.

He didn't let her. Eric placed his hands on either side of her sweet bump. "I should have been there from the start."

"Oh," she said again, the tension bleeding out of her body. "You aren't mad?"

"I thought I was going to give you my true intentions and you'd bolt on me. You're it for me, Carys." Her hands slid over the top of his and he felt her body shudder with a sob.

"Guess this explains why you're sipping Shirley Temples instead of daiquiris."

She laughed. Eric looked into her face then, seeing the relief in her watery eyes. "I promise it's yours. I'll understand if you want a DNA test though."

Eric shook his head. "No, sweetheart. I know it's mine."

"I don't want to open that box with you thinking I'm trying to secure an easy life or a meal ticket. Or for you to feel obligated. You don't owe us a thing, Eric."

"You're wrong. I owe you everything," he said with conviction. "Besides, have you looked up military divorce rates? I'm not offering you an easy life at all. But I can promise to make it worthwhile."

"I didn't think it was the kind of thing I should tell you over email," she said awkwardly. "But you have a right to be upset I kept it from you when I didn't have to." She sounded embarrassed now, and he hated the way her shoulders slumped and her gaze fell from his.

"Sweetheart. The fact you are here says all I need to know. If you hadn't come I would have never known." The thought of being a father and not knowing gave Eric a pang of despondency. She could have kept this from him so easily. On impulse, he leaned forward and kissed right over her belly. It was one of many things he was sure had changed as their baby grew inside Carys. "Thank you."

"Can we go upstairs now?" she asked timidly. "Please?"

"You know what that word does to me. Let's go."

———

"COME ON, SWEETHEART," Eric said as soon as the door to the honeymoon suite closed. "Let's talk through everything before I get carried away with myself and take you along with me."

She laughed nervously—nerves he hoped to remedy—as he led her to the bed by the hand. He'd dropped his bag at the door, uncaring where it landed for now. Carys was scared, and she took priority. Eric didn't know much about pregnancy, but he did know a stressed mother wasn't good for the baby.

Eric climbed to the center of the bed, fluffed a few of the massive pillows up against the headboard, and made himself comfortable for however long this was going to take. "Right here," he called out to her and patted the spot next to him. Carys was still standing shyly at the edge of the bed, her arms crossed under her chest protectively. From Eric's view, all it did was make her low-cut dress heave with her swollen breasts.

"Okay," she said hesitantly.

"Let me hold you while we talk out all your worries, sweetheart." He watched as Carys came to sit beside him against the headboard, doing her best to keep her indigo colored dress from showing too much leg. The effort amused him, given how much time he'd already spent admiring those legs before burying himself between them.

And making a baby.

Once he had her tucked under his arm with her head resting on his shoulder, he reached across with his other hand and placed it on her bump, gently rubbing. He kissed the top of her head and breathed in her floral shampoo. For the first time in five months, Eric felt *whole*.

"I don't want you to accept me because of the baby, or the baby because of me," she murmured. "I need you to want us both, or I can't do this."

"The baby is one more reason to love you, Carys. Its proof I didn't imagine you, or our time together."

"You love me?"

"Madly," he said. "Enough to drive my entire platoon crazy. Ruben said I'm a moody SOB when I'm in love. Completely insufferable."

Carys let out an amused hum.

"Where do you live?" he asked.

"Nowhere, really. I've been staying in my old room at my mom's house since I graduated," she said with complete misery. "We don't really see eye to eye on a good day, and then this happened," she patted her belly for effect. "Now we *really* don't agree."

He smiled to himself. "And where is your mom's house *located,* sweetheart."

"Right, sorry. It's in Ojai, California."

"Fuck. You've been a three hour joy ride away this whole time," he said.

"What? Wait, that's either Twentynine Palms or Camp Pendleton, right?"

"I'm impressed. Camp Pendleton, I bought an interesting house in Oceanside. Most of the neighbors are military too, so we're pretty good about looking out for each other."

"Oh, good. Twentynine Palms sounds miserable."

Eric laughed. "Trust me, it is."

"Interesting how?"

"Hmm?"

"You said the house is *interesting.*"

"It's got an upstairs income suite, or it could be used as a separate entrance guest apartment. I doubt I can do it justice. You'll have to see it for yourself." *Please say you will be seeing it for yourself.*

They talked about what they liked about living in Southern California, and the things they could live without. Carys told Eric about her six years of college in LA, and Eric told her about his first five years as a Marine, being deployed more than he was home.

"It's better now," he assured her. "I still get sent out, but my current job is more balanced. I actually had time to accumulate decent furniture the past few years," he added dryly.

Her stomach interrupted, gurgling loudly.

"When was the last time you ate?" he asked.

"I've been picking—"

"Picking?"

"I've been nervous since I packed my bags to come here. I'm not starving myself, but food hasn't been very appealing," she confessed.

"And now?"

"I'm so hungry I could cry," she said, her voice warbling at the end as she *did* begin to cry. "Damn these hormones!"

Eric didn't dare laugh or smile, but it wasn't easy. "The last thing I ate was stale pretzels on the flight over. How about we order up some room service?"

"Yes, please." She sniffled.

He kissed the top of her head and reluctantly released her. They didn't speak again until the food arrived, pausing their conversation and opting to remain curled up together on the bed until they had refueled. Eric was exhausted, his internal clock completely out of whack from all the globetrotting. He woke to the rich smell of authentic Mexican cuisine, only then realizing he'd nodded off.

"Sorry," he said. "I didn't mean to sleep."

"I don't mind. I drifted off too, but the sound of room service knocking at the door woke me," she said, shifting the last items off the trolly and onto the table as she spoke. "I'm tired from the trip here, and you did the trip and then some."

Eric forced himself onto his feet before he passed out again. "Yeah, it's been a long week of traveling and it's what —Tuesday?"

"Wednesday," she corrected. "Come eat with me."

She didn't have to tell him twice. They both dug in, the first few mouthfuls hitting his stomach before the spices could register on his taste buds. Eric took a long drink of water and sat back for a moment. When he retrieved his cutlery, he forced himself to slow down. The kitchens at the resort were award winning, and after months of uninspired, budget friendly chow hall, he wanted to savor both the meal and the company.

Carys sat across from him, taking small bites. Eric worried she was still too emotional to eat a substantial amount, but she finished her plate. She hadn't scarfed down her food last time either, but this was different. It was methodical. Even when she drank, Carys took several small sips.

"Are you feeling okay? Don't force yourself to eat for my benefit," he added.

"I'm fine. If I eat or drink too fast I get terrible heartburn. Pregnancy," she said with a shrug. "It has its ups and downs. I was hungry though. I feel much better now."

So did Eric. Sustenance had sparked his brain temporarily back to life. Not the way a good sleep would, but enough to make sure he knew where they stood before he crashed again. He thought about what else needed to be said here and now as he cleared the dishes back onto the trolley and pushed it out into the hall.

"We've talked over a lot already, but how are you feeling

about *us,* sweetheart?" He was hoping for the best while internally preparing himself for a brush off.

"Us," she said. "Hmm. The three of us?"

"That's the idea."

"I meant what I said about the test."

"And I told you I don't need one." They were standing at the foot of the bed, and he reached out to pull her to him. Carys's arms wrapped around his waist, squeezing tight. "Do you know what the baby is? Boy or girl?"

"You've missed so much already, I wanted to save something special for you," she murmured from where she was pressed against his chest, her cheek settled over his sternum.

Eric hugged her tighter, trying to swallow around the lump of emotions in his throat. She didn't have to do that, but he was grateful she had. Her desire to include him in the pregnancy before he even knew about it further confirmed to Eric they were on the same page.

"I'm going to suggest something completely crazy. Crazier than meeting me here again after only a week together." His voice was gravelly and forced, his tone lower than usual from all the emotion he was trying to process. "Let's be a family, Carys. Come live with me."

"On one condition," she said, pulling back so she could meet his gaze. "If we're going to do this, let's shoot for the moon, Eric." She held up her hand between them and opened it up, revealing the velvet box he'd given her downstairs.

He took her face in his hands and kissed her properly. Then he took the box and opened it up, facing her. "Marry me, Carys. I still don't know your last name, but I'd like to give you mine. *Please."*

"I see what you mean about that *please.* It's got some power."

"Not much, given you haven't answered the question," he said pensively.

"Yes, Eric. I was yours before I ever laid eyes on you."

Screw the ring.

Eric slipped one hand behind Carys's neck and kissed her with all the ravenous hunger he'd been fighting since he arrived.

Chapter Twelve

CARYS

She hadn't been lying when she told Eric pregnancy came with ups and downs. The heartburn was a downer, but now that she was with him again, Carys could take her out of control libido off the same list as her decidedly craptastic hormonal side effects. The way Eric was kissing her sealed the deal for Carys. She'd made the right choice in coming back.

It was impulsive—some would say stupid—agreeing to marry him on the spot. Carys had been clever about arranging her life, scheduling every last detail, except for two things. Mexico, and Eric. She wouldn't say she'd been lifeless before, but with him she felt *alive.*

Eric pulled out of the kiss too soon for her liking, and she moaned in complaint. "I'm not done kissing you, I promise."

"Then why did you stop?"

"Because you crushed the ring box when you leaned into me, and my finger is pinched in the hinge," he said with a laugh.

"Oh! I'm so sorry!" she cried, leaning back. She hadn't even looked at the ring. The devotion and affection in his expression as he asked her to take his name meant more than any bobble, and she didn't want to miss a moment.

Eric flipped the box back open and moved his finger out of the way. "What do you think?"

Carys looked down at the open box for the first time. The inside of the lid read Gustav's Custom Jewelry in gold calligraphy, right above the most beautiful ring she'd ever seen. It was a cushion cut tanzanite solitaire—almost the exact shade of indigo as her dress—set in rose gold.

"You had this made for me?" she asked as her eyes welled up.

"As soon as I got home, I asked Gustav to help me with something special."

"It's beautiful."

Eric took the ring out of the box and lifted her left hand. As he slid it in place, he said, "I had a feeling you wouldn't be a diamonds kind of girl."

She wasn't. Her mother was known to hum the tune "Diamonds Are A Girls Best Friend" as she adorned herself to leave the house, but they held no appeal with Carys. She preferred a little color, something that felt more natural and less flashy. "How did you figure me out so well in such a short time?"

"I paid attention," he said, kissing her knuckles before placing her hand over his chest. Carys admired the way it caught the light. "Gustav suggested rose gold to bring out the sparkle, whatever that means. I don't know much about jewelry, but he showed me a color wheel and—"

Carys laughed. "Sorry. I wasn't laughing *at* you. I'm just so…happy. Nobody has ever put this much thought into something for me before, except maybe Vinny."

"And I thank the stars for Vinny every night, or I'd never have met you."

"It's true."

"Let's elope," he said, catching her off guard.

"What? Eric, we can't elope!"

"Of course we can. They have a whole package deal for people who come here specifically to get married. We can arrange it at the front desk."

"You're serious?"

"I've already shocked everyone I know by chasing after you. And your mother doesn't sound like she believes I'm any good. We really can't do any more damage to everyone's expectations and opinions," he said with humor.

"To be fair, she thinks men in general don't deserve women," Carys said with amusement.

"She's not wrong." He laughed, his accompanying smile melting her resolve. "We don't deserve women in the least, but I'll try every day to prove I'm the right one for you. To deserve you and our baby."

She smiled up at him. "Okay. Marry me in Mexico, Eric."

He sealed their agreement with a kiss, his soft lips brushing over hers until they tingled. She moaned, needing so much more. Eric nipped softly at her bottom lip, and Carys ran her tongue over the seam of his mouth as he did in invitation. *Kiss me like you did before.* He took it, deepening their kiss into everything she'd craved from him and more. His tongue danced with hers, both soft and commanding at the same time, triggering a surge of heat throughout her body.

Carys stripped off the light cardigan she'd paired with her dress, revealing the low cut V in the back. "Touch me," she begged against his lips. "Please." He groaned, then began feathering kisses down her jawline toward her ear, his hands finding their way across her exposed backside.

Eric nipped her earlobe before whispering, "I'm going to touch all of you, sweetheart."

"Oh."

Carys could feel Eric and nothing more. A hurricane could slam into the resort and the only storm she'd register was the emotional one coursing between them, five long months in the making. His hands across her back were heavenly, his touch causing her to arch into his chest and tip her head to the side so he could kiss farther down her neck.

"Did you wear this just for me?" His lips were against the pulse point of her throat and made her shudder with delight.

"Yes."

"I can see your warm golden skin in the mirror behind you," he said, nipping her collar bone gently. "And your reactions when I touch you. Especially *here,"* he said, trailing his hand down her backside. She gasped as his fingers spread across her lower back, pulling her firmly against his erection. "You're stunning, Carys."

"I missed you," she whispered. *I love you.*

He pulled her toward the bed gently, stopping to tug her dress over her head before he laid her out across the pillows. "How do these come off," he asked, grazing a hand across her breast.

"Like this." Carys showed Eric how to remove the backless bra she'd worn. As soon as he peeled back the cups, her nipples hardened painfully.

"Look at you," he said with wonder. "They're darker," he said, running his fingers around her areolas before cupping both her breasts, filling his hands. "And larger."

"And more sensitive," she said seductively. "They ache. All of me aches."

"Tell me what you need, sweetheart."

"Please touch me," she begged.

"Yes, ma'am." He was stretched out beside her, still

completely dressed, while she was down to her little panties. "How would you like to be touched?"

"With all of you." She looked pointedly down his body and then back up at his face expectantly. Eric took the hint and stripped slowly, his smile turning devious. God, he was amazing. How had she survived five months without him?

"Say it one more time for me, sweetheart."

"Please, Eric. Please fuck me."

He settled down off to her side, his torso curved over her so he could pick up where he left off at her collar bone. Eric kissed his way down through the valley of her breasts. It felt so *good.* With one hand on her swollen belly, Eric ran his lips over both her breasts in turn, stopping at the top to lave his tongue over her peaks before sucking down on them. She moaned as her breasts grew heavier and began to tingle in a new way.

Eric gently released her second nipple with a look of interest and surprise on his face. "That's new," he said, rubbing his thumb around the bead of moisture on her tip. Carys blushed.

"Oh. Um…"

"Don't be embarrassed. You are growing a person. Some things are different, and I like it," he assured her. Carys relaxed.

"My doctor said it could happen, I just didn't expect it," she said quietly.

Without dropping her gaze, he swirled his tongue around her nipple again, his fingers working the other one. It was sexy to watch him, and another rush of tingling flushed through her breasts and right down to her belly. Her nipples beaded up again, and he smiled with satisfaction. "Amazing. *You're amazing."*

She was going to burst. Carys scissored her legs together,

trying to control her need. Her thighs were already slick with arousal, just from him playing with her nipples and the way he reassured her she was still desirable to him. Eric noticed her movement and moved his hand down to her mound, his soft lips moving down over her belly while his other hand continued to fondle her breasts.

"I love you," he whispered over their baby, and Carys felt tears of joy break free as her emotions surged. Eric kissed her belly with tenderness, *reverence*. She was so caught up in watching him, she hadn't realized his hand had gently parted her legs until he stroked up her thigh.

He cupped her sex, humming with satisfaction. "Now *this* I remember well. Wet and ready for me."

She wanted to say something sexy back, but he pinched the nipple he'd been working with his fingers, and all she could manage was, "Yours," as bliss coursed through her. She bucked her hips against his hand desperately while Eric gently soothed her nipple with tender strokes of his tongue.

"I'm coming back for these later," he said, before moving his body down between her legs. He looked up at her as he slid a finger inside, his finger curling against her walls enough to make her whimper.

"More please."

He added another finger easily, her arousal creating more than enough slip. "I don't want to hurt you. I need you to come on my fingers first, sweetheart. Then I'll give you what you want."

Carys nodded through the delirium of her lust. Eric didn't keep her waiting. With his second hand on her bump, he worked his fingers inside her until she was grinding her hips against his hand, crying and begging for more. He swept his thumb across her nub and she detonated, screaming his name as her core clenched around his fingers.

Once the orgasm ebbed away some, she asked, "Wh-when did you take my panties off?"

Eric laughed. "I can't reveal *all* my secrets. Best to save a few for later."

He slowly pulled his fingers from her, holding them up to admire the way they glistened in the dim light of the room. Then he licked them clean. Carys licked her lips as she watched.

"Have you ever tasted yourself?"

She shook her head. "No."

He slid a finger back inside her, swirling it around before removing it slowly. "Open," he said softly. Carys did, sticking her tongue out when his finger touched her lips. "Everything about you is sweet."

She wasn't sure about sweet, but as she sucked his finger into her mouth, she would certainly say there was a distinctive tang to it. To *her.* She hummed gently as she pulled her head back, releasing his finger.

"Jesus. You aren't even trying to be sexy," he said, watching her swollen lips. "Damn."

"Eric."

"I know," he said, leaning over to kiss her. His shaft was hot against her belly, and she rubbed up against it as she kissed him back. "I don't want to crush you," he said between desperate kisses. "Think you can ride me if I help?"

Chapter Thirteen

ERIC

When they'd been intimate before, it had been a frenzy. Carys hadn't had the patience for a lot of foreplay, so Eric was enjoying every moment of her writhing at his touch now. He wasn't sure if it was the hormones or because she knew they now had all the time in the world together, but *damn*. Those little whimpers she made as he touched her had him primed and ready.

The sight of her greedily sucking his finger into her mouth with her juices on it. *Fuck*. She was gorgeous. And she was *his*. Eric had known he wanted a family eventually, but he never would have guessed he'd be this turned on at the sight of his baby growing inside a woman. The fact it was Carys was beyond his wildest dreams.

"Think you can ride me if I help?" He watched her for any sort of unease as he asked.

"I want to try," she said carefully. "The doctor told me as long as I was comfortable, we wouldn't hurt the baby."

Good to know. Eric made a mental note to explore all the ways he could keep her *comfortably* satisfied. He was going to enjoy it.

He slid to the head of the bed, sitting up. Carys rolled toward him and onto her knees before straddling him. She looked down at his cock, taking it in her hand and running her thumb through the pre-cum at his tip before pumping him with firm strokes. Eric growled with satisfaction.

"I'm ready for you, sweetheart."

Carys looked at him mischievously before lifting her hips and positioning herself so his cock sat at her entrance. She slowly rocked and swayed, enough to coat his head and drive him crazy. In retaliation, Eric leaned forward and sealed his mouth over one of her nipples, pulling it in deep. She breathed in sharply, and he smiled as he drew back, gently sucking and tugging her sensitive tip until her body began to tremble.

She was whimpering again, little sweet nothings and incoherent pleas he didn't think she had control over. He ran his hands up her thighs to her hips and held her in place as he thrust up carefully, sliding in halfway before he yielded to her tightness. "Ease yourself the rest of the way, sweetheart. I'll help you."

She lifted slightly before surprising him by sitting down until he was fully seated inside her, both of them moaning with pleasure. Carys rocked and swayed her hips, grinding against him. Eric gently thrust his hips up until her pleas for more snapped his resolve. They worked together, Carys lifting up while Eric thrust deeper as she came down.

"Need you," she panted out. "So close."

Eric rolled his hips up harder, watching as her eyes rolled back in her head. "Eyes here, sweetheart. Look at the man you're marrying while you take what you need." Her glassy eyes met his, her sweet lips swollen from their kisses and red where he'd nipped them. "Come, Carys."

He shifted one hand to the back of her head for support,

gripping his other hand into her hip firmly as he pumped up into her as hard as he could, her lithe body bouncing as he slammed into her. Her walls tightened until it was almost painful around his cock, causing Eric's spine to tingle and his balls to tighten. "Now, sweetheart."

She shattered again as he released his seed, crying out as she tensed, then slumped like a rag doll in his arms, while he pumped into her until he too was completely spent. Eric tenderly pulled her to his chest and leaned back into the pillows and headboard, semi reclined with her above him, his cock still throbbing inside her.

"I love you," she murmured.

Eric's heart ached with relief. He moved her hair off her face, stroking it across his chest as he rubbed her back and pressed kisses gently to her crown. He breathed in her floral scent again, filling all his senses with proof she was real. Proof she was *his*. He looked down to where her left arm hung limply down her side, his ring prominent on her hand.

"I am going to worship you every day of our lives," he vowed. "In all the ways you can be worshipped. Until the only thing you can say for sure is your husband loves you for you. Loves you enough to have known you were it from the moment I set eyes on you."

She tipped her head back and kissed the underside of his jaw tenderly before nestling back against his chest. He held her as their breathing slowed back to normal. She let out a sigh and pressed herself against him. Eric remembered her doing this when they first met too. Carys craved the feel of their bodies touching, skin to skin.

He hugged her tightly to him, forgetting about her bump until a strange feeling struck his stomach. Eric wasn't sure at first, maybe he had imagined it. But no, it came again. "Carys?"

She looked up at him. "Can you feel it too?"

"Is that the baby?"

"Yes." She blushed happily. "It moves most the hour or so after I've eaten, or anytime I'm active."

Eric slid down the bed and rolled to the side, already missing the feeling of her channel as soon as he pulled out of her. But some things were more important. He placed his hands on her belly and waited.

"Talk to our baby, Eric. It can hear you."

"Hey," he said. "I'm sorry we haven't met before. In my defense, it was your mom's idea, and I'll never agree to something so preposterous again." He rubbed his hands gently across her skin, wondering if the baby really could hear him. "I'm your dad."

Saying it aloud for the first time was surreal. *I'm your dad.* Eric was a dad. Carys was his, and they were going home a family. It was insanity, and it was perfect.

The baby kicked hard, and Eric startled. He looked up at Carys, who was smiling as tears streamed down her face. "I knew you would love us both," she whispered as the baby kicked again. Eric covered her belly in gentle kisses before leaning up to take her mouth with his.

He kissed her slow and deep, until she was panting and wiggling against him.

"Again. *Please.*"

————

AS MUCH AS he'd wanted to stay up all night getting reacquainted with Carys's body, Eric literally couldn't. Near three days of solid travel had taken its toll. They kissed and groped their way into an opiate like state of bliss before falling asleep wrapped around each other.

When they woke *twelve hours* later, Eric's morning wood was nestled up against Carys's backside. They had turned in their sleep until they were spooning; her soft body curled up, using one of his arms as a pillow, while the other wrapped around her body, his hand over her bump.

The honeymoon suite faced the ocean same as their first room, and though the sun had long risen, Eric had slid out of bed long enough to open the patio doors, allowing the sound of the waves to wash over them, if not the first hues of daylight. He curled back up behind Carys and gently made love to her in time with nature.

While the night before had been saturated with a desperate need—to reaffirm the burning connection between them—now they moved with love and tenderness. Eric cradled her fullness, caressing her swollen chest and belly as he drew out her pleasure. He tipped her head toward him and leaned forward over her shoulder so he could swallow all the delicious sounds she made. Her little pleas and shudders were food for his soul, and when she found her release he followed her.

By the time they emerged from their room showered and dressed, breakfast had passed. They settled in for lunch side by side at a shaded patio table off the sand, a pamphlet explaining onsite weddings between them. Eric was surprised how natural it felt, discussing an elopement with her. Sleep had done more than deepen the passion between their bodies upon waking.

It seemed to have settled everything between them, so much so, the only thing that made sense at all was laid out before them in the brochure.

"What about witnesses," Carys asked, pushing her empty plate away. "We didn't bring anyone with us this time."

"They will cover those too," he reassured her.

"I wish Vinny and Ruben could be here."

Eric agreed. He'd always thought Ruben would stand up with him on the big day. But then, he also thought he likely wouldn't get the chance, at the pace his love life had previously progressed. "He couldn't have made it anyway. He's using his reintegration leave to spoil *Carla.*" He didn't bother keeping the distaste from his voice.

"Vinny is on tour with her dad. If it goes well, they were talking about joining up on a USO tour. I guess this is what was meant to be for us," she said, her tone even and calm.

He placed a hand on her bump and said, "Guess so."

"I'm still waiting for the dream to end," she murmured. "I'm going to wake up alone and never know what happened to you, what could have been. If it was the baby or *me* you couldn't stand the idea of."

"That's just the Caribbean air getting to you, sweetheart. Give us a year, and you'll be wishing you'd stayed home this week," he teased. "You don't know if I'm tidy or sloppy. If I put the dishes in the dishwasher right away or leave them all over the house until they look like science experiments gone wrong. Maybe I have an entire room set up for my collection of pet tarantulas, and I expect the baby to share with them. Or perhaps—"

She quieted him with a finger over his lips. "Or perhaps you are an orderly Marine at home too, who will put his boots away in the closet where I won't trip on them when I'm so huge with this baby I can no longer see my feet. *Maybe* you adore me enough never to make me question if our home is safe to live in, free of bachelor messes and hazards."

"Maybe," he said quietly. The baby moved under his hand, a sharp staccato beat striking his palm. "I think the baby is on my side."

"Not a chance." Carys laughed; all traces of anxiety gone. "So, what *is* my new name?"

"Come with me," he said, taking her hand and helping her up. "I have to tell them when we apply for a marriage license."

Eric led Carys to the front desk, where they were directed to the office of the events coordinator. An hour later, they had everything set for a wedding on the beach that evening.

"Carys Rose Parker, huh?" Eric said back in their room.

"My mother said I looked like the loveliest little rose bud when I was born," Carys said, rolling her eyes. "Carys means *love,* so I'm a lovely rose in a park. Except she wanted a variety she could prune to her liking, and instead got an independent, stubborn, wildflower instead."

"Is that such a bad thing?" he asked.

"It is if you have control issues." She shrugged her shoulders.

"There will be plenty of things out of my or *our* control while I'm in the military, you know."

"I understand your job has its challenges, but I'm not afraid. There will still be plenty of things we get to choose for ourselves. How to raise our baby, how many babies. The way we run our home and how we prioritize and organize our life together. And it's temporary, Eric Blackwood with no middle name." She smiled at him as she sat down on the bed.

"It left a big gap for my other name," he joked.

"Your nickname is only four letters long," she deadpanned.

Eric joined her on the bed, turning sideways so he could kiss her temple. "Do you want to make one up for me? We'll have to get your name changed anyway. I could always add something extra to mine."

She shook her head. "No, I *do* have a gift for you

though." Carys pulled away, her bare feet quietly padding across the floor to her dresser—he'd been damn proud she'd unpacked her bags as soon as she'd arrived. Carys removed a small envelope from the top drawer and brought it to him. "These are for you."

Eric took the envelope, noting the *Ojai Imaging Center* logo on the front. "Are these pictures of the baby?"

"They are, and something else," she said, picking up her phone off the mattress. "Listen to this." Carys tapped her phone a few times, all smiles as a whooshing sound came from the built-in speaker. "They gave me a recording of the heartbeat so you could hear it."

"Wow," Eric said, closing his eyes and listening. He felt the mattress dip beside him as she sat, taking his hand in hers. "Thank you."

"Do you want to know the gender?" she asked softly.

He thought for a moment. Did he want to know? Did it matter? He opened his eyes and looked down at the envelope in his hands. "I think so," he said hesitantly, "as long as you want to know."

"Honestly, I've been chomping at the bit. They can tell really early now with a blood test, but I couldn't bring myself to do it without you," she admitted.

"Then let's find out," he said, pulling the flap of the envelope out of the tab securing it.

The top images were various body parts. Eric looked at legs, feet, arms, and a sweet little profile of the baby's face—all labeled, thankfully, or he'd never have known what he was looking at. He ran a finger gently over the shape of the baby's face, humming with pride. "It has your cute little nose."

Carys snorted. "Yeah, okay. All babies have little noses, Eric."

He stared at the image. *Nope. That's the exact profile I woke up to, in my arms.* He kept his thoughts to himself.

"Last image is gender!" she singsonged, bouncing on the bed with her hands around his bicep.

Eric flipped over the last image.

"I knew it!" she squealed.

"Uh…" He had no clue what he was looking at.

"The label is under your thumb."

Right.

Chapter Fourteen

CARYS

Carys wiped her sweaty palms on her leggings again, a shaky breath escaping her. She was married and about to be a mom. None of that had been scary. Formally meeting her husband's best friend as his new wife?

Utterly terrifying.

"Ruben is going to love you," Eric reassured her—again.

"Yeah," she said, her voice coming out high and squeaky. "Yeah." *Because it's totally normal to come back from vacation with a new wife and baby you didn't have when you left. Totally normal.*

Eric's phone chirped out a text notification. "He's already parked and waiting at the baggage carousel."

Carys wanted to run away, but her *husband* had tucked her neatly under his arm, his hand rubbing up and down her bicep in a soothing way. She knew it was completely irrational—one more thing to blame on the hormones—to fear Ruben's reaction. Their first meeting as he bailed out of Mexico prematurely had been pleasant, and she'd thought at the time his free spirit was a great balance to Eric's more contemplative pace of living. Ruben was fun.

But fun people still get suspicious when a stranger shows up married to their best friend and claiming to be pregnant with his baby. Even in her mother's Hallmark movies, her situation wasn't a winning combination for acceptance.

"Slow! Over here, man."

Eric steered her in the direction of Ruben's voice, her arms wrapping around his waist. She was too short to see over the crush of people pushing their way through baggage claim, but she could see his distinctive arm waving in the air off to one side. Ruben had found a pocket of near empty space against the wall, the throng pushing by a solid five feet away from him.

"My. Man." Ruben said exuberantly. "And the lovely Carys. Didn't I tell you I'd be seeing you around when we met? Eh?"

"You did." Her nerves eased up now that Ruben was a few feet away, his megawatt smile lighting up his face.

"Ruben, this is my new *wife,*" Eric said, turning to face her, both his hands resting on her upper arms. "Carys Blackwood, you remember Ruben Holt." In her peripheral, she could see Ruben's jaw hanging open. "And *this,*" Eric went on, sliding his hands down Carys's arms and around her bump, "is your future goddaughter."

The smile on Eric's face filled Carys with both relief and butterflies. Their last five days in Mexico had been put to good use. She felt prepared for what this new life would be like for her. As nervous as she'd been to tell him her feelings, he'd done a lot to help put all her worries aside for now.

"Woooo-yah! *I'm an uncle!*" Ruben shouted, startling Carys out of her reverie and drawing looks from several people close by. "Oh, man. I'm gonna be a fun uncle. *A funkle.* Hell yeah!" He threw a fist in the air, bounced on the balls of his feet, and let out a celebratory holler Carys imagined could only come from the love child of Matthew McConaughey and Chris Rock—and it strangely worked on Ruben.

She let out an awkward, nervous giggle, her body trembling from relief now instead of fear. Carys let go of her husband and threw her arms around Ruben, pulling him in tightly as tears ran down her face. "Thank you, Ruben."

"Hey, now. Those better be happy tears soaking my favorite shirt, *Missus Blackwood*. I don't need no trouble from your old man," he teased.

She stepped back, releasing him. "I was really scared," she blurted. In her efforts to choke back a sob, snot shot out her nose, sticking to her upper lip and threatening to slide to her mouth. *"Ugh.* Great, now I'm the snot queen."

"Here, sweetheart," Eric said softly, his arm coming into view from behind her with a tissue in hand. She took it, blowing her nose.

"All hail the queen," Ruben said as they moved toward the baggage carousel together. "And my *niece,"* he purred sweetly. "Our very own Oceanside royalty."

"Sorry I ugly cried all over you," she said. "And almost used you as a hankie."

Ruben *pisht* her with a wave of his hand. "Man, ladies have it way harder than we do. I respect that."

Once they were buckled into Ruben's huge truck and on their way, Carys fell asleep against Eric's shoulder in the back seat. Subconsciously, she recognized the sound of their voices conversing, but nothing they said registered in her mind. She hadn't expected Ruben to be so excited, much less welcoming, and the adrenaline crash wiped her out.

When Eric gently shook her awake, Carys felt disoriented. They were parked in a driveway, and Ruben was already hauling her bags up to the front porch for her. She smiled to herself. He was a good guy, Ruben. She hoped they'd see a lot of him.

"Hey, now. Don't be making heart eyes at my friend, sweetheart." Eric kissed the top of her head.

"I'm just grateful," she said, arching her back as she stretched out. "He's a keeper."

Eric helped her down from the truck and walked her to the front door, which was already open. "Welcome home, wife." Carys shrieked in surprise as Eric scooped her off her feet to carry her over the threshold.

This is so much better than Mom's Hallmark movies.

———

"SHOW ME AGAIN," Vinny said with a heavy sigh.

Carys held up her hand in front of her tablet again so Vinny could see her ring, blushing prettily. "I love it."

"I bet; it's exactly what you would have picked yourself. I can't believe he had a custom ring made for you after *one week* of fucking your brains out."

"Lavender!"

Vinny laughed. "Oh, come on, Carys. Your life is so textbook fairytale perfect right now, it's sickening."

"How's the life of a rockstar going?" she countered, not wanting to make Vinny feel like she was rubbing in how wonderful her life truly was right now.

"Decent," she answered, looking away from the camera.

"What's his name?"

"What, who?"

"Yeah, *who.* Don't play dumb with me. What's the name of the reason you can't look at me right now."

"Brooks."

"Like Garth Brooks?"

Vinny snorted sardonically. "If only. No, his first name is Brooks. I'm not sure I caught his last name."

Which means they were fucking against a wall before she asked for it, Carys thought to herself. "Is Brooks in the band?"

"No, he's the band manager's assistant. And *fuck me,* can the man make a cappuccino."

He's probably fucked her everywhere but a bed by now. Carys shook her head. "You don't even like cappuccino, you matcha loving freak."

"He's converted me." Vinny sighed wistfully. "Anyway, it's a road thing, you know? Plus, my dad thinks he's a tool, so I'm just having a bit of fun behind his back," she added, waggling her brows.

"You're twenty-five, Vin. And your dad doesn't care, so long as you find someone who will treat you right and make you happy." The unspoken end to that sentiment was *the way he was with your mother.* "And since when does your dad use the word *tool* as a descriptor?"

"Whatever. Hey, are you celebrating tomorrow?"

"It's freaky how well you remember things."

"Hell yeah. Three months since you eloped, and I got to watch your mom completely break down in hysterics when you showed up for the rest of your stuff with your new husband." Vinny laughed. "I knew he was a keeper."

Carys had gotten a lot of raised eyebrows and slack jaws as Eric introduced her to his colleagues and friends, but nobody had gotten weird about her suddenly appearing in his life, obviously pregnant. Her mother on the other hand, had taken the news poorly. While Eric and Vinny helped box back up what little she'd unpacked when she'd moved back in after graduating the month before, her mother had turned purple screaming at her in the living room about how she was ruining her life.

With her meager belongings tucked into the bed of Eric's truck, he and Vinny had come back in to fetch her right as Carys's mother let off about how abusive military men were because they were conditioned to violence, and she wouldn't take Carys or the baby in when it happened. Eric had wrapped his arms around Carys protectively and then promptly told her mother she was never to speak to *his wife* like that again.

Unused to being corrected by anyone, her mother stood there sputtering in shock, as Eric tenderly turned Carys to face him and kissed her until her body was rubber. As they turned to leave, he'd informed her she was welcome to call and apologize to Carys whenever she was ready.

Carys wasn't holding her breath for the call.

Vinny had skipped down the walkway back to her own car humming "Ding Dong the Witch is Dead" from the *Wizard of Oz*, pausing to give Carys a tight squeeze before she drove off in her baby, leaving Eric and Carys laughing on the curb over her antics.

"I'll be down the next couple weekends to set up and host your baby shower, don't forget," Vinny said, pulling Carys back into the present.

Right, still on a video call. Focus.

"I'm so excited to see you! And you have to meet Ruben. He just bought the house across the street from us."

"Eric's bestie, right?"

"That's the one."

"Looking forward to it. I gotta get to sound check soon, so put the baby on."

Carys rolled her eyes but moved the phone so it was pressed against her torpedoing middle. Vinny crooned out the lullaby *Lavender's Blue,* a tradition she'd started the moment Carys told her she was pregnant. The baby knew her voice and popped a foot right into the microphone in what Carys liked to think of as a hello.

After they said their goodbyes, Carys went back upstairs to the nursery, where she'd been painting the walls a soft robin's egg blue. The trim was done in white, and she had been acquiring a kaleidoscope of pastel accents in the form of art, pillows, rugs, curtains—anything she took a liking to. In the second garage at the back of the property, Eric had set up an area for her to work on refurbishing a dresser she'd thrifted.

She had wanted to start job hunting right away, but Eric talked her out of it. Carys had spent an extra year in school, opting to take her classes slower a few terms so she could manage to pay for her education without debt. It had been hard, but with the help of grants and scholarships, she had managed. He insisted she take some time off to focus on herself and adapting to military life before putting her education to use.

Carys had halfheartedly argued out of a sense of obligation to contribute, but deep down, she was grateful. Because deep down, she was also exhausted. With all her time her own for once, she was enjoying transforming their very white interior into something homier and more personal.

Aside from the nursery, she'd taken advantage of the burst of energy she'd gotten in her second trimester to paint as many rooms as she could before she ran out of steam—or her belly made it impossible to reach. She'd so far left the warm oak trim alone, opting for coordinating warm, light shades of soothing colors to bring a richness to each space.

Their bedroom was done up in soft lilac and pale buttercream. She'd used the same cream down the hallway and the staircase and kept the ceilings white, so they didn't feel heavy or cave like. The living room was a lovely, creamy sage color, picking up where the buttercream ended at the bottom of the stairs. Carys might not have been so driven to paint if Eric's reactions hadn't spurned her on. Every time he came home to a new something or other, he made her feel like she could do no wrong; with his *I never would have thought of that color,* and *you are making our house a real home, sweetheart.*

Carys loved all the little quirks of the property, and there were plenty of them. It was situated on a rare double lot, giving them a substantially sized yard, for starters. Eric had told her the original part had been the main homestead back when the area around it was undeveloped land. The house itself was an interesting mesh of add ons and adaptations, from the bulk of the second story to the second garage at the back of the property and the income suite that spanned both garages with an attaching hallway.

If Eric had brought Carys home to some perfect mausoleum he expected her to maintain, she would have been intimidated. The home they now shared instead brought her am immense amount of comfort. A man who could see the potential in a home like this and strive to improve it would be the sort to work hard towards building their marriage strong too.

She hoped, at least.

Eric had built a pergola over the back deck off the kitchen shortly after he bought the place, creating a shaded area between the add-on office space and the second story breeze-way. At the base of the posts, he'd planted native California Honeysuckle and encouraged it to grow over the beams for shade. The pink blooms smelled heavenly in the summer and attracted hummingbirds. It was already their favorite place to sit and talk about their days, beneath his handiwork with the solid decking he'd also constructed beneath them. She'd caught him looking at tree swings online the other day, and she smiled every time she remembered it.

How much her life had changed in eight months—for the better.

It wasn't what she had imagined settling down would look like for her, yet she couldn't regret it. From their immediate connection in Mexico that grew antidotally via email, finishing her education, and the pace with which they had married and settled in together, it was a lot to cram into two thirds of a year. To be expecting their first child as well…

No, it wasn't how Carys had seen her life progressing. But any other way would have deprived her of Eric, and for that, she was grateful. To be known by any other name than Carys Blackwood would have been a tragedy now that she knew what the moniker came with. The love and attention of her husband was priceless.

Chapter Fifteen

ERIC

"Sweetheart, I'm home," Eric called out, sitting down on the bench Carys had added to the hall leading from the garage into the kitchen, along with storage for shoes and outerwear. He'd never admit it, but she'd been right about the floors needing less cleaning now he was taking his shoes off at the door.

"I'm out here!" she hollered from the back deck.

When he stepped outside, she was sitting on the bench swing with a bowl of fruit balanced on her belly and a lemonade in hand. She'd been obsessed with lemonade the past month, along with wrapping herself up to sit on the swing he'd built himself the same time he'd installed the pergola it hung from.

The autumn air was nice today, but being on the coast it sometimes grew chilly in the evenings. Eric had gotten a fluffy blanket for her to use outside that was easy to wash, so she wouldn't ruin anything fancy if it was forgotten out there. Between critters and the elements, it wouldn't take much to destroy something fine.

"How was your day?" he asked, slowly lowering onto the

swing beside her. Carys immediately scooched closer, and his arm automatically went behind her.

"It was good. I got the poly on her dresser today. Give it a week to air out, and you and Ruben can haul it up to the nursery. I should have her room done by then too."

"You are getting close to your due date. I think you should slow down on all this painting," he said, concern tinging his voice.

"I know, but I can't help it. I feel like I need to be constantly doing things. And besides, I'm *enjoying* myself. Making this house our home has been more fulfilling than I ever imagined," she said. Carys turned her face up to his expectantly.

Eric gently kissed her lips, soft pillowy touches that quickly led to something more heated. As her belly had grown, so had her libido. They had to get creative now to keep her comfortable and supported, but all in all he'd never had more sex in his life.

And he wasn't complaining.

"Mmm," he said, pulling back before he forgot what he needed to talk to his wife about. "We're getting a new neighbor."

"Oh! Is someone moving out?"

"Sort of. The Browns next door have a mother-in-law suite they rent out to single military. They just finished updating it and their new tenant is Perez," he said.

"Oh."

Carys knew all about Perez. Everything about their life together had happened so fast, Eric had spent a lot of time telling her as much as he could so his past wouldn't create any new anxiety for her unexpectedly. With the way Perez had acted down range after he had declined to extend their casual sex agreement from the previous deployment, it wouldn't surprise him if she was set on starting drama. He hoped not, but he wasn't holding his breath. She was still barely cordial at work on the occasions they had to speak at all.

"And there's more. Ruben proposed to Carla," he said, distaste filling his mouth. He never did see what Ruben saw in her, especially after she'd strung him along in college. She was the spoiled daughter of a Navy admiral, an only child brought up in a world where she said jump and everyone around her asked how high, including her otherwise strict father.

"Oh...joy." Carys wrinkled her nose, looking as if a skunk had fouled the air. "I guess there goes the neighborhood."

Eric laughed. "I know. At least this way we can keep an eye on the situation. I don't trust her any more than you do."

Carla frequently stayed over with Ruben at his apartment, and after they had run out of legitimate excuses, Eric and Carys had twice agreed to a double date. Both times they watched with horror as Ruben pandered to her every whim. Her every bitchy, self-entitled demand. Being Ruben, he'd done it with a smile.

"I still don't understand what Ruben sees in Carla."

"Nobody whose met her does," he said.

Carys let out a sigh full of resignation. There was nothing more to say. They had agreed Ruben was in for heartache if he kept pursuing her, and rehashing it again changed nothing.

Eric's eyes followed Carys's right hand to her belly, where a foot was pushing hard enough to make her cringe. They watched as the baby pushed harder still, until you could see the shape of the bottom of her foot through Carys's light cotton top, moving from right to left before disappearing again.

"That was one hell of a stretch," Eric said with amusement.

"She's running out of room," Carys agreed. "It's neat to see her little toes poke out like that, but it doesn't feel great."

"We're in the home stretch, sweetheart," he said. "She'll be the best Christmas gift anyone has ever given me."

Carys was due early December, but the doctor she was seeing in Oceanside now had told them due dates were more guesstimates, give or take two weeks. She could arrive anytime between Thanksgiving and Christmas, but first babies tended to cook a little longer. The news had been hard on Carys, given all the Braxton hicks contractions—or false labor—she'd been having lately.

Eric looked on helplessly as she breathed through the pain, doing his best to comfort her through them. He felt helpless, useless. She had assured him his presence did wonders, and the new dad advice books he'd been secretly reading on his lunch breaks told him likewise. He was doing everything he possibly could for both of them, but it didn't feel like enough.

He was a Marine, damn it. Eric was used to putting his boot down and getting the expected results.

And he hated seeing his wife in pain.

God help him when she went into labor.

"Vinny will get here on Thursday," Carys said offhandedly, breaking the comfortable silence that had settled around them as they gently swung, each with a hand on her belly.

"You know, we could offer her the apartment," he said. "I'm not comfortable renting it out to a stranger, but it's got enough space for her and her stuff. I could even enclose the shed attached to the back of the second garage and move the door from the outside into the garage itself. With a little sound proofing, she could use it as a downstairs studio space to store her instruments and do all her social media stuff."

"I would love that, but I don't think she'll go for it. Maybe someday. Thank you for offering it to her though."

"Mmm. I'll get a head start on the shed idea anyway. Just in case."

Carys laughed. "You're just making new projects for yourself, so you feel like you have some control around here."

Nail, hammer. Little building projects helped Eric feel less useless as he watched Carys do all the real work growing their daughter.

"I built the pergola and swing out here *just in case* I ever had a family to enjoy it with too," he deflected. "I like doing useful things."

"If you would like to be useful, help your wife up and feed her."

"With pleasure, sweetheart."

———

"I KNOW you aren't sold on Carla, but she's the one, man. I know it," Ruben said between bites of his lunch.

He'd come into Eric's office with a peace offering—takeout from their favorite pub—and unknowingly forced Eric to stow away the latest book he'd picked up on being a dad. He'd gone a little crazy with the self-help books the past month. But unlike everything else he'd ever done in his life; babies didn't come with instruction manuals or a 101 class. Ruben had already side eyed him last week when he stopped by for lunch and noticed a stack of parenting self-help books, suggesting Eric was panicking.

Which he was. Carys had reached thirty-six weeks and

would be considered full-term from here on out. At any time in the next six weeks, she could go into labor. Carys was cleaning; Eric was reading. Between them, he hoped they had all their bases covered in time.

If it was even possible.

"I'm the last one to cast stones, Ruben. Carla just seems…" *Like a complete bitch.* "High maintenance."

"I don't mind," he said, smiling wide. "I like taking care of her."

"Then I wish you nothing but the best."

"That's great, man. Because I came to ask you to be my best man," he said. "What do you think? We're doing the full military brouhaha. Mess dress and sabers and the whole shebang. Can I count on you?"

"Of course you can," Eric said between bites. "I wouldn't miss it. Have you set a date?"

"April fifth," he said.

Eric choked on his half-chewed food. He turned his head to cough into his elbow until he could gasp in enough air to sputter, "Ruben, that's only four months away!"

"And a few weeks," he added with a shrug, his smile going lopsided. "We've been on and off for almost ten years. I want her to move into the house with me as soon as its ready, but she wanted to be traditional and officially go from her father's home to her husband's, even though she left for college and all. The Admiral's house is still her home."

The Admiral. For fucks sake.

"Are you ever going to call the man by his name?" Eric asked.

"Sure. Soon as he gives me permission."

Jesus. He's out of his mind.

"You really think he's going to grant it?"

"Sure, once he sees I'm the right man to take care of his princess."

"You don't think, given your long history with Carla, he should have crossed that bridge already?" Eric said warily. "You were eighteen and twenty when you first got involved, and even when you haven't been a couple, you were still around her all the time."

Ruben was thirty, same as Eric. Carla had come on the scene the end of their sophomore year. She'd been legal about twelve seconds and was still a high school senior when she caught a ride to her future university for Greek Week—AKA party central on any American college campus. Ruben had fallen in lust immediately. Eric had blamed it on the booze back then, but his friend hadn't been drunk all of the last decade, so he honestly couldn't explain his attraction or dedication to her since.

"I'm not worried," he said with ease.

"You only proposed a month ago. Are you sure you want the stress of planning something so big in only a few months? Especially with all the holidays coming up." Eric reminded him.

"Slow. You got married the day after you proposed."

"I also *eloped.* We didn't go all in on sabers and mess dress," he said dryly.

"It's going to be fine. Stop worrying. Oh, and no strippers at my bachelor party. I'm only interested in one woman from here on out," he proclaimed.

This is going to be a shit show, Eric thought to himself as he smiled wide for his friend. "I know how you feel on that front at least."

Chapter Sixteen

CARYS

"Eric!" she called out as fluid ran down her legs. "We aren't practicing anymore!"

Thankfully, she'd made it downstairs before her water had broken. Carys wouldn't want to brave the steps like this. She could hear Eric's feet pounding down the staircase toward the kitchen, where she was standing in front of the sink, gripping the rim. When she looked up, he was wearing a towel around his waist and his face was half shaved, the other half still covered in white lather.

"Shit. Uh…"

"She's not gonna fall out on the floor. You have time to put pants on." She tried smiling, but an oncoming contraction morphed it into a grimace. "Call Vinny," she said through gritted teeth.

Carys's mother still hadn't called to apologize. Most days she was relieved, but right now, the yearning to be comforted by her mom was strong. Eric's parents had retired to Vermont, and still hadn't flown out to meet her. She got the impression they weren't happy with their only son's choices regarding marriage and family.

It was just them, and the family they had made for themselves.

"Right," Eric said, snapping out of his panic. "Pants. Vinny. Car. Do you need anything?" he asked as he removed his towel, folded it in half, and placed it on the floor so she didn't slip in the puddle forming below her. Carys carefully lifted her feet one at a time so he could arrange the towel, so she was standing on it.

"No, just hurry."

"On it," he said, and she watched him dash out of the kitchen completely naked. Eric returned in under five minutes, his face half smooth and half shadowed where he'd wiped off the shaving cream instead of finishing the job. Carys waited, as Eric put on his sneakers and brought over her slip-on sandals—the only shoes that still fit over her swollen feet.

"I managed to get a hold of Vinny and Ruben," he told her as he pulled the car out of the garage and pointed it toward the birthing center. "Ruben said he'd tell our boss. I will need to make it official with an email once we get you checked in. And Vinny was with her dad in LA, so she shouldn't be long in getting here."

"Thank you," she said with obvious relief. Knowing Vinny was on the way made her feel better already. She'd read in books some new dads faint during delivery. Carys didn't think Eric would be one of them, but if it happened, he would be at the mercy of the nurses. Vinny would get her through until Eric could be revived.

Eric moved a hand over her stomach and stroked it gently once they were on the freeway. "Daddy can't wait to meet you, Maya Blue. But if you could give Mommy a little time to get situated safely with the birthing team, I'd sure appreciate it."

Maya Blue Blackwood was born in a birthing pool twenty-seven hours and nineteen minutes later on Thanksgiving morning.

Carys thought she'd been a little *too* accommodating to her father's request.

———

"ALL DONE, SWEET GIRL," Vinny cooed over Maya, who lay on her changing pad. "Look at you, so pretty."

Carys watched from the corner of the nursery, grinning. She knew what was next. Vinny would scoop up her goddaughter—whom she insisted on changing when Eric was out running errands—and sing Maya her song as she danced her over to Carys for her feeding.

"I still can't believe you named her after the place you got knocked up," Vinny snickered as she placed Maya in Carys's arms.

"Hey! It's more than that and you know it," Carys said, giving her best friend a harmless stink eye. "I fell in love with her father as he dragged me up those ruins and daquiried and dined me over authentic Mexican food."

"Daquiried and dined?" Vinny said with amusement.

"I sure as hell wasn't drinking wine down there."

"True."

"I'm more concerned about the mental lapse I had with Blue, after the lullaby you are always singing her—well, and the beautiful beach waves we watched with the dawn."

"You could have gone with Lavender," Vinny said with a shrug and a smile.

"Uh-huh. Just straight up name my kid after you? Your ego is big enough," she said.

"Oh, sweetheart," Eric said, coming in the room. She

hadn't even heard him come inside; she was so exhausted. "Let's go nap with Maya in our bedroom."

"Eric, she's never going to sleep on her own if you keep insisting on family sleep sessions."

"Come on, sweetheart. You are overtired and frustrated right now. This is still new. It's okay to let me hold you—both of you—whenever you need the support. That's my most important job right now."

She did need soothing. All the soothing. And naps.

Eric helped her out of the rocking chair she'd reupholstered herself and led her across the hall to their room. Vinny followed with Maya, waiting for Eric to get them both situated on the bed before passing her to Eric, who placed the baby on Carys. With the swaddled mound on her chest, Carys leaned back into Eric's embrace with a long yawn. She was going to miss this when he went back to work. He was so hands on with Maya.

"I don't know if I could do this without you," she said quietly. "It's so hard, and you are such a good dad. A good *partner.*"

"We're a team, Carys. Whether I'm home or not, you are never alone." He kissed the side of her temple. Carys felt like he'd read her mind, putting her insecurities to rest without her voicing them. "But to be on the safe side, I asked Vinny if she could stay through the holiday break, until her next tour kicks off."

Best.

Husband.

Ever.

Carys fell asleep with Maya snuggled close, the two of them tucked safely against their personal hero.

"RUBEN STOPPED by while you were out with Vinny," Eric said as he carried in the groceries. "He was really sorry to miss all of you."

Carys finished washing her hands, shut off the kitchen tap, and dried her hands. "Has he even *met* Vinny yet?" she thought out loud.

"I haven't even glanced him coming in and out of his house," Vinny said, breezing into the kitchen to hand off the baby for feeding. Vinny had stayed on for extra baby time partly to help out and also because the tour she and her dad had signed on for was a long one. It would be at least six months before she would be able to visit in person, and Vinny took her role as Maya's godmother seriously.

Carys was going to miss her when she had to leave. They would video chat and text like always, but somehow Carys anticipated it wouldn't be quite the same now the baby was here.

"He's been spending every spare second scraping together this damn wedding." Eric practically growled out the word *wedding*. Being the best man meant he had been further exposed to the bride and her flights of fancy. The extra time together had not improved his opinion of her if the scowl on his face when he returned home afterward was any indication. "Every time he updates me on her must haves, I'm more and more grateful we spontaneously eloped," he said, winking at Carys before ducking his head back into the fridge with more perishables.

"I'm just miffed," Vinny said, putting her hands on her hips. "We share the duty of godparent, and I don't even know what he looks like."

That reminded Carys, she needed to have some personal photos framed for their home. They would look great lined up on the mantel—eventually. When she was less sleep deprived and had time to pick out some favorites. If their family couldn't be around personally, Carys would make sure they still had a presence. Maya gurgled in her arms, reminding her she was supposed to be nursing.

"Well, as much as I don't love Carla, I *do* love Ruben. I really hope he gets what he needs from this relationship in the end," Carys said.

Christmas came. Ruben did not. Ditto for New Years. It was unlike him not to pop over. He had been living across the street in his new house for a few months, and yet they rarely saw him even in passing. They saw the lights on in the evenings, so he was coming home regularly. Eric worried about his friend more than he let on, and Carys was beginning to wonder if something terrible was afoot, and Ruben was avoiding them in order to prolong some inevitable fallout.

Only time would tell.

Chapter Seventeen

ERIC

Vinny stood at the front window, watching Ruben's house through the sheer curtains Carys had hung to—ironically— keep out prying eyes. *They certainly don't keep prying eyes in,* Eric mused to himself as he glanced over at his wife's best friend from the couch. She was humming something under her breath as she observed, but he couldn't quite make it out.

He wished he could hear the tune. Vinny was a musician down to her marrow. If anyone ever wanted to know what was on the woman's mind, they need never ask. She'd either be playing, humming, singing, or tapping out a song matching her mood, or posting her life's reflections on her ArtBeat account. She was an open book.

"Something interesting happening out there?" Eric finally asked.

"No," she answered simply.

"Am I so bad to look at after six weeks staying with us, you can't stand the sight of me now?"

She turned to him with a smile. "That's what I like about you, Eric. You know how to laugh at yourself."

"If only I could read minds," he said, shifting his attention to his sleeping daughter. He was holding Maya while Carys took a nap. "I wonder what she's thinking."

Vinny came and sat beside him, reaching out to briefly stroke Maya's nose. "She's thinking this big world isn't so bad with her badass auntie here."

"You're probably right," he conceded. "Her parents are a little crazy. I hear they don't plan out any of the important details in life."

"Some people operate better with spontaneity guiding them," Vinny said. "Others thrive within rigid structures. Religion, social constructs, set schedules they create for themselves to keep life predictable. If you are never surprised, you can't be caught off your guard."

"Some surprises are good though," Eric bantered back. "You have to take the good with the bad."

"Only good here," Vinny said, smiling at Maya.

"What's bothering you, Lavender Blume?"

She sighed. "Honestly, I'm torn. I am really looking forward to this tour, but I don't want to leave you guys either. I know Carys is doing a lot better, and she's an *amazing* mom, despite her self doubts."

"But."

"But Maya has two godparents, and it's really pissing me the hell off the one who moved in across the street has been MIA."

Preach, sister.

"Our family is small, Eric. I know you think of Ruben as a brother, and Carys and I are ride or die friends for life. But with Maya here, that's still only five people. Family should show up. Given we built our family from love over blood, I can't help believing it's even *more* important we do what we can for each other."

"Hopefully things settle down after the wedding," he

said. Vinny cocked a brow in his direction, making him chuckle. "Yeah, I don't believe that either. Wishful thinking."

"You're worried about him."

"He's my best friend. Of course I'm worried. Between Carys's mother and my parents, we really only have the two of you, like you said. What little blood family we have left isn't exactly stepping up. You and Ruben are our family, and family sticks together. I agree with you whole heartedly." *Which is why Ruben's behavior is so difficult to tolerate. Marriage should add to a family, not break it apart unnecessarily.*

It still smarted Eric how Carys's mother hadn't come down off her high horse. At the same time, it was her loss and his gain. He would never take them for granted like that, but he still believed in his core she should have embraced her daughter's choices, even if she didn't agree. Looking down at his own daughter, he couldn't imagine giving up on her for something that made her happy.

"Don't you have sisters?"

"I do, but they live on the east coast, and they are a lot older than me. I was born when my mother was forty-three," he explained. "My sisters were already out of the house by then. I have a niece two years *older* than me."

Vinny snort laughed. "I can't even imagine that."

"She'll be okay," Eric said after a long pause. "You've been so supportive of her, of *us*. It means something. I'm grateful for you, Vin."

"I definitely got my money's worth out of our trip to Mexico," she teased, attempting to hide her discomfort over his direct praise. Eric had already figured out she didn't like attention drawn to her good deeds, but he'd be an ass if he didn't say something. "And you certainly did *change the world,"* she said, referencing the Eric Clapton song she'd hummed when they first met. "For me and for Carys."

Something settled between them as they fell into comfortable silence.

We're friends now, he realized.

"Chinese takeout for dinner? My treat," Vinny said.

"Deal."

————

"SLOW!"

Eric turned to look out his garage door at the familiar voice. Ruben was jogging across the street, already out of his uniform and dressed casually.

"Hey," he said. "You haven't been over in two weeks."

"I've barely been *home* the last two weeks, man. Between cake sampling and all the menu, venue, officiant stuff, I am officially having nightmares over buttercream frosting and having to settle for a cross eyed JP who sounds like the guy from *Princess Bride*."

"I thought Carla didn't want a Justice of the Peace?"

"That was before every other option refused to officiate without several weeks' worth of premarital counseling," Ruben said. "We just don't have the time."

"How did she take the news?"

"Eh. Not bad."

Eric had seen Carla on her "best" behavior. *Not bad* was probably similar to a weekend getaway in the sixth circle of hell.

"About your bachelor party," he segued, not wanting to talk about the bride overly long. "I have it all set up for the second weekend in March. I can't move the date again, so consider yourself locked in. I already told the guys."

"Awe, yeah!" Ruben hooted, bouncing on the balls of his feet as he was prone to do. "Looking forward to enjoying something I *didn't* plan."

Eric laughed. This was the Ruben he knew, cracking jokes and getting excited.

"Can I come in and see Maya?"

"Of course. You missed Vinny again though. She had to go to LA for the next four days to get things squared for her upcoming tour."

"That's right," Ruben said, nodding. "Carys said she's a musician."

"Yeah. Touring is fun for her, especially the one coming up because her dad will be playing too."

"Oh, family business. That's cool."

"Yeah. She has a top trending ArtBeat account as well. Vinny was telling me she makes enough off her affiliate links to support herself. She tours because playing live is food for the soul," Eric said, shaking his head as a smile curved his mouth upward. "She reminds me of you sometimes."

"Gotta tend to the soul, Slow. But I doubt we will have much in common, musically. Aside from both loving music."

Eric knew he was making a false assumption, but he didn't say a word. He hoped he got to see the look on Ruben's face the first time he heard Vinny riff on her guitar though. The more time he spent with Vinny, the more he liked her.

Eric had already sat down Carys and explained a few harsh realities about being military, especially if you deploy. You *have* to have wills and advanced directives on file. There is no way around it. Shortly after Maya was born, he'd made an appointment with the legal office to update his own paper-work and get Carys's started.

The easiest choice had been naming Ruben and Vinny

joint custodians of Maya and any future children they had should anything happen to them. Now if only they could get the two in the same room and discuss it. Eric understood Ruben had bitten off too much for himself with Carla, but this was about his daughter, and he needed his best friend to step up. It wasn't lost on Eric that *Vinny* had called him out last week.

"I can't believe she's already three months old," Ruben said from behind him as they entered the house through the garage.

"She woke up yesterday too big for the last of her 'new baby' clothes, and I thought Carys was going to drown herself crying as she packed it away," Eric said.

Ruben chuckled. "I bet. You having more then?"

"Kids? Hell yeah." Eric smiled at his friend as he got his shoes off and his overcoat hung. "I wasn't sure I'd be a dad at all, and now I'll take as many as she'll give me. Don't tell her this," he said, dropping his voice, "but I finally understand the appeal to barefoot and pregnant in the kitchen. Carys is a fucking goddess pregnant. Seeing her all rounded out, growing a person we made together—nothing compares."

"All right. That's not creepy or possessive at all," Ruben said.

"You'll see," Eric said with a grin. "It's different when it's *your* wife and baby."

"That's not really in the cards, man. Carla doesn't want kids," Ruben said as they crossed the kitchen, his voice tinged with tension—and sadness.

Eric stopped right before the doorway into the living room and turned to face his friend. "Are you okay with that?"

He shrugged. "Carla's going to be my wife. It would be shitty to make her do something she doesn't want to."

It's fucking shitty she knows you want kids and is manipu-

*lating you into sacrificing the experience to satisfy her need
to be the center of attention.*

"Okay," he said, turning back toward the living room.
"Come on in and have a seat, brother."

Carys came down the steps with Maya as they were
settling into the couches. Eric was grateful her timing had
prevented an awkward silence between them, her smile
cutting through the tension left behind after Ruben's
confession.

"Look at you!" Ruben cooed, his arms out in invitation.
Carys gladly handed Maya over to him and took a seat next to
Eric. "My little princess can hold up her head and everything!
Your Funcle Ruben missed you, baby girl."

"She is *not* calling you funcle, Ruben," Carys lightly
chastised him.

"You totally are," he stage whispered to Maya, who gifted
him with a gummy smile and an impressive amount of drool
right down the front of his shirt.

———

"ALREADY?" Carys said, her voice sounding small and
frightened.

"It's only two weeks, and Ruben will be right across the
street."

Carys snorted. "No, he won't. I don't even know why he
bought that house, because he sure as hell isn't living in it,"
she said caustically.

She had a point.

"He won't let you down, sweetheart. I already talked to
him about it," Eric said, trying his best to put her mind at
ease.

"I'm not sure I'm ready."

"You made it through half your pregnancy alone, with what sounds like killer morning sickness. I have complete faith you will handle yourself fine for two weeks."

"The morning sickness wasn't that bad," she huffed.

Eric pulled her in close and kissed the top of her head before murmuring into her crown, "that's not what Vinny said."

"Fucking traitor." Carys buried her face into his chest, her arms coming up around his back. "When do you leave?"

"The day after Ruben's bachelor party."

"Okay," she said, her voice muffled by his body. "Two weeks. It'll be a mini training for me too, a taste of what the main event will be like."

"That's the spirit."

A two week training exercise on the east coast was the least of Eric's worries. Talk of deployment was in the air.

How was he going to tell Carys he'd likely miss Maya's first birthday?

Chapter Eighteen

CARYS

"Good morning, my sweet girl," Carys said in her happiest tone. "You look perky this morning."

It was day three of Eric's TDY—temporary blabidyblah, meaning leaving but not moving—and her spirits were low. She'd slept next to him every night since he came for her in Mexico, even after Maya was born at the birthing center. Her sleep was off from his absence, coupled with a baby sleep regression breaking Carys's already poor sleep into even smaller chunks.

Maya didn't seem to be suffering from her sudden change in sleeping habits in the least. She smiled up at her mother same as she always did, the dark waves of hair she'd inherited from her father sticking every which way around her head.

How come babies look adorable with bed head, but adults look like they stuck a finger in a light socket? It was completely unfair. She hadn't even managed a shower since Eric left.

Vinny: How are things? Don't lie. I know when you lie.

Carys huffed as she read the message. "Your aunt is a pain," she said to Maya with false cheer.

Carys: It's hard to sleep alone. I miss him.

There. Find the lie in that, Lavender.

Vinny: And…

Carys: Stop reading between the lines!

Vinny: Stop hiding all the important stuff there and I will.

Carys: Fine. If I feel this shitty after three days, what will I do for months without him?

The dots on the screen bounced and disappeared several times before Vinny's reply came through.

Vinny: One day at a time. One minute at a time if that's all you got. It's never easy being the one who is left behind, but Eric would scorch the earth to get back to you and Maya. Believe in his love and devotion and take it as slow as you need to.

Damn.

Vinny would know. Her dad had been out touring a lot when she was small, until her mother had died. He'd slowed down then in order to raise his daughter, but Vinny was still well aware what it felt like to have a loved one leave.

And one who never came back.

Carys: Thanks, Vin. I know you're right, but it's hard. Every little thing Maya does is bittersweet because he isn't here to share it with me.

Vinny: I feel that way when I babysit her. You aren't special.

Carys laughed. "Bitch."

Vinny: Soon as this tour is over, I'll come stay awhile, okay?

Carys: We'd like that.

Eric liked Vinny. He'd told Carys so several times while

she'd been here. She'd known she couldn't be with a man who didn't like her best friend, but everything with Eric had been so *fast.* If he and Vinny had discovered they hated each other outside brunch on the Caribbean, it would have destroyed Carys.

Carys: btw saw your ArtBeat video yesterday. "Play Date" by Melanie Martinez? Who burned you this time?

Vinny: Let's just say, I have reaffirmed my belief crew members are trouble.

Carys: I liked the whole split grid thing. How many instruments are you proficient on now? And jeez, woman! Doing your own backups. Damn. I wish you would pursue a career as a headliner. You have the skills.

Vinny: You know how I feel about my career, Carys. The second it's not fun anymore, I'm walking. That's a lot harder to do as a headliner, with tons of people depending on you. I can walk from a bad vibe as a touring band member.

Carys: You know what you should do? Get your dad to do a grid video with you. I'm thinking The Eagles.

Vinny: Yeah…no. I gotta go.

Carys: Liar.

Vinny: Dad says I need to be early to sound check.

Carys sighed with a shake of her head. She smiled down at her conversation with Vinny. No way she had sound check this early in the day, but Carys knew Vinny was sensitive about her dad. He didn't do social media at all and while he loved watching Vinny's videos, he didn't like her posting so much of her life online.

Scooping Maya up, Carys headed downstairs. She wiggled her nose, hoping she could bewitch a caffeine IV bag to materialize in her kitchen. No such luck. She'd been too tired to prep the coffee pot and set the timer on it last night. Eric usually did it, so it wasn't her habit.

Drats.

Maya lunged at her chest with a soft baby grunt.

"Okay, okay. I hear you," she said as she shifted the baby to one arm. "Second breakfast is served, my little Hobbit." Eric did so much to lighten Carys's load when he was home, and she missed all the little things she realized she'd taken for granted. Necessity had forced her to learn to do things one handed lately.

Like make coffee. *I miss my man.*

Was she feeling sorry for herself? Absolutely.

As she topped up her second mug with her favorite creamer, Carys heard the loud sound of heavy doors slamming out front. She shifted Maya in her arms and grabbed her mug before walking to the front window. Outside, a moving truck was parked at the curb between their home and the Brown's next door, the ramp already down in front of their driveway.

From the back of the truck, a woman of average height and above average ass sway sauntered down the ramp like it was a runway, carrying a box. She was fit, her naturally brown colored locks streaked from the California sun swinging in time with her hips from her high ponytail.

Sonja Perez.

Eric had told Carys his old deployment fuck buddy would be moving in, but they hadn't known when. Just her luck it was happening while Eric was away. Sonja had obviously showered that morning. The old clothes hugging her body still had far more sex appeal than Carys did right now, with her greasy hair, milk crusted shirt, and an old pair of Eric's PT sweats.

But Eric doesn't want her. *He wants me. Everyone has a history. Her being next door doesn't mean a thing for us. What means something is Eric breaking his slow and steady nature to make sure we're a family, making me the exception to his otherwise cautious existence.*

Carys popped the baby up onto her shoulder and rubbed her back as much to calm Maya as to reassure herself of Eric's steadfastness, her mug growing cold on the window ledge as she distracted herself. Carys burped, bounced, and kissed Maya. She told her daughter how loved and wanted she was by her parents. She soaked in the sweet smell of baby, her warmth and softness.

And she watched.

We're a family.

If she said it enough times, perhaps she could vanquish the insecurities bubbling up as she watched her husband's ex-lover sashay her way into the neighborhood like it was built for her. A knock at the door startled Carys out of her downward spiral.

Before she could get to the door, she heard the key turn in the lock.

"If it isn't the queen and princess of Oceanside," Ruben said smoothly as he let himself in.

"Hi, Ruben."

"Milady," he said, bowing dramatically. "May I make a suggestion?" She nodded. "Get thee away from yonder window, my queen."

Carys sighed, her eyes burning with unshed tears. "I saw her at the Christmas party. I don't know why her moving in is such a killer."

"Because she's a bitch with an agenda. V12 said he heard her talking shit, about taking back what is rightfully hers. Be careful, Carys. Don't give Perez any reason to come after you, because she will," he warned.

"Eric usually has such a good read on people. *Why her? How?* She's got homewrecker written all over her, Ruben."

Ruben rubbed the scruff on his face, looking thoughtful. "Honestly, I used to think she was on the DL myself. I don't know, something about Slow. I don't think she's used to being the one left behind, you know? Eric went to the Caribbean and came back celibate over some beach bunny, when she was counting on him for a good time down range. Scuttlebutt is, she expected him to get his heart broken. Instead, he went back for the girl and came home married. Jealousy does bad things to good people, man."

"I got a bad feeling, Ruben."

"I don't blame you. But guys like Slow don't throw fast balls if they aren't sure. He knew from the start you were a home run, and he was willing to do whatever it took to make sure you and Maya were his forever," Ruben said with a conviction she rarely heard from him.

"Thank you," she murmured after a long pause.

"Come on," he said, holding his arms out. "I took the day off. Go take a long, hot shower and put on something that makes you feel like the queen you are. Maya and I will be down here waiting."

"Waiting for what?"

"I'm taking you out to lunch. No arguments," he added when Carys opened her mouth to protest.

She couldn't help the genuine smile pushing up her cheeks as Ruben took Maya and shooed her away. How could she have ever doubted him? When it mattered, Ruben showed up. Given he was weeks away from an elaborate wedding he was planning on the fly, she knew his time was precious. And he'd earmarked today for them.

"Ruben Holt, you are one of a kind," she said over the banister as she began climbing the stairs. "Thank you."

He smiled up at her from the couch with a slight nod.

Then went right back to his face making competition with Maya.

Carys's feet moved with the energy of someone who'd slept in that morning as she readied herself for lunch out.

———

"WHEN I CAME DOWN, he'd already changed Maya and dressed her up in the cutest little romper. He must have brought it with him special because I know I haven't seen it before," Carys mused over the phone that night.

"I'm glad you got out of the house, sweetheart. You deserve it."

"I can't wait for the weather to warm up, so we can put Maya's swing under the pergola. She's going to love it. And I'll get to see the flowers in bloom this year," she said wistfully. "The backyard is going to be a dreamland when spring and summer finally return."

Eric laughed. "I built it all for you."

"We hadn't met yet when you built it."

"I built it for the *possibility* of you, then. In hopes I'd have someone to share it with."

Carys felt warmth spread all over her, the love in his tone suffusing her body with everything she'd been missing. "I know. Thank you."

"Maybe it needs something else, what do you think?"

"The backyard?"

"Yeah."

Carys thought for a moment. "No, it's perfect for now. We'll need a play structure before next year though. Maya will need a safe place to be active and explore, and if her pregnancy was any sign, the next one will be rough too. I'd rather be sick at home than a public park."

"The next one?" His voice was low and rough, like when he called her to bed. Carys's core clenched, and she felt herself go damp.

"Yeah," she said softly. "I was thinking we could start trying after her first birthday."

The noise Eric made next set her heart racing, her breath coming out in short little pants. "Say it," he rumbled.

"Please, Eric. Put another baby in me."

"Fuck, sweetheart. I can't wait."

Chapter Nineteen

ERIC

Every time he thought about his wife over the next ten days, he remembered the sound of her voice—soft and sexy as she pled on his command—asking him to put another baby in her. It was torture. And it was divine. A euphoric hell he battled all day, his cock more than ready to fulfill her request immediately.

When Eric finally made it home, he slipped in as Carys was putting Maya to bed. He watched through the half open nursery door as she tucked their baby into her crib, softly humming the lullaby Vinny had gifted Maya in the womb.

She was perfection. Every statue of every fertility goddess *ever* had been carved with her in mind, Eric was sure of it. Carys lifted her hand to the edge of her tank as she moved away from the crib, clearly intent on fixing her shifted top. "Leave it," he said in a low, husky whisper. He wanted her exposed to him.

Her gaze went up to him, her body ridged for a moment before she realized who was watching them. He saw the heat rise in her eyes as she locked on to his face. Her hand slowly dropped to her side, leaving her breast still exposed as she padded to his side on silent feet, closing the door behind her.

"I thought you would be home really late, practically tomorrow," she said low under her breath. He followed her shadow into their room and closed that door too.

"Sometimes planes break. I didn't want to promise I'd be home at a decent hour, only to get delayed," he confessed. Eric's hand drifted toward her peaked nipple, his thumb grazing over it as he palmed her. Carys pulled away, weariness seeping from her.

"I can't tell you the last time I showered. I'm pretty gross." She looked down at her feet, but he could still read the embarrassment flushing her face in the dim light from her bedside lamp.

And he would not stand for it.

Eric quietly sidestepped her, dropped his bag by the closet door, and headed into the bathroom. He began drawing her a bath, then returned to the bedroom where she was standing in the exact same place, frozen except for a single tear glistening as it tracked down her cheek.

"Come here, sweetheart." He opened his arms, stopping right before her.

Carys shook her head.

"Carys Blackwood, step into your husband's arms," he murmured, a hint of authority in his tone. This time, she did as he asked, although reluctantly. "You will never be gross to me. It's not possible."

She collapsed into him then, an exhausted sigh involuntarily warming his chest as she did. Her voice came out muffled from where her face was pressed into him. "I missed you."

"I missed you too." His voice turned coy. "Especially after you asked so nicely for me to put another baby in you."

He rolled his hips into her belly, his hardness obvious. "I've been fighting to keep myself in check ever since."

"How can you want me like this?"

"I'll take you however I can get you, sweetheart. But I can tell you need more from me than a few orgasms. That's why the bath is filling. I'm going to pay homage while I scrub you clean, and when you are relaxed and feeling more yourself, *then* I'm going to carry you to our bed—where I expect you to direct me in exactly how you need to be satisfied."

She shuddered against him, her breath hitching. "Yes, please."

Eric slid his hands around his wife's hips, his hands reaching under the hem of her tank to the waist band of the old PT sweats she'd stollen from his drawer and caressed her soft skin. "I love it when you wear my clothes." His voice was husky, possessiveness wrapping around his vocal cords and infusing his speech with pure sin.

He watched Carys's pupils dilate with need as his hands slid up her body, taking the tank with them. Her arms automatically lifted for him, and he tossed the top aside before his hands wandered back down her torso towards *his* pants. Dropping to his knees, he tenderly kissed her abdomen before dragging the sweats down to her ankles, panties and all. "Step out," he said.

Now that she was bared to him, he said, "Look over my shoulder, sweetheart. What do you see?"

"The mirror. *Us.*" The tension in her voice made his cock jump.

"Do you see the way you have your husband on his knees for you, Carys? Ready to do anything and everything to please you."

She nodded, her lips parting as she began to pant softly. Her nipples grew erect, so enticing. But she didn't feel like herself yet, and despite his not giving a damn she thought she was *dirty,* he knew she wouldn't like him catching one between his teeth before taking a mouthful to enjoy.

Not yet, at least.

Eric stripped rapidly, his brown eyes focused on the lust filled hazel orbs aimed back at him. He led Carys to the bath, holding her elbow as he helped her step inside. He followed, taking a seat behind her and reaching for the hand held wand to wet her hair.

It had been a long time since he'd washed his wife in the bath. They showered together often, but tonight he was more than happy to pamper her, soaking in all her little moans and sighs as his fingertips massaged shampoo into her scalp. Eric could see the way Carys's shoulders visibly dropped as the tension left her body beneath his touch.

"Lean back, sweetheart. Your hair is done." She wiggled her ass against his hard on as she relaxed into his chest, the whisp of a smile raising her cheeks. *"Tease."*

Carys let out a soft chuckle. "Never. You know I'm a sure thing."

Eric smirked as he reached for the sponge and her favorite body wash. "You certainly know how to keep me interested, sweetheart," he said as he lathered the sponge and began stroking it across her body. As his hands glided across her, he teased her sensitive tips, watching with satisfaction as they further hardened and Carys moaned beautifully. When he'd thoroughly washed and teased every other inch of her body, he moved back up her thighs to her apex.

"Eric." She took one of his hands in her own and guided it up and around her.

"You want me to keep you from moving?" he asked as his left arm reached across where she'd placed it, his hand gripping her bicep firmly.

"Yes," she whimpered.

"Anything you want, sweetheart." Eric swirled two fingers at her core before pushing inside. She bucked against him, and he tightened his hold on her as his fingers took up a vigorous pace, stroking her walls as she tightened up around him. "Whatever you need," he added as she bucked her hips up into his hand again, harder this time, her hips gyrating against his palm as he worked.

"You! I need you!" she keened as her orgasm struck. Carys gasped before letting out a soft moan.

Eric's chest filled with pride, even as the rest of his blood surged south. He'd told her to direct him, and she had. "I think you're ready to take this to the bed, sweetheart."

———

ERIC KNOCKED on Ruben's door, his mind flooded with concern. In the three days he'd been home, he'd spent every second he could with Maya, so Carys would have time to do things for herself. Even if all she wanted was to sit in their bedroom with a book. He was proud of how she'd handled his time away, but he still needed to be sure of a few things.

"Hey, man!" Ruben said as he opened the door. "Come on in. You want a beer?"

"I'm good, thanks." Eric followed Ruben into his sparse home, noting the dining room full of boxes. "What's all that?"

"Ah, yeah. Carla has been sending me home with boxes every time I see her."

"Why doesn't she hire a moving company and save the both of you the trouble?"

Carla's dad was an Admiral in the Navy. He had both money and the reputation of being a good man—fair and honest, but still scary as fuck if you crossed him. Carla was his reason for breathing, and therefore spoiled. No way was the Admiral going to like her packing her own boxes.

Ruben shrugged. "She said this was easier for her. She wanted to be sure nothing broke of value. The rest will be brought over later."

The rest? Half the room is full already. It's not like she's bringing a lot of furniture.

Eric swallowed his concerns for the umpteenth time since Ruben got engaged and nodded in false understanding. "S'pose it makes sense."

"Have a seat, man. I'll be right back."

Eric settled down on Ruben's couch. It was worn to perfection. Not saggy but broken in enough to make it really easy to fall asleep if you sat there too long. Before Carys, Eric had done so countless times back at Ruben's old apartment. He'd wanted Ruben to either take the upstairs apartment at his place or move in as a roommate, but he'd insisted that was as over as their years in ROTC.

In hindsight, Ruben had been right.

Just the thought of Carla being in his home during hers and Ruben's on and off again relationship made Eric cringe. Then the thought of bringing Carys home as his wife to a roommate—Eh, no thanks. Some things are more than a friendship can withstand. He was stupid about women, but Ruben nailed it in the friendship department.

"Here you are," Ruben said, handing Eric an opened beer. "Nice and cold."

Eric took the bottle without mentioning he'd turned down the offer.

"Thanks again for keeping an eye on my ladies while I was away," he said instead, taking a slow sip of his beer. "She was a lot less frazzled on the phone at night the days you stopped over."

Eric watched as Ruben took a deep pull off his bottle. He wasn't making eye contact or smiling. If he had to guess, Eric would say his oldest friend was blushing, which was saying something since he was more or less black as midnight.

"Yeah, man," he finally answered, his tone almost somber. "You know I'd do anything for you and yours. I love them like family."

"I know you do, but I'm grateful all the same." Something was bothering Ruben and Eric wasn't going to give him an easy out. "You're family to us too, brother."

Ruben closed his eyes. He was sitting forward at the edge of the couch opposite Eric, his elbows propped on his knees and the beer bottle rolling back and forth between his palms before him. *Nervous.*

"I gotta tell you something, and I don't want to." Ruben's voice came out pained.

"Then don't." Eric countered easily, taking another sip. The beer had gone sour with the mood in the room, and he set the mostly full bottle down on the coffee table.

"I have to, man. But it doesn't mean I like it."

"Then get on with it. What does Carla want now?" Eric said, sarcasm and disappointment dripping from his words.

"All this time I've been here with them instead of helping her plan the wedding every spare second... *Fuck.* She's worried Carys will need too much help with Maya at the wedding."

"Because you were helping her through our first separation after Maya was born, she thinks Carys can't handle our daughter for an *hour?* Are you fucking kidding, Ruben? You know Carys is an amazing mother. Carla won't even realize they're there," Eric seethed.

"I know. It's her big day, Slow. She wants it perfect. In her mind, that means all my attention, and no children present at the ceremony to distract or upset the other guests. It's nothing against you or anything—"

"The hell it isn't! Ruben, she's been a jealous bitch every time you come around, which isn't very often because she's got you by the balls. Now you are asking me to tell my *wife* she can't come to a wedding ceremony I'm standing as best man for?" Eric snorted derisively. "That's bullshit."

"Of course, Carys can come," Ruben assured.

"But not with our *daughter.* Not with *your* goddaughter. I've tried being civil and understanding, but not with this. I'm sorry, Ruben," Eric said, standing. Ruben rose from the couch at the same time, his face marred with sadness and desperation. "You are going to have to find someone to take my place."

Ruben stared at him, his bloodshot eyes wide. He really looked like hell now that Eric could take him in properly from two feet away. A twinge of sympathy took the edge off the heat under his collar, but at the end of the day, Ruben had chosen a selfish woman to marry. It wasn't Eric's fault, and he would *not* play Carla's games.

"I'm sorry, brother."

"Yeah, man. Me too."

———

CARYS PACED THE LIVING ROOM, too wound up from what Eric had relayed about his talk with Ruben earlier to be still. He sat on the couch, slumped back dejectedly. Everything about this was *wrong.* He knew Ruben wanted Maya at the wedding. Hell, Ruben had picked out a special dress for Maya, so she would match her "Funcle Ruben" on the day.

"First Perez moves in next door, now this. I can't believe someone so cold and selfish will be Ruben's wife," she muttered.

Eric grunted his agreement.

"I mean its *Ruben.* He's the most affable person I've ever met, aside from maybe Vinny. He didn't even blink when you brought me home. I was so afraid he would think you'd lost your marbles, but no. Not Ruben. He welcomed me and Maya both like long lost family. He isn't *this* guy," she continued. Carys stopped her pacing and turned to face him. "I'm so sorry, Eric. I understand why you walked away, and I appreciate it. But it couldn't have been easy."

"Honestly? It was the easiest thing I've done since I married you. I don't want to watch the train reck. I *can't* watch. He's my best friend and this wedding is a mistake." Eric shrugged. "Leaving Maya at home was not a viable option, and he knew it. Even if we had someone we trusted to care for her, she's too young for solid food and she won't take a bottle. I'm not leaving our baby with a stranger who can't feed her to attend a wedding I don't believe should be happening in the first place. I know it sounds dramatic, but our family comes first. Ruben knows we are a package deal."

Even as the truth poured out of him, Eric knew this was only the beginning of what could very well be the end of his most important friendship. Ruben had been his brother in everything but blood since they had met, and Carla had never liked Eric being around or stealing his attention.

Chapter Twenty

ERIC

"You wanted to see me, sir?" Eric asked, stepping into his commanding officer's office. Colonel Greer had a steady head on his shoulders, and Eric had a lot of respect for him.

"Close the door, would you?" Eric did, then took the chair Greer offered with the wave of his hand. "I wanted to talk to you about your future, Slow."

"Okay." He hoped he was coming across as confident and not scared shitless. These talks went one of two ways, and there were no gray areas.

"I'd like to recommend you promote this year," Greer said.

"Sir? It's several years before I'm due for consideration."

"I know, but you have potential. The thing is, you will have to commit to a lot of travel, if you catch my drift."

Greer studied Eric as he spoke. It felt like some sort of test, although for what Eric couldn't tell. He'd always gotten a good vibe off his boss, but right now he was completely unreadable.

"I appreciate your faith in me, sir. As you know, I have a family now. I'm happy to be considered later when I'm rightfully due for the honor, so I can spend more time with my wife and daughter before more responsibilities are added to my plate." Eric could tell it wasn't the answer Greer wanted, but he couldn't understand why.

"I can respect that, Major. I remember the early years of marriage and fatherhood. Busy times."

"Yes, sir." Eric couldn't help but smile. "Precious moments I'll never get back."

"Yes. Well." Greer sat forward in his seat, leaning on his desk. "You are in for the long haul, yes?"

"It has always been my intention to retire a Marine," Eric confirmed with a nod. "This is my family too."

It must have been the correct answer this time because Greer sat back in his chair again, his posture more relaxed. "Very well. Thank you for stopping by."

Or maybe not the right answer at all.

Strange.

Eric made his way down the hall, toward the front door. V12—so named because *Vorderstrasse* was too damn long to say or write—had asked him to meet up for lunch. They often worked together, and Eric considered V12 a friend. The medic was also a friend of Ruben's, and Eric knew V12 had replaced him as Ruben's best man.

He wouldn't be taking any bets on what V12 wanted to talk about over lunch, given the wedding had taken place the previous weekend and Ruben was on leave for his honeymoon.

"Pull up a seat," V12 said jovially as Eric approached him. "I went ahead and ordered our usual."

Eric couldn't help but compare his friend's greeting to the commander's twenty minutes ago. Similar on the surface, but completely different in reality. "Hey, thanks. How have you been?"

Zeke Vorderstrasse wasn't one to mince words. He called it like he saw it, and Eric appreciated that. Except for right now, when his buddy was looking at him with pity and amusement. "I'm good," he finally said, drawing out his words. "Better than you are about to be."

"This about my new neighbors?" Eric said with a fake smile.

"Eh. Yes and yes."

"Helpful. Why two yeses?"

"Because Perez has not moved on from your brush off."

"It's been over a year. I can't help she took the arrangement as invitation for more eventually even though I was clear what she could expect," he said with a shrug. "If I go talk to her, she'll get the wrong idea."

"I agree," V12 said. "She's been nasty lately. Has she given you any trouble since she moved in next door?"

"Not a peep," Eric said.

"On to the second 'yes' then," he said. "The newly acquired Mrs. Holt."

"How was the wedding?" Eric asked softly, nodding at the waitress as she set a pizza in the center of the table and plates in front of each of them. They thanked her and waited until she was out of ear shot.

"I don't think you are going to see a lot of Ruben at home," he said quietly. "The whole wedding was…uncomfortable."

"How so?" Eric asked between bites.

"Hmm." V12 chewed as he considered his answer. Eric waited. "Her bridal party was full of lovely young ladies, but none were as *advantageously* presented as the bride, for one. And she was smug about getting her way in regard to what made *her* day perfect."

"You mean pushing Ruben hard enough for me to back out."

"I agree she doesn't like you, but I think it goes deeper than that. Carys is a lovely woman, Slow. Your baby is damn cute too. I got a strong vibe last weekend the bride doesn't like *any* competition. Not in looks, and certainly not where Ruben's time is concerned. Don't be expecting them at any cookouts you host this summer," he said dryly.

Eric contemplated V12's words. As ridiculous as it tracked, it fit with the last thing Ruben had said outside of work—the night Eric had quit the wedding. Carla didn't want any attention taken from her on her special day. Except V12 was telling him she wouldn't tolerate anything she considered competition at all. *Ever.* Certainly not the baby girl Ruben gushed over or his best friend's wife, who happened to be a total knock out—even if Carys didn't realize it.

"Fuck."

"Indeed, my brother. Indeed," V12 said with a sympathetic nod of his head. "I'm worried about our boy."

"Yeah."

"And I need you to know, Perez was a bridesmaid." Eric's head snapped up, his brows competing for which stopped their upward trajectory first. V12 nodded his head again and continued. "She was down toward the end of the lineup, but it looks like they know each other from somewhere else, and they seemed chummy."

"You think Carla's playing Ruben?"

"I'm certain of it, but I couldn't tell you how. Something doesn't smell right though, other than her two hundred dollars an ounce perfume."

They continued eating in contemplative silence for a few minutes. When the pie was gone and their plates cleared, Eric leaned back in his chair. "We're watching our boy, right?"

"Like a damn hawk."

———

ERIC WANTED V12 to be wrong. A week after Ruben returned, he watched through the sheers at the living room window as the last of Carla's boxes went out with the recycling. He'd seen the lights on late at night in the room over the garage, a feminine form setting the room up—alone—every night as he locked up. He had yet to see Ruben, except rare glimpses of him gophering about for his wife, a manic smile on his face.

If that's wedded bliss, I'd rather swallow a bullet, he thought to himself. The open, carefree love of his own home grew even more endearing to him when he looked across the street.

"He'll be back," Carys said from behind him. "Just as soon as the ink is dried on their divorce papers. Yesterday I heard her screaming at him over the phone. What a bitch."

Eric turned away from the window and pulled her into a tight hug. Carys added a kiss, and he took it deeper. The moan she gave him tasted like everything he knew love was supposed to be. He backed her into the wall beside the fireplace, canting his hips into her and tipping her face up to his.

"Maya still sleeping?"

"Uh-huh." She panted.

"You get that birth control thing finally settled yesterday?" She nodded, and his cock thickened painfully inside his uniform. "Good."

Carys was wearing nothing but her bathrobe, having come down for her first cup of coffee. Eric took the mug from her and set it on the mantel with one hand as he untied her robe with the other. She reached for his belt and he could feel her hands trembling with anticipation.

"I'm not going to be gentle, sweetheart."

"Take what you need," she offered, her voice quivering as much as her hands were.

He did. As soon as she shoved his pants down, boxer briefs and all, he grabbed her lush ass and lifted her up. Carys wrapped her legs around his waist and angled her hips so his tip lined up with her core. Then she used those legs to pull him into her, slamming down so hard it almost hurt from how tight she was.

"Carys. Fuck. My whole body is burning for you, and I haven't even moved yet."

In response, she nipped his earlobe and ground her hips while her channel tightened around him further. She was playing dirty. Eric squeezed her ass tight enough to leave handprints and pulled back slowly, watching her eyes glass over with lust.

He crashed into her quick and hard, his mouth covering hers before her screams of ecstasy could wake the baby. Their first baby. *Please, Eric. Put another baby in me.* Eric pounded into her, devouring her mouth as she strangled his cock. It was rough and powerful, the stress and emotions they'd both been dealing with coming to the surface rapidly.

Carys tensed against him, pinned to the wall by his chest. He squeezed harder, tipping her hips and angling his own at the same time, knowing he was perfectly positioned to set her off. The guttural noise she made as her come ran down his sack snapped Eric's shaky control. He spilled into her but managed not to allow himself more than a release of pressure. It damn near hurt to pull back, but he knew he'd be settling for bliss instead of nirvana.

They both needed more. The kind of detonation that

would make the Manhattan Project's test range look like kiddie sparklers in comparison.

Eric turned from the wall and carried Carys to the edge of the couch.

"You did it again, didn't you?" Her voice was thick and heavy, a lust induced sleepiness coating her tongue.

"I did. On your knees, sweetheart. Arms over the back of the couch," he directed, having pulled out to reposition her. "That's it. you know what to do."

Carys straightened her spine and used the back of the couch to leverage and support herself as Eric slid back into her from behind. He reached around her body and cupped both her breasts firmly as he slowly built his pace back up.

"My perfect wife," he groaned out. "God damn I love your body."

She whimpered softly against the couch cushions as he massaged her breasts with his hands, a yelp turned moan filling the room when he pinched her nipples without warning. They were so much more sensitive while she was nursing, and he took advantage. Another practiced tug sent a shiver down her spine to her sopping core, which quivered around his cock.

"Eric," she groaned, fighting to keep her volume low. "Please. I need you."

Wordlessly, he picked up his pace. His knees almost gave out, but Eric managed to stay upright. The fire from before returned, thrumming through him as a lightning storm joined in. *Nirvana.* This time he didn't hold back. Eric roared out his orgasm, satisfied when he felt her follow him over.

Without pulling out, he turned them so they would collapse together on the couch, his arms holding her close. They lay spooned together while he ground his cock inside her until the aftershocks subsided.

His pants were still around his ankles, but she had shed her robe between the wall and the couch. The feel of her softness tucked against him like this—if he closed his eyes, he could hear the waves of the ocean crash against the Mexican sand. He could smell coconut and salt in the air.

"Did I hurt you?" he murmured into her ear.

"No," she said. "I needed it too."

"I don't think I've ever been that rough with you before."

"You haven't, but I liked it. Maybe not all the time, but it was a great release just now."

The alarm on Eric's watch chirped.

Shit. I'm going to be late to work.

Chapter Twenty-One

CARYS

"I don't know, Vin. He's still him, but all this shit with Ruben is messing with his head." Carys was stretched out on the couch, enjoying a few minutes of tranquility while Maya napped. Or she had been, before her phone rang and startled her out of her reverie.

"They still not talking?"

"Nope. Eric said Ruben got pulled for a special task, so they aren't even working in the same building right now. Unless they take the recycling to the curb at the same time, he doesn't see Ruben at all." Carys could tell by the way Vinny had gone quiet she was silently seething on the other end of the line. "It makes for some amazing sex though."

Vinny laughed. "Now *that* I believe. Angsty sex always has a little extra oomph. Maybe not as much as makeup or breakup sex, but damn close."

Carys rolled her eyes. She didn't believe in makeup or breakup sex, and Vinny knew it. But then again, Carys hadn't put much effort into men before Eric, so what did she know? She'd never find out anyway. They didn't fight—at least not on the level Carys knew Vinny instigated with her paramours —and she was going to die happily married to Eric.

"Hussy," she said playfully.

"Saints and sinners, Carys. I know which has more fun," Vinny singsonged back. "Change of subject. How is Maya?"

"Huge. Loving the summer weather. She crawls over to the back door and bangs on it until I take her out to her swing. She's getting a lot of fresh food options too. We go to the farmer's market and pretty much buy everything that makes her drool."

"So, everything."

Carys giggled. "Yup. How can I say no to that face, Vin?"

"You can't. I can't. Eric can't. Nobody can tell her no because she's so damn perfect." Vinny's obvious pride over Maya made Carys smile.

"Will you make her birthday?" she asked hopefully.

"Fuck, yeah! The tour manager tried adding a few dates, but I told him he'd have to find someone else for those days. I was there when our girl was born and I'm not missing this milestone for anything. Not even a bunch of horny GIs who fuck like Eros gave them lessons."

Carys's laugh came out as a cackle, her head thrown back and a few tears streaming down her face. "Eros was the god of *love.* I think his brother Himeros is more your speed."

"Is he the god of mojo or something?"

"You could say that. *Technically* he's the god of sexual desire. But hey, invite Dionysus and you'll have yourself one hell of a Greek orgy."

"God, woman. Is all that blather smart people foreplay? Does it get you two in the mood?" Vinny teased.

"Nudity gets Eric in the mood. Sometimes not even that. I just have to be available." She grinned to herself with satisfaction, her core aching at the thought.

"Even though you had a baby crazy fast, you guys are still in a honeymoon phase."

Carys blinked a few times while Vinny's words sunk in. "Oh, wow. I guess we are! I hadn't thought of it like that."

"Enjoy every glorious moment of it, before he knocks you up again. It's bound to happen," Vinny advised.

Carys didn't bother telling Vinny how hot the sex had been while she was pregnant. She'd probably taint the memory by saying something about hormones or attribute it to Eric's long abstinence over deployment. Because for Vinny, five months without sex should elevate you to saint-hood and requalify you as a virgin. Carys snorted to herself.

"What's so funny?" Vinny demanded.

Shit.

"Oh, are you still on the line? I thought I heard a beefy GI in the background pleading for your challis to accept his sweet, godly nectar."

They both pealed with laughter.

———

ERIC CAME HOME LATE that night. Maya was already down for the night and Carys had been finishing her evening wipe down of the kitchen when she heard the gentle hum of the garage door opener doing its thing. She listened to the sound of Eric's truck coming to a stop, the engine cutting off with the familiar faint clicking sound. He closed his car door quietly and waited for the garage door to shut again before coming inside.

He looked gutted.

"Hey," she said cautiously. Carys had moved from the sink to the doorway of the mud room off the garage, where Eric sat removing his shoes. "You okay?"

His silence told her more than words ever could.

"They're sending me out. I tried to swap for the next rotation, but we don't have the manning for it right now." His voice was low and filled with disappointment.

"When do you leave?" she asked in a small voice.

"November eighth."

She sucked in a sharp breath. "You'll miss Maya's first birthday."

"Yeah. I will." He tucked his boots away and reached out to her. "Come here, sweetheart."

Carys went to him, sitting in his lap on the bench. She knew it was going to happen eventually. He hadn't deployed in almost a year, and if there was one thing Eric had been from the start, it was open about what his job entailed.

"I've never had something I was scared to lose before."

"You can't lose us, Eric. We'll be right here waiting for you."

Even if you never come back to us.

They sat there until Eric's stomach complained before silently moving to the kitchen. Carys warmed up the plate she'd set aside for him and waited beside him as he ate. He put his plate in the dishwasher when he was finished and took her hand, pulling her to a stand.

Eric led Carys to bed, where he slowly used his body to bring her pleasure, before falling asleep wrapped around each other. Even tucked snuggly in his arms, Carys dreamed she was Humpty Dumpty from Maya's nursery rhymes book—and nothing in the world could keep her heart from shattering as it struck the ground. His last deployment she'd been busy finishing college. Instead of focusing on the full ramifications of what could possibly happen to Eric, she'd been studying her ass off and mentally preparing for what would happen if he didn't choose her and Maya when she returned to Mexico.

The emailing had been a taste of what a life could be like with him, but things were on a whole other level now.

Now she was his *wife.* The life Eric had given her was more than she thought she'd ever find, and her world revolved around their little family. Sure, she spent her days alone with their daughter, but she spent her evenings with her husband. When the mom gig got hard, Eric was there to assure her she was doing a wonderful job. And when that didn't go the way he wanted, he moved on to other ways of taking her mind off whatever was upsetting her.

Naked ways, usually.

What would she do without him here in the evenings? Especially since Ruben would likely be going with him; not that he was present now, even living across the street. The dread of being alone for months on end made for shit sleep. Carys's dreams crossed into darkness—millions of ways things could go wrong, ways she would fail as a mother and wife without him home.

When she faced the mirror the next morning, she looked like a raccoon after a Greek row kegger. Not that she'd ever participated in Greek Week, but she'd certainly seen the tell-tale repercussions on her peers. Carys splashed a little cold water onto her face and patted it dry before going downstairs to start the coffee.

"Here, sweetheart." She looked up to find Eric standing at the counter, her favorite mug steaming in his hand. *I'm so exhausted I didn't even smell the coffee on the way down.* "I even remembered the shells you add to the grounds."

Carys let out a snort as she reached for her coffee, a smile following it just as she knew he'd planned. "Nutmeg."

"Right. Nutmeg."

She took a tentative sip, careful not to burn her mouth and ruin the experience. He made a mean cup of joe. Carys let out a heavy sigh, dropping her shoulders, and relaxing her posture. She hadn't been this tense since she'd waited for Eric at the bar top table in Mexico, asking all the ancient Mayan juju in the area to deliver the father of her child to her. And then something occurred to her.

"You aren't buttering me up, are you?"

"Should I be?" he asked with his roguishly panty melting half smile. She stared at him patiently over her mug as she took another slow sip of coffee. "Maybe a little."

"I'm not going to like this, am I?"

"I *hope* you will."

"A little early, don't you think?"

"That's not what this is about," he said softly. "You remember Zeke?"

She did. Great guy. Medic. Was *not* fond of Perez. Carys adored him. "What's he got to do with it?"

"A year ago today, we met back up in Mexico. I was terrified you wouldn't show. Instead, you handed me an ultrasound envelope and told me I was a father. It ended up being the most important day of my life." Carys lifted a brow in contest. "Yes, more important than marrying you, although it's a narrow victory. I swear it." Eric lifted his hands in the air, palms out like she'd asked him to prove he hadn't stolen candy from the 7Eleven.

"Uh-huh."

"You picked me that day, sweetheart."

"I picked you the first time I set eyes on you," she murmured. Eric's eyes went molten as he pulled her closer, wrapping his arms around her waist and pressing his forehead to hers.

"Me too," he said, his voice raspy with emotion. "But I didn't know it until I found you sitting in the bar, and you didn't know I felt the same."

Well, he's got me there, she thought.

"What's Zeke got to do with it?"

"I asked him to come watch Maya tonight for a few hours, so I can take you out on a date. He loves babies, and he's got the CPR thing down. I figured with Vinny out on tour, he'd be the next best thing. What do you think? Will you go on a date with me, Missus Blackwood?" Eric pulled his head back enough to meet her gaze as he asked.

The eagerness in his eyes was hard to miss. So was the sexy little half smile he was leveling at her. Not to mention they hadn't gone out much since Maya was born, and never without her.

"Okay, *Mister Blackwood,*" she said slowly. "I'll go on a date with you." She quirked her head to the side, analyzing him through squinted eyes for a moment before adding, "And if you are lucky, I might even put out."

"Oh, I'll make sure I'm lucky," he said.

Chapter Twenty-Two

ERIC

"Oh my…" Carys speechless was a beautiful thing. Eric watched his wife as she took in their surroundings. "Eric."

"It's not the same beach, but we do get to enjoy the surf while we take in the sunset."

"It's gorgeous."

"I asked for a patio table." He gave her hand a gentle squeeze before lifting it up to kiss the back of her hand. "It's as close as I could get to those mornings we shared the sunrise."

Minus the bed, privacy, and amazing sex.

He led her over to the hostess stand before his mind took a sudden turn down Sexy Way and got lost. There was time for that later when he could do something about it. Right now, his focus needed to be with her. Eric pulled out his wife's chair for her, enjoying the way she blushed softly at the gesture. He half listened to the specials while he stared at her.

Once the hostess was gone, he reached across the little table for two and took Carys's hand. "I love you."

With his next trip down range coming up soon, he couldn't say it enough. Eric knew his wife. She'd shook and cried most of the night, despite how firmly he'd held her to him. They weren't ready for this.

Nobody was ready for this.

There is no manual for leaving your family behind for the first time. He'd deployed many times in his nine plus years of service, but not like this. Not when he had someone to miss. Not when he had a growing baby at home who would be blazing through her milestones without him.

In some ways, he thought he was the lucky one. Eric would be busy every waking moment he was away. Carys would be home, surrounded by his presence but lacking it too. His shoes would be by the door. His scent in their room. Every moment Carys wasn't occupied with Maya, she'd be staring at the evidence of her absent husband.

Him.

Eric usually looked forward to this part of his job. It was hard but satisfying. This time it was just *hard.* He'd give just about anything to stay through the year, but Colonel Greer said he was the only one available for it. Eric had to leave.

On the bright side, V12 told him Perez would not be joining them. Eric didn't like her chilling next door, waiting like the snake she'd become, for the perfect moment to strike —he hadn't forgotten V12's warnings over her jealousy towards his wife. But at least Carys didn't have to worry about her putting the moves on him while they were gone and stirring up trouble. Besides, the Browns were good people. He didn't think they would tolerate any bullshit from their tenant.

How much trouble could she possibly be?

And with any luck, he'd have enough down time with Ruben to talk some sense into him. All in all, he *should* be happy. Everyone on his team was cream of the crop. Even the first timers had proven themselves well. After a few months under the wings of the repeaters, they'd be even better assets to the team.

It was best case scenario, minus one detail. He couldn't take his family.

"Eric," Carys whispered across the table. "There are no prices on the menu!"

"It doesn't matter," he said easily, stroking the back of her hand with his thumb. "Order what you like, sweetheart. I knew what I was in for when I made the reservation."

She let out a nervous breath that made him smile. Carys had expected to use her degree and bring in a substantial income of her own after college. She still struggled with the idea of living off his income alone and was ever the frugal spender after years making ends meet while she finished her education. The last bit didn't bother him. The not feeling free to spend *their* household money however she saw fit drove him crazy.

Even after Maya was born, he'd had to get Vinny involved before Carys would go out and buy new clothes that fit her. She'd been prepared to make her maternity wardrobe work until she fit into her regular clothes again and wouldn't hear a word from him on the subject. Vinny on the other hand had no quarrel with taking his credit card and his wife down to the mall—or insisting her college clothing was not what she'd feel comfortable in now she was a *mother*.

New lifestyle.

New clothes.

End of story.

Without Eric or Vinny around to break her out of those habits, would Carys remember to take care of herself? How was *he* going to take care of her from afar?

There was always some trash talk among the wives of his colleagues. They hadn't been as warm in welcoming her into their community as Eric had hoped. V12 had heard a few of them talking at a backyard party a few weeks ago—one they hadn't been invited to—about Carys. It had been unflattering and ignorant, but it still burned to know a clutch of the louder wives chittered away to anyone who would listen about the situation in the Blackwood home.

They didn't believe Maya was Eric's daughter. To them, Carys was an opportunist who'd gotten herself in trouble and latched onto the first income she could sink her claws into—his. The same women who had cooed over Maya at the holiday party and gone on and on about how much she looked like her daddy were still trash talking his wife to all and sunder when she wasn't around.

And they made damn sure she wasn't.

Eric didn't blame his fellow Marines. When put between a rock and a hard place—your own wife's happiness and or forced inclusion of another man's family—it made sense they would choose what made their own household a nonhostile zone. It didn't make it suck any less. He'd put too much faith in the experienced wives helping Carys get her footing. Instead, she'd become gossip fodder.

Even if Maya had come along after they were wed, Eric finally understood Carys wouldn't have been a shoo-in with a lot of the wives because she came out of nowhere. They didn't take her seriously because they had eloped suddenly— to their minds suspiciously—and the other wives saw no point investing time in someone they expected would leave as suddenly as she arrived.

It's not like the military community wasn't rife with lovesick guys marrying piranhas only in it for a way out of wherever they came from. He understood where the prejudice originated. Eric was still appalled it had been applied to *Carys*. She was well educated and grew up nearby. She was capable of supporting herself and had been prepared to do so if things had gone differently.

"Why are you staring at me like that?" Carys asked, startling him back into the here and now.

Where he *belonged.* With his beautiful bride.

"I'm so fucking proud of you, Carys," he said with conviction. "No, that's not it. I'm in *awe* of you." She stared at him, her lips parting with surprise. "I don't know why you married me, but I will be endlessly grateful for your singular lapse in judgment."

Carys let out a soft laugh. "Are you kidding me? I'm still blown away you didn't walk the second I stood up from the table. You never doubted Maya is yours…" Her eyes shone with the tears she was fighting back. Carys squeezed his hand firmly. "Your unwavering faith in me from the beginning. Eric, I've *never* had that. Not even from Lavender, and certainly not from my mother."

"And here we are, a year later." His voice was rough with emotion.

"Yes. Both still amazed the other saw anything in us at all apparently." She gave him a small smile before growing serious. "Maya would have missed out on so much if you hadn't come. Or if you had walked away."

"Never. If I'm breathing I'll be fighting my way home to my girls, sweetheart."

An immense calm fell over Eric as he looked at his wife. The love and devotion radiating from her was more than enough to put him at ease. He wouldn't be like so many of his buddies in the past, coming home to an empty house and a Dear John letter on the counter, dusty from how long it had been sitting there.

Carys and Maya were going to be fine.

At least as fine as they could be while going through the

Big D.

———

DINNER HAD BEEN AMAZING. They walked down the beach as the last rays of sun gave way to the inky night, stars flickering across the night sky over the water. As the Pacific gently broke against the still sun warmed sand, Eric let the moment fully permeate his senses. The way the smell of Carys's shampoo came to him on the salty air. The flick of loosed tendrils of hair dancing across her face. The cool grit of the wet sand beneath their bare feet when they drew closer to the water. The faint remnants of the wine she'd had at dinner mixed with *her* when he kissed her long and deep.

"I am addicted to you," he murmured in her ear. "Everything about you. I can't believe you're mine."

"Touch me. Please, Eric."

"Not here. I won't be able to stop."

"Come on, we can go down by the peer. The tide is out, and nobody will see us in the shadows," she purred, her voice sultry and warm against his throat. *"Please."*

Something animalistic rumbled through his chest, releasing from his throat as a low, needy, possessive growl. *Fuck it. What my wife wants she gets.* He knew exactly the spot to take her where they would have relative seclusion from anyone else out for an evening stroll.

"Not by the peer, sweetheart. Come with me," he commanded, pulling her to his side and turning away from the more populated stretch of beach.

They hadn't far to go, but with the way his dick was throbbing against his zipper, it sure as hell felt like a 5K. They rounded a section of beach where the rock curved in like a bowl, shielding them from view and the wind. Eric spotted a slab of rock worn down by elements, the surface still radiating heat from the sun.

"Here," he said, pulling her up onto the slab. "What do you need?"

"Take me hard," she said without hesitation, her hands gliding over his chest beneath his shirt. "And then when we get home, draw it out."

As soon as Eric sat down beside her, she threw a leg over his lap and centered herself, her knees on either side. Carys had his slacks open and her soft palm caressing his length before he could ask anything more. He shifted his hips enough to slide his pants out of the way, his bare ass grateful for the warmth still in the stone beneath them.

He couldn't completely see what she was doing with the skirt of her dress in the way, but he had a good idea where she was taking him. Her hand guided him against her warm, slick, *bare* folds. "No underwear?" She shook her head and smiled at him.

Then she rolled her hips, working her wetness across his shaft until he was seeing more stars than were in the sky above them. Eric slid his hands up her dress to her hips and guided her higher, until the head of his cock notched into her opening. He held her there, gyrating as he kept her hips steady, preventing anything more than the tip of his cock from entering her. He waited until she shook with the same desperate need as his own before pulling her down flush to his own body.

With his teeth, he tugged down her bodice. Carys reached up and pushed her bra cups out of the way for him, her perfect breasts bouncing in front of him. Eric gripped her hips firmly and began plowing up into his wife as she used her legs and hips to help. His tongue swept across her nipples, drawing a shaky moan from her.

"Shhh, wife. You have to be silent so we aren't caught. Now pinch this beautiful nipple right here," he said, pausing to sweep his tongue around it once more in direction. One of her hands moved swiftly to her straining peak, supporting it with her hand as her fingers glided up and pulled on her tip. Her breath hitched and her walls fluttered around him. "Good girl, sweetheart. I can tell you're close."

He wrapped his mouth around her other peak, alternating laving his tongue with pulling her areola completely into his mouth. Her channel clenched down on him, and he sucked a little more, testing her boundary between pleasure and pain. She was sweet in his mouth, some of her milk flowing from his efforts.

The world around them disappeared. It was just Eric and Carys, their bodies fused together in pleasure. Carys switched hands, dropping the breast he'd told her to pinch so he could give it the same treatment while her other hand continued to work the nipple he'd released. Eric greedily attacked her other breast, occasionally nipping her tip before soothing it with his tongue. Then he was sucking again, gently tugging as he buried his face in her chest.

All the while he continued to thrust into her from below, while she rode him hard and swirled her hips as much as his grip would allow for. Carys arched into him, her second hand moving from his shoulder to the back of his head. He felt rather than saw her head falling back. Eric pulled her hips forward hard the next time she came down on him and nipped her tip at the same time.

She came apart around him, her core squeezing his cock so tightly his vision blurred. He let out a low groan as he let himself go, almost forgetting he was supporting her weight through her own release. He kept them from falling over, but it was a close thing.

When she could hold herself upright again, Eric gently washed both her breasts with his tongue before fixing the top of her dress while she panted quietly.

"Mmm," he moaned as she pulled off him. Carys did him a solid, cleaning him up same as he had done to her before tucking him back into his slacks after he yanked them back up. When she was done, he cupped her face in his palms and kissed her tenderly, with all the reverence he held for her.

"You did so well, sweetheart," he praised her. "Not a peep, and I know staying quiet was difficult because I felt it too. When we get home I expect all those moans and whimpers you saved to fill our bedroom while I worship my wife properly."

"Yes, please."

Chapter Twenty-Three

CARYS

He was gone. It felt like yesterday Eric was doing his due diligence showing her how much he loved the body that had made him a father on the beach. He'd done it all over again on their first anniversary; singing his praise for her body as well as her soul. Showing how deep his love flowed for her, an endless, bottomless well he promised to her and the family they were building together.

Vinny was right. They were still very much in a honeymoon phase, despite the sleep deprivation of early parenthood. But all things must end, no matter how amazing they are.

Like knowing where your husband is sleeping at night.

Literally.

Wherever they were and whatever they were tasked to do, Eric had not been allowed to share anything with her. With so much unknown to her, it had made his leaving that much harder. Celebrating Maya's birthday a few weeks early, so Eric could participate…

All Carys could think was, *keep smiling. For Maya, keep smiling. She may never get another birthday with her father.*

It was a horrible way to live.

Carys watched the rain turn the air misty through her back door as she sat at the table with her morning coffee and let out a heavy sigh filled with melancholy. It had only been a month, but it felt like a year. She envied the wives who were free to up and leave. A lot of them had traveled for Thanksgiving or were planning on going home for Christmastime celebrations so they wouldn't be alone.

She wasn't alone—no young mother really was—and she had no interest in seeing her own mother. Vinny had come early enough for Maya's true birthday, and her dad had joined them on Thanksgiving as a surprise. They were enough for Carys, and it was more important to her Maya have *genuine* people in her life than a *lot* of people in her life. She couldn't have asked for more.

Now if only she could cancel Christmas.

Carys preferred to focus on Eric's homecoming. She understood it was a long way off, but all the whispers in the dark before he left had her nearly vibrating with anticipation. The sweet nothings and blush inducing promises he'd made as he ran his hands over her body every night danced through her subconscious, creating a vibrant and lurid dreamscape that ended with his happy smile as her body swelled with his seed again.

And they were more than ready.

As soon as Eric got home, it was on. She couldn't wait to go through a whole pregnancy with Eric, and the feeling was mutual. He'd caressed her stomach the night before he left, trailing kisses across her belly. *When I get home, I'm putting another baby inside you, sweetheart. Since you asked so nicely.* Remembering his words and the intense arousal pouring off his body as he said them was a delectable form of torture.

She finished her coffee and made herself rinse the mug and put it in the dishwasher, so the job wouldn't pile up on her. Then she slowly walked back upstairs to her bed and collapsed onto her heating pad. As she settled, Vinny's notification tone went off. Carys reached over to the edge of her nightstand where her phone sat on the charging pad.

Vinny: Hey. Any better today?

Carys: Not really. I forgot how shitty periods are. I mean, they came back pretty quick after Maya was born, but they weren't much. The last couple have made me feel like a bomb went off inside my uterus.

Probably not the best analogy right now, she thought after she'd sent the message. *Jesus, are bombs a problem where Eric is?*

Vinny: Fuck. I'm sorry, Carys. You never have had periods less than crow like mayhem.

Carys: Ha. Ha ha. A murder of crows. Cute, Vin.

Vinny: I do what I can!

Vinny: How is Maya?

Carys: She watches her good morning and bedtime messages Eric recorded before he left all the time. I can tell she's confused why he's in the screen though. Even after a month, she still looks around, wondering why he isn't coming in to hug her. I don't know how people survived this before technology.

Vinny: They wrote letters and mailed pictures. I'm sure back then they wondered how people did it without those things, too. Back when men went into battle and they might come back in a month or a year or a decade.

Or not at all, Carys's mind filled in. Yeah, that would suck. Not knowing if your partner would ever return. It wasn't consistent, but Eric was able to call her when he had decent Wi-Fi, and sometimes he'd get up at odd hours so there was enough bandwidth on the shared service to video call. Carys had taken a screenshot the first time, of Maya's big drooly smile while her daddy told her how much he missed her. She'd sent Eric the image after they ended the call.

Carys: I'm trying to be positive…but it's hard.

Vinny: I wish I could be there with you.

Carys: I know you would if you could. Tell me something good, Vin. Something new.

Vinny: How about new*ish?*

Oh, hell. Now what?

Carys: Okay?

Vinny: I ran into Jake on tour. We've been hanging out.

Carys: Translation: fucking. Isn't he the one that got all weird because he can't play as well as you can?

On any single instrument, she added in her head with a smirk. She hadn't met Jake, but he'd sounded like an asshole from the start.

Carys: I thought you were trying not to be involved with other musicians. You said it never worked out and wasn't worth the trouble.

Carys: Or all the extra STD screenings.

Vinny: Ouch! Don't quote me to me, Carys. That's unfair. I've grown. Jake has grown.

Carys: First evidence those Swedish penis pumps work?

Vinny: OMG. *laughing emoji*

Vinny: Fair play. And *no,* but he's certainly gained skills with the perfectly average sized dick he has.

Carys: That just means he's a manwhore. And you know it. I'm happy if you are, Vin. But please be careful. Sometimes they are exes for a reason.

This wasn't going to end well. Every time Vinny broke her own rule about dating fellow musicians—or anyone she was touring with, for that matter—it got progressively uglier during the fall out. Vinny was an amazing person but devalued herself in relationships. Worse, she allowed the guys she dated to devalue *her*. And while Carys would never say it to her face, she knew in her marrow it was because Vinny inwardly struggled with her looks.

Vinny wasn't just a pale eyed, blonde haired beauty. She had Albinism. Her skin was milky white, her hair the perfect platinum white blonde every California girl strove for at the salon but couldn't fully achieve. Her eyes, ironically, were the most beautiful shade of lavender. Vinny was a knockout. She *acted* like a knockout. But deep down, Lavender Blume was still working the *fake it til you make it* mantra like her life depended on it.

Being in the music industry, she was a fascinating addition on stage. Vinny's talent was real as her looks, but she knew her looks had gotten more doors opened to her than her talent. She wasn't an idiot. Which was why her ArtBeat account and the income she generated through it was so important to her. The first few years, she'd done it with a lot of mood lighting and shadowing, where you couldn't actually see her well enough to tell she didn't have a molecule of melanin in her body. She'd refused to show herself in full light until after she'd garnered half a million followers on principle.

They wrapped up their talk, Vinny insisting on an update in a few days, and Carys promising she'd be kept up to speed on the goings on in Oceanside.

———

"WHY IS IT SO *COLD?*" Carys muttered through her chattering teeth as she bundled her way downstairs, all the blankets from her bed wrapped around her. She had to step carefully, since she'd stollen Eric's slippers the day after he left, and they were way too big.

Carys rounded the banister and headed toward the mudroom off the garage, where the breaker box was. She checked to see if anything was tripped. Then she found the breaker for the furnace and flipped it off and on just in case.

Nothing.

So much for an easy fix.

She went out to the garage to check the furnace. It wasn't running and felt cold to the touch. She wasn't an expert, but it didn't feel like a good sign. Carys grabbed the necessary tool to open the access panel out of Eric's tool chest, grateful for both his organization and forethought to show her what went where and what it was good for. Once she had the access panel off, she looked at the labels on the inside of the panel.

Why couldn't they have put this information on the outside? Ugh.

"If unit is not engaging, check the view window below for code…" she read aloud to herself. It seemed simple enough. Wait for a two second pause, then count the number of times the red light inside blinked before the next two second pause. There was an answer list under the instructions, next to the diagram pointing out where the tiny window was.

Because heaven forbid the damn thing be easy to locate when you were about to go into hypothermia and had a baby inside recovering from a cold.

Carys awkwardly located the indicator, careful not to send herself into shock by contacting the freezing cold concrete floor. Even with Eric's faux fur lined, rubber soled slippers, she could still feel the chill under her feet. She waited and counted. Five.

"Reset needed," she read off the panel. All she had to do

was push a *tiny* red button, also hidden from view. She looked at another diagram, showing her where the button was. It was even more inconveniently located than the indicator window. She shoved the screwdriver into the tiny opening and pushed the button.

The furnace kicked on a second later, and Carys smiled to herself triumphantly as she put the screwdriver away and went back inside. She got the coffee pot going before starting a fire in the living room fireplace, hoping it would help the furnace bring the main living area back to livable from dark side of the moon cold.

Seriously. Carys could see her breath in front of her. She was so thankful she'd put one of those little infrared heaters in the nursery to keep Maya's room consistently warm while the rest of the house was kept cooler at night to save energy. At least her baby was sleeping comfortably this morning.

As she sat down at the table with her first cup of coffee, Carys's phone pinged. She answered the message immediately, smiling giddily as she waited for his call to come through.

"Hey, sweetheart. How are you?"

"I'm okay. I miss you," she said.

Eric's eyebrows furrowed. "Why do your lips look blue?"

Did they? Oh. She told him about the furnace issue, but not to worry.

"If it keeps acting up, there is a magnet on the fridge from the company who installed it. It's still under warranty," he reminded her.

"How are things with you?"

"Hot. Wish I was there to warm up the bed for you instead." His eyes flashed with desire, and she felt her core clench.

"Me too," she said, feeling a blush creep over her cheeks.

"I have to tell you something you won't like, but hear me out, okay?"

The look on Eric's face did not agree with the nod he gave her. "Okay."

"My endo is really bad again," she said shakily. "They want to do surgery."

"I thought the pregnancy gave your body a chance to clear out a lot of the mess from inside and gave you a break from the endometriosis growing?" he asked.

Carys had been honest with Eric from the start. Maya hadn't only been a surprise because she'd been on birth control at the time, she also had a condition where her uterus didn't properly clean itself out during her periods, causing a buildup of tissue over time and affecting her fertility. It also made her periods absolute hell. The endometriosis was part of that hormonal Molotov cocktail, adding to her discomfort. Eric had done serious research into the condition after she'd told him about it, shortly after they'd returned to California together from Mexico.

"It did, but it wasn't as long lasting as we'd hoped. There is a concern I will miscarry if the excess isn't cleared, and she suggested we do laparoscopy at the same time because it can cause problems outside the womb too. Sort of get it all done with so it's easier to manage with supplements and other therapies for a while," she explained.

"Why didn't you tell me before I left?"

"Honestly? I didn't want it to be the focus. I have all the time in the world to get it sorted before you come home. There isn't anything you could do for it anyway."

"I could have held your hand," he countered gently. "And gone to your appointments with you. I could have taken care of Maya so you could get the rest you will need to heal."

Carys's heart swelled. "I love you so much, Eric. Thank you for wanting to do those things for me."

"You're my wife, Carys. That's the job. When do they want to do the procedure?"

"Next week. Mrs. Brown said she would be happy to come over and watch Maya for me, and her husband said he could drive me to the procedure and back home. It's all outpatient, so it won't be a huge disruption for Maya."

"Okay," he said, letting out a deep breath. "That's good at least. I still don't like you doing it alone, but I hate you being in pain too."

Vinny was still on tour, and with Eric and Ruben both down range, the neighbors were her only real option. She didn't like the idea of leaving Maya with a total stranger, and Mrs. Brown was a grandmother now. She loved babies, and Maya loved her. It wasn't the ideal situation, but it was what it was, and she was grateful for the help. If a hospital stay had been involved, she would feel differently about it.

As it stood, she mostly wanted it over with so her body was fully healed and her cycles more predictable by the time Eric returned. It was her first surgery, and she was nervous. But the love she had for her family was stronger than her nerves.

Chapter Twenty-Four

ERIC

To: CrayonLover@mailwarrior.net
From: ByAnyOtherName@Eden.com
Subject: Tell me a story

I was thinking about you last night as I fell asleep. (Like always, in case you were wondering if it was a one off.) I fell into a familiar dream, where you are twirling me around on the patio in Mexico for the first time again. Only this time Ruben was there. I know, he really was there that night. But usually, my dreams stay focused on you. The change reminded me of what Ruben had said, and I wanted to ask you:

What did Ruben mean when he said you never made it past dating? You must have had girlfriends before you took a *wife*. Even the name he calls you partially reflects the way you paced your life before me, which doesn't fit the man I married in many ways—save that smile of yours.

Tell me the story of *you,* Eric. You before me. Please.

To: ByAnyOtherName@Eden.com
From: CrayonLover@mailwarrior.net

Re: Tell me a story

That's not much of a story, sweetheart. But since you said please, here it is. I was a gangly, pimply youth. No, I mean it. Laugh all you like, but I believe the appropriate term is "late bloomer." I had a first love, of course. Mary. She was exciting and vivacious, a lot like Vinny if you took away the soul and beating heart at her core. Instead, Mary was malicious, but my hormone engorged brain didn't see it until it was too late. Mary made a fool of me; in a way few fifteen-year-old boys could easily recover from. After that, I stayed away from girls until my senior year of high school. Kate was opposite of Mary. Instead of too much, she was…not too little, but maybe *bland* is the kindest word. We didn't have a lot in common, and looking back, I think it was a convenience for both of us to have someone to attend events with more than mutual attraction. We got along fine, but that was the extent to whatever we had.

College was just that. More school. Girls had been cruel in high school, and I wasn't eager to make an ass of myself to amuse one any more than before. I dated plenty, but as soon as they would get heart eyes, I would politely disengage and fade into the background until they lost interest. I wasn't at school for a girl; I was there to secure my future. Given how the trauma of Mary haunted me through all of high school, I wasn't eager for a repeat. Dating became something more transactional than emotional in my twenties. I was safer that way.

Right until I wandered into a bar in Mexico, aged thirty, and saw the same sort of ass I hated in school all over the sweetest *woman* I'd ever seen. You aren't a girl, Carys. You're a woman. *My woman.* And sweetheart, I was waiting for you the whole time and didn't know it. My hesitancy before you came into my life was rooted in my own understanding of myself. I knew I would know you when you came along for what you are.

My wife.

My life.

———

"I'M SORRY, SHE'S *WHAT?*" Ruben's jaw was agape, his eyes wide with disbelief and worry. "Man, that's crazy. I don't care if it's all outpatient, she should wait until we are home to help."

"I agree, but this isn't something she will negotiate on. I don't blame her for wanting the relief, but I don't like her being alone with Maya when she should be focused on healing either." Maya was into all sorts of things these days, and Eric didn't think Carys was going to be moving as fast as she expected the first week or so.

"Slow. You have to talk some sense into her."

He shook his head. "I tried. She thinks this way is better, so we can get pregnant again right away with less chance of a loss."

"Did it occur to her this would affect your job performance? You are going to be a total asshole while you are worrying over her. In fact, I think I'm going to have food poisoning that day," Ruben added with a nod. "Get myself out of the line of fire."

"Thanks for the support," Eric said dryly.

"I'd ask Carla to help, but she's not really the nursing type," he said, his tone apologetic.

She's not the type to put anyone above herself, Eric said mentally. Out loud, he said, "The neighbors are solid. At least she will have them, and it's better for everyone if their tenant stays away."

Perez had been quiet since she moved in next door, and Eric didn't like it. Quiet was not her style, and after V12 informed him of her friendship with Carla, he worried what the two of them might cook up while he and Ruben were too far away to protect his family from their venom. After enough times in a combat zone, Eric knew not to trust or draw solace in silence from the enemy. As much as he hated lumping Perez into that category—she was a damned good medic and an asset on a mission—she had been far too backhanded since he got married to place her anywhere else on his list.

"Fuck, man! What about Vinny?"

Eric laughed. "I can't believe you *still* haven't met her."

Ruben's familiar lopsided grin emerged. "It is weird. I mean, we share a godchild. And she visits a lot. Seems like I'm always just missing her."

"Yeah," Eric said. "Vinny can't leave the tour right now. She asked, but she's contractually obligated to do so many shows, and she hasn't hit the threshold yet."

Vinny had reached out to Eric with her concerns before he'd had a chance to ask her himself. Neither of them liked Carys's plan, but even together, there was nothing they could do to persuade her. After several days of sporadic messaging, they both unhappily concluded they weren't going to win this one.

"Did I tell you she diagnosed and fixed the furnace the other day?" he asked, needing a subject that wouldn't drive him crazy.

"I'm not surprised. Carys isn't one to sit around," Ruben said. "Carla on the other hand. She'd have called a repair man and bought a new parka to wear until they arrived."

He said it like it was nothing, but Eric wondered. "Does it ever bother you? The way she throws money around?"

"Nah. I like taking care of her. You'd do the same for Carys," he added, looking at Eric pointedly.

He nodded in agreement because he would—if it were necessary. A single day without heat in southern California did not require an entire ski ensemble to survive. Carys was made of heartier stuff than that. Plus, she'd already been prepared. Between the fireplace in the living room and the electric heater in Maya's bedroom, she had it covered. If things went on more than a day, she would have moved the heater to the master bedroom where she and Maya could sleep together and been just fine.

"I'm proud of her. The first month has been fucking brutal on both of us, but she's making it work. How is Carla doing?" he asked, more to be kind to his friend than because he actually cared.

"She's great, man. All smiles and surprises when I get to video call. Mmm! My wife is *fine.*"

"Do me a favor and—"

"The sexy things she likes to wear for me. *Dayum.* She had on this little black number last night that had me grateful one of the Air Force guys had let me use his private room." The Colgate smile Ruben gifted Eric told him all he needed to know about the direction the call had gone in.

"I was going to say, *don't tell me about it.*"

"Oh, my bad. Sorry, Slow." His growing smile indicated that was a lie.

"Liar."

Ruben laughed. On the way over, he'd teased Eric mercilessly over how hot FaceTime sex could be. Eric was more concerned about the completely unsecure wireless internet they shared, and how unlikely it was those video chats remained private. The idea of someone other than him watching his wife get off made him want to snap the offender's neck.

No way in hell was he going down that road. It was partly why he'd never kept a girlfriend long term before, opting to have a temporary and exclusive partner while he was in the field. Granted that hadn't worked out so well in the end for him either, but at least some cyber perv hadn't recorded him getting his jollies off for their own repeated future pleasures.

An alarm went off, and they sprang into action.

One month down, five to go.

So long as they kept their heads on a swivel and followed protocol.

———

Carys

She should have waited. Everything would have been so much better if she had only listened to Eric and Vinny. Even Ruben had delicately suggested Carys wait until at least Vinny could be there through her recovery.

The surgery had gone well, and she was healing nicely. If Maya still took two naps a day, she'd probably be fine. The trouble was Maya didn't sleep well at night if she took two naps now, but Carys needed those naps for herself. *And* the same bedtime as Maya. Healing was draining.

The first week had been a doozie, but she'd planned for it. Carys had made plenty of extra food the week before she could pull out of the freezer and reheat with minimal effort, and about a dozen of those crock pot freezer meals she kept reading about on mom blogs. The leftovers were dwindling, but she was feeling well enough to remember to pick out something for her slow cooker the night before and move it to the fridge to thaw a bit overnight…and was she ever grateful Eric had bought a house with a laundry chute.

Week two had been better. This morning, she'd woken feeling much more herself, excepting she was freezing. *Again.*

Carys went out to the garage, popped off the access panel on the furnace and counted the blinky light thing. Same as before. Her screwdriver again had a quick run in with the red reset button, and the furnace chugged back to life. She really should call the service company to come diagnose why the thing kept kicking off, but it wouldn't be today. Probably not tomorrow either, because it was Christmas Eve, and that cost extra.

Which reminded her to take out the little Cornish hens she'd decided to bake for the occasion. There had been so many leftovers from Thanksgiving, Carys had put some of them in the deep freezer to make Christmas even easier. They would have a beautiful little feast tomorrow, just her and Maya.

Now she was moving around, she realized she felt pretty good. Two weeks seemed to have been her needed resting time to bounce back. Maybe today she would take Maya out to admire all the decorations around town. They didn't need anything, but one of the parks nearby had been tressed up beautifully. Carys smiled to herself. Yeah, that was what they needed. A nice day out, for more than a few perishable items at the grocer.

She hopped in the shower, really enjoying it for the first time in weeks. Maya would be up soon, and she wanted to be ready to get out the door. Once Carys had dried her hair and pulled on something cozy and comfortable for walking in the chill of December, she went to wake up the baby. She was surprised she'd slept in so late, but that wasn't completely unnormal. Maya always slept more when she was teething or growing.

Carys's smile vanished as she looked down into the crib at her daughter.

"Maya," she called, gently shaking her. "Maya, wake up." She shook her a little more frantically, then lifted her up with all the efficiency of experience, cradling Maya's dead weight against her shoulder. She was burning up, her back damp with sweat. Maya's shallow breaths wheezed slightly as she exhaled.

No. No, no, no. We are not doing this.

She'd had a little bit of a cough last night, but nothing to worry about. Carys had figured the cold she'd had a few weeks ago had maybe left her a little sensitive. This was no cold. She quickly changed Maya into something dry, checked the diaper bag was adequate, and gave a dose of fever medicine before nearly leaping down the stairs and out to the garage.

With her hazard lights on, Carys wove her way through traffic as quickly as she could through the holiday traffic to the nearest emergency room. The admitting nurse brought her straight through to the back, which was both comforting and terrifying. They only did that if you were really bad off. The attending called up to pediatrics, and they were on the move before Carys had managed to set down Maya's diaper bag.

It wasn't until after they had admitted Maya into pediatric intensive care for RSV Carys realized she was still wearing Eric's slippers.

———

"MISSUS BLACKWOOD?"

The voice was accompanied by a gentle yet firm hand on

her shoulder, pulling Carys out of her doze next to Maya, her body in a chair with Maya's little hand in hers on the bed. She sat up with a start, turning to face the night nurse. She blinked twice before realizing the woman had been addressing her.

"Yes?"

"You have a visitor."

A visitor? She shook her heavy head. "No, that can't be right. My husband is deployed."

The nurse smiled patiently. "All the same, I was sent in to find you."

Carys looked over at her daughter. Maya looked so frail still, with all the monitors and tubes around her. But she had recovered some of her coloring, which gave Carys hope. She'd been pale and blueish when they had arrived yesterday morning.

"I promise you will be notified if anything changes, ma'am."

Carys nodded and stood. "Okay." She hadn't left Maya's side since she was admitted, and she didn't want to leave her now either.

Once she was in the hall, she looked up to find a shock of silver white hair and jean clad legs. She would know that person anywhere, even from behind. Without her permission, Carys's feet took her right past the nurse fast enough you could almost call it a jog. "Lavender!"

Vinny spun around in time to catch Carys as she stumbled forward, nearly face planting it right in front of the nurse's station. "It's okay, Carys. I got you." She leaned into her best friend and quietly began to sob.

"I was so scared we'd lose her." Her words came out jerkily between sobs.

"No way. A great mom like you? Maya is so lucky. You knew exactly what to do and got her the care she needed right away," Vinny said with quiet conviction. "I'm here to take care of *you* now."

"What?"

"Go home, Carys. Get some real sleep before you are the next person they need to admit."

"But Maya—"

"Has her godmother now. Take a moment to fortify yourself for whatever comes next, Carys."

"How did you even get here? You're supposed to be on tour."

"Don't worry about it right now. It's kind of funny though. I'll tell you after Maya comes home. Promise."

Carys let out one of those really gross sob laughs, complete with tears and snot and she suspected a bit of drool. She was a mess. "Okay. Okay, I'll take you to Maya."

Chapter Twenty-Five

CARYS

"Are you *serious?*" She laughed uncontrollably as she watched Vinny take their Christmas turned New Year feast out of the oven.

"Can't make that shit up," she said. "I've met some really strange people in the industry, but nobody quite like him."

"I thought the lead singer was supposed to be all hot headed and full of themselves…and cocaine. And whiskey."

"Duke is a vodka man," Vinny said. "Maybe that's where he went wrong. Instead of downing Old Fashioneds with Brendon Urie, he was taking shots out of…*an area exposed* when groupies are really good at doing hand stands and the splits at the same time. Huh," she said with a pause, looking up and off to the side in thought. "That would be an interesting thing to poll—pun intended—how many strippers, hookers, and escorts were gymnasts and cheerleaders in their youth."

"Yeah, but Vinny. You said the guy had to cancel his tour because he had *two* STIs in his throat at the same time and literally couldn't sing."

"That's not the shocking part," she said as she turned off

the oven. When she turned back to Carys, her eyes were alight with glee. "Duke thought because they overpoured the shot glass he was positioning in the cranny of the moment that the alcohol would *cleanse her* so he couldn't get any kind of diseases."

Carys's jaw hung open in disbelief.

"Yeah. I probably had the same look when the manager told us what happened. Duke thought he had the world's worst strep. We knew he was struggling the past few weeks, but he showed up to sound check the last day and could barely speak, much less sing. His 'strep' was actually gonorrhea."

They both exploded in laughter. Much needed laughter. Maya had been in the hospital for five days, and Carys didn't know how she would have pushed through without Vinny's support. Maybe she should send a care package to Duke for prematurely terminating her contract with his idiocy.

When they finally settled down, Carys asked the question that had been niggling at her brain all evening. "He wasn't someone you got involved with right? Or someone Jake shared with? I'm not judging, Vinny."

"I know you aren't. And no, I never crossed paths with him sexually, or any other way. Not even a handshake. We don't share mics or anything, so the chances of me coming into contact with his fluids is pretty low. We weren't even on the same tour bus."

"Okay."

"But I'm smarter than that, so I already had a full workup done to confirm I'm clean. Just in case we swapped water bottles or something."

"Oh, good. That makes me feel so much better." They had dished up themselves and were now moving back to the dining table. "So, what is Jake doing right now?"

"He went to see his family back east somewhere, and then he's coming back to LA. I found a little one-bedroom place. Really cute. Security gate, two parking spots which is practically unheard of in that part of town. And most importantly, I can pay for it with what I make with my ArtBeat account."

"Sounds ideal. You won't have to store your van at your Dad's anymore," Carys said warmly.

"Nah, I'll still have to deal with that situation. Otherwise, Jake won't have a place to park."

Carys lowered her fork and stared at Vinny. "Wait, he's moving in with you? Vin, it's been like two seconds."

"Maybe, but I've known him a long time. It's not like he's a stranger."

"Vin—"

"It's not your choice, Carys," she said firmly but not unkindly. "Jake and I are already lined up to do a lot of work around town together, so it will even be beneficial."

"I'm sure you're right and everything will be great," she said. *Great for Jake,* her mind tacked on.

"He's a good guy. I hope you get to meet him before another tour pops up. Jake can be a lot of fun."

It sounded like Vinny was trying to convince herself more than Carys, but this time she shoveled a heaping forkful of mashed potatoes in her mouth and smiled at her friend. While thinking about the potatoes, of course—they were as delicious the second time around. If she thought about Jake, she'd make what Vinny called her "squishy face," and she'd know Carys was trying to be nice.

Friends supported friends.

Carys wished Vinny had taken her up on their housing offer instead though.

"Okay, let's do this," she said, needing a change in subject before she stuck her foot in it. "New Year's Eve! What do we want to accomplish in the next year?"

"I'd like to continue growing my following and maybe score an international tour with the USO this year. The one Dad and I did stateside was so much fun," Vinny said around a mouthful of her dinner roll.

"I'd like to never see the inside of an emergency room again...and a baby."

"Really?" Vinny cried, bits of food falling out of her mouth. She wiped her face off with a napkin and washed down her food with some water before turning back to Carys. "Oh my god, Carys! Maya is going to be the best big sister. Now I understand better why you insisted on doing the surgery alone. I'm still mad about it, but I get it."

"I was having some really bad pain too, especially when I was trying to do anything with Maya. It was necessary anyway," she said, shrugging it off like it hadn't been nearly as hard as it had proved to be.

"Eric must be so excited to get to experience the whole process this time."

He was. Every moment, from conception to birth. And Carys was just as excited to not feel like a nervous reck the first half, wondering if she was going to be a single parent or not. She let out a sigh of contentment before shoving another bite into her mouth and chewing vigorously.

"He is," she finally replied. "But what man doesn't look forward to months of sex?"

———

VINNY HAD STAYED with them through the first week home; long enough to make sure Maya was fully recovered and help Carys catch up on things she'd struggled with during her own recovery. A few hours after she'd left for LA, there was a gentle knock on the front door.

"Can I help you?" Carys asked the pleasant looking woman standing on her porch.

"Hi, Missus Blackwood. My name is Beth. Your husband hired me before he left."

"Hired you to do what?" Eric hadn't mentioned anything to her. Had he? She pulled her phone out of her pocket and checked the screen. It had been on silent, and she'd missed a text from him earlier. "Oh! You're a massage therapist."

"Yes. He asked me to come by once a month during the afternoon. Mister Blackwood said it was naptime, so you wouldn't have to stress over a sitter."

"That's...true. Wow. I had no idea he'd set this up." Carys was overwhelmed with emotions, gratitude and love at the forefront. After the past six weeks, she needed someone to care for her desperately. Tears welled up in her eyes, burning as she fought to keep them from falling—which made her nose start running. *Gross.* "Come on in, Beth. You can call me Carys."

"Okay." She picked up a long, somewhat flat carrying case Carys hadn't noticed before because it had been propped up next to the door out of sight. "It's my massage table," Beth explained when she saw her looking.

"Of course. How about we set up in the office. Plenty of space, and it's quiet back there. Do you need anything?"

"I've got it all here with me, thank you," she said, following Carys.

A freaking massage! Carys couldn't remember the last time she'd even had a pedicure, much less a full body massage.

"We were meant to have an earlier appointment, but I

understand you had surgery," Beth began as they entered the office.

"I did."

"I'm going to have you fill out a questionnaire since it's your first time, and then we'll get started."

Ninety minutes of bliss later, Carys waved goodbye to Beth and collapsed onto her sofa happily. She felt good. Sincerely good. Beth had worked her over carefully and thoroughly, making sure to check in with Carys as she went along. Since they had missed an appointment, Beth had split the time between the next two appointments to make up for the lost hour Eric had already paid her for.

Which meant Carys would be getting another ninety-minute massage next month too.

She consulted the clock before deciding now was as good a time as ever to try talking to your husband located in an undisclosed location. A text wasn't enough. Eric picked up right as she was beginning to feel the disappointment of not reaching him.

"Hey, sweetheart. How was your massage? Did you like Beth?"

"I loved her. Thank you so much, Eric." A little sob escaped. "I was having a hard time, especially with Vinny leaving for LA today. I just—I don't deserve you."

"You're right. You deserve *better.* I'm sorry you have had to do so much on your own, sweetheart. It has been killing me, being away while Maya was so sick."

"Yeah." It had almost killed her too.

"We didn't get into what happened with her tour, but when Vinny messaged she was done early and headed your way, I cried like a damn baby. Fuck, Carys. It hurts so much.

I should have been there for both of you." Eric's voice was full of despair.

"None of that. Everything we have is because of *you,* Eric. Kids get sick. Ours decided to be an overachiever this go around." Carys thought for a moment on what could possibly help Eric out of his wallowing. "She didn't tell you what happened to end the tour?"

"No, why?"

Carys filled Eric in on what had happened, enjoying the way his face lit up and the deep tenor of his laugh. Then he called in Ruben, and Carys told the story again. By the end, the three of them were laughing near hysterically, barely able to keep themselves upright.

"You doing better now, Carys? Is our princess back to normal?" Ruben asked when he finally caught his breath.

"She misses you guys, but yes. She's much better. When we got back from the hospital, she grabbed for your pictures off the side table where she nurses and planted slobbery wet kisses on them. It was so sweet."

"Awe, she knows her Funcle!" Ruben hooted. Carys rolled her eyes. Try as she had, the moniker wasn't going anywhere. "Give her kisses back from me, will you?"

"Of course, Ruben."

"I've gotta go, man," he said to Eric. "Shift starts soon. Bye, Carys."

"Bye, Ruben. Be safe." He flashed her his blindingly white smile and disappeared himself.

"I love you, sweetheart. Counting down the weeks until we're together again."

"Me too," she said quietly. "I miss you so damn much. Be safe for me, Eric. Promise me. Please."

"I promise."

———

TO: CrayonLover@mailwarrior.net
From: ByAnyOtherName@Eden.com
Subject: New beginnings

I can't believe it's March already. At the same time, it feels like it's taken an eternity, waiting for these months to pass. Time moves differently when you are away.

You are still my reward for making it through this strange paradox wherein the earth purposely circles the sun in a lazy manor, elongating the time it takes for you to come home to us. I know you think I can do it alone, but I can't. Not without the spark of hope you give off, gleaming like a beacon and guiding me safely until *you* stand before me again, instead of the flicker I grasp so desperately in your absence.

I love you, Eric.

And I need you, always.

Chapter Twenty-Six

ERIC

Five months, twenty-nine days, eleven hours, and three minutes.

That was how long it had been since he held his family, give or take a few seconds. Nearly six solid months in the bowels of hell while his wife took down obstacles like a heavyweight champion matched with a gnat. He was so damn proud of her.

But it was a talk for later.

Right now, he was searching for his wife in the crowd. He knew he would find her right where he'd left her and Maya when he departed—it had worked well enough in Mexico, he'd used same tactic when he left this time too. The crowd parted, and there they were. When he got close enough, Carys put Maya down and let her run in her little toddler rhythm straight to Eric. He dropped to one knee and caught his baby girl up, kissing her rosy cheeks and smelling her sweet baby goodness as she giggled happily. Three more strides and he was able to pull Carys into him as well.

He was finally home.

Eric murmured his love in Carys's ear while she clung to

him, too emotional to speak. He held on to his girls like a favorite daydream, precariously balancing the moment with the fear it wasn't real and he'd blink himself back into a war zone.

"Daddy!" Maya squealed, squeezing his neck as tightly as her little arms could. "Daddy, Daddy, Daddy."

"Hello, my sweet baby girl. You look so precious today."

"She picked out her own outfit," Carys finally spoke. "She's been watching a lot of *Monsters, Inc* and thinks Boo is the coolest ever."

"That explains the OshKosh, pink shirt, and pig tails," he said with a chuckle.

With his other hand, he tipped her face up to his and planted a kiss promising a whole lot more when they had privacy. The heat in her eyes made it extremely hard to stop, but Maya's weight reminded him it wasn't the time.

They began walking back to his truck together, Maya sitting in the crook of his left arm and still lovingly clinging to his neck, and his wife walking beside him. He wished he could put an arm around her, but Eric had to drag his giant wheeled bag behind him. They were most of the way across the airfield when a whistle made them pause.

"Hold up, Slow!" The sound of boots hitting the blacktop drew closer, until Ruben came into view through the crowd.

"Fuckle!" Maya yelled, drawing looks from nearby.

"Princess Maya!" he answered, coming to a stop. *"Fun-cle,* sweetness. *Fun cuh el."* He said it slowly and repeatedly. "Your very own fun uncle, princess. Funcle Ruben!"

"Fuck 'Uben!" she repeated back with typical toddler gusto.

"Only if I find my wife," he replied, giving Maya his most winning grin. "Good try, Maya. We'll keep working on it."

"Ruben," Carys said sternly, narrowing her eyes at him. "This is *exactly* why I didn't want you calling yourself *that.*"

Ruben bowed dramatically. "My apologies to the queen of Oceanside."

"Uh-huh." She was still shooting darts out her eyes at Ruben, but the smile winning out showed her true feelings. Carys loved how much Ruben loved Maya, and how easily he had accepted them both from the start. They all knew she'd get over the taboo toddler tongue tie he'd dubbed himself eventually.

"You look good, my liege. What merriment can we expect at the royal court for this auspicious occasion?" Ruben continued with a haughty air.

Carys rolled her eyes. "As nobody here *likes* me, I'm going to keep my king to myself for at least the next week. After that, maybe a small something. I haven't decided yet."

Sounded like heaven to Eric. Days playing with his daughter, nights worshipping his bride.

"Woah there, Slow. Put those bedroom eyes away until you get home, man."

"Shut it, Ruben." It was said without malice, one brother to another. "Where is Carla?"

"She's running a little behind," he said with a shrug. His smile held but Eric saw the disappointment in his eyes.

"Do you need a ride home? I think we can spare the time to swing your way," Carys said kindly. Eric would be rewarding her for making light of it so Ruben wouldn't be embarrassed by the offer.

Ruben looked down at his phone for a minute, swiping around. His jaw clenched, and Eric knew what it meant. She wasn't coming anytime soon.

"That would be great, actually. Looks like she got stuck behind a wreck on the way back from her dad's house. I'll go grab my bag." Ruben turned and walked away without making eye contact.

"She wasn't out of town last night," Carys murmured to Eric soon as he was out of earshot.

"I didn't think she was." He let out a frustrated sigh. "I can't believe she fucked up his homecoming though. I thought she'd overdo the glam and make a scene or something, but not showing up is unforgivable. Ruben had a bad trip."

"I wish you were talking about hallucinogenic mushrooms."

"Me too."

If only war was so kind as shrooms and paranoia.

Eric swung wide into Ruben's driveway and put the truck in park. He'd missed his truck. The smell of it, all the memories he'd made with it. Mostly at the hardware store, but still. You can't bring home building materials without a truck.

"Thanks for the ride," Ruben said with false cheer. He turned to Maya and kissed her outstretched fingers before pretending to gobble them up. Maya giggled. "Be good, sweet princess."

Eric got out of the truck with him to drop the gate, full well knowing Ruben could lift the bag over the sides of the bed if he wanted to. "You can come over anytime. The girls don't change that. If anything, they'd kick my ass if I allowed it to," he said to his friend as Ruben slowly pulled his bag to the tailgate and hefted it over his shoulder.

"I know. It'll be fine, man. She's on her way."

Ruben looked ready to break, and Eric wasn't going to push him over the edge. Instead, he nodded his head, clasped hands with him in the casual way they had for years and got back in his truck quietly. Carys had already pushed the garage door opener when he was talking to Ruben, so as soon as he disappeared into his house, Eric backed down the drive and kitty cornered right into his own garage.

"Is he going to be okay?" she asked after he killed the motor.

"I don't know," he answered honestly.

Carla had not been kind to Ruben during his deployment. Eric wasn't going to spill the beans he did know about, nor would he ask what Carys had picked up on across the street in their absence. Things would come to a head on their own and it was more important they be there for Ruben when it did than have him think he'd get nothing more than an *I told you so* from his oldest friend.

"But I do know what I want to spend the rest of my day doing, and it has nothing to do with the neighbors," he added, his voice dropping low and gaining a huskiness.

"Right. A nap," Carys said playfully.

Eric put Maya to bed himself. Carys had said she'd do it, but he insisted. Frankly, he'd *missed* it. She was so big now and he had missed so much. She had been cruising the furniture when he left, now she was running. Maya had an opinion on certain things too, like what she would wear and how she wanted her bed arranged. Her little vocabulary was gaining every day.

He'd almost fallen asleep himself as he rocked her, proving his wife correct yet again. Eric was exhausted. After silently closing Maya's door, he walked down to their room, where Carys was waiting for him in her bath robe. He could hear the shower running in the ensuite.

"Close the door, please."

He did.

"I'm going to show you how much I appreciate all the

massages and little tokens you sent to me while you were away. Strip," she ordered.

Eric began peeling off his clothing, watching Carys watch him as he did. The way she nibbled her bottom lip made his blood hot. He was well on his way to a full salute when his pants hit the floor.

"Time for a shower," she said, her gaze locked with his as she turned her body and walked toward the bathroom. Her robe hit the floor right before she crossed the threshold.

Eric followed, catching up to his wife with a handful of long, purposeful strides. He pressed his erection against her back and breathed in her scent. "I missed you, sweetheart."

She took his hand and led him into the shower, backing him under the water. Her hands moved over him. It was both loving and sensuous. A groan echoed out from his chest. Next she soaped him up, wordlessly continuing the perfect agony of her hands gliding across his fatigued body. When he was all rinsed off, she took a step back, pulling him with her.

Carys turned Eric's body where she wanted him, then put her hands on his shoulders and guided him down to sit. "When did we get a bench in the shower?" *And how did I miss it on the way in. Oh, right. Naked wife.*

"I had it installed to make things easier. Like shaving my legs," she said coyly, dropping to her knees between his thighs. "And *this.*" Her hands slid up his thighs to his shaft, drawing another groan from him. "Relax, Eric. Lean back and let me love you."

Her mouth joined her hands, her tongue first circling the head of his dick before she took him into her. Eric watched as she hollowed her cheeks and relaxed her jaw, then took him as deeply as she could before slowly drawing back. He reached for her, and she shook her head. *No.* He dropped his hands to his sides and was rewarded with a smile with her lips still wrapped around him, which was sexy as hell.

Carys bobbed up and down his shaft, her hands working his base as she did. He closed his eyes and relaxed the way she wanted him too, enjoying the feel of her confidently owning the moment. He heard the sound of a bottle opening and lazily cracked one eye to see where that was going.

"Trust me. Relax."

He closed his eyes again and let out a heavy sigh. It wouldn't take much more if she kept going at this pace. Eric liked blow jobs as much as the next guy, but this one was different. He could feel it. The way she was building him up...

"Fucking heaven," he groaned as his body sagged down on the bench further. He might slide right off, the way she was melting him with her touch.

A euphoric high began building as she continued, changing her pace and technique seemingly at random, never letting up. One of her hands moved down to his sack. He white knuckled the edge of the bench, trying to keep from touching her, afraid she'd stop. *God, it's so fucking good.*

With one hand working him in tandem with her fantastic mouth, he hardly noticed the way her second hand explored. The buildup was beginning to overwhelm him and, "Sweetheart. I'm going to..." His words were cut off by the newness of what she was doing. "Carys," he grunted, realizing what was in the bottle he'd heard her opening.

Lube.

She pressed one, then two fingers inside him, gently finding her target before she doubled down. Carys worked him inside and out, pushing him right over into the most explosive orgasm he'd ever had in his life. Eric's whole body tensed right before he let out an involuntary roar. His spine tingled, toes curled, chest heaved—until his body sagged again while his wife swallowed him down, gently slowing her pace to a languorous goodbye. She removed her fingers before slowly pulling off his drained member.

"Welcome home, Eric."

"When I can think again, you are going to tell me where you learned that finger trick," he said with a grin. "Jesus, Carys."

A lesser man would be worried right now.

But not Eric. He let his wife guide his spent body to the bed without bothering to towel off, then collapsed into a deep sleep with her body wrapped around him. He'd get the story on the butt thing later.

Chapter Twenty-Seven

CARYS

Every day they did something fun as a family. The sound of Maya's giggles and exclamations as she explored the world left a look of wonderment on Eric's face. Probably on Carys's face too.

Once Maya had come home from her scary brush with RSV, things hadn't really improved. They kept right on happening. Her car stopped working, but she'd been lucky enough to have Eric's truck to get around in while it was being repaired. The furnace had to be reset twice more before she finally called in the HVAC specialists to figure out what was causing it.

A leaky pipe had made it necessary to rip out the master shower and redo the entire thing. She'd ordered more of the same tile—Eric still had a box in the shed, thankfully—and Vinny recommended a bassist friend who did remodeling as his day job. Since it had to be redone, Carys decided she was going to make it worth the trouble. Hence, the new shower bench.

Of course, after she'd given Eric his little surprise home-coming treatment on it, she'd never look at the built-in the same way again. She didn't think he would either. After a few days, Eric had finally gotten around to asking her how she'd known where to find his prostate and what exactly to do with it.

"I used to work at a sperm bank part time," she deadpanned. "Ever see the movie *Road Trip*?"

"Try again, Missus Blackwood."

When she stopped giggling, Carys explained about a roommate she'd had once who was attending nursing school at the time and had been doing a rotation with a proctologist in town. It wasn't nearly as fun a story as working for a sperm bank, but it was the boring truth. The first time her old roomie had watched the doctor at work, she'd come home and blurted out the whole scene in detail, using a fake patient name. To get her through it, they had looked up what a *pleasant* exam might be like. The idea was she'd feel less frantic—and embarrassed—if she could believe the patients enjoyed the experience.

Carys had paid attention.

"You never did it to someone else? *Ever?*" he asked with a hint of skepticism.

"Never wanted to before. But you're my husband. If I was ever going to satisfy my curiosity, it would have to be with you. And judging by the way you reacted, it was a good time," she added smugly.

"I'll show *you* a good time, soon as our daughter goes to sleep tonight," he whispered low against her ear. Then he sat back and eyed her nipples poking through her shirt. *Damn it.*

"Yes, please," she said in her most sultry tone.

He bit back a groan. They were at the park—not exactly the right place for this level of flirting. Although the sight of Eric with Maya only reminded Carys how much she loved her husband.

And how much she wanted another baby with him.

There wasn't time to think about anything outside their little sphere of bliss. The domesticated side of Eric turned her on as much as anything else he did, and she found herself dragging him off to various corners of their home for sex over the littlest of things.

"If I had known putting the toilet seat down turned you on so much, I would have capitalized on it a long time ago," he teased. Carys reminded him Maya would only be asleep another half hour at best, and he threw her over his shoulder like a caveman, hauling her off to their bedroom.

Where he fucked her like a bit of a caveman too.

It was amazing how much they got done and how often they left the house, given how often they were at it. If she didn't start it, Eric would. Carys was swollen and tender from how often he took her in a day and loving every second of it. She'd never had this much sex this often before, not even when her pregnancy hormones with Maya had her pawing at Eric the moment he came home from work.

The last weekend of Eric's reintegration leave, Carys invited Zeke—or V12, as they said at work—and Ruben over for a casual afternoon. They sat around on the back deck under the budding honeysuckle and watched Maya play in the yard. *If you want to know the measure of a man, watch how he treats children,* she mused to herself.

While Carys was setting out an easy meal of burgers, chips and salad, the menfolk were out on the back lawn making asses of themselves to Maya's delight. Ruben caught up his goddaughter, giving her a swift toss in the air—then abruptly called for Eric after catching her, holding Maya out at arm's length while he made a face. Someone needed fresh pants.

Eric took Maya from Ruben with a laugh and bounded

across the yard and deck to the kitchen door. "Hey, sweet-heart. Smells good."

"I'm guessing Maya doesn't."

"She does not," he confirmed. "I'm going to go clean her up before we eat."

"Okay." She paused to watch Eric disappear toward the staircase. He really did have an exceptionally nice ass.

"I am so glad that man found you," Zeke said behind her, a low chuckle emerging. "He is much better off."

Carys laughed off her embarrassment at being caught checking Eric out. "I'm the lucky one."

"If you say so."

"I do."

"Well, as someone who knew Eric before he went to Mexico and came back with his heart between your teeth, I think we'll have to call this one a draw."

"Agreed," Ruben said, coming in through the sliding door behind Zeke.

"Of course *you* agree. Nobody else would be brainless enough to let you name yourself *Funcle.*" Zeke and Ruben laughed over her comment while Carys mean mugged Ruben in jest. "The food is ready. Why don't you two help your-selves. I've already started Maya's plate."

"All right, Scarecrow," Ruben said.

Carys's brows hit her hairline with surprise. Ruben usually wasn't one to make the snarky comebacks. That was Vinny—when she was in the mood to do it. But taking her self-deprecating remark into the land of Oz on her..."Scare-crow, Ruben?"

"You started it. I'll call it like I see though, Missus Black-wood," he said, letting his Georgia upbringing slide in with a soft twang. "You are far from brainless. Maybe blinded by light."

"And revved up like a deuce?"

Ruben grinned. "All right. Try this. You were *addicted to love* at the time, and now it's too late. The name Funkle has stuck."

"Manfred Mann's Earth Band *and* Robert Palmer tonight, huh?" *He and Vinny will quiz each other to musical death if they ever freaking meet.* "On a roll tonight. Still not getting away from the scarecrow comment, Holt."

"Ouch. It's Holt now? My humblest apologies to the queen."

"Stop kissing my wife's ass," Eric said lightly as he reentered with Maya. "You're gonna give V12 some pineapple shaped ideas."

"Pineapple?" Carys asked, physically perking up alongside her curiosity.

Zeke and Ruben both let out one of those snort laughs, decreasing their visible ages by at least a decade each. It was cute, seeing them acting boyish—except the part where it was at her expense. They turned to Eric expectantly.

"You don't know about pineapples?"

"Other than how to mix them with rum or grill them, apparently not," she quipped, crossing her arms over her chest. It pushed her cleavage up, and she smirked when she caught Eric staring down her V neck top.

"Go on, man. Tell your wife about *pineapples.*"

Eric gave Ruben a dirty look. "It's a symbol."

"Like the bat signal?" she couldn't help but ask.

Zeke put a hand over his mouth to hide his grin.

"Yeah, if you are looking to share an evening with other couples," Ruben blurted out.

"It's so swingers can easily identify other swingers," Eric said, still glaring at Ruben as if *he'd* been the one to bring it up, and not himself.

Carys felt her jaw drop open. She looked between the three of them, trying to feel out if this was a preorganized prank. And *holy shit,* they were completely serious. Her surprise melted away into manic glee. She giggled, chortled, and then full-on belly laughed.

"That's fucking amazing!" And she kept on laughing.

Throughout the rest of the evening, she kept randomly breaking into giggles and whispering *pineapple* to herself. The guys watched her with fascination, and maybe a little bit of trepidation—like she needed a mental health assessment or something. The end of the evening probably did not help reassure them of her sanity.

"Zeke," she said low and serious at the front door as he and Ruben were walking out. "I need you to know something important."

He nodded. "Sure, Carys. What's up?"

"A pineapple will always be fruit to me. Delicious, sweet, tangy fruit. So, if I mix up some cocktails next time or serve up a fruit salad, it's not a come on."

Then she slammed the door in their startled faces and ran up the stairs to laugh hysterically into her pillow.

Military life was wild.

———

"YOU DIDN'T KNOW ABOUT PINEAPPLES?" Vinny laughed.

Carys shifted the phone to her other ear so she could more easily wrangle Maya into her clothing. She was being wiggly as hell today, and Carys was trying not to get frustrated with her for being what she was—a toddler.

"Of course, *you* know," she huffed.

"My life is ahhh…more varied than yours. I meet a wider

range of people out on the road," she said. "It's pretty common with musicians."

"Sex, drugs, and rock'n'roll," Carys said. "Maya, baby. Be still, please."

Instead, Maya arched her back and pushed hard with her legs, nearly overpowering Carys's grip on her.

"I've got rehearsals to get to anyway, Carys. I'll let you go so you can tackle the wiggle butt."

"Yeah, no kidding." They said goodbye and Carys set down her phone right before Maya made another attempt at launching herself off the changing table. She was really getting too big for the thing. "Maya Blue!" she cried in frustration. "Let me dress you."

"I got it, sweetheart," Eric said as he came into Maya's room. Carys let him take over.

"Great. The diaper bag is already stocked and ready to go. I'll get the picnic out of the fridge and into the cooler then."

"Okay, we'll meet you at the car. Right, Maya? We'll see Mommy at the car." His tone was sweet, the smile he gifted their daughter more so.

Carys's ovaries *ached.*

This. Man.

Everything about him turned her on. She'd been worried the time apart would create issues, but instead she felt like they were even stronger now. He anticipated her needs and frequently stepped in with Maya. Some men shirked the dirtier part of fatherhood, but not Eric. He would change diapers without being asked. Laundry, picking up, changing out the linens.

Carys felt like she'd won the lottery. There was no weird gender roll bullshit. Eric was an equal partner in all things. As she walked down the stairs to pack up lunch instead of the baby, she couldn't help smiling. After six months of doing everything herself, it was a relief to have him home to share the workload of their family.

When they pulled into the parking lot of the aquarium half an hour later, Carys could already smell Maya. It was *bad*. Air out the car and warn passersby of the olfactory danger about to immerge kind of bad.

"Where is the diaper bag?" she asked him, frowning when it wasn't in the usual place she kept it on the floorboard.

"I thought you grabbed it."

Is he kidding me right now?

"No, I told you it was all packed up and ready to go. With you. And Maya. *To the car* you were already headed down to while *I* packed up lunch."

He shrugged like the smell in the car wasn't about to register on one of those smell-o-meters they used to detect nuclear threats. "I assumed you were going to go back up for it."

"Why would I need to go back upstairs for a bag that was already packed and ready for you to bring down to the car *with the baby*, Eric?" She knew she was letting too much frustration bleed into this conversation, but it was hard not to.

It was the first time he'd taken Maya to the car since he got home two weeks ago, and she hadn't exactly told him about all the routines in place to keep her sane while he'd been away. She was too busy enjoying him being there, allowing herself to be relieved he was safe at home. Eric didn't know she always packed the diaper bag right before she changed Maya to leave, then carried them out together so she didn't have to worry about forgetting the bag. Why would he?

And yet. Why *wouldn't* he?

It had been sitting right next to him, packed and ready to

go. She had told him it was ready to go, damn it. It felt so obvious.

"It's okay, I saw a Target on our way in, maybe half a mile back. We'll swing in real quick," he assured her, putting the car in reverse.

"It's not okay. There is more than diapers and wipes in there, Eric." There was also a change of clothes, a wet bag, teething supplies, Maya's favorite stroller lovie and blanket, medicine in case she got sick while they were out…

Oh, God. What if she gets stung by a bee or something while we're out? I won't even have a first aid kit. The nearest children's hospital is a good hour away. She could die this time.

"Maybe we should go home," she snapped. *Better safe than sorry. There will be other days for the aquarium, and Maya is only nineteen months old. She'll never know we skipped it.*

Eric put his hand on her bouncing knee and gave it a little squeeze, stilling her beneath his touch. "We've got this, sweetheart. Let's just go to Target."

She'd obviously had those grateful, totally in sync, so glad he was home to share the burden, thoughts too soon.

Chapter Twenty-Eight

ERIC

His wife was *freaking out*. Over a diaper bag. It was all new territory and Eric had no fucking clue why it had set her off like it had. He'd seen a panic attack before, but not from his wife. Not even when she was trying to tell him she was pregnant. Incessant nervous rambling, sure. But panic? Not Carys.

Not until today.

He put the car in park outside the Target he'd remembered passing on the way out before unbuckling his seatbelt. "I'll only be a minute."

As he sped walked through the bright red doors, his eyes scanned for the baby section. Seeing kids clothing, he figured it was probably in the same direction, and adjusted his course down the main aisle. There it was, calling to him like a beacon of marital hope. He turned up the diaper aisle and skidded to a halt, his brain going numb at all the boxes and boxes and *boxes* of different products—all designed to catch literal shit.

Fuck. What do the front of Maya's diapers look like again? Carys kept them in a cutesy little basket, so he'd never even seen the box. Diapers for sensitive skin, overnights, organic, fragrance free, odor lock...and each came in different sizes, which seemed to be weight based. He'd just been carrying her, so he was pretty sure he could guesstimate the right size. Now which type?

After fumbling around, he finally grabbed a small package of what he thought looked like the diapers Carys kept on the changing table. Next was wipes. And somebody shoot him now because this area was no better than the diapers. *Think. What does the bag she refills the warmer thing look like?*

White. She bought a box with several giant refill bags in it at a discounted price, and all the labeling was on the box, damn it. They had a textured pattern stamped on them, but he had no reason to memorize them before now. He did know one thing for sure; Carys didn't like a lot of smells. She'd told him early on there wouldn't be a bunch of baby powder scented crap—no pun intended—in their house.

He grabbed a small pack of wipes with a resealable lid on them claiming to be free of fragrances and made of ninety six percent water, and almost choked when he saw the price tag. *That's what it costs for water rags to wipe an ass? Jesus.*

On his way back up the aisle toward the checkout, he saw something he did recognize—the diaper rash ointment at home did have a recognizable label on it—and grabbed a travel sized tube of it. Eric rushed through self-checkout and back out to the car, giving Carys his biggest *we've got this, nothing to panic about* smile as he climbed back behind the wheel.

"Did you get her a new outfit?" Carys asked. "There is no way that smell stayed contained."

Fuck. She was right. Maya was ripe, which usually meant a big mess.

"No, but I will," he said, releasing the seatbelt again before he could click it in place.

Eric went back into the store twice more before Carys seemed calm and satisfied enough to head back to the aquarium. He felt like he'd just run a gauntlet, and he honestly wasn't sure if he'd won the right to believe he'd been spared from elimination. There was so much tension in the car right now, pouring off her in the passenger seat.

Where had his easygoing wife disappeared to?

———

THINGS GOT PROGRESSIVELY WORSE over the following weeks. The only thing Eric was confident he still did right for his wife was sex, which there was still plenty of. It was everything else at home that had gone to shit. He didn't understand how six months could change *so much.*

Even though he'd remembered all the key things Carys looked for in a diaper or anything else in contact with Maya's skin, the brand of diapers he'd chosen had been a different brand, and Maya had developed a horrific diaper rash while they were out. Carys had been near hysterical that evening when they stripped her for her bath. When her usual remedies didn't work as well as she'd hoped in relieving Maya's discomfort, Carys had put her in a dress and let her run around in the yard most of the day bare bottomed.

Apparently the best cure for a rash that bad was fresh air. Who knew? Certainly not Maya's *father.* If it weren't for her mother, the poor kid would still be chaffed and bleeding on her most sensitive areas.

A few days later, he accidentally mowed over the emerging bulbs Carys had planted as a surprise. They were still under the last of the debris left behind from winter, which he'd told her to leave for him to handle since it was good mulch come spring. She'd cried until her nose was red as a beet, her eyes swollen and puffy. Eric felt terrible. Even more so when she told him Maya had "helped" her plant them last fall on the sly…and they had chosen ones that would bloom around Father's Day.

He'd thought Maya could sit up on his lap on her own without help, which was *mostly* true. The sitting part was fine. The *lunging forward* part had caught him off guard. Realizing her favorite lovey was on the floor, Maya had reached down for it faster than Eric could react and fallen forward hard, striking her head on the coffee table.

She'd had a lump on her forehead for days, and the last bits of yellowing from her healing bruise were still there to taunt him with his failure after a solid ten days of healing.

Carys never blamed him in so many words, but it sat between them—the proverbial elephant in the room, and like an idiot he kept on feeding the damn thing. He wasn't trying to make things worse, but every time he attempted to do something helpful it backfired spectacularly.

He didn't understand his own family anymore.

"Why are you so mopey?" Ruben asked. He'd come back from helping another team out yesterday and had been giving Eric weird looks ever since. He'd known this visit was coming. "Slow? You okay, man?"

He let out a heavy sigh while rubbing his face. "Not even close."

"What's up? Did I miss something while I was out of the office?"

"No, it's *home* that's gone sideways. Fuck."

Ruben laughed lightly. "You're kidding, right? Carys adores you, man. The way she looks at you…let's just say more than one man here is jealous."

"Seriously?"

"Why do you think the wives are all still so bitchy toward her? They see her as competition, Slow."

"Huh. Here I thought it was because we eloped and they didn't want to take the time to get to know someone they didn't expect to be around this long," Eric said sarcastically.

"That too," Ruben admitted with a shrug. "Still, she's more than proven herself. That's not really enough of a reason at this point."

"And how do you know all this, bearer of gossipy wisdom?"

Ruben rubbed the back of his neck, a sure sign he was embarrassed. "I overhear them talking when Carla invites them over."

Right. Carla invites all and sundry, but I have to miss my best friend's wedding because she's jealous of my wife and baby. Eric wondered how much of what Ruben had overheard had been slowly planted in their heads over time by Carla, convincing them Carys was a threat that should be kept at a distance so she couldn't inflict damage by ingratiating herself with their husbands.

She was certainly petty enough.

Not that Eric could tell Ruben any of those suspicions.

Fucking love goggles.

"How nice for Carla, she could make friends easily within the group," he said instead.

"I think it helps being a military brat and all," Ruben thought aloud. "It's not a new dance for her."

Unlike Carys.

"True."

"Look, you want some time alone? I could come over one night and watch Maya. Maybe you two need to get out of the house and do something nice together. Carla has a lady's trip planned this weekend, so I'll just be twiddling my thumbs at home anyway," Ruben offered.

Eric thought it over for a moment. "That's probably a good idea. Let me talk to her and see what she says."

"Sure, man," he said as he turned to go. "Let me know."

"Close the door, please."

Eric sat quietly in his office thinking things over. Ruben had a good idea. They'd been out with Maya plenty of times, but Eric had yet to sneak away with Carys alone. The more he thought about it, the more he realized it wasn't just something he *should* do, it was something he *wanted* to do. If he could take Carys out and get her to relax, maybe she'd be in a place to talk to him about what was going on with her.

He picked up his cell phone and did a quick search, pulling up a listing he'd utilized plenty while he was away.

"Hi, I need to place an order for delivery. Today, please. Yes, I know there is a fee for rush orders, that's fine." Eric smiled to himself as the woman pulled up his information in her computer. "Yes, I'm still here. No, I don't want to repeat a past order. What can we do within the usual budget featuring plenty of indigo?"

Chapter Twenty-Nine

CARYS

Carys wasn't feeling overly hospitable as she opened her front door. When she looked up to see a familiar white van at the curb, she perked right up. *Only good, pretty things come from that van.* In the half second it took her to register why someone was risking waking Maya from her nap, she'd managed to put a genuine smile on her face for the delivery driver.

They passed their usual banter while Carys signed for the delivery. When she looked up, clipboard outstretched to return, her breath caught. "Oh, wow."

"Your husband has great taste," the driver said with a nod. "The florist had little input, aside from what was readily available."

Carys thanked her as she took the flowers, then shut the door with her hip while she buried her face in the blooms. They smelled heavenly. Her body erupted with pleasure, those familiar butterflies only Eric could inspire deep inside threating to fly off with her. She took them to the kitchen table.

No. Just...no.

The coffee table was next, but she was afraid Maya would do something alarming—like try to eat them. She certainly didn't want to hide them away or leave them where they would be easily knocked over or bruised in passing. Her eyes locked on the mantel.

Perfect.

There were so many varieties of flowers, she couldn't name them all. Roses and lilacs she knew. All of them were stunning, and the sprigs of greenery added were the perfect touch to break up the different shades of blues and purples, allowing each stem to shine like a crown jewel. Carys was so moved by the gesture; she felt her face dampen with tears.

Eric had pampered her plenty while he'd been away, but not since he returned. Carys hadn't realized how much those little surprises meant to her until now. She hadn't cared for being spoiled in the past. But she'd never been with someone who would be away for so long before either. The little care packages he'd sent at random and the monthly massages had reminded her she was just as much on his mind as he was on hers while he'd been gone.

She was not out of sight, out of mind.

She was his wife.

She was *beloved.*

The clock on the mantel struck the hour, startling Carys out of her revery. Maya would wake soon. If she wanted a shower before Eric came home, it would have to be now. Especially if she was going to show him how much the gesture had meant to her. *I can't even remember the last time I shaved my legs.*

Cleaning herself up didn't feel like enough, but it would have to do. Carys had already decided on leftovers for dinner, in an attempt to make space for the next thing Maya would hardly pick at before chucking it to the floor. There was no time to change her mind and whip up something more gourmet.

As she turned on the water and began stripping, she glanced over at the shower bench. Memories of what she'd done to Eric the day he came home immediately sprung up, making her core ache desperately. He hadn't so much as flinched when she'd moved her fingers over his hole, and as she remembered how bold and confident his trust had made her feel while she brought him pleasure, she wondered what else she could do for Eric.

Now *there* was a way to show him how much the flowers meant to her.

"How about a date this weekend?" he murmured as he nestled his face in her hair. She could feel him inhaling her scent. "Would you like that?"

"Mmmm," she managed, her tone warm and silky. "What about Maya?"

"Ruben will be free."

Eric pulled her impossibly closer, given they were already pressed together. They'd just made love—twice—and hadn't actually parted. Carys had slid down his chest like melted candle wax, her body conforming to his completely. He'd pulled one of her legs over his hip as he rolled them sideways, still intimately connected. Now he held her, nuzzling her hair between tender kisses across her crown.

"She'll love that."

"But will *you?*" he asked, his tone betraying his underlying worry.

"Of course," she said easily, punctuating the words by rolling her hips into him. "I love spending time with you. It's just harder because…"

"Because we had a baby so soon," he finished her thought.

"I don't regret her for a second, but a little more time being the center of your universe before having to share your attention would have been nice," she confessed.

"I feel the same way."

"You do?"

"Yup. Completely jealous of all the time our daughter has you to herself. It's been far too long since I came home from work to find you naked and spread out on the bed waiting for me when I came up to change." His voice grew huskier and he ground his hips toward hers as he spoke. "Whimpering your little pleas as you spread your legs in invitation."

"I love you, Eric. I'm sorry I can't show it better right now."

"None of that," he said with firm patience. "I know you love me, sweetheart. I just wonder if you *need* me."

She tipped her head up until they locked eyes. "Of course I do. How could you ever think otherwise?"

"This whole house—our family—runs by your schedule. I don't know if I have anything to contribute," he said, working hard to hide deeply rooted anguish from his expression.

And failing.

"Please," she whispered. "Don't ever believe I can do this without you."

"You've proven you can, Carys."

"No. If anything, I know how absolutely lost I am without you." She shuddered, dark thoughts pulling her out of her post sex delirium. *The thought of a life without him…a life where he doesn't make it home one day.* Her eyes welled with tears as her throat constricted painfully around the softball sized sob forcing its way up. "Don't ever leave me. I can't—

you don't—nothing would ever be right again," she stammered.

"Nobody can promise they'll never leave, but I promise I'll never leave you by choice."

Eric took her face in his hands and kissed her deeply, feeding his light back into her and vanquishing her insecurities back to their shadows. Carys could feel him hardening again inside her and began to slowly move against him. He rolled above her, his mouth never leaving hers as he worshipped her.

Slowly.

Reverently.

Making a promise he *could* keep.

———

"THOSE ARE GORGEOUS," Vinny said. "I kinda hate you right now."

"I hate myself," Carys said. "He thinks I don't need him, Vin."

"Rubbish. You've never had so much purpose in your life as you do now, and it's not because of Maya. It's because of *Eric.*"

Carys let out a sigh. She was right. "I was having a crap day before these arrived yesterday. Now I'm feeling melancholy when I look at them, because instead of the thrill they gave me when they were delivered, all I can think about are the things he said in bed last night."

She switched cameras as she dropped down onto the couch, knowing it was safe for Vinny to see the hurt she couldn't hide.

"It's just a thing. A bump. You guys are solid. I'm not

even convinced this little hiccup in his *reintegration* has broken your honeymoon phase," she insisted.

"Ugh. I don't know, Vin."

"You still having sex?"

Always the blunt one. At least with me.

"Yes. Why wouldn't we be?"

"Lots of sex, Carys. Not once a week on a scheduled night."

"Yes. We have sex all the time."

"How often?"

"Lavender!" Carys could feel her face blazing with embarrassment.

"See, still in the honeymoon phase," she insisted. "I can tell by the maroon shade of your face, there is plenty of random, uncontrollable fucking still happening."

"How is what's his face?" she threw out, desperate to change the subject.

"Jake is…good."

Uh-huh. He's still an ass.

"The apartment is set up nicely, I just wish we were home more to enjoy it together." She tacked it on in a way a lifetime of friendship told Carys there was more to it, but she wouldn't push. She'd already shared her concerns over rekindling something with Jake.

"I'm glad you like your apartment," she said earnestly.

"Yeah. Um…my dad found this really sweet gig out in Nashville. We'd both go out together. I mean, it's been so much fun actually touring with him. We were talking about renting a trailer and towing my car behind the van, so we don't get stuck with one car out there. I'm not sure, but there might be some recording opportunities while we are there," she gushed.

The way her face lit up on the screen while she spoke

lifted Carys's spirits. It was great she had such a solid relationship with her dad now they could do music together all the time. He'd been around enough to teach her as a kid and instill all his passion, but Vinny surpassed him in ability now and they both knew it.

"Sounds like a dream. When do you leave?"

"A couple months. I figured I'd come down for a week or so first. What do you think?"

"I think you better mail your goddaughter some great postcards from Nashville, so she can read them when she's older. It's hard when you are so far away, but I'm really proud of you, Vin. You can stay as long as you like before you head out," she said hopefully.

Chapter Thirty

CARYS

"A vineyard? For the *weekend?* I don't know, Eric. We've never left Maya overnight before."

"It's going to be fine. Zeke and Ruben are perfectly capable of watching her overnight," he said casually. "They are going to have a blast with her."

"Are you sure?"

"Of a two to one ratio? Yeah, I'm sure," he said with amusement this time, a slow smile pulling up on his face. It felt like she hadn't had very many of those since he came home, and the effect melted her into a gooey mess on the inside.

"Okay. If you think they can handle her, I trust your judgment. They've both watched her a few hours here and there. I'm sure as a team, nothing can go wrong," she said, surprised she meant it.

"Then it's settled," he said, giving her a little smolder to go with his grin. "I get you all to myself from Saturday morning until Sunday evening."

Carys didn't believe for a second he'd won a room for the weekend over the radio. For one, Eric wasn't the type to call into the station. If she had to guess, he'd done the same he had in Mexico and gotten lucky with someone else's cancelation. But if pretending he'd won some sort of contest made him happy, she'd go along with it.

Honestly, she was too excited to *care* how he'd gotten the room. He'd done it for her, for *them*. It wasn't the first time he'd pulled this particular rabbit out of his hat, but she'd never thought there would be a repeat performance. How do you top what ended up being their wedding trip? Booking the honeymoon suite by luck alone and then eloping...

The stars had aligned under the Mayan night sky to make it happen.

"I guess I better decide what to pack," she said softly, her body thrumming with the promises swirling between them. "It's only three days away."

"The room came with a few packages," he said. "You'll want something casual but nice for Saturday afternoon."

"When are the guys coming over?"

"Ruben said he'd walk over whenever we were ready to head out. V12 will come over after breakfast."

She'd have to pull something out of the freezer. If she started today, she could prep enough food for them to eat over the weekend. All they would have to do is—

"Stop."

"Stop what?"

"Mentally cataloging the pantry," he said warmly. "They can both cook. Maya will be fine."

"How did you know?"

"You had your grocery list face on."

"That's not real."

Eric laughed deeply as he leaned into her across the couch. "It is. And it's incredibly sexy."

She snorted. "Now I know it's not real."

"Mmm. Watching you figure out how you are going to take care of the ones you love *is* sexy, sweetheart. The way you prioritize others shows how genuine a person you are. Nothing sexier than a giving woman." He closed the distance between them, gifting her a languorous kiss that had her toes curling inside her slippers. "Especially when everyone who meets you is jealous you're *mine.*"

"Get your ass to work before I rip your uniform off and make you conspicuously late," she said, her voice raspy with need.

He took her hand over the bulge in his lap while he stared at her like a wild beast trying to decide where to best begin his feasting. She gripped him over the fabric, watching his eyes darken as she did.

"I'll chance it."

———

Eric

"It's going to be a great weekend," Ruben said with a wink. "For all of us."

"Funcle!" Maya yelled, throwing herself out of Eric's arms and toward her godfather as soon as he was in the door Saturday morning. Ruben gracefully caught her up before Eric completely fumbled her like he had the ball his first and only season of peewee football.

"That's right, princess! Your Funcle Ruben is here. We are going to have the *best* time together," he said to her brightly, his smile captivating Maya.

Eric knew Ruben's general disposition made his smile all the more appealing to Maya. Ruben was genuine in his love for her, and Maya adored Ruben too. But there was more there, and Eric was curious to see how Maya's purity would help heal parts of Ruben, as well as how his presence would shape Maya as she grew.

It never ceased to amaze Eric how much Ruben would tolerate from her. If anyone else drew attention to his vitiligo, he'd either cringe away or give them a death stare. As Maya became more observant, she began to note things with the innocent curiosity of youth. Last time he was over, she'd pointed to her polka dot shirt and then to Ruben's exposed neck and said, "Dots!" He was Maya's dark, polka dotted knight in shining armor now.

And everyone knows a princess needs a knight in her corner.

Carys bounced down the stairs, her excitement tripping down the steps along with her, right into Eric. He reached out as she hit the landing, pulling his wife into his side, kissing her temple. It was going to be so good having her to himself again for a few days.

"All ready," she said cheerfully. "Are all the bags in the truck?"

"Everything you set by our bedroom door. All that's missing is you, me, and the giant duffle you call a purse." She slapped his chest playfully. Eric let out a little *oof,* as if she'd hurt him. Carys giggled.

"You two have a good time," Ruben said, drawing their attention back to him. "And don't worry about us. We've got everything in hand."

"Do you remember everything I showed you yesterday?" Carys asked.

"I do, but if something slips my mind, I'm sure it's in the detailed two page report you put on the fridge for me." Ruben smiled reassuringly and Eric felt Carys relax further into him.

"Thank you so much, Ruben. I'm really excited."

"You have a great weekend, my queen. Nobody deserves the time off more than you."

"Awe," she said, placing a hand over her heart. "You're gonna make me cry, Ruben. Enough of that." She leaned forward and kissed Maya's cheek. "Be good for your godfather, sweet girl. Mommy loves you."

Eric leaned in and kissed Maya's other cheek before navigating Carys out to the garage, where the car awaited. He opened his wife's door and handed her in, then buckled her seatbelt for her. He planted a lingering kiss on her soft, pillowy lips before he eased back and closed the passenger door.

It would only take a few hours to get to the vineyard, where he'd already arranged for early check in. He had some things on his mind for before their wine tasting and tour that afternoon. Then again, between the tour and dinner. And after dinner…

If he didn't get his libido in check, he was going to have blue balls before they left Oceanside. *Calm the fuck down. It's not like she turns you down at home.* It wasn't the same though. At home, Carys felt the need to reign in, out of fear her cries would wake Maya. At the vineyard, he could watch her fall apart the way he craved.

As they made it out onto the more scenic roads with less traffic, Carys turned off the radio and turned to him in her seat. "You look tense."

"I *am* tense."

"Are you nervous," she asked as a coy smile took over her face. "Or are you needy?"

"Probably a little of both."

"Oh, dear. We can't have that."

"I'll be fine."

"You aren't though. I can tell by the way you are white

knuckling the steering wheel. And the way you keep shifting in your seat."

Shifting in my seat? Am I?

"I can't stop thinking about all the things I want to do to you this weekend," he admitted.

"Me either."

"Yeah?"

"Mmm. In fact, there is something I've been dying to do. Something I think will help us both relax for the drive." Carys moved the shoulder strap of her seat belt behind her and leaned forward on the bench seat toward him.

"What are you doing, sweetheart?" Eric's need for her to touch him was beginning to outweigh his wits. The feral way she was eye fucking him was about to push him over.

"Set the cruise and scoot your seat back a bit so I have room to work," she said as she slid her hand across his lap and tugged open his fly.

Is she serious? There wasn't a lot of traffic out here, and the truck was high enough off the ground nobody would see her. Eric did as he was told.

"Hands at ten and two, Eric. We don't want you distracted now, do we? Focus on the road."

"Jesus, sweetheart. When did you become such a tease?" she hadn't been this way since before Maya was born.

Carys slid close enough to descend on his lap, pulling out his achingly hard manhood with nimble hands before twirling her tongue around his tip. Eric groaned, his right hand moving down to lace into her hair.

"Ah ah. Ten and two, Eric," she singsonged.

Fucking hell. He pulled his hand back and gripped the steering wheel again. "You're killing me, here."

"Be good and I'll make it all better."

Eric constricted nearly every muscle he had as his wife

bobbed up and down in his lap. He wanted to touch her so badly, but every time he released the steering wheel to reach for her, she popped off and *tsked* him. The only thing he could do was thrust up as much as his seatbelt would allow as she took him deeper and harder, until his cock was slamming into the back of her throat while her moans of pleasure vibrated right down into his balls. Carys used her hands to help bring him to the edge, her wet mouth slicking him enough to make every stroke feel like silken torture. He groaned out a warning, bucking his hips up harder as she slammed down one last time, her throat contracting hard enough to milk him dry. He felt her swallowing him down, working him until his body relaxed.

"What did I do to deserve you?" His voice was hoarse and heavy.

"You can pay me back when we get to our room," she said softly as she tucked him back into his pants.

She scooted back over to her side of the truck with a happy little sigh, but he didn't miss the look of longing and need in her eyes as she did so. It was a look he was well acquainted with on her. Carys still set him on fire after two years together. Granted, they had spent half that time apart because of his job.

Still, he knew how it went. Guys coming home from a short trip or deployment to an empty house. Carys wouldn't do that to Eric, and he was grateful she was devoted and determined enough to wait it out.

"I'll do more than *pay you back.*" It was a dark promise he was already planning out his execution to.

"I know you will."

An hour later he led her into the resort side of the vine-yard and right up to their suite. Thanks to technology he could use his phone to get into their room and skip the front desk completely. He dropped their bags onto the dresser and immediately prowled over to her.

"Is this where the predator catches his pray?" she asked coquettishly.

"No. It's where I take all the time we don't have at home to worship my wife." She blinked at him in surprise, her mouth falling into an O. "If you like, I can devour you later, sweetheart."

She shrugged playfully. "I think I'd like a reminder on how you earned the name *Slow* for now."

He showed her. Gently at first, cupping her face in his hands as he feathered his mouth over hers before deepening it. Only when she was trembling did he begin to back off, murmuring sweet things while he undressed her. Eric scooped her up and took her to the bed. His hands drifted over her body as he kneeled over her.

"I can smell you, Carys. Did your little trick on the way here turn you on?"

"Yes."

"I could have gone right off the road without knowing it, you had me so wound up."

"You were already wound up. I brought relief. Eased your suffering." She said it so innocently, but he could see how much was hidden behind her words through her reactions to his touch.

Eric dropped to his elbows and settled between her legs, his hips grinding his cock along her folds. He looked down, appreciating her cream coating him. "Beautiful. My wife is beautiful." He continued to grind against her clit, his hard length growing slicker the longer he worked her. As he continued to torment them both, his hands slid up her arms to her hands, grasping them firmly against the mattress by her face, and watched her writhe.

Carys's lips were swollen and rosy from kissing, her cheeks perfectly flushed and eyes wide, her gaze hazy as she moaned his name. He slowed his glide through her folds, dragging out her pleasure until she was arching off the bed.

And he waited.

Watching her with wonder and love, his body pinning hers to the soft bed.

And waited.

"Eric. *Please.*"

He felt his smile lift, his cock throbbing with her plea. "For you, sweetheart. *Anything.*"

Chapter Thirty-One

CARYS

Nearly two hours later, Carys floated her way down to their scheduled wine tasting on Eric's arm. No amount of road head would ever show her gratitude for the way he'd completely unraveled her upon arrival. She ached wonderfully, each step a reminder of how well he'd drawn out her pleasure.

She had overheard some of the other wives saying they took a weekend away every time their husbands returned from a deployment. At the time, she thought it sounded terrible. Why wouldn't they want to be home with their children, the whole family together for the first time in months? She understood now.

Perhaps that had been part of her problem the past three months. They had plenty of sex, but there was never enough time to do what they'd just done. To openly explore and worship each other like there was nothing and nobody else in the world who mattered. He'd done something similar when he'd come for her in Mexico, and Carys knew a large part of her ease in eloping had been the way Eric had physically shown her how affected he still was by the passion and love which had bound them when they met.

It made sense he'd had problems when he came home. Maya wasn't the same little person he'd left behind. Even Carys was different, but instead of experiencing their growth alongside them, Eric had come home to a complete cluster. She could admit to herself she'd made it worse by trying to ignore how much it hurt he didn't have the answers for anything as readily as she expected, or the same knowledge she'd gained caring for their daughter alone.

Carys's emotions had been all over the place. Burning love and desire, yes. But also, desperation and exhaustion. She had wanted to hand Eric the reigns and rest, but he simply couldn't give her what she needed at first. Surviving his return had in some ways been *harder* than the actual deployment had been.

All those burdens melted away now as Eric pulled back the high back chair at the tasting counter and helped her into it. Instead of taking the seat beside her, he stood close at her side. The heat from his body was comforting, a joy she hadn't had enough of lately. By the way he was curling his body toward her, Carys realized he was probably feeling the same way.

Lesson learned.

Carys and Eric were extremely physical with how they loved one another. From now on, she would tell him when she felt she needed more from him. Maybe over dinner, she could bring it up. He needed to know she cared when he was listing away too. They were *not* two vessels passing in the night. They were *one,* on a mutually agreed upon destination. There was no dingy aboard. They would figure it out or go down with the proverbial ship.

"Oh, this is my favorite!" she said, wiggling in her seat as the sommelier explained the bottle of wine they were beginning with. Carys didn't like a lot of wines, but this one she quite enjoyed when she was in the mood.

Eric smiled beside her. She caught a faint shake of his head. "Why do you think I wanted to come?"

She lifted an eyebrow and stared at him.

"I meant to the vineyard," he said low against her ear.

"Sure, you did. Had nothing to do with the massive bed we both came all over upstairs."

"Better not let anyone hear you talking like that, sweetheart. Those dirty words are only for me."

"All of me is only for you, Eric." She felt her face heat as she smiled up at him. "Thank you. I had no idea how badly I needed this time with you until you offered it."

"Noted."

They clinked glasses and took a sip. Eric looked down at the glass appreciatively, but Carys wrinkled her nose at the taste. It wasn't the same as the bottles she bought at the store. Maybe it was the temperature she kept it at or how she poured it through an aerator instead of letting it breathe on the counter a few hours like the winery did. Oh, well.

Her focus shifted more to what the sommelier was saying, about soil conditions and how it changes the health of the vines and therefore the flavor of the grapes produced. She hadn't put much thought into how a good wine came about before, and felt herself getting lost in the fount of knowledge she'd landed in.

"You don't seem to be enjoying this," Eric said halfway through the tasting list.

"I am, but more the information than the wine itself," she said with a submissive shrug. She was still taking small sips from her glass, but most of it either went to Eric or the pour out bottle on the counter.

By the time it was over, her stomach was unsettled. At dinner, she quietly ordered some ginger ale with a dash of raspberry syrup and a splash of cream. It was as close to an Italian soda as she'd get, given she hated the traditional base. It was more to ease her digestion than anything else. But they were on a special trip, so why not dress it up a little?

The food was amazing. Their afternoon activities had left Carys ravenous. She cleared her plate and still wanted dessert. Eric ordered it to be delivered to their room and stood to take her back.

"Why can't we eat it here?" she pouted.

"Because your dress has entirely too much cleavage and I need to put my mouth on you right fucking now." His words were low, the feel of his warm breath against the shell of her ear igniting her core.

Oh. She let out a giggle and took his offered arm without another peep. She could feel her thighs slick with her arousal as they walked back to their suite. Carys had brought a lovely tea length dress to wear to dinner and had ducked into the bathroom to remove her panties before they went down to eat, leaving Eric none the wiser.

She felt sexy, with the air brushing her wet, swollen flesh as her skirt moved with each step. By the time they returned to their room, she was nearly panting for him to find her bareness. Eric eyed her with a mixture of curiosity and arousal. "Are you okay, sweetheart?"

She shook her head.

"Anything I can do?"

She nodded.

He quirked his mouth on one side. "Can I incorporate dessert into it?"

"Please."

———

IT COULD BE A COINCIDENCE. All of it could be a wild *thing,* something that happens from time to time. Yet as she laid wide awake in Eric's arms while he slumbered deeply beside her, she knew in her heart it wasn't.

The things she had begged Eric to do to her after room service had left coupled with how the wine tasted funny and her ravenous appetite weren't wholly unfamiliar. Not to mention how sensitive she'd been feeling all day, and even Friday, now she thought of it. Both her emotions and her body seemed to be constantly burning with energy.

After Eric texted Ruben *again*—seriously, Maya was fine —about who knows what, she'd decided not to say anything. He seemed to be taking the night away a lot harder than Carys was. Even at the wine tasting, she'd seen him pull out his phone a few times to send a message. It was sweet, and somewhat amusing. He really did not like them both being away from Maya. Ironic, given he'd planned this whole weekend for them.

Eric had done sinful things with their dessert, making a mess. Which led to more sinning in the shower. Carys's core burned for him at the thought. They'd hardly left the bedroom except to go to the tasting and dinner, yet she craved him so much it hurt right now. She buried her face in his chest and inhaled his maleness deeply, a soft whimper escaping unbidden. The soft hair tickled her face as she filled her senses with him.

"Sweetheart," he murmured. *Shit. I woke him up.* "You're practically humping my leg. You can wake me if you need me."

"I need you," she said, huskiness dominating her voice. "I can't help it. Sorry I woke you."

"I'm not," he said, rolling her up above him.

Without hesitation Carys took him inside her with a sharp, hungry cry. They moved together, a synchronized undulation that turned frantic as sparks of desire and pleasure spread through her entire body. Eric rolled her to her back and wrapped her legs around his waist before pounding into her swollen heat. She snapped, screaming his name as her body convulsed around him. She felt the warmth of his seed inside her and smiled deliriously.

"I don't know what's gotten into you, sweetheart, but I'm not complaining," he said, still buried inside her. She could feel him throbbing—or maybe that was her.

"You did."

"What?"

"Eric." She took his face in her hands and kissed him tenderly. "I think we did it. I think I'm pregnant."

His face morphed into a cautiously hopeful smile. She couldn't help it. Carys felt her own smile growing.

"Already? Fuck. God, that's the best news."

"I don't know for sure, it's just a feeling."

"Were you pretty sure last time?"

"Actually, no. I didn't think it was possible. Vinny was the one who went for a test. I only took it to prove her wrong." Carys laughed at the memory.

"Then I'll get you a test," he said, slowly pulling out of her. She missed him already. "So we can be sure."

"Now?"

"There is a pharmacy five minutes away. You stay here. I'll be right back." He smiled at her boyishly, the sureness of youth setting him in motion.

The wrong motion, given he was headed out of the bed and into his clothes. She groaned at the loss of him. "It's three in the morning. Can't you wait until *real* morning?" she asked, reaching out to him from the bed.

"It is real morning. You just said so. And there is no way you can tell me you think you're pregnant and then expect me to go back to sleep." He tucked her in tightly and kissed her. "I'll be back in twenty."

He was back in fifteen.

She took the test.

But even then, Eric didn't go back to sleep until dawn. He was too consumed with worshipping her body *again*...in celebration.

This time, everything will be different.

Chapter Thirty-Two

ERIC

Eric shook his head, but it did little to break the need to lay his head on his desk for a nap. He stood, hoping pacing around his office would make him more alert. It hadn't worked earlier, but it was worth a try.

It didn't work.

"Man, you look like hell," Ruben said.

Eric hadn't even noticed his arrival. From the looks of it, Ruben had been propped up against the doorframe for some time, watching him with amusement. He was so damn *tired.* How the hell was Carys doing this?

"I feel like hell," he finally answered. "Baby isn't even here and I'm not sleeping."

Ruben laughed. "You wanted to be there for the whole process this time, Slow. Did this one to yourself."

"Even so, it was different with Maya. I can't keep up."

"Are you *seriously* complaining about too much sex?"

"Yes? I don't know. I need *sleep,* Ruben."

"Won't be long now," he mused.

Eric collapsed back into his chair with a groan. If he'd

known their weekend at the vineyard was going to set a precedence for the following months, he'd have incorporated more *sleep* into their weekend away. Carys had enjoyed sex when she was pregnant with Maya, and rarely had turned him away. This time, she was insatiable.

Every day was an occasion to celebrate lately. He'd enjoyed it at first. What man wouldn't? Their anniversary had been memorable, to say the least. Maya's second birthday too. Halloween, Thanksgiving, Christmas, New Years, Groundhog's Day…and nearly every day in between.

He'd nearly volunteered for a TDY just to get some sleep. *Nearly.*

"Think you can take a few more weeks?"

"Do I think I can take *seven more weeks* of sleep deprivation? No. Fuck, I miss Vinny."

"What's she got to do with it?"

"When she visits, she takes Carys out to buy baby things and I get to nap."

Ruben threw back his head with a deep belly laugh. Somehow, they were never around at the same time and Eric would forget they only knew *of* each other. It was strange, given Ruben was across the street and Vinny came down to stay most of her spare time. At first he'd found it funny. Now he was dumbfounded how the two had continued to miss each other for the past *two years.*

"Pick a name yet?"

"No. Maya was so easy, I guess it was bound to be the opposite with her brother."

"Maybe it's the sleep deprivation, man," Ruben teased.

"Could be. What are you doing here, anyway?"

"Just checking in. If you want I can come over tomorrow."

"Tomorrow?"

"Yeah, man. It's the weekend."

Shit, was it really Friday? "Uh, sure."

"How about I take their royal highnesses to the park while you get some sleep?" Ruben offered.

"Fuck, yes." Eric scrubbed his face with his hands. "Sounds like heaven. Hey, before you go, are you still off a week from Tuesday?"

"Yeah, I took the day off for Carla's birthday but she's going to see her dad, so…" Ruben looked away, glancing down the hall like he'd heard someone coming.

It killed Eric to see Carla brush off all Ruben's attempts to spend time with her since they returned. It seemed like everything he attempted, she managed to have a reason she couldn't make it, always promising next time.

And never delivering.

"Think you could watch Maya? Carys has an appointment with her birth team, and it will go much easier if we don't take her. Last time she nearly took out the computer swinging some toy around." Eric cringed at the memory.

Maya was sweet as sugar, but she was a typical toddler. She was smart and into everything. Unfortunately, all her curiosity often brought mayhem in its wake. Ruben and Zeke did a great job of redirecting her energy into things that didn't require an insurance claim.

"Funkle and princess time!" Ruben said, bouncing on the balls of his feet while pumping a fist in the air. Eric smiled through his exhaustion at his friend. "Sounds like a great way to spend a day off to me."

"Thanks, Ruben."

"See you tomorrow," he said before heading out.

Tomorrow. I'll finally get some sleep. Eric couldn't wait.

———

"IT WAS wonderful of Ruben to watch Maya today," Carys said on their way home. "He's been around a lot more since your last deployment."

"Yeah," Eric said, his heart hurting for his friend. "It's good to have him around, but I can't help wondering what the hell is happening in that house."

"We agreed not to push him," Carys said gently, placing her hand on his thigh in quiet support.

"I know." It didn't change the bad feeling he had. Eric worried how long it would take Carla to finally break Ruben, and if he'd ever recover.

Ruben genuinely believed he was in love with his wife. Eric knew better. He also knew it was up to Ruben to get himself out of his one-sided marriage. Carla wasn't steadfast toward him. The multiple times they had been on again in the mostly off again delusionary decade Ruben called their *long courtship,* Eric had seen more than enough evidence to believe she wasn't faithful. When he finally found out, it was going to devastate Ruben.

Eric was not looking forward to it. Yet the longer things continued between them, the worse it would be for Ruben in the long run. There was only so much he could do for his friend to begin with, and none of it would be beneficial until Ruben realized what he'd aligned himself with through marriage.

"Come now, Eric. Let it go. We have so many good things to celebrate right now," she said, placing his hand over their son as he kicked from inside her. "Probably should think of a name soon, don't you think?"

"Freddie."

"Be serious."

"Vinny would like it."

"Vinny would also understand the reference and make his personal nursery rhyme 'Fat Bottomed Girls'," she said dryly.

"No way. It's got to be 'Bicycle Race.' Think how epic it would be if he became a professional BMX rider," Eric bantered back.

"No Queen inspired names, Eric."

He chuckled softly as he navigated his way onto the freeway. "All we have is a middle name. That won't do."

"Not my fault. I've made *numerous* lists of names for him, and you have hated them all."

"Carys. *Gregor?*" He shook his head. "What period drama were you watching when you jotted that one down?"

"I wasn't!" she cried with outrage. Then more softly, "It was a documentary."

Eric laughed. "About what, the Russian Revolution?"

Carys turned to look out the passenger window with a sniff of what he was sure was meant to be distain. *Bingo. Time to cancel the History Channel.*

"Anyway, what have you offered? Outside of secret little puns to further ingratiate you with Vinny. It's not like she hasn't been rooting for you since we met—best friend stealer!"

"Yeah, right." Eric nearly snorted but kept himself in check. "You two have been thick as thieves since birth. I'm lucky to be allowed a view through the window of your secret girl club now and again. It's only a matter of time before Maya is old enough to be let in, and then it will be me and little Freddie here against the world." He gave her belly a soft pat.

"And they say women are dramatic." Carys let out a long

suffering—and if Eric was consulted, extremely dramatic—sigh as she shook her head. "And stop calling him Freddie. That's not his name."

"Of course, sweetheart," he said, hoping she believed him sincere. "It was only a suggestion."

"We'll figure it out," she said, seeming to rally from the frustration. "Ruben calls him the little princeling."

"Are you surprised? He dubbed you the queen and Maya the princess of Oceanside thirty seconds after we arrived back from Mexico."

"No, it's very…"

"Very what?" Eric glanced over at Carys beside him, worried something was wrong. She was leaning forward, her eyes focused upward and her expression tight with concentration. "Carys?"

"Sorry, I could swear someone was up on the overpass ahead," she said, sitting back in her seat and wrapping her arms around her swollen belly protectively.

The hairs on Eric's arms stood up.

"Are you okay?"

"Ye—*Eric, look out!*" she screamed, throwing herself back into her seat.

His mind had time to register nothing but the smoothly flowing traffic before everything went dark.

———

ERIC CAME TO SLOWLY, a sharp ringing in his ears. Faintly, he could hear shouting and someone pounding on his window. Farther away, sirens were blaring. The smell of burnt rubber and smoke came to him next. He opened his eyes.

The airbag had deployed.

"Carys?" His voice came out weak, his body still struggling to grasp the physics he had just experienced.

They had been clipping right along in traffic on their way home from…

"Carys?" His voice came out stronger this time.

Then suddenly, everything snapped back. The ringing in his ears cleared, his eyes focused. Carefully, he reached out to the passenger seat, his head cautiously turning to take her in.

There was so much blood.

Too much blood.

"Carys!" he screamed. "Talk to me, sweetheart." He carefully grasped her forearm and gave her a squeeze. Her arms were cradling her belly limply. "No. No, no, no. Carys."

A burst of fresh air hit him as the back window was broken. "Hey, buddy. You need to keep still. You could have neck trauma."

Hands grasped him carefully from behind, keeping him still, his head pinned against the headrest with gentle firmness.

"EMS is on the way. They are going to have to cut you out, though. Your door is stuck," the stranger said.

"No, no. Let me be. My wife," he choked out. "My wife is pregnant. God, there is so much blood."

Another stranger gently opened the door beside Carys, carefully looking her over. She reached out and Eric panicked. *"Don't touch her!"*

The second man stopped, his hand floating near Carys's neck. "Can I check her pulse? I won't hurt her."

"Yes," Eric relented, needing to know she was alive. "Please. Is she okay?"

"Pulse is weak, but she's alive," he confirmed. "Do you remember what happened?"

"No, I…" Eric took a deep breath, his body shuddering on the exhale. *Adrenaline rush,* he thought to himself. "She thought she saw someone on the overpass, but I didn't see anything. The traffic was moving fine, and then there was a huge crash."

He eyed the windshield for the first time, taking in the ragged hole in the middle, caved in toward his wife.

"Something hit the windshield," he said, realization dawning. From the looks of it, it was something *big.*

"You got lucky," the man behind him said. "The cars behind you managed to avoid a pileup. It will make it a lot easier for EMS to get you out quick."

Lucky?

How the fuck was this lucky? *My pregnant wife is unconscious and bloody beside me, and our son…*

Eric choked back a sob.

She had to be okay. How was he going to tell Maya her mother and brother were never coming home again?

No.

That wasn't acceptable.

Carys was going to make it, and so was the baby. They *had* to make it. Eric repeated this over and over to himself, refusing to believe in anything less. He would *not* lose them.

"The bleeding," he said, rolling his eyes to the stranger kneeling by Carys. "Where is it coming from?"

"I don't know. I'm sorry. She's got some cuts on her face, but I'm an engineer. I don't want to tell you something that isn't true," he said, but by the way he wouldn't meet Eric's eyes, he knew it was a partial lie.

It was bad.

Eric's eyes roamed as far as they could with the man behind him trying to keep his head still. Her face was bloody, yes. As was her shirt, which made sense. Head wounds tended to bleed a lot but that didn't always mean they were life threatening.

What sent him into a deep panic was the bit of floor visible below her airbag—or more specifically, the growing puddle of crimson between her feet.

No.

Chapter Thirty-Three

ERIC

Nobody had been willing to tell Eric anything helpful at the scene once EMS arrived. They had taken Carys first, carefully extracting her and rushing off as another fireman replaced the bystander behind Eric and began stabilizing him for his own extraction.

But he had seen the blood-soaked upholstery in her seat before they pinned his head into place. It didn't take a doctor to know that kind of blood loss jeopardized their son. "Save my wife," he'd called as they took her away. All he'd gotten in reply was an affirmative nod from one of the paramedics.

This isn't happening.

He wanted to believe it, but the backboard he was now strapped to didn't lie. No matter how hard they tried to ease his ride to the hospital, Eric begged they radio the other ambulance and ask about Carys.

Was she okay?

Was their son alive?

All he saw was red. *Blood red.* His mind was soaked with it, his right hand stained from where he had reached out to touch Carys's arm.

"Please," he called out to the doctor who met them at the emergency room door. "My wife. She's almost thirty-four weeks pregnant. I need to know if she's okay."

"She's being seen to right now," he said kindly. "Someone will update you as soon as we know something."

"Is she alive?"

"She was when she came in two minutes ago. That's all I know. Now I need to look *you* over," he said firmly.

Eric begrudgingly allowed himself to be assessed. The sooner they got done, the sooner he could demand an update and call Ruben. They should have been home by now.

Six hours later, they told him he was fine, aside from some minor lacerations to his face and arms they had glued shut, and warned him he would likely suffer from whiplash. The next time he woke, he would need to move slowly until he knew what all was hurting. He nodded and went to wait in another part of the hospital for Carys, who had been taken for emergency surgery.

"Hey," Zeke said, wandering into the waiting room and taking a seat next to Eric. "Ruben called me."

Eric nodded, his emotions strangling whatever words he might muster up. What was there to say anyway? Carys was still in surgery.

"It's okay to be upset, Slow. Don't be stoic on my account."

"I can't do this," he stammered out. "I can't—*my wife*—they don't know if the baby will make it."

Zeke put a hand on Eric's shoulder and squeezed. "Then don't. We will sit together and wait for news on Carys and the baby together. You don't have to do a thing right now."

———

"HELLO?"

"Vinny," Eric said, his voice harsh. There was loud music behind her.

"Hey, hang on," she said, and a few seconds later the sound was barely audible. "What's wrong?"

"Are you back?"

"Sure am. And free as a bird, so tell me what's up because you don't cry, and it's freaking me out, Eric."

"There was an accident. Carys is in the hospital."

"I'm on my way," she said. He could hear her footsteps heavy on what sounded like a staircase, a faint echo to her words. "Where am I going?"

"To the house," he said. "I'm headed home to clean up and relieve Ruben, but I want to be back before she wakes up."

"See you soon."

Eric hung up the phone, aware when Vinny said *see you soon* he could anticipate an arrival time defying speed limits and logic. Relief coursed through his body. Ruben had to go back to work, and the only other person he could trust with Maya was Vinny.

Which would allow him to focus on Carys.

He stopped at the nurse's station and let her know he'd be back. Carys was still under sedation and her nurse assured him he had time to clean up and rest.

Rest.

Who can rest when their wife and baby are clinging to life by a thread?

It turns out, Eric could. No sooner had he relieved Ruben and taken a quick shower—throwing away his bloody clothes from yesterday—he passed out on top of the bed. He startled awake three hours later, the faint sound of Vinny waking Maya in her room like a jolt through his system. There was only so much adrenaline a man could take in so short a time. Eric sat at the edge of the bed, rubbing his bare chest, and going through the breathing exercises Carys did during labor to calm himself.

Breathing techniques she wouldn't need again.

He stumbled down the stairs ten minutes later in sweats and an old T-shirt, his heart nearly breaking at the sight of Maya helping Vinny make his coffee the way he like it. She turned to him with a sad smile.

"Hey," she said, and Eric immediately felt his eyes burn as tears tracked down his face. Vinny set Maya down in her booster at the table with some breakfast and took him into the living room. "Let's have it, Eric," she said soothingly as she pulled him down to the couch.

He told her everything. Joking around about what to name the baby, Carys's curiosity over a shadow on the overpass, and waking up to the sound of chaos and the metallic tang of blood in the air.

"Do they think she will make it?" Vinny asked softly through her own tears.

"Yeah. It's going to be hard, but she made it through surgery. The doctor said if they could get the bleeding to stop, she'd more than likely recover."

Or at least her body will recover, he thought to himself. *She'll never fully recover from what it cost emotionally.*

"Thank you for calling me, Eric. I would have come no matter what. Even if I'd been on the other side of the world, I'd have come." Vinny squeezed his hand tightly. "You're my family too."

He nodded. "Yeah. Family."

"Okay," she said, withdrawing her hand and standing. "What do you need? Let's see. I'll go up and pack a small bag for Carys. Her favorite bathrobe, real underwear. We can put in a picture of Maya too. Maybe some toiletries. And we'll do up a bag for you too, Eric. We're going to be good here, so you can focus on our girl."

Eric stood and pulled her into a tight hug.

"Thanks, Vin."

———

Carys

There was a soft caress against her palm. *Eric. I'd know his touch anywhere.* Nothing else felt familiar. The air was too dry, without a hint of the flowers over their deck floating in through the open bedroom window. And the light. Even with her eyes closed, the lights were too bright.

What is that noise? Beep. Beep. Monitors? Am I in labor already?

Her eyes fluttered open heavily, the feel of Eric's touch tightening on her right hand helping to ground her. She was in the hospital.

"Hey, sweetheart. I'm right here." His voice soothed and alarmed her simultaneously. He was here with her, but he sounded so forlorn and helpless.

"Eric?" she rasped, slightly turning her head toward him. She hissed in pain.

"Careful. Here, let me get you some water." Eric held a straw up to her lips while she sipped slowly. "Don't move too much. You are going to be sore for a while."

"Where is Brendon?" she asked in a panic as her left hand landed on her empty belly. *Where is our baby?*

"He's okay. They have him in the NICU," Eric assured her. "Brendon?"

"I had a dream about him. Our little prince. What happened?"

"Do you remember our checkup yesterday?" he asked. She gave a slight nod. "On the way home, we were in an accident."

"The shadow," she said, her drug addled memory grasping onto the last hazy detail she could remember. "Overpass."

"Yeah," he said, his voice rough with emotion. "Someone threw a rock over the overpass fence into oncoming traffic. It smashed through the windshield. The police think it was part of a gang initiation. It hit closer to you than me. I'm so sorry, Carys. I tried to swerve but it happened so fast—"

"Shh. You didn't throw the rock."

"There was so much blood," he said. She studied him silently as his face crumpled with emotion. "I thought I'd lost you both."

"What about our son?"

"He's early, really little. The nurse said he's about four and a half pounds. His lungs are good for his age, but he's in NICU for more extensive monitoring due to why he was born so soon and how little fat is on preemies. He'll be here a week or two, but he's strong—like you."

Carys let out a little sigh of relief; the most her battered body could handle. As long as her family was okay, so was she. "Good."

"Carys." The way her name came off his lips, as if she had actually died, sent goosebumps over her body. "You were hurt the worst. The blood. It took a long time for them to stop the bleeding. You were in surgery for hours. A few intestinal bleeds, you have a lacerated liver. It's going to take months for you to recover."

"What else?" Her instincts told her he hadn't said the worst of it.

"When they took out the baby, your uterus had ruptured. They couldn't stop the bleeding."

They took my womb.

"No." She shook with rage and denial; pleading with her look for Eric to tell her she was wrong in her assumption.

"I'm sorry, sweetheart. We can't have any more babies." The desolation in his face drove his words deeper, shredding her carefully stitched together body more than anything else could have. This wasn't the plan.

No more babies.

The soul shattering wail that escaped her brought a flood of medical personnel into her room. They fussed and soothed and then—nothing. Her mind floated back into the drug induced void she'd emerged from.

Carys welcomed it.

Chapter Thirty-Four

ERIC

"She knows everything," he told Vinny softly, as if his voice would stir Carys after the sedatives they'd pushed through her IV ten minutes ago. "It didn't go well."

"We knew it wouldn't. Better she hears it from you than a stranger though."

"I know. It didn't make it hurt less to watch her fall apart at the news. They had to sedate her so she wouldn't reinjure herself. She must hate me."

"Not a chance, Eric." Vinny said with a snort. "Carys comes alive around you."

"We hadn't put a cap on how big we wanted to grow our family. I guess it's decided now," he lamented as he watched his wife breathing in the bed beside him. Her cheeks were still streaked from her tears. At least the medication gave her a respite from the pain of her disappointment.

"Well, I have some *good* news. I'm finally taking you up on the income suite. You do what you need to do, and I'll be here no matter what. I already ordered a car seat for Maya, so she can ride in Auntie's car now I'll be around all the time."

Eric's whole body sagged with relief. *Thank fuck. I don't know how to do this.* "That's…that's great, Vinny. Thanks."

She *psht* in response. "I was getting bored of LA anyway. Now I get to spoil my girlie here and help our family. Everybody wins."

"Oh," he said, sitting up a little straighter. "I forgot to tell you; Carys named the baby. She said she had a dream about him, and when she woke up, she asked where Brendon was."

"Brendon Blackwood," Vinny tried. "I like it."

"Brendon Ruben Blackwood," Eric said. "Maya's middle name honors you, so we gave this one to him."

"I think he'll like that," she mused. "Not that I've ever met the man. It's totally a guess."

Eric had a feeling they'd be meeting soon enough with Vinny moving in. At some point, it was bound to happen.

"Oh, I know his song! If I send it to you, will you play it for him?" Vinny asked with unbridled glee.

"If they will let me, yes." Eric smiled softly. Leave it to Vinny to perk him up. "I bet Carys will love it when she wakes back up."

"I'll record it right now and send it to you soon as it's done. 'Kay, bye!"

He said goodbye and ended the call feeling a little lighter. With her help, Eric could balance time between home and the hospital. Carys wouldn't have to be alone until she was allowed visitors who liked to climb and bounce on others.

Eric's phone pinged, a specific tone he'd set up for Vinny. He opened the text and saved the video clip before playing it.

It was Vinny singing a beautiful version of "Behind the Sea."

How did I know it would be a Panic! song, he thought to himself.

———

Carys

"Can I hold him? Please?" she begged the nurse.

"I'm sorry, Missus Blackwood. He can't leave the NICU yet. As soon as we can safely get you down there in a wheel-chair, we will let you hold your baby."

"But what about milk? I need to feed him," she insisted, ignoring the desperation she could hear in her voice.

"He's being given donated breast milk right now, per your husband's request, in addition to anything you pump. I know this is hard on you," she said gently. "But we can't risk moving either of you too much until you are ready."

Carys allowed herself to cry. Beside her, Eric enveloped her hand between his own. "Can I hold him? Would someone take a picture for her to have until she can go herself?"

"I don't know since I don't work on that floor. But I can ask for you," she said, and left the room.

"This is shit, Eric. I want to hold my son," she cried.

"I know, sweetheart. I wish I could make it happen for you."

After her drug regulated nap earlier that morning, she'd woken to somewhat good news. Vinny wasn't just watching Maya, she was staying for good. Eric had already told the hospital their baby's name, and Vinny had sent him a sound clip for Brendon.

Brendon meant prince. Her little prince. Her *very* little prince, from what Eric had told her. She still hadn't seen him since Eric had been more focused on organizing the chaos than snapping a picture. Carys couldn't blame him for that, but she did want to see her son.

"I need to try pumping again," she said forlornly. Carys

hated using a breast pump. It hadn't worked well for her with Maya, and now she had the added difficulty of trying to nurse a preemie. Tiny babies have tiny mouths, and memories of falling asleep in Eric's arms while he cradled her and Maya while she nursed flooded her mind. He'd been the only thing to settle them both enough to make nursing work in those early days.

How was she going to do it again? With a baby so much smaller? Most of Eric's paternity leave would be used up in hospital, although his boss had already assured him he could take an extra week of regular leave without issues. Vinny too, would do everything she could to help Carys with the children.

Carys knew it was the trauma and hormones, but she couldn't help being a little angry with Eric. He hadn't walked away with nothing—she could tell he was hiding whiplash best he could, and he had a few stitches across the right side of his face where they'd had to remove bits of glass, and there was some visible bruising—but compared to her, he may as well be injury free.

Internal bleeding, a stollen uterus, and what they promised would leave minor scaring since a plastic surgeon had been on hand and offered to stitch up her face and neck. Her mind was numb to the true extent of her own injuries. All she wanted was her baby boy, who should still be safely growing inside her for two more months.

There were moments pure hatred coursed through her at whoever had done this to them. Maya could have been left an orphan. Eric could have been left a single parent. Or worse—if Brendon had made it but she and Eric had not. Carys knew Vinny and Ruben would never let anything happen to her children, and all the necessary paperwork was in place if the worst should happen.

So why did it feel like the worst *had* happened and she'd survived?

Why wasn't she grateful to have her life and her family?

Why would someone throw a rock off a fucking overpass onto a freeway full of cars going seventy-five miles an hour?

Eric said he'd spoken to the police, but Carys wasn't ready to hear their theories yet. None of them would matter. She couldn't change the damage done with any of the cut and dry facts they would dole out.

They had stitched her up, but she was still hemorrhaging with grief on the inside.

Carys remained silent as Eric gently helped her connect to the breast pump. He held her hand and showed her all the notes and pictures Vinny had sent about Maya's morning. Even the still frame of her daughter laughing didn't break the frost hardening around Carys's heart. She ignored the concern on Eric's face.

It wasn't his fault.

She couldn't bring herself to care.

He was there, and it was easier to tune him out along with everything else than accept her losses. Even when he praised her for what she'd been able to produce to feed the baby, she barely looked at him.

I want my son.

Give me my son.

The ancient ways of Mesopotamia suddenly seemed fair. An eye for an eye. The hatred burning where her womb used to be demanded she be allowed to castrate the man who did this to her. Slowly, with as much pain as possible. She should be allowed to leave the bastard a eunuch, as incapable of bringing life as she now was.

She sincerely hoped his dick would rot off—and for it to be an agonizing process.

TEN DAYS LATER, Brendon ticked the last box on his to-do list and was allowed to go home. They had kept Carys in the hospital with him, so she could be nearby. Finally holding her son had brought her some measure of peace. He was small, but he was doing well. They were still supplementing with donor milk, which broke her heart.

What kind of mother can't feed her baby?

It's the hormones talking. I am *feeding my baby; he just needs extra right now. We will go home, and things will get easier.*

Moving around still hurt. She was safe to go up and down the staircase slowly, but they didn't want her to carry more than ten pounds. In other words, she could carry the baby, but not the toddler.

Before, Maya had been enthralled with her brother. She delighted in watching him move around under her little hands and kissed him as often as Carys would let her. It was yet another thing stolen from their family.

Maya screamed and wailed constantly for Carys's attention, even with Eric and Vinny around to pick her up. The jealousy in her angry little face as she watched *anyone* carry Brendon was enough to test even Eric's patience. More than once, he'd taken Maya to Ruben for a "Funcle date," since Ruben was the only one she felt was still hers alone.

The backlash stunned all of them. Maya had never been prone to fits in her life. Ruben had snuck over a few times long after Maya's bedtime to make sure she didn't see him holding Brendon. Carys had insisted at first he shouldn't pander to it and Maya needed to get over it, but in the end, she relented.

"A lot happened, Carys. Princess needs to feel like

someone is on her team until she comes to terms with all the changes. Look at it from her perspective. Her momma left for the afternoon and came home days and days later, bandaged and barely walking, and she was told she couldn't hug Mommy too tight, or even sit in Mommy's lap. But her brother *can.* She feels replaced. Until she calms, I would rather her still feel like I'm still only hers," Ruben had said gently.

While neither would say what had happened, Ruben and Vinny had finally met while Carys was still in the hospital. The tension between them was thick, and Vinny was the first to shoot Ruben a dirty look and dismiss him. After years of looking forward to dinners with both of them, it still wasn't going to happen anytime soon. Ruben was as quick to go home when Vinny came down from her apartment as Vinny was to stare him down until he left.

Not that Carys had a lot of energy to put into whatever had set them at odds. She had an angry toddler and a baby who was going to starve to death if she didn't figure out how to feed him enough. Vinny and Ruben would sort themselves out over time, or not. As long as neither of them made more drama in her home, she didn't care.

Six weeks after the accident, Carys collapsed on her bed in exhaustion, weeping and ugly. Snot and tears and saliva smeared her face as she released her anguish while curled up in a ball in the middle of her bed. She didn't care.

She was too broken to care.

Eric came home from work and found her there, shivering atop the blankets. She didn't know when she'd last showered. Her hair was greasy, and she could smell herself. *No wonder Brendon doesn't want to nurse. His mother is repulsive.*

"Sweetheart," he called out to her as he crawled across

the bed and wrapped his body around her. "Please. Talk to me. Let me in."

"My milk is drying up. I can't feed our son," she said blankly.

"Then we can see about more donor milk or formula, Carys. It doesn't matter how he's fed, so long as he is."

"It matters to *me!*" she shouted, her body trembling in his arms. "I should be able to feed my own baby, Eric!"

"I'm so sorry, Carys. I know you're disappointed." Eric leaned forward to kiss her temple, but she turned away from him.

"Don't. I'm disgusting."

"Carys," he said firmly, sitting up and roughly spinning her to her back. "Enough. You can't keep doing this to yourself. This isn't what I wanted either, but I'm fucking trying. We're supposed to be *partners,* but I get more support from our friends than my *wife.* I love you. You will *never* be disgusting to me, Carys. But this has to stop. Now. I need my wife back, damn it."

He pressed his mouth over hers roughly—a kiss full of angst and agony—before abruptly pulling away and striding into the bathroom. She heard the shower turn on and then he was back, already stripping out of his uniform.

"What are you doing?" she asked when he began pulling her clothing off after his own lay in a heap on the floor.

"I'm taking care of my wife. Whether she wants me to or not."

Chapter Thirty-Five

ERIC

Watching Carys fall into depression was akin to surviving daily assassination attempts to his psyche. This was more than the *baby blues* her doctors asked about. Not that it mattered, because she looked those same doctors square in the eye with a smile and said she was *great*.

Bullshit.

The very last thing his wife was right now was great.

The physical scars were healing well; faded to a pale pink. In time, they would be nearly undistinguishable. Even the faint line down the side of Carys's face would all but disappear, having been expertly repaired by a sympathetic plastic surgeon at no cost, since their insurance wouldn't cover his services. If these were the only scars he had to worry about, Eric could breathe easy.

Between the loss of her womb and failure to feed Brendon with her own body, Carys was spiraling out in front of him. No matter how hard Eric tried to console and reassure his wife her value to him and their family was far more than these things, she was emotionally beyond his reach. Even after she was cleared for sex, it was several more weeks before she begrudgingly allowed Eric to touch her.

He had been gentle at first, not wanting to be too aggressive after what she'd been through. As time passed, they fell back into a more regular pattern of intimacy like they used to have. Eric had hoped all his efforts worshipping his wife's body the same as he always had—for him, she was as desirable and attractive as the day they met—would help reinforce his words and bring her back to him.

Instead, he often heard her crying softly in her pillow afterward. When he asked the next day if she was sore or if he'd hurt her, she assured him he'd been as attentive and thorough as usual. While he knew she was telling the truth, he could also see something else in her expression when she spoke.

Something new, and wretched. She was his wife, but she also was not. Her body still melted under his touch, and yet she didn't seem to *enjoy* sex the way she once did. He instigated, she did not. Carys was worth far more to him than a living doll to pleasure himself with; yet his frustration still brewed until it turned into bitterness.

How do I fix us?

"She won't let me in," he told Vinny one afternoon. It was Saturday, and Carys was inside napping with the kids. Eric had gone to Vinny's apartment in search of answers, or support if it was all she had to offer. "I try, but it's like she doesn't enjoy anything anymore. Not our family, or outings, or even sex. I don't know what to do to break this depression."

"I thought it would have broken by now too," Vinny admitted. "She's never been depressed a day of her life until now. The only time I see her smile at all is when she's with the kids, and even then it's forced."

"What do I do, Vin?"

"I'm not sure there *is* something you can do on your own. When is her next appointment?"

"Next week. They want to be sure the last of her internal injuries are clear."

"She's going to be pissed, but I think you need to tell the doctor about the depression when you go in. She needs to get into counseling and probably take some medication for a few months while she sorts her shit. She'd never take medication while nursing, but since that didn't work out…"

Vinny didn't need to say more. Carys cried every day while she washed Brendon's bottles.

Eric let out a frustrated sigh. "Yeah, you're right."

"I'll see if I can't get her to open up when we are alone too. We'll figure it out, Eric. Don't give up."

"I can't give up on her."

"Me either."

He'd returned downstairs to his own living room and sat quietly, rolling their conversation through his head. It helped having Vinny back him up, especially since Carys was likely to think they were ganging up on her when shit finally hit the fan. Eric worried she'd feel more isolated and alone, but if they didn't get her the help she truly needed, he hated to even contemplate the consequences of doing nothing.

Carys deserved so much more than what she currently thought of herself.

To make matters worse, Ruben and Vinny were still avoiding each other, repelling like oil and water anytime they came close to contact. If Ruben was coming up the front, Vinny was sure to disappear out the back door toward her own abode. And soon as he left, she'd reappear like she hadn't bolted out the back to begin with. The whole thing was odd.

The only thing healing alongside Carys's physical wounds was Maya's attitude toward her brother. Now that she could cuddle her mother again and be picked up, her grudge had lifted. Maya had even taken to climbing under the baby gym with Brendon and showing him how to make things rattle and crinkle. She'd tell him what colors he was looking at and point up to the mirror where both their faces could be seen.

At four months old, Brendon was thriving. He was still a bit small but quickly growing, catching up to his full-term peers in both size and milestones. Their pediatrician assured them nobody would ever guess his early arrival by his first birthday.

All this brought comfort to Eric. Carys…less so. Speaking of their son's age only reminded her he had come early, forcing every date out of sync with when it *should* have been.

There was no winning.

———

"HOW DID IT GO?" Vinny probed.

"About as well as you would expect. She went through every emotion imaginable in about thirty seconds, from denial and sadness right on up to unadulterated fury," Eric replied.

"And?"

"She finally broke down in tears, confessed she was struggling but thought she'd been hiding it well, and *maybe* she needs a little help for now."

Vinny rolled her eyes. "Maybe my ass."

"Yeah."

"So, she's going to try medication and counseling?"

"She is. The medication is already picked up, the counseling will take a little time. We have to go through the list of providers covered by military health insurance first and get her on wait lists. Carys said she'll give anyone a try so long as it's a woman. Given what she's lost, I can't deny that's probably for the best."

"As long as she tries, it's a relief."

"I miss my wife, Vin."

"I hear you." Vinny studied him a few moments, her expression thoughtful. Eric wasn't any good at keeping secrets anyway, but under her scrutiny, even less so. "What else is wrong?"

"I got called into Greer's office today," he admitted.

"And what did the boss man have to say?"

"We're headed down range in four weeks."

Vinny's eyebrows shot to her hairline. "Oh, fuck. They couldn't replace you with someone else?"

"Unfortunately, not. The guy who was supposed to be going broke his leg doing some advanced level hike trying to impress his new girlfriend. *She* is advanced. He should have been on flat terrain, from what V12 told me. The guy is a complete klutz. I *am* the replacement."

"Nothing sexier than falling off a mountain," Vinny said with a snort.

"Especially when you are aiming to impress someone who has hiked the entire Pacific Crest Trail—all 2,650 miles of it from Mexico to Canada."

Vinny pealed with laughter. "Idiot."

"Carys is going to lose it when I tell her."

"I'm sorry, Eric. Thanks for the heads up though."

"I've seen your concealed firearm. No way I'm risking you accidentally shooting me when she starts screaming because you thought our house was under attack," he said with amusement.

"Smart man."

Eric had wandered back downstairs into the main house after they spoke, ready to embrace the chaos of bathes and bedtime. He loved both. There was something wondrous about tending to his children's basic needs that left him feeling full.

But tonight, he would have to tell his wife he was leaving. The same wife he'd convinced to address her mental health only this morning. Eric dragged his feet through the bedtime routine, soaking up the love and sweetness as much as he could before he faced the music.

The worst reaction he could imagine as he walked down the hall and into their bedroom had been screaming or crying. As it turned out, he realized there was something much worse. Silence.

Carys sat on the bed with her huge doe eyes on him and didn't move a muscle. He wasn't even sure she'd blinked as he explained why he was set to leave in less than a month. She could have been secretly elated with the news behind her poker face.

Eric knelt before his wife and took her face between his palms. "I'm sorry, sweetheart."

Nothing.

So, he did what he had done every evening for months now. Eric stripped himself and his wife and hauled her off for a shower. He washed her meticulously before quickly scrubbing himself down so she didn't get cold on the bench waiting.

Then he tucked her into bed and lay beside her—his gaze on the ceiling with her back turned to him—while she quietly cried into her pillow.

Eric silently broke right along with her.

———

"YOU READY, MAN?"

"No."

"Come on, Slow. It's going to be a quickie, four months."

"Four months away from my family while my wife is fucking falling apart right in front of me, Ruben," Eric barked. He didn't want to leave, and everyone knew it.

"We can't change the job, man. At least she won't be alone. Your tenant will keep an eye on things," he said with a note of bitterness as he mentioned Vinny.

"What the fuck happened when you two met?" It wasn't the first time Eric had asked either of them. At this rate, he doubted he'd ever know. "She's a fun woman. I don't get it."

"We have obviously been acquainted with different sides of Miss Blume," he said ambiguously. "Maybe you have to meet her in Mexico to get a warm welcome. Hell, if I know."

"Evasive as ever," he mumbled.

"Carla said she's going to try harder this time to include Carys when she throws her little spouse parties. Maybe that will help." Ruben smiled hopefully.

Eric did not reciprocate.

He already knew Carla was blowing smoke up Ruben's ass.

"Do we have a set departure yet, or are they still fucking around with the timetable? I'd like to make it to Brendon's six-month appointment if I can." Not only that, Carys hadn't driven anywhere since the accident. She wouldn't even pick out a new car to replace the one they'd been driving the day everything went to shit. Vinny would take her, but Eric wanted to take in as much as he could before he had no choice.

"I'll ask Greer," Ruben said. "She'll be okay, Slow. I know this has been really rough on you guys, but you did good, man. You got her help. It's just going to take time."

"I hate not being here for her while she figures it out. We barely had our shit figured out when I came home the last time before she was pregnant. Now we can't even…" *We can't even talk about how I need to hurry back and put another baby inside her.*

Fuck, this sucks.

"Hey," Ruben said low, leaning across Eric's desk until they were face to face. "You are *not* going to lose your wife. I know that look. Cut it out. No more feeling sorry for yourself, man."

Eric let out one of those pained laughs you can't control when you are fighting back tears. He was a Marine, damn it. He was tough.

"Yeah. Thanks."

Chapter Thirty-Six

CARYS

Eric was leaving and Carys was numb—or she had been the day he told her. Since then, whatever the doctor had prescribed to help her feel again had cracked her heart right open.

Was it helping the depression she still didn't want to admit she had? Yes and no.

Sure, she was feeling more like herself. Life felt less like a void and more like something she wanted to participate in. It also meant she had to address the way she felt about Eric leaving so soon. There was an abundance of things she still needed to tell him.

Before the medication, she told herself keeping quiet protected him from the heartbreak and disappointment she felt day in and day out. With the medication…Carys couldn't lie to herself anymore. The way his eyes subconsciously studied her anytime they were in the room together, and how his breathing didn't deepen into a proper sleeping rhythm until long after she stopped weeping into her pillow were truly happening.

It was a problem.

Damn it.

Of all the things she didn't want to do, emasculating her husband was at the top of her list. She *should* be honest with her husband, but what if it ultimately did more harm than good? Now that she couldn't have more children, fear he'd look elsewhere to continue his family had a chokehold on Carys every time she tried to speak up.

He was her husband, and she loved him more than anything. At her second appointment with her new counselor, Carys finally spoke her truth.

Sex was different.

She wanted the mind bending, thought paralyzing bliss Eric had always delivered...before. Time had not helped. Doctors had not helped. Carys was ashamed of herself. *What is wrong with me? Why can't I feel like I did before? How can an orgasm be so empty?*

The counselor had listened patiently to her agony, somehow hearing Carys's words through the blubbering and nose blowing accompanying her hushed words. It wasn't fair. Was she broken?

No.

"The uterus is a muscle," her counselor had patiently explained. "It contracts during intimacy, creating a more intense orgasm. Sex can still be fulfilling, but you will have to get creative if you are looking for the same high you had before."

Before.

And after.

Why did they have to be so fucking different? So difficult? So...anticlimactic?

All she wanted was one damn thing to return to normal. *This* thing. Carys wanted to fall into her husband as she always had, knowing her reactions spurred him deeper into his own pleasure. Of all the ways her body had let her down as of late, this was the final straw.

She had to tell Eric.

It almost felt pointless. Why put this on him right before he deployed? It's not like it was something he could fix or even begin to address in a few short weeks. But the thought of him leaving thinking she wasn't interested anymore, or maybe he'd done something wrong, was even worse.

She wanted their honeymoon phase back—yesterday.

———

"SWEETHEART," he said, pulling her in close beside him and kissing her crown. "You can tell me anything. I want you to be satisfied too."

Eric was leaving in ten days. After talking it over with Vinny, Carys finally had gotten up the nerve to sit down and tell her husband what was bothering her. Some of it was obvious—it would be a long time before she wasn't tormented by her lost ability to carry a child or having to give up nursing their son—but there was no way for Eric to know her sexual satisfaction if she didn't tell him.

"I thought you were struggling with the internal healing, or maybe the depression was making our sex life less fulfilling for you lately. I never would have guessed it was something physical. We're going to figure this out, Carys. I promise."

"It isn't awful for you? I mean, it's different inside me. Can't you feel it?" She voiced her fears with wide eyes, searching his gaze for any sign he was about to lessen the truth into something easier for her to hear than the full truth.

"No, sweetheart. You are as perfect as the day I met you. My fingers can tell the difference somewhat, but my cock can't. And honestly, the longer you heal the less noticeable it is. Making love to my wife is a damn privilege." Eric turned his body sideways onto the couch, scooting down and pulling Carys on top of him. They lay there like that, Carys's head pressed over his heart, the familiar sound reassuring her he was still hers.

"I'm still...desirable?"

"After what you have been through, I'm more in love with you than ever. Your body, your mind. I know it's been hard on all of us, but I have drawn my strength from *you,* wife. I've seen Marines go through far less and bitch a helluva lot more."

Carys giggled, her heart releasing the last band of anxiety constricting it as she did. Eric still wanted her. There was hope. "I think you are overstating, husband."

"Not even close. Call Zeke if you don't believe me," he teased. "He's the medic."

"I'm sorry I haven't been attentive to your needs lately."

"Shh. None of that," he soothed, his strong arms squeezing her firmly against the plain of his chest. "We are looking forward, not dwelling on the past. How can I help you?"

"I don't know," she said in earnest. "We've always had such an intense connection. I still respond to you—"

"Damn right you do." He smirked.

"But my climax falls short now. It's nothing like it was, and since they can't give me back what I lost, I don't know how to be less frustrated."

"We could try new things. Not just positions, other things too."

"Like what?"

"Different kinds of toys and lubes. More foreplay. What

are you comfortable with, sweetheart?" His suggestions caught her off guard.

"I…I don't know, Eric. You're leaving. I never replaced my last vibrator after it kicked the bucket. I don't know what I might like other than you."

"That's the point, isn't it? We get to learn what you like and need all over again." His voice pitched low, and she felt his cock harden between them.

"Is this turning you on?" she asked, lifting her head up to meet his gaze.

"Fuck, yes. I get to relearn how to pleasure your beautiful body. By the time I'm done with you, you'll forget why you were ever upset to begin with."

Shit. That panty melting smile of his. Mmm.

"Vinny has the kids," she said coyly.

Eric slid her up his chest and kissed her until she was breathless while she ground her hips down onto his stiff cock. The relief from his reaction made Carys want to try.

He still loved and wanted her.

"Eric," she moaned.

"How long do we have?"

"Couple hours," she panted.

"It will have to do," he said, hoisting her upward so he could stand. "Bedroom. Now."

Eric half carried Carys up the steps in his haste. His determination stifled her anxiety, leaving her no time to fret unless she was interested in tripping on the stairs. This amazingly sexy, caring man was going to take his time with her, like they were still new and not three years into their marriage.

Her libido began to rekindle, the old spark of need flaring to life under his touch for the first time in months. It wouldn't be perfect. She might not get all she needed. The only thing that mattered was the determined look on Eric's face as he slammed and locked the bedroom door behind them before lunging to remove her clothes.

"I'm going to edge you with my mouth," he said gruffly as her shirt hit the ground somewhere. He laid her back on the bed with her knees bent over the side. "Lift," he prompted as he grabbed the waistband of her lounge pants. The cool air hit her abruptly as he yanked them down, causing her to gasp. "Fuck, Carys. You want this too. God, you're so wet."

"Yes." It came out as more of a breathy moan than a word.

Eric dropped to his knees in front of her at the edge of the bed. "Feet on my shoulders, sweetheart. That's it. Shimmy your hips down. It's been months since I tasted you."

With that, his mouth was on her. Carys moaned as his tongue caressed her folds before he sucked her nub between his lips and grazed his teeth over her. Without any obvious rhythm or pattern, Eric made love to her with his mouth. As soon as she began to feel herself building, he'd shift, sometimes pausing.

"Look at you, all glassy eyed," he said between nips at her folds, which he soothed with his tongue. "How am I doing, sweetheart?"

"G-good," she moaned.

"Only good?" he growled against her. "I better try harder."

Two of Eric's fingers slipped inside her, immediately curling into her G spot. His mouth suctioned down onto her with gusto, nipping and sucking in tandem with his fingers curling inside her. Faster, slower. Languorous, then enthusiastic. Eric continued to adapt as her body began to writhe under his ministrations.

Her toes began to tingle. Carys's eyes went wide as the sensation she'd missed began to reappear. "Eric!"

His eyes smoldered as he looked up at her. "Play with your nipples. Pinch them. Show me what feels good."

She hesitated at first, but the look in his eyes erased all her reservations. They had always stroked each other. The voyeuristic nature was new, and more thrilling than she had anticipated. She grasped her full breasts and squeezed upward toward her tips, awed by the way his pupils blew out watching her. *He likes this too.*

She continued to play with her breasts, experimenting with her gaze locked on Eric's while he continued to eat her. His fingers began to twist as they curled, dragging her wetness to her opening. His thumb swiped through, gently massaging it around—down. Carys's eyes widened with surprise when she realized he was asking her permission. She nodded her consent.

Slowly, Eric worked his thumb over her back hole. She shuddered, the newness sending a nervous thrill through her. It had been a long time since she'd felt this turned on, and she was ready for anything he wanted to try with her body. His mouth slowed again, allowing her to relax as he worked his thumb deeper.

With his fingers above and thumb below inside her, he began to massage the wall separating her on the inside. Tingles erupted across her whole body this time, and she let out a heady keen as she gripped her breasts harder and flexed her hips harder against his mouth. With his eyes trained on her the entire time, Eric brought Carys her first remotely satisfying orgasm since the accident.

She screamed his name, her body clenching and trembling. Before she'd come down completely, he removed his mouth and fingers and flipped her over, his thumb still in place, and plowed into her swollen core with enough strength to make her grateful she was bent over the end of the bed.

Her orgasm began to crest again with the change, Eric pounding into her with all he had. His thumb pressed in as far as it would go, and his other hand slid up her spine into her hair.

As soon as Eric found purchase against her scalp, he gave a firm tug. Carys pinched her nipples hard, arched her back and hips against her husband, and let the magic word pull her into bliss with him. *"Please,"* she cried out. He roared with his release, shouting his praises before stilling over her.

"You know what it does to me when you say please, sweetheart," he murmured over her spine before pressing a kiss to her shoulder.

"Mmm. Looks like you're not the only one who likes butt stuff, Eric." A breathy laugh worked its way through her straining lungs as she thought back to her welcome home surprise when he'd returned from his last deployment. "Perhaps I need to return the favor soon."

"Hearing you scream my name again was reward enough, sweetheart."

Chapter Thirty-Seven

ERIC

After working his wife into a sexual frenzy, Eric celebrated by taking her to the shower and washing her tenderly before carrying her back to bed. He held Carys tightly to him, willing his dick to behave. Her curves melded to his frame like warm clay, the heat from her well fucked core distracting as hell against his hip bone with her leg wrapped around his waist.

"How did I do?" he asked genuinely. "Give me some feedback. What worked, what didn't. Don't hold back. My wife *will* be satisfied."

"Mmm. I need to think about it. Right now, I'm just relieved." She pressed her pillowy lips against his sternum, trailing kisses up and across his collarbone before ascending his neck to nip his ear playfully. All the while, her heat continued to torment him. "It will never be the same, but you made me feel so good. I really didn't think it could be that good again."

"Only good? That's twice now. I'm going to have to work harder."

"No, this was perfect. Gives us something to look forward

to when you return," she insisted.

"Carys," he groaned. "If you keep working yourself over my hipbone like that, I'm going to have to fuck you," he warned, flexing his hips up so his hard shaft bumped her low belly. "I'm trying to gather data here."

She giggled, and he relished in the sound after its long absence. "Sorry."

"Liar." He pushed her hips down as he flexed himself into her again, this time pushing against her back hole. She gasped, her face flushing beautifully. "Wow. That really does get you going. Should have tried the back door a long time ago from the looks of you right now."

"Something to look forward to…maybe." She flushed deeper, burying her face in his chest again.

"Carys," he said firmly, gripping her chin with his thumb and finger and tipping her face up to his. "I love you. We can both think about what sex will look like now and write down hard passes and interests. If we don't like it, we don't have to do it again. But we are going to figure this out because you deserve to be satisfied in bed."

She was quiet, her round glassy eyes locked with his. "I liked you watching me touch myself," she said softly.

He'd liked it too. Watching her follow his commands had been more empowering than he had anticipated. "What else?"

"The…edging. By the time you let me come, my body was on fire. I felt it all over, waves of pleasure. And the way you slammed into me before I stopped…"

Fuck. Pounding into her tight, swollen heat. I knew it would feel amazing after the way she nearly broke my fingers clenching down, but god damn. I feral groan escaped his throat, and she grinned up at him.

"You liked it too, huh?"

"Impossible not to. You strangled my cock with your

cunt." She took in a sharp breath, her pupils dilating and lips parting softly. "Oh, sweetheart. Did you like what I said?"

She nodded.

More dirty talk.

"Anything else you need to tell me before I flip you over?" Now he understood what had been holding her back, Eric was determined to push both their boundaries to keep her satisfied.

"I think you were right about trying different lubes later."

"Noted."

———

THEY STOOD on the tarmac together, waiting for Eric's signal to board. He had spent an hour rocking Brendon in his sleep that morning, his heart aching as he detailed everything about his son to memory. Now the boy slept in his stroller while Maya clung to him.

"Don't go, Daddy!"

"I'm sorry, baby. If it were up to me, I would stay home. Sometimes we don't get what we want." He breathed her in, the sweet smell of the shampoo Carys washed her hair with mixed with that something you only get with small children. "I love you so much, Maya. I'm going to miss you the whole time I'm away."

"Hey, princess," Ruben said from beside him. "Can I get a hug from my favorite girl?"

Maya had already told her godfather she was mad at him for leaving too, but there was nothing to be done about it. Her innocent heart still loved him, and she reluctantly let go of Eric's neck and leaned into Ruben's embrace.

"If I'm your favorite, why are you married to Carla?" Maya demanded.

Eric nearly choked. Even with the little contact she'd had with Carla, Maya couldn't stand Ruben's wife.

"Because I was born too soon for you, princess. We'll have to fix it in our next lives." She nodded firmly, with all the bravado of one who knew what was what.

Eric kissed the tears from Carys's face, gently cradling her head in his hands. "I love you," he murmured. "Don't doubt it for a second, sweetheart. And keep working on those lists," he added, the slow pull of a smile creeping up his face. She nodded.

"You too."

"Oh, I've already got a head start. There is a present on the bed for you. Open it when you get home."

"What kind of present?"

He leaned into her ear and whispered, "The naughty kind."

"Okay, you two. I'm going to wind up with heat stroke being this close to you. Cool it down," Vinny barbed from the other side of them—the opposite side Ruben was standing on.

"I love you," Carys said, ignoring her friend.

Eric kissed his wife softly and let her go. They were in a good place. He'd spent the last week home experimenting with her body, creating a base for them to build on when he returned. Her mood had leveled out and she was smiling again. Vinny was here to support her.

There was nothing else he could do for her until he returned.

"That's the signal," Ruben said, kissing Maya's cheek and handing her back to Carys. "See you in four months, princess. Bye, Carys."

"Bye, Ruben. You guys take care of each other."

Eric gave Vinny a quick embrace and a nod before turning to walk with Ruben. He was feeling sorry for his friend after his wife refused to get out of bed and give him a sendoff. Eric had finally gotten Carys to purchase a new vehicle—an SUV this time with a lot more room—and they had given Ruben a ride. Vinny had climbed into the third row and kept her mouth shut while Ruben rode in the middle next to the kids.

It was bullshit. But it was what it was.

"She's going to be good, man," Ruben said as they climbed aboard the transport.

"I know she will be. And she's got Vinny here now. Not sure what happened in LA, but I'm grateful for her. We would have been completely fucked since the accident without the two of you."

Ruben grimaced. "Uh. Yeah. I'm happy for Carys she's here too."

Eric turned his face away so Ruben wouldn't see him smile.

What the fuck happed when they met? It's been months and they are still at odds.

"I like her new wheels," Ruben said. "A proper tank to haul around precious cargo."

"Yeah, replacing her sedan with something beefier was the only way to go. That thing has more safety features than I can count."

"And I see she chose blue."

"The closest shade to indigo she could get." Eric chuckled. "She likes what she likes."

"It suits her. And the ride was great heading over here."

"Are you okay, Ruben?" Eric turned to his friend beside him, watching him fumble his seatbelt so he wouldn't have to square up. "You've been a little melancholy lately. And right now, you are over focusing on Carys's new truck, which is also unlike you."

Zeke dropped into the seat on the other side of Ruben, effectively caging him in on the center seating row. "This to do with the drama low key buzzing around the water cooler?" he asked quietly.

"It's just talk, man. You know how people get. Can't stand how miserable they are themselves, so they have to go start shit for others." Ruben's tone straddled a fine line between defensive and his usual joviality as he attempted to brush off whatever the scuttlebutt was.

"You know your business better than I do," Zeke conceded. "But if I were you, I'd pay attention."

"What's that supposed to mean?"

Zeke shrugged casually, like they were debating the best way to cook a steak. "I'm surrounded by women in medical. I hear a lot. And right now, the loosest lips in the building are in a position to know firsthand. You understand?"

"Perez is running her mouth," Ruben said with annoyance.

"Yeah."

"Why can't that woman get orders?" Eric said with irritation.

"How is she as a neighbor?" Zeke asked.

"Quiet, actually. After the first six months, Carys finally stopped waiting for the other shoe to drop. The Browns say she's a model tenant. Clean, friendly, pays her rent on time. I hardly see her, even in passing," Eric admitted.

"I see her," Ruben all but sneered. "She's always attending the girl's weekends Carla likes to host. They drive together most of the time, so Perez will come help my wife pack before they head out."

Well, V12's firsthand comment makes sense now. Perez probably sees Carla more than Ruben does. Especially given how often he's been free to take Maya lately.

"Is she coming?" Eric asked.

"No, she is benched at the moment due to injury. Should make for an easier trip for all of us," he offered.

By the look on Ruben's face, Eric wasn't sure he agreed.

What was happening between Perez and his wife, and how long had it been going on? And why the hell hadn't Ruben talked to Eric about it? It was clearly bothering him more than he wanted to let on.

"How is your cousin?" Eric asked.

"Enzo?" Zeke looked to Eric for confirmation. Eric nodded. "Good as can be expected. He's been moved to a station where they respond to a lot of dark shit. I think it's been harder on him than he wants to admit."

"Does he like being an EMT still?"

"Oh, yeah. He loves his job. I worry though, you know. I don't care how old we get, Enzo is still the same fool who thought any girl who let him carry her backpack was his girl-friend back in the day."

"Not you," Ruben chided. "V12 is too jaded to fall in love."

"I'm not jaded, I'm realistic. Love is a lot of hard work. It means choosing that person every single day, even when you aren't sure you like them at the moment. I've had my share of ladies, Ruben. I'm not running into anything long term without serious consideration." He paused and side eyed Eric around Ruben, one eyebrow popping up. "We can't all be as lucky as Slow, here."

"No," Ruben said with weighted finality. "We can't."

Eric had a gut feeling this deployment was going to be make or break for more than his own marriage.

Chapter Thirty-Eight

CARYS

"What the hell is that?" she asked as Vinny stormed into her room with *three* black plastic shopping bags.

"It's your new kit."

"My what?"

"We are going to figure out how to get your motor running again!" she announced, lifting the bags up and giving them a little shake.

"What did you do, Vin?" Carys was completely mortified. Her bestie had obviously gone to some sort of sexy megastore and bought out their inventory on her behalf.

"Now that you are feeling better and more communicative, I decided it's time to bestow all the wisdom I have gained as a single musician on the road with a strict no fraternization policy." Carys gave her a stern glare. "Most of the time, anyway."

"I don't care what you do when you are lonely on tour buses, I am *not* getting a sex ed class from you, Lavender."

"Eew, no. My gate only swings one way, and it's definitely into the pasture of dicks." She set the bags down on Carys's bed and turned each over so the contents would spill all over her mattress. "I got you a little of everything, so you can decide for yourself. Feel free to ask questions, but there will be zero in person tutorials. Even I have limits."

Carys smirked. *No, you don't. Limits. Ha!*

"What's this?" she asked suddenly, picking up the gift box Eric had left on Carys's pillow.

"I don't know," Carys said, waving her hand at the shiny foil in Vinny's hands. "As you can see, I haven't unwrapped it yet."

"What do you *think* it is?" she asked, wiggling her eyebrows.

"No clue. Now put it down. I'm saving it for later." *If I can't curl up with my husband, at least I can look forward to his gift at bedtime.*

Vinny dropped it back onto the bed and moved on to the mass of packaging she'd spread out. "Well, what do you think?"

Carys picked up a brightly packaged something and read the label. "What the hell is a Taco Tickler?"

"Oooh! That's a good one. I have high hopes it will work out for you. I've replaced mine—"

"Do not start telling me how often you have to replace your sex toys, Vin!"

"Fiiiine." She pouted. "But for the record, you will want to pair it with this," she added, tossing a bottle at Carys and scampering away.

"Great. Now she's giving me lube advice too."

Knowing there was nothing wrong with a healthy curiosity was one thing, having it piled up all over your bed was something else. Carys stared at the heap of unsolicited toys, her eye catching something caution yellow peeking out from the bottom. She reached out and grabbed it, tugging it forward.

It was a book. "Masturbation for Dummies," she read, her face heating. *Fucking Vinny. I bet she was cackling when she added this to her purchases. Just because I'm an intellectual.*

Although if she was honest with herself…she would feel better *not* adding anything pertaining to sex into her web browser history. She really hated how much Vinny had anticipated her there.

The sound of Eric's alert tone chimed, and Carys reached for her phone.

Eric: Open your gift yet?

Carys: I was saving it for later.

Eric: Open it, sweetheart.

Carys let out a groan. *Fine.* She reached over for the box, tearing away the paper and opening the lid.

Carys: Am I supposed to wear these when you come home? Not very sexy for panties.

Eric: Pick them up.

She did. They were kind of heavy. Not in a thick kind of way, but actually weighted in the crotch. "Oh my god!" she squealed, nearly dropping them.

Carys: Why do they vibrate?!!!

Eric: So I can play with you while I'm gone. I can control the vibrator with an app on my phone.

Carys's jaw hung open in disbelief while heat simultaneously flooded into her core. She wanted this. The few days they had been able to explore before he left weren't enough. She wanted Eric. She *needed* Eric.

Eric: I'm going to tell you when to wear them, sweetheart.

Eric: and it won't be while you are alone at home.

Carys's hands trembled as she held the panties in front of her, despite the vibrator being off at the moment. He was going to edge her from half a world away…

She looked over at her new Taco Tickler. *Guess I'll be needing you after all.*

———

BY THE TIME Carys had sorted through all Vinny's purchases and stored them away, her embarrassment had given way to gratitude. She wondered if Vinny knew about the panties Eric had bought but decided probably not. As weird as it was, Vinny was trying to help Carys find her new norm and love her body again. She was just a bit more aggressive than most people's best friends.

The three items that had interested Carys the most were set aside, two of them charging inside her nightstand where Maya wouldn't find them. She'd snuck into her own bathroom like an idiot, placing the toy cleaner she'd found inside her shower behind her shampoo, where the black bottle wouldn't wink at her from across the room.

When did I become a prude?

Maybe this would be okay. Eric had said he'd be up for almost anything, so this was her opportunity to hone her… what? She eyed her nightstand, where the bright yellow instruction manual for her body was hidden in the lower cupboard. She'd flipped through it quickly, but the nervous excitement she'd felt had freaked her out.

She wasn't broken.

There was nothing shameful about craving sexual satisfaction.

Her husband still wanted her.

Three years of marriage, two kids, and she wasn't even thirty yet. Carys had expected to be working in some high end corporate job by now, but her actual life as a military wife and mom had been far more fulfilling than she'd ever imagined. Her mother would say she was a threat to feminism, but her time in Oceanside had cleared her head on a lot of things she'd been raised to believe.

For one, being a feminist didn't mean hating or hating on men. It was a belief they should be on equal grounds. Never in her life had she felt more *equal* than she felt with her husband. Deployments were hard, and she wasn't looking forward to this one any more than she had the last two.

But.

Carys felt more valued in her life. Even when it had been time to make a move with his career this past spring, Eric had included her in the process. She'd overheard plenty of wives snarking on their partners over moves they didn't want and hadn't known were on their list of options. Eric hadn't done that to her. He'd brought home their best options and discussed the pros and cons of both for their family as well as his career.

They had decided a move in place was the right call for both. They loved their home here in Oceanside, and since an opportunity was available to keep them there, Eric took it. Given the way life had exploded on them only weeks later, Carys was so glad they hadn't attempted to move while she was pregnant.

If her mother thought her life now was damaging to women everywhere—well, it wasn't like she'd ever called with the apology Eric insisted Carys deserved. Her mother could suck it. And so could all the other ideals she'd instilled in Carys as a young woman. *Ladies do not do obscene things to themselves, Carys. Know your value and never debase it with carnal desire.*

No wonder her mother was so uptight and bitchy. She probably hadn't had an orgasm in decades.

Since she'd started counseling, Carys had thought of her

mother frequently. Aside from her irrational fear at first Eric wouldn't want her anymore, memories of her childhood and adolescence had sprung forth like a plague. Carys didn't want to be alone and angry like her mother. Now she was an adult, she realized how much of it her mother had likely brought upon herself with such a bad attitude.

Her counselor had assured her she was too focused on having a more fulfilling and joyful life of her own to repeat the mistakes her mother had made. It wasn't in Carys's nature to be bitter.

But was it in her nature to take her own pleasure?

A week had passed since Eric left, and he'd neither told her to wear the panties, nor had she experimented with her special lady toys. Her curiosity hadn't died, but every time she peeked into the drawer a shyness came over her. What if she couldn't do it? Even if she read the self-help book cover to cover, what if she couldn't find a level of sexual satisfaction that was gratifying again?

It occurred to her that while she was not afraid of her body, she *was* afraid she would fail—a sensation she hadn't dealt with on this level since she finished her education. It meant too much to her. She hadn't even reached a woman's sexual prime yet, but what if she had already peaked?

———

"HEY, do you mind if I add a few things around the apartment?"

"It's your apartment, Vin. You know we don't care what you do so long as it isn't trashed. Besides, what could be more damaging than all those guitars you decoratively hung across the back wall of the living room?" Carys smiled and shook her head. Some people hung art. Artists apparently hung the tools of their trade.

Although she did have a gorgeous classic Stratocaster her dad bought her last Christmas. Even Carys would have displayed that beauty.

"Okay, well if you hear noise on the roof, it's just me running lines," she said.

"Lines, huh? I don't advise snorting coke off my roof. Might not go well with asphalt."

"You're a dork," Vinny said with a laugh. "That would be *doing* lines. I'll see you later."

"You only have permission for rock and roll on this property!" Carys shouted at her backside. "Leave the sex and drugs for the road!"

"I'd have to meet someone to have sex!" she called back over her shoulder before the back door closed behind her.

"At least you aren't afraid to have sex with yourself," Carys mumbled as she went back to washing the dishes.

She missed Eric.

She missed the way Eric would help her do the chores she hated the most, so they would be done faster—like the dishes, the grocery list, meal planning, and yard work. Oh, and the trash. She really hated taking out the trash. He was so good at swooping in with a fresh bag before Carys even asked, she hadn't realized how often the trash actually did need taken out.

On the bright side, she'd decided to host a gathering with the other spouses who were dealing with deployment. Plenty of people had moved on to other locations, and Carys had a lot of hope the incoming families would be more welcoming.

If nothing else, less hostile was still a step up.

Eric's job transition also meant she was moved into a different circle of spouses. Nobody would bat an eye when

Carla wasn't invited because she was still in the old group with the rest of the pernicious Barbies.

Saturday would be a simple luncheon potluck with a handful of other moms with littles. Carys was excited to get to know them better, and hoped Maya would enjoy making new friends her own age. Brendon was teething, but nothing was perfect. If she was ever going to make friends within the community, she had to stop using day to day life as excuses to back out. Especially since she had Vinny here to help this time.

She was lucky.

As Vinny went flouncing across the backyard with the ladder, Carys laughed. She looked incredibly serious about whatever she was up to. Once Vinny was set on something, there really was no talking her out of it. Carys had learned not to bother by middle school, but it still brought a smile to her face. Sometimes Vinny's motives were beyond what she could figure out on her own.

Like why she needed a ladder to get on the roof.

————

TO: **CrayonLover@mailwarrior.net**
From: ByAnyOtherName@Eden.com
Subject: At home
What can I say, Eric? I'm trying. Therapy helps. Vinny… means well, and I appreciate her so much. I'm here, at home.

Without you.

I'm not sure that's even possible. Home *is* you, Eric.

I feel so much, sometimes too much. Missing you, trying to understand myself better and work through my own shit. At home. Alone.

With a collection of items I'm still too afraid to even look at for long.

I'm scared. What if therapy doesn't stick in the long run? What if my body is so disconnected from the rest of me no amount of tingly lube or kinky lists can save me?

What if I lose my home? Lose you...

I know it's the depression talking, but still. What I would give for you to be home, reassuring me I'm not a lost cause the way only you can. It's like that old song, you remember? The way you smile, how you look at me. Your hands always ready to catch me. All the things you say when you say absolutely nothing at all.

I'm just going to listen to that song on repeat and remind myself I have that. As long as I have you, I have all I will ever need.

To: ByAnyOtherName@Eden.com
From: CrayonLover@mailwarrior.net
Re: At home

I feel all those things, sweetheart. I'm right there with you, all the way. Home is you and the kids. I don't want anything else. I don't *need* anything else. Keep talking to me, Carys. I'm listening, and I'm on your side even when I can't physically be *by* your side.

You have already come so far. I'm sure at times it feels like you are stuck, but do me a favor? Take a moment to think back a month or two. How did you feel then? How do you feel now? Acknowledge that progress, sweetheart. You are already changing your world, and in turn, mine is finally spinning again.

Because you are my world, Carys. I don't want to do life without you.

Chapter Thirty-Nine

CARYS

"Hi, Marcy! Thanks for coming," Carys said, holding the front door open for her guest. "Do you need a hand?"

"Nah, you know what it's like. The best way to forget something is to let someone else help."

"Amen, sister." Carys thought back to the trip they'd taken to the aquarium when Eric hadn't grabbed the diaper bag assuming she would since he had brought down Maya. "We'll be out back today, but feel free to drop anything you don't need outside in the living room."

"Thanks. And thank you for organizing this," Marcy said as her bags thudded to the floor beside her. "It's hard being the FNG."

The fucking new guy. Yep, I know a thing or two about that curse.

"Where did you PCS from?"

"Virginia. He was doing a joint task thing out there. I'm loving the break from east coast pacing. Everyone is in a hurry! California has been so much more relaxing."

"I'm from nearby, so I can't say I'd know. There is

nothing quite like it though," she said with a dreamy sigh. "Hey, Marcy?"

"Yeah?"

"I know PCS means 'move,' but what does it *actually* stand for?" Carys asked. "I gave up a long time ago understanding the lingo. It seems the same letters mean something different from place to place and job to job, but at least this one is universal."

"It means *permanent change of station.* And I hear you. Mike is always trying to tell me about the can of soup he works in, and I can't follow any of it. Like you said, they change offices or locations, and the same things mean something completely different. Nobody with littles has extra brain cells to waste on *that.* "

"Hey, Carys!" Vinny called from the back door. "Can I talk to you?"

Carys excused herself as Marcy settled in. "What's up?"

"There is some sort of *soiree* going on across the street. How many people are coming?"

"Marcy and Hailey are already here, so we're only waiting on Alexis," Carys answered.

"They like to double park and block the street. I think we should make sure everyone is backed into the drive so it will be easier to leave later. I'm not leaving, so I don't care if my car is blocked in out back," Vinny said. "I was thinking of offering to repark their cars for them."

"That's a good idea. Thanks, Vinny."

Vinny disappeared out into the yard to ask Hailey where she was parked as Marcy came up behind Carys with her son on her hip. "Your friend is gorgeous," she said. "Those eyes of hers. Must be hard for her to enjoy being outside though."

"Albinism has made her life interesting, but I can't say it's slowed her down much. And you know, given the shade of her eyes, you would *think* that's why they named her Lavender," Carys mused.

"I wondered what Vinny was short for."

"She's always been a little tomboy rocker. I'm glad she didn't stay in her Avril Lavigne phase for long though. That much black eye makeup on her complexion was not complimentary to her beauty or her reputation. I mean, it *could* have been. If we hadn't been in middle school with zero consistency past a daily poke in the eyeball with our mascara wands."

They laughed softly together, watching Vinny's gleaming white locks blow in the gentle breeze as she waited for Hailey to pass over her car keys.

"Nowadays, all these kids have YouTube tutorials. I'm thirty, and I don't know how to contour—but my eleven-year-old niece does. What happened to painting your lips with blue nail polish and roll on body glitter that smelled like Fruit Loops?" Marcy mused.

"I know what you mean. Rushing off to the mall after school in the hopes you could find the perfect combination of fine *and* chunky glitter lip gloss. Mine had to be watermelon flavored. You?"

"Peaches and cream," she said with a laugh. "And the funny thing is, you won't catch me eating anything peach. I don't like them at all."

Once the cars were all moved into the driveway and the kids were occupied in the yard with Vinny, they began to unwrap their contributions. Alexis had been fifteen minutes behind schedule after one of her kids needed an emergency bath. The four mothers all nodded at each other knowingly.

Kids were kids. Sometimes, you had to roll with the punches.

"That's why I suggested we meet at eleven anyway,"

Carys said. "We all know by the time the munchkins cooper-ate, there is always an hour delay."

"Ah, yes. Planning for the delays in order to make sure food is ready on time. My superpower," Hailey chided. "Samson gets hangry when he doesn't eat on time."

"You have a son? I thought I saw you with two girls?" Alexis—Lexi—asked.

"I *do*. Sam is my husband," she said with a smirk. The others grinned with her. "Isla and Ellie couldn't care less so long as they are occupied."

"Juan starts gaming with his brothers online after work and forgets to eat," Lexi said, shaking her head. "He says it's a fast metabolism, but I swear he's so skinny because he's starving. He's going to have to make some changes when they get back. I grew up at a family dinner table, and so will our kids," she insisted, rubbing her stomach. "No more stuffing in a few bites between rounds. The girls are old enough to pick up on it."

A sliver of longing lodged in Carys's heart, missing the way it had felt to grow a human inside her. *I got to do it, though. I got to make two perfect babies with the love of my life,* she reminded herself. Lexi's third baby was wonderful.

Plates full, they moved out to the patio. The kids who were mobile were sitting around Vinny while she made up little songs about their names, occasionally strumming her favorite acoustic guitar. The rest were mostly napping on bouncers in the shade, within arm's reach of their mothers.

The toddlers were called to eat, Vinny opting to sit beside them so the moms could relax a bit more, and something akin to bliss fell over them all. Carys had always wanted other wives to connect to, and after three years, she finally felt like something *good* was happening.

After they ate, Vinny and Carys spread out the sprinkler

mat in the grass for the littles to play in. Poor little Mason didn't know what to do with so many girls bossing him around, but Marcy kept shoving him back into the fray.

"He'll be happy when his baby brother is big enough to join," Carys mused. *And Brendon,* her heart wished. She was having a wonderful time and hoped this was the first of many such lazy afternoons.

"I hope so," Marcy said. "Miles is so chill compared to Mason. But hopefully once he can get around a bit more, he'll get more curious and help Mason channel his energy for good. Or at least stop being afraid of girls," she said with a snicker.

"Do you know what you're having, Lexi?" Hailey asked.

"No, Juan didn't want to know. It's killing me though. Buying gender neutral everything isn't nearly as much fun," she groused.

"How did you all meet?" Carys asked.

"College sweethearts," Marcy said.

"He dated my cousin first," Hailey said with a wicked grin. "But he didn't date her long."

"Juan came into this diner I was waitressing at every day for a year, always at the same time between the lunch and dinner rushes," Lexi said with a smile. "He'd order a cup of coffee and ask me for a date every time, but I turned him down."

"Not forever, obviously." Vinny laughed from near the kid's table.

"No, after a full year I finally said yes. Making him wait was worth it, just to see the look on his face. I thought to myself, 'he's a scholarship kid who can't afford to get distracted. You can't be the reason he fails.' But he finally wore me down. The day I said yes, he fumbled the full mug of fresh coffee I'd just given him, and it splattered over his arm. He still has a faint mark from the burn." She grinned, her hands cradling her bump as she remembered the moment she gave her husband a chance.

"That's so sweet," Marcy crooned. "You took him by surprise."

"Yeah, but he did too. Even when we were living paycheck to paycheck, he found the most amazing things for us to do together. Movies in the park, late nights up playing cards during semester breaks. Juan can be a charmer. And according to him, his grades improved when we started dating, because he wanted to impress me."

They all let out a laugh.

"What about you, Carys? How did you meet Eric?"

"Oh…" *Why didn't I think of that before I butted into their own stories?* "We were in Mexico."

Vinny stared at her. "Don't short them."

Carys relented, telling them about the trip Vinny had made her take, and how Eric had rescued her from a creepy frat boy at the bar, then later from sleeping in the hallway while their other travel companion banged in the girls' shared hotel room. By the time she got to their reunion five months later and subsequent elopement, they were all swooning.

"That's the most romantic story I've ever heard," Hailey said. "And you never had cold feet?"

"It went too fast to have cold feet. Besides, I was pregnant. The way he dropped to his knees and kissed his baby…" Carys felt herself blushing, her core heating with her face. "There wasn't a doubt in my mind he was the one. We just clicked."

"I lost my bestie to a worthy man," Vinny lamented.

Carys snorted. "Yeah, a man who asked you to move in for *years,* even made a space off the back garage for you to store and play your instruments."

Vinny grinned. "Yeah, all right. I gained the best brother. Eric is great, and he treats you well."

"What about you, Vinny? Got a special someone?" Lexi probed.

"No," she said softly. "This is the first time I've been in one place for so long in forever, with zero plans to go out on tour. I'm a touring musician," she explained. "But after the USO tours I did, I can see why you all went for a man in uniform," she said, wiggling her brows suggestively.

Carys had a thought, as she watched her friend interact with her fellow wives. She'd be good at this. Vinny didn't mind moving, or long travel. If she ever decided to settle down, a man who was also often on the road would likely be a good fit for her.

After the way Vinny had helped bring her and Eric together, maybe Carys should weed out some single gents from Eric's crew for Vinny.

When it was time to pack it up, Lexi came in frustrated her car was blocked in.

"Seriously?" Vinny huffed. "They blocked the *drive-way?*" She strode off around the back side of the house and up the long drive from the back. Carys could see out the front window through the house, a perfect view of her friend stomping her way up Ruben's front walk and pounding briskly on the front door.

Carla opened up after the fourth time Vinny set to pounding with her full fist. There was a heated exchange before Carla slammed the door in Vinny's face. She pivoted on her heel and abruptly marched back to Carys's house, mumbling all the way. "Stupid hussy," Carys overheard as Vinny reached for her phone.

"Don't worry ladies," Vinny said with a smile. "We deal

with this sort of thing in the music industry all the time. I'll have you all free in a jiffy."

Within half an hour–a rather short turn around, given the non-emergent situation—the police had come by to issue parking tickets to the two luxury cars blocking the driveway, a tow truck pulling in as the officer was leaving.

"You fight dirty," Marcy said. "I like it."

Chapter Forty

ERIC

"Man, what the hell is going on back home?" Ruben said, dropping onto the seat across from Eric. "Carla is losing her shit right now."

"Carys said things have been going well," he answered with a shrug. "She even had some people over last weekend."

"So did Carla, but she said 'the bitches across the street ruined my whole vibe,' whatever the hell that means," he said, using air quotes and doing a frighteningly good impression of his wife when she's on the rampage.

"Did you ask her to clarify?"

"Of course I did."

"But she wouldn't?"

"She said she was too distraught to go into details."

"Ruben. You know Carys didn't start anything with Carla. She hates unnecessary confrontation. So does Vinny, for that matter."

"I don't know, man. It's been a month, and she's already on a bender. I hope it blows over before we get back."

Unlikely. Carla isn't one to let go, even if she has to hold onto her grudge for months, waiting for the right audience.

"Vinny said things went smoothly too, so I don't know what Carla is on about. Sorry."

Technically, Eric wasn't lying. He hadn't been home last weekend to know firsthand what exactly had happened, and he'd learned back in college never to assume what got stuck up Carla's ass when she was in one of her moods. But if he had to take a shot in the dark over what it was this time, he was pretty sure it was Vinny's response to Carla rudely calling her *Casper* and telling her to "float on home like a good little ghost" when Vinny asked her to have her friends unblock the driveway.

But it was only a guess.

"Why do you look like someone egged your grandma's house?" Zeke asked, sitting down next to Eric as he pondered Ruben's body language.

"I *wish* it was something you could fix with a damn hose, man." Ruben shook his head. "I don't want to talk about it. Tell us about you."

"I had the privilege of doing the inventory today," he answered dryly. "Exciting stuff."

"I had to reprimand a cocky little fucker out here on his first tour," Eric added. "I hope you are stocked on all the critical items, because at the rate this kid is going, you will be patching him up soon."

"Let me know, I'll give him *my* first timer—who is also out to make this tour hell—as his personal nurse," Zeke said, grinning from ear to ear.

"You got plans for your down day, V12?" Ruben asked.

"Nah. I'll probably talk to Enzo, go to the gym, maybe read a book. Not much to do out here, but the solace of my bunk will be nice. I'll be lucky to get another day off before we go home," he said.

Eric and Ruben nodded knowingly. Deployment wasn't

an office job. The hours were long, and the shifts were endless. Down time was as precious as rack time, and they all knew not to take it for granted.

"What about you, Slow? Got plans after your shift ends tonight?" Ruben pressed.

"I'm hitting the rack early so I can wake up for some quality time with my wife," he said, a satisfied smile slowly pulling up his face. "Figured it was time I surprised her."

"I do not want to know," Zeke said, standing. "That smile says dirty things."

Eric laughed as his friend walked away.

———

Carys

"Go," Vinny said. "You don't want to take Brendon out with this earache, and Maya is moody as hell today. This is why I *live* here."

Carys let out a sigh. "Thanks. I know all that, I'm just not used to having the help."

"I know you aren't, but you do now. So go enjoy your grocery shopping alone for a change, and I'll hold down the fort."

She nodded. "I need a shower first. I smell like baby puke."

Carys went upstairs to her room, turning on the shower to warm as she stripped. She needed to stop at the pharmacy for the baby too. Maya needed more vitamins since she refused to eat the grape flavored ones Carys had accidentally grabbed last week. Not that she blamed her; Carys thought grape flavoring was nasty too.

Eric: Good afternoon, sweetheart.

Carys's heart melted with the unexpected message. She knew he should be asleep right now.

Carys: Hello, handsome. Everything okay?

Eric: Just checking in with you before you go grocery shopping.

Carys: How did you know I was getting ready to go to the store?

Eric: Because you have a schedule. When do you leave?

Carys: After my shower.

She wanted to tell him all about poor Brendon's ear, but there was nothing he could do from so far away. He didn't need the extra worry.

Eric: Wear your special panties. Tell me when you leave the house.

Oh, shit. He wants me to wear vibrating underwear to the grocer.

Carys let out a shaky breath as she reread the message over and over. She'd wondered when he'd bring them up, but this was a situation she hadn't predicted. He'd said they weren't for when she was alone, but this...was unexpected. She pulled them out of her drawer and held them up.

Just looking at them made her curious, but like the toys still hidden in her drawer, she was nervous too. Intimidated even. *You are going to where these big girl panties to the store, and you are going to let your husband have this moment. Even if it isn't good, it will make* him *feel good to try.*

Yeah, that was so not the helpful mental pep talk she thought it would be. Who was she kidding? She wanted to like those panties. She wanted to like all the things she'd been too afraid to try. Same as he'd pushed her to open up about her struggles with recovery, Eric was pushing her to rediscover her sexuality.

In the grocery store.

On a Thursday.

Heaven help me.

After the world's fastest shower—her whole body was tingling with curiosity and need—Carys barely had herself patted dry before she quickly stepped into her panties. She debated what she should wear, but in the end chose her favorite jeans. *Oh. Well. Hmm.* The seam running up between her legs pushed the vibrator against her, causing a pulsing to join Carys's needy tingling.

And Eric hadn't even turned it on yet.

Her hands were shaking so badly from anticipation, she missed the hook on her bra twice. As she went to close her lingerie drawer, she saw her cup inserts that were meant to keep you from nipping through thin tops and decided to use them. The last thing she needed was to have her nipples crack the case at the deli counter because she leaned on it for support through whatever she was about to experience.

Sweatshirt?

T-shirt?

Something flowy?

Jesus, how do you dress for potential public orgasms?

She thrust her hand into her closet at random and yanked out a thicker V neck cotton tee. *Perfect. Not too hot, hopefully enough coverage.* She didn't want anyone seeing her flushed, so she decided to pull her hair back, but not up, to hide her ears and neck somewhat. She was so nervous, she thought she'd throw up.

In a good way.

Is there a good way to throw up?

Finally, she let out a nervous breath and headed downstairs.

"You okay?" Vinny asked.

Carys froze. "Yeah," she said, glancing at her friend across the kitchen from the mud room as she shoved her feet into her favorite sandals. "Why?"

"I don't know. You look…anxious? No, that's not right."

"Oh. Maybe a little? Eric messaged he has a surprise for me, and with you here and the monthly massages, I guess I can't help wondering how he could top it." She laughed nervously, then cringed.

Vinny staired at her a few seconds before saying, "That makes sense. He loves to spoil you. Have fun shopping. I'll double check the pantry and supplies in case we forgot something on your list."

"Great! Thanks, Vin." Carys grabbed her purse and keys and headed into the garage.

Carys: I'm in the garage now.

His reply was immediate.

Eric: Mmm. You were fast. Are you anxious or excited, sweetheart?

Carys: Both? I think.

I light thrumming against her sex made her jump at first. The vibration added to the pressure of her jeans, pressing the toy harder against her clit and forcing Carys to bite back a moan. *How will I survive this in public?* It stopped a few seconds later.

Eric: Now you know what the lowest setting feels like. I hope growing up near Hollywood honed some acting skills, sweetheart. Don't let anyone know this is anything but a regular trip to the store.

Right. I almost collapsed in the garage just now. Ha! Don't let anyone know…

It was a quiet ride to the grocer. Carys couldn't help shifting in her seat, feeling the pressure of the toy grinding against her with anticipation. Eric didn't turn it on again while she was driving. He didn't text. Knowing it was coming but not knowing when had her amped up. His little tease had been way too good.

She needed more.

Halfway through her list, she barely suppressed a jump of surprise when the toy turned back on. It was the same frequency as before; except he left it on this time. Carys took a deep breath and kept walking down the aisle, her list trembling in her fingers. Right as she felt she'd regained her composure, the feeling intensified.

And then it stopped. Carys was filled with a rush of both relief and disappointment. *Was that it?* She turned up the next aisle, trying to keep her focus. If it was all Eric wanted to give her, it was sweet he had tried. It *had* been enjoyable, albeit brief. When she got back to her SUV, she'd text him she'd like to do it again.

Carys was at the deli counter trying to be polite to the random old lady who always seemed to be there at the same time—she was widowed and lonely—when the delightful pressure of the toy exploded into a new sensation. It began more intensely than either time before, and slowly shifted through intensities, growing and lessening at a gentle rate that had her absolutely *throbbing.* She quickly said her goodbyes best she could without seeming rude and beelined for the children's vitamins.

All the while, there was a full-on Mardi Gras parade happening against her sex. Or at least that's how her body interpreted all the sensations coursing through her from the tips of her toes to the tips of her hair. *Can you feel hair? I know I'm feeling my hair.* Like the sensations were being channeled over different frequencies all over her; each reminding her of a different instrument. Low, slow base. A little tenor saxophone vibrato. The blast of a trumpet. Carys wanted so badly to strip off her shirt and earn some beads, right there on the bread aisle.

I gotta get out of here. Fuck, fuck, fuck…

Tried as she did, she couldn't help the way she shifted on her feet at the register. In her peripheral, she could see the cashier giving her a funny look. Carys was usually friendly with the lady, but today she couldn't even make eye contact, much less speak. Not with all her focus on keeping herself from toppling over the edge while she entered her debit pin on the keypad.

She turned down help from the bagger for the first time ever and speed walked to her car alone, popped the back and nearly threw the groceries in, with the exception of the eggs —although it was a close call. The cart return was next to her, so she was back in the driver seat almost as quickly as the lift gate closed itself. With shaky hands, she reached up and started her SUV.

Carys: Holy shit, Eric! I'm not going to make it.

Eric: Are you in the car.

Carys: Barely.

Eric: Leave the sunshade in the windshield. Your windows are tinted.

Carys: I am NOT getting off in the grocer parking lot! I will never be able to shop here again!

Eric: Suit yourself, sweetheart. Drive safely.

He didn't need to add an emoji for Carys to know he was smirking. She yanked the sunshade out of the window and tossed it into the backseat instead of folding it up like usual. Her body trembled all the way home. Now she was seated again, the seam of her jeans forced to toy tightly against her needy clit. She couldn't help from slowly grinding her hips down as she navigated home, the occasional whimper escaping.

I'm so grateful for tinted windows right now.

As she turned up her street, the toy stopped. Somehow, she managed to back into the garage. Carys pushed the button to open the back hatch and opened her car door…right as the vibrator began pulsing again. She slid off her seat to her feet in pure agony. Without pausing, she ran into the house, dropping her purse along the way and muttering something to Vinny about the groceries as she passed her in the kitchen.

Carys moved as silently as she could up the stairs and into her bedroom, locking the door behind her. Her entire body was quivering now, and she could feel beads of sweat drip down her back. *Get away from the door.* She went to her bathroom and closed that door too, leaning back against it and pulling her phone out of her pocket.

Carys: You're so mean. Fuck, Eric. I need you.

Eric: I'm right here.

The intensity settled into a steady rhythm, somewhere near medium—she thought. Thinking was near impossible right now.

Eric: Are you home?

Carys: Yes. In the bathroom.

Eric: Close your eyes and put your hand over yourself, sweetheart. I want you to grind until you come for me.

He didn't have to tell her twice. Carys put pressure over the thickest part of the seam of her jeans and pressed, gyrating her hips to create an overload of sensations. She was *soaked.* Next to her on the counter was Eric's aftershave. She reached for it, flicking the cap off and giving it a little shake to release the scent before putting it back and closing her eyes. With his smell lingering around her and his command in her mind, she whimpered and shook until her body exploded with euphoria. Carys's hand continued to jerk between her legs as her knees gave out. She slid to the floor with her back to the door, crying out her husband's name.

Her phone buzzed beside her from where she'd dropped it on the floor. She picked it up.

Eric: Still with me, sweetheart?

Carys: Eric. *Again.*

Eric: Strip and turn the shower on. I need a picture.

Chapter Forty-One

CARYS

She stood in the shower, trembling all over. After what she'd experienced, Carys was no longer afraid. Somehow, Eric had anticipated her needs from what little she'd shared with him right before he left and immediately decided he'd find a way to give her back what she craved.

Long, intense pleasure leaving her entire body tingling and limp.

And he'd done it with special underwear from across the globe.

Her shampoo bottle was shoved aside so she could reach the lube she'd nervously hid behind it with the cleanser. After stripping, she'd grabbed the toys she'd left in her nightstand, including her Taco Tickler. The suction cup phone holder she used on her vanity to make it easier to follow hair tutorials was now on the shower wall. Carys set up her phone in the holder, nervous yet anxious to give Eric something back. She opened the camera and started recording, doing her best to ignore it once she'd made sure the frame was set so he'd see her on the shower bench.

He wanted to watch her come undone.

Something new. A sensation exciting, but not scary.

She'd settled on a small plug. It was sitting on the bench with the other things she'd picked, and the lube. Carys sat down at the edge of the shower bench and spread her legs wide.

"Okay, Eric. Since you were good to me, I'll be good to you," she said to the camera.

Without a moment of hesitation, she began her exploration.

———

Eric

Holy fuck.

It was the third time in a row Eric watched the video Carys had sent him. The beautiful, sexy woman he'd eloped with flickered back to life, right before his eyes. He'd opened the video on his tablet so it was easier to see, zooming in on her face as she fell apart calling his name.

He was so fucking *proud* of her.

And so fucking *horny.*

It was going to be agony, waiting three more months to sink back into his wife. He wondered if she'd surprise him with more videos. All he had hoped for was a timid nude, but this was beyond all. Those magic panties had been worth every penny to see her so satisfied again.

As the video came to an end, his phone chimed. He set down the tablet, hoping it was something else from Carys.

Vinny: Is everything okay?

Huh?

Eric: As far as I know. What's happening there?

Vinny: Carys came home from the grocery store acting

really weird. She's had her fair share of tired mom brain, but this was nothing like that. She'd mentioned talking to you, so I wanted to make sure there wasn't something I should be aware of.

A slow smile pulled up Eric's face. He wondered exactly how flustered Carys had been by the time she got home.

Eric: No, we had some quality time. Nothing bad. What happened when she came home?

Vinny: Well…for starters, she ran past me like her pants were on fire, talking gibberish about the groceries needing unloaded.

Vinny: Then when she disappeared upstairs, I went out to the garage to unload everything, and she'd parked the SUV crooked in the garage. The gate was open, her door was open, the *garage door* was still open, and the engine was still running.

Eric's grin turned wicked. *Ohhh, she was that distracted, huh?*

Vinny: I re-parked the car, shut it down, unloaded and closed everything up. Then I put her keys and purse away, since she kinda flung them toward the table when she came in. Once the groceries were put away, I gave her some time. When she didn't come down I went up to check on her.

Eric: And? Was she okay?

Vinny: I think so? She was passed out on the bed in some of your clothes, with a big smile on her face. And it smelled like you. The same smell when you get out of the shower. I think she sprayed your cologne or something.

Vinny: I mean, she looked pretty content and blissed out, but the whole series of events was weird AF.

Eric laughed out loud this time. Glancing down at his paused tablet screen, he admired the *bliss* on Carys's face as she came.

Eric: Good.

Vinny: Good?

Eric: I'm glad the time I made for her helped her de-stress.

Understatement, he thought, smirking.

Vinny: Okay, I guess. So, you don't think I need to keep an eye on her?

Eric: No, she just needs rest. I'm sure she isn't sleeping well at night with Brendon's sleep regression. Can you set a water bottle on her nightstand please?

He'd zoomed in far enough to see her arousal dripping down her thighs, plus whatever she sweat and her first orgasm before the shower. Carys needed to hydrate.

Vinny: Yeah, sure.

Vinny: I hate how attentive you are from far away. Seriously, Eric. It's been three years. Have a flaw already so we singletons don't have to feel so fucked with the dating pool.

Vinny: It was cute the first couple years, but the perpetual honeymoon phase is starting to make me sick.

Eric laughed again as the door to his shared room opened. He sent off a cocky comment to Vinny just to rile her up before saying goodnight and set his phone on the charger. If Carys was sleeping, there really wasn't any reason to have his phone out.

The familiar sound of Ruben collapsing onto the bunk next to him had him pulling back the sheet he'd hung so nobody coming in saw him in his corner, stroking off to his wife.

"You okay, Ruben?"

"Not even a little, man." Ruben blew out heavily, and Eric could see and hear the frustration emulating from him even in the dim light. The rest of the guys in this section were mostly on shift right now. The few around were all dead asleep. It was as private as it was going to get.

"Do you want to talk about it?"

"It's my dad."

Eric couldn't help thinking at least it wasn't Carla this time. "What about Abe?"

"He's not taking his heart medication. They messed up his Medicare again—or Medicaid?—and now it's not covered at all until the paperwork is fixed. Without it, there is a strong chance he'll have another heart attack. I just want to cover it while he waits for the red tape to get sorted, you know? I'm good with money. He and Mom taught me how to be smart like that. I can afford to help."

"But he's too proud to let you help," Eric filled in. "A lot of people in his generation are like that."

"I know, and I get it. But he's *it,* Slow. It's me and him now. I hate he can't see how much it will help me to pay it, knowing he's less likely to have a medical emergency while I'm down range." Ruben scrubbed his face with his palms a few times before sliding his hands behind his head, clasped at his neck with his head tipped back. His whole body radiated with concern.

Eric didn't mention Carla *technically* was also a Holt as well now. Something was off between them, and Ruben's attitude of late told him he was about done with his wife's shit. Not claiming her as a Holt just now only confirmed for Eric where Ruben was mentally with his marriage, even if he wasn't ready to admit it.

"Ain't nobody ever told Abner Holt anything. *You* taught me that," Eric said with a hint of amusement. "I know it hurts."

"I miss my mom so much. Especially when he gets like

this. Mom would have told him to let me help," Ruben insisted.

Eric had never met Ruben's mom. She'd passed away years before they met, and while he'd gotten a pretty good idea who she'd been in life while they drank their way through college, he also knew it was the one wound time couldn't heal for Ruben. Her death had been senseless negligence on behalf of the same medical teams and systems failing his father right now. Ruben's life had taught him not to trust the system, and Eric agreed with him.

Being poor and black in Georgia did not get you the same level of care as white people got. Even more so for women. There was plenty of research to prove it. Ruben's mother was all the proof he needed—her passing had been preventable.

"I'm sorry, Ruben."

"Yeah."

"And he still won't move in with you?"

"Hell, no. He and Carla are oil and water. But he also won't leave the grimy little slum he's stuck in since that's where he has all his memories with Mom. He told me once leaving would be akin to forgetting her."

"The neighborhood has gotten that bad?"

"Lately? Yeah. It was never great, but it's getting worse. The last time I was out, I counted three newer drug houses within two blocks of the house. He shouldn't have to worry about a drug run gone bad leaving him to bleed out alone after a stray bullet goes through the wall of his home." Ruben dropped his arms and shook his head with disgust. "He's a good man. He deserves better in his retirement."

"Maybe something will change his mind. All we can do is hope he's safe and his medical stuff gets sorted in the meantime," Eric said.

Ruben nodded solemnly.

"Carys sent me a picture of the kids earlier today. They're getting big," he said, clearly using the subject change to move on from his frustrations.

Eric agreed. "I hate missing out on Brendon's first year. Makes me feel like a shit dad."

"Yeah. The shittiest." Ruben rolled his eyes. "That's why you have a new play structure hidden in my garage until we get back. Because you are a *shit dad.*"

"My dad never had any energy for me," Eric admitted. "Not sure if it was him or because I came so late in their lives. I try to give Maya and Brendon the things I wish I'd had, you know? Not the *stuff,* the *time.* I'm going to love being able to play outside with them more. We'll have a swing for both of them now."

"It will make it nice when Funcle Ruben babysits, for sure," Ruben said cheerfully. "I'm gonna sack out, I think. It's way too fucking late."

"Agreed." Eric was glad Ruben wasn't trying to pull him into a round of Spades first, like usual.

"Do me a favor?"

"What?"

"Wait until I'm asleep to proceed behind that sheet." Ruben waggled his brows at Eric, a shit eating grin taking over his face.

"Fuck off," Eric said gruffly, yanking down the sheet and throwing it in Ruben's face. "Asshole."

Ruben's low chuckle eased Eric's concern for him. "No brother like a military brother, Slow."

"Yeah, yeah."

Eric rolled away so he was facing the wall, mostly so Ruben couldn't see his grin.

As he stashed his tablet under his pillow and settled in, Eric thought again on his childhood. He was in his mid-thirties now, so he knew age wasn't really a factor in why his father had been so distant growing up. Eric's mother had been nurturing, but not in an overly affectionate sort of way. Nothing like the way he saw Carys tend to their own children. Even his sisters had a more distant relationship style of parenting.

He wondered if it was something he simply needed *more* than the rest of the Blackwoods seemed to. The cuddling and kind words that flowed freely in his own home was something he couldn't wait to get home to. His wife was warm and giving. His children were curious and engaged. Overall, the life he'd build for himself was pretty fucking amazing.

It was more than he'd thought could exist in a home before he met his wife. The more he thought about it, the more he missed them. Even Vinny, with her mysterious rocker ways and quick wit, always ready to zing him when she was in a playful mood.

He couldn't get home fast enough.

———

TO: **CrayonLover@mailwarrior.net**
   From: ByAnyOtherName@Eden.com
   Subject: Wow
   Sir, you have started something dangerous.

   To: ByAnyOtherName@Eden.com
   From: CrayonLover@mailwarrior.net
   Re: Wow
   I may have started it, but *you* will be my undoing. You are a goddess, sweet wife of mine.

Chapter Forty-Two

CARYS

After the grocery store, Carys finally caved. She promised herself she'd try one new thing a week from the massive dump of toys Vinny had brought her when Eric left. It was still intimidating—before Eric, she'd buried herself in work and school and rarely had taken time to focus on herself like this—but it was also *liberating.* There were so many disappointments attached to *that day.* No more babies, all the unwanted scars reminding her of what she'd lost and almost lost.

Recovery had been hard both mentally and physically. When intimacy proved to be another thing she couldn't find the same joy in, part of Carys had broken. If she hadn't confessed to Eric, there was no telling how bad the depression would have gotten. She shuddered at the thought, and not in the *good* way she had when he'd destroyed her inhibitions with vibrating panties.

They were halfway through this deployment, and despite all the recovery and counseling she was still working through, it was easily the easiest one so far. Vinny was here, and she finally had positive connections with the military community through Marcy, Hailey, and Lexi. Since the first time they gathered, they'd gotten together at least once a week. Her new friends loved Vinny so much, they'd even added her to their new group chat.

Things were going well.

Or as well as they could with whatever standoff was happening between Vinny and Carla. Carys didn't have to ask to know Vinny had placed Carla as numero uno on her shit list. Whatever had been said when she went to ask about Carla's friends moving their cars was still heavily on Vinny's mind. It had inspired some interesting content on her ArtBeat account, to say the least.

Today was full of promise though. They were going to a gathering with all the families in Eric's new squadron. There was going to be bounce houses for the kids, a potluck, games —kind of a mini family carnival. Carys had always avoided these events before, after the first few went poorly. Now she was excited. Even if she left with the same number of friends she showed up with, the point was *she was showing up with friends.*

Finally.

"Carys!" Lexi called across the parking lot, waving frantically.

"I don't see a husband with her. Let's see if she needs a hand," Vinny said, turning Brendon's stroller in Lexi's direction.

"Where's Juan?" Carys asked when they reached her.

"TDY. *Again.*" Lexi rolled her eyes. "He made a bunch of tamales before he left though. I brought a few trays for the potluck."

"Ooooh," Vinny and Carys both said.

"Do you need help carrying anything?" Carys asked.

"Can I put my purse in the stroller on the way in?" she asked.

"Sure." Carys took the bag from Lexi while Vinny rearranged the bottom basket to make it fit.

"Thanks, ladies," Lexi said, hefting up two big trays. Vinny closed the back of her car for Lexi, and they headed inside together. "The girls are inside with Hailey."

Marcy was already inside at the potluck tables, and they found Hailey over by the bounce houses, trying to get Ellie to take off her shoes.

"Eleanor! Look inside, baby. *Nobody* is allowed to wear shoes inside. See? It's not only you. I promise nobody will steal your pretty pink bow slippers," Hailey said. The conversation must have been going on a long time because she wasn't calling her daughter Ellie like usual.

Maya walked up to Ellie and gave her a hug. "Let's go," she said, kicking off her sandals and climbing inside. Ellie immediately did the same, following her friend into the bounce house.

Hailey's jaw dropped. "I have been fighting her on this for *fifteen minutes,*" she seethed.

The others laughed beside her.

"Boys aren't like that," Marcy said. "Seems like I can't keep Mason *in* his clothing, much less shoes. See?" She pointed into the corner of a different bounce house, where her son was trying to bounce and take his shirt off at the same time.

Vinny walked over to the side of the safety mesh, calling to Mason. He immediately stopped and flashed her a flirty little boy smile. She said something that made him take on a serious expression, nodding his little head. Vinny put her hand against the screen for a high five, then turned back.

Now it was Marcy's turn to look incredulous. "How the hell…"

"I'll never tell my secrets," Vinny preened. Behind her, Mason had fixed his shirt and gone back to exclusively jumping. "Auntie powers. It's a gift."

They stood watch over the big kids while they bounced, the babies being passed around when they weren't sleeping in the strollers. When the kids were ready, they moved on to the craft tables and games before circling back for lunch.

"Your tamales are all gone!" Vinny pouted.

"Don't worry," Lexi said. "I asked Juan to make some just for us. You'll be home Tuesday, won't you?"

"Yesssss!" Vinny whooped, bouncing on her feet and pumping a fist in the air. It reminded Carys of Ruben, and again she wondered what had happened when they met to make them hate each other so.

"There is a cake walk in the back," Hailey said.

Carys scrunched her face. "I'll pass. But I can watch the wee ones while you all do it."

"You don't like *cake?*" Marcy gasped.

"I love cake. *Homemade* cake. From scratch. They make you buy everything you donate anymore, or people use box mix and canned frosting," Carys said, making a gagging gesture. "Gross."

"I miss your mom's cakes," Vinny lamented. "She made the best cakes on our birthdays."

"Oh, did she pass away?" Hailey asked gently.

"No," Carys said, her voice hardening. "She didn't agree with my marrying Eric, and it got heated."

"She hasn't talked to any of us since," Vinny added. "But it's her loss. The kids are amazing. I've never seen my bestie so happy, and Eric treats her like a goddess."

"She hasn't even *met* the kids? *Que perra,*" Lexi huffed.

Vinny snorted. "You can say that again."

"Okay. *Que perra,*" Lexi repeated.

Carys had heard enough Spanish living in southern Cali not to need a translation. As much as she hated to agree, she found herself nodding. "It was a real let down, but Vinny and her dad never second guessed my marriage or the conditions we married under. And honestly, without constantly having to explain myself to her, I've never been more confident in myself, or felt more loved. Sometimes we have to hurt in the short term to heal in the long term." She shrugged. "Mom is an angry, controlling person, and she made her choice."

Vinny stood with Carys while the others duked it out for a cake. None of them won, but it was fun to watch them fight dirty against a bunch of kids. After three rounds, they all gave up. Vinny promised to make some sort of cake for Tuesday, leaving everyone satisfied.

The kids all clamored for another round in the bounce houses, so they collectively headed back toward that side of the room. As they spoke, Carys saw Eric's old boss talking with his new boss. She wondered what would bring Colonel Greer here and hoped everything was going well in the old unit. It hadn't been a good fit for her friends wise, but Ruben was still working there.

As he turned to leave, Greer saw her and waved. Carys waved back with a smile before turning back to her friends.

"Uh oh," Marcy said.

"Hmm? What? I'm sorry, I was looking around and lost the conversation," Carys admitted. "What did I miss?"

"Do you know Greer?" Marcy said under her breath.

"Yeah, Eric worked for him before he transferred. Why?" Marcy looked at Hailey, her eyebrows furrowing. Hailey shrugged. "What am I missing?"

"He has an open marriage. A *very* open marriage. His wife doesn't even live here," Marcy said.

"Okay?"

"Him singling you out like that isn't a good thing," Hailey said.

"He's known for taking up with just about anyone, Carys. Please be careful around him. He can be very charming when he wants to," Marcy said. "This isn't the first place we've been stationed with him. He doesn't have a good reputation out of uniform if you know what I mean."

She didn't know, but Carys also wasn't sure what to say. *Is it a pineapple thing? But that is a couples' activity. If his wife doesn't even live here, then...* "Oh. Well, I'm sure it's nothing. It's not like I'm going to run into him all the time."

But it wasn't lost on Carys later on, when they were all crossing the parking lot to go home, and Greer was sliding into a familiar car.

"Was that the neighbor's car?" Vinny said once they were all buckled and Carys was pulling out of the parking lot.

"Looked like it to me," Carys said quietly.

"Why would Eric's old boss be getting into a car with Sonja Perez?"

"I don't know. Maybe his car is at the shop or something," she said, but even as she spoke, it felt wrong. *Why, indeed?* The things Marcy and Hailey had told her came to mind. She knew Sonja had no issues taking up with guys from work, since she'd been with Eric as a fuck buddy before he met Carys—and hadn't liked him walking away after he had met her.

It wasn't their business. Was she curious? Sure. But ultimately, Carys knew nothing good would come from sticking her nose in anything involving Sonja. She didn't need the drama.

———

THE FOLLOWING DAY, they took the kids to enjoy a particularly nice section of the beach located on the installation. It was more peaceful, given tourists weren't allowed. They had played in the waves and built sandcastles most of the afternoon. When Maya started getting cranky, it was time to pack up.

The kids were both asleep as soon as the car was in motion, but with Vinny in tow, Carys decided she'd take advantage and run into the commissary on the way home. Usually, Eric would go in after the odds and ends she loved that were either too expensive at a regular grocer, or not available anywhere else.

Vinny was more than happy to work on her laptop in the SUV while the kids slept, and Carys ran around as quickly as she could grabbing all the things she'd been missing since Eric deployed. By the time she reached the frozen section, her cart was considerably fuller than she had anticipated. But there was always room for her favorite ice cream, especially when Vinny was baking a cake the next day. She was so focused on deciding between two different flavors, Carys hadn't realized a man had approached her.

"We meet again, Missus Blackwood," Greer said.

The fine hairs all over her body immediately stood on end —and it wasn't because she'd been standing in front of an open freezer for too long. "Oh! Hello, there."

"Twice in one weekend. I must be lucky," he said, his voice dropping low.

Is he flirting? No, I really need to stop listening to the girls' idol gossip. This is crazy.

"I'm not sure my obsession with Tillamook ice cream is lucky," she said.

"Lucky for *me,* since I have the pleasure of seeing you." He stepped in closer. "How have things been at home, Carys?"

"I miss Eric," she said immediately. "It was hard having him leave so soon after the accident. Especially since he's moved to another job."

"Yes, well. Needs of the military unfortunately come first," Greer said, leaning into her.

Okay...maybe they weren't crazy. This is uncomfortable.

"We're on the tail end now," she said, forcing a smile and shoving her cart so she could navigate it between them and regain some distance. "He'll be home soon."

"I know Slow is handy. If you need anything at all," he continued, his eyes scanning her body as he spoke, "I'd be happy to come over and help out."

"That's very generous of you, but I would never insult my best friend like that. She's quite handy too, and lives with us," Carys said pointedly.

Stop eye fucking me, you creep. I can't believe I thought you were a good person all this time. Gross.

"I'm happy to help her too," he said, his voice dripping with innuendo. He licked his lips as he stared at her chest. He casually stepped in closer, putting a hand over one of hers on the handle of her cart. Anyone who came around the corner would think he was simply showing concern, but this close, it was impossible to miss the heat in his stare. "I know you married under...*unusual* circumstances, Carys. I'm a discreet man. Nobody would ever need to know."

"You think because we married quickly it was for convenience," she stated flatly.

"Wasn't it? You were pregnant, jobless. I don't blame you. Slow is a good sort of guy. I know he cares, but it's okay if you are lonely. Even when he's home." His hand squeezed hers before he gave it a condescending pat. "Think about it."

Greer smiled at her before sauntering off.

What in the actual fuck?

It wasn't surprising he knew she'd been pregnant when they had eloped. Eric hadn't been embarrassed about how they met or married in the least. But the fact his commanding officer had so grossly misinterpreted—probably willfully—the love and satisfaction they found with each other as partners and lovers was sickening. Where was this coming from?

Back in the parking lot, she quietly loaded her own groceries with Vinny's help and began the short drive home to Oceanside. It wasn't until Vinny spoke she realized how uncharacteristically silent she'd grown in her introspection.

"You okay, Carys?"

"Hmm? Oh. Yeah, I just...saw someone in the store who caught me off guard."

"His name wouldn't happen to be Greer, would it?"

Carys glanced over at her in surprise. "How did you know?"

"He was parked in front of us. He waved at me as he climbed into his tiny dick mobile and *winked.* With *smolder.* It was disgusting." Vinny's face pulled in like she'd accidentally taken a shot of rot gut instead of Patrón.

"He offered to come over and *help out,* " Carys admitted, her voice soft and tone clear on what exactly that meant to him. "And was clear he'd be happy to service us both."

"What a pig. Are you going to tell Eric?"

"No," she said quickly.

"Why not?"

"He doesn't need that on his mind while he's out facing God knows what, Vinny. I'll tell him when he gets home, but not before. Besides, I heard Greer is leaving soon. I'm not interested in creating drama."

Vinny crossed her arms over her chest. "I think that's a mistake, Carys. But I won't say anything…so long as he doesn't ask me directly. But I won't completely lie to Eric. I respect him too much."

"I know, Vin. Thank you."

Soon as the groceries were put away and the kids had dinner, Carys was going to take a long shower and scrub off the lingering ick clinging to her from the unwanted attention.

Chapter Forty-Three

CARYS

"Eeeeew! What a pig!" Alexis cried.

"That's what I said," Vinny agreed. "As Lexi so elegantly said, 'what a pig.'"

"I'm not surprised he was that bold, but in the *commissary?* And to go for both of you…ugh. New low. He can't PCS fast enough," Marcy said.

Hailey simply shook her head. "I'm ready for cake."

All the kids had run themselves out in the backyard and were now sleeping in the living room while a movie played in the background. The adults had settled around the dining room table where they had some privacy but could still keep an eye on the tiny tornadoes sacked out on the floor through the doorway between the rooms.

"It was creepy. I've never been hit on like that. There were some idiots in school, but wannabe Abercrombie models and frat guys are not the same as older men with distinguished careers who could absolutely *tank* your husband's career without an afterthought." Carys sighed heavily.

Vinny handed Carys the ice cream scoop and carton of

Vanilla Bean she'd picked up the other day. As Vinny plopped healthy wedges of her decadent chocolate and caramel custard cake onto plates, she handed them to Carys so she could add the ice cream and a little shake of maple sugar and cinnamon. Lexi collected the finished confections and took them to the table.

"I'm glad we warned you," Marcy said right before shoving a bite into her mouth. She groaned loudly, prompting the others to giggle over how indecent she sounded. "Holy shit, Vinny! Where has this cake been all these months? Who needs a man when you can eat *this?*"

One by one they all took a bite, their moans joining Marcy's.

"I'm glad you warned me too," Carys finally said between bites. "Not sure I would have been prepared to deal with it if you hadn't."

"What is this called?" Lexi said, licking her spoon seductively.

Carys laughed. "Yeah, Vinny. What do you call this cake?"

"Better Than Sex Cake," she said in a sultry voice, slowly tipping her head sideways as she drug her fork from her mouth down her neck and cleavage.

"Ignore her. In honor of some political BS in the art community, she did a version of Dove Cameron's song 'Boyfriend' for her ArtBeat account this morning. She's rocking her inner lesbian hard today," Carys said.

"Just because my gate only swings one way doesn't mean I can't find beauty in those with different hinges," Vinny proclaimed proudly before stuffing a giant forkful of decadence into her mouth.

"Uh-huh. Explain Lisa then."

"Hey! It was senior year, and she was *smokin'* hot.

Nobody is truly a hundred percent hetero, Carys. We all have our exceptions. Lisa was mine. She's still the best kiss I've ever had." Vinny sighed in a way most people reserved for celebrity crushes before taking another huge bite. "Fuck, I need to get laid."

They all cheered in agreement as they stuffed their faces.

"The cake deserves the name," Hailey said. "I'm so glad Samson is home tonight."

"Juan won't be back for another week," Lexi whined.

"And you are hornier than you've ever been in your life, aren't you?" Carys teased.

"Yes! Stupid TDY!"

"I couldn't stand to be touched the first time I was pregnant," Hailey admitted. "The second time though…I made up for it."

"I was the opposite," Marcy chimed in. "Sex crazed right up until the day Mason was born. With Miles, Mike so much as looked at me and I was already telling him off," she mused.

"Really?" Vinny said. "I always thought that was shit Hollywood made up."

"The way they portray birth on screen should be illegal," Marcy said, rolling her eyes. "But the hormones making your sex drive and food tastes go haywire is completely true. It is a time of polar opposites and most of the time you can't even understand why. It just *is.* "

"Amen," Lexi said, rubbing her expanding middle. "What about you, Carys?"

"Oh, I was insatiable as ever," she said, unable to hide all her sadness. "I loved being pregnant. The sex, knowing I was growing a person. Knowing I was growing something Eric and I made together… It was the ultimate aphrodisiac."

Hailey leaned in from beside her with a hug. "I'm so sorry that was taken from you."

"Yeah." Everyone knew about the accident by now, and the loss of her fertility. The fact all of them embraced her instead of making her feel pitied was so important to Carys. She threw enough pity parties for herself without so called friends adding to it.

"I'm not sure babies are in the cards for me. I'd have to find someone I clicked with," Vinny said from her other side. "I love kids, but I love music and my car and my *freedom*... A baby would mean no more touring for a few years, at least. I'm not sure I'm ready for that."

"You've never met someone you considered a family with?" Hailey asked curiously.

"Nope. I really wanted it to be the last guy, but I should have known better. Right now, I belong here. It's the first time I've been in one location long enough to decorate since I graduated from high school. I like it," Vinny admitted. "I like all of *you.*"

"Well, that settles it," Lexi cheered. "We need to find you a Marine! Or at least a military man."

"She already had her fill when she did a tour with the USO," Carys teased, bringing on a round of cat calls.

"That was a damn fine tour." Vinny smirked. "But two nomads on different trajectories will not make a happy home together. Uncle Sam doesn't care where my next gig is. And if there are children, it won't matter if I'm touring or not. When they have to leave, they have to leave. They aren't really cohesive career paths, especially with little ones."

"I've seen a lot of Dear John letters over the years," Marcy concurred. "Often from a spouse you wouldn't have guessed was struggling. It's good you know yourself and are realistic about your wants and needs, Vinny. I respect the hell out of you for it."

They sat around moaning over the last scraps of dessert after that, slowly consuming their weight in chocolate and sugar. Once the dishes were all loaded into the dishwasher and everyone else had left, Carys and Vinny went through the bedtime routine together. Baths were had, teeth were brushed, kisses and stories and songs begged for until Vinny and Carys finally escaped downstairs.

"You're really not sure about kids?" Carys asked, flopping down next to Vinny on the couch.

"I don't know," she answered. "I always thought I'd be a mother. My albinism is genetic, and while I've been fortunate to have the milder side effects associated with it, maybe my kids won't be so lucky if they get it too. It's not probable, but it's not impossible."

"I think those are healthy concerns. You should only have kids if you really want to," Carys said.

"And there is always adoption," Vinny said. Even if I don't marry, I think I'll keep that in my pocket. If I adopt older kids, I could even take them on short tours with me. It could be a lot of fun."

"You could put together your own family band," Carys said. "Your dad would love that."

Vinny rolled her eyes. "He'd want to be our manager."

———

TWICE MORE IN the following month, Vinny reported she'd seen Greer leaving the neighbor's house at odd hours of the night. "They're shacking up," she insisted.

"Probably. Kind of pisses me off he had the nerve to say what he did to me regarding both of *us* when he is obviously spending time with *her.*" Carys had seen him one other time in Target and promptly headed for the checkout before he could approach. She wasn't interested, and never would be.

"Pig," Vinny muttered.

"I'm glad Eric will be home in a few weeks."

"Me too. Maybe Ruben will get his skanky wife in check."

Skanky?

"That's pretty strong talk, Vin."

"Truth is truth. She's not an honest woman, no matter how much Ruben spent on her wedding ring."

"You know something I don't?"

"Yes."

"Care to elaborate?"

"No."

"Vinny, you aren't going to take whatever it is out on Ruben are you? That's not fair. He can't help what she does while he's gone."

Vinny looked at her with fire in her eyes, but she didn't comment. Carys wasn't sure if it was because she had so much to say on the topic she didn't know where to begin, or if she'd crossed into straight up petty vindictiveness. Either way, it put Vinny in a foul mood without Carys pushing for details.

"Let's talk about your reunion," Vinny said a few minutes later.

"It's the same as always," she said with a shrug. "We'll go get him and come home."

"Nope."

"What do you mean *no?* We can't exactly skip town!"

"Of course you can. I'm here, and the kids will be fine. Find a romantic something somewhere and book two nights."

"You're crazy. One, maybe. Two?" She shook her head.

"Carys, listen to me," Vinny said, turning sideways on the couch so she could face Carys straight on. "You have done so well these past three months without him. You made friends finally, and I know the counseling has helped a ton. Go spend a couple nights with your husband alone and show him how okay you really are. You need this. Eric needs this. The kids will be fine with me."

"Are you sure?"

"Let me put this another way. One of us should be getting fucked senseless. It's obviously *not* going to be me. I *demand* it be you."

Carys laughed. "Blunt as ever."

"I love you. Go spend some time bonding with your husband. In fact... I think you should consider a second honeymoon for your next anniversary. Brendon will be over a year old, and Maya will be in preschool by then part time. You should bring it up with Eric while you are hydrating between fucks."

"You really are impossible."

"The last time I demanded you travel, you met Eric. Obviously my intuition is better than yours."

"And thank God he is who he is, because that could have ended with me scraping by as a single mother with my own mom barking up my tree to find a *nice guy* who will forgive my transgressions," Carys huffed, rolling her eyes.

"Does it upset you she didn't apologize or make amends?"

"Sometimes," Carys admitted. "She's my *mom.* It would absolutely decimate me if Maya or Brendon disappeared from my life. Especially if there was something I could do to make amends. I'd be swallowing my pride and doling out whatever apology they needed."

"Honestly? It surprised me she never called. It's not like

you changed your phone number. Even my dad is disappointed in her," Vinny admitted.

"There is only one Quincy Blume, and I'm lucky to have him as a surrogate parent. And you too, Vin. I guess in the end, I know exactly who my family is."

"Even if it hurts sometimes."

"Especially when it hurts."

————

"SERIOUSLY?" she asked, shock rippling through her body. "Why would anyone let another under their skin like that? Javier is going to be crushed."

"I thought the same," Marcy said. "It's like our conversation yesterday breathed it to life. When I went to take the trash out this morning, there was a moving truck pulling up outside Javi and Bella's house. She was in the yard looking grimly determined with their youngest on her hip while her mother barked out orders to the moving company."

"Eric always talks about how *solid* they are," Carys said sadly. "Did she tell him she's leaving?"

"I don't think so. Hang on," she said, before the sound of her voice muffled. Carys could faintly hear her on the other end of the line calling out to Mason about something. "Sorry. One of these days that boy is going to maim his little brother."

Carys smiled to herself. There had been several moments she'd felt the same way about Maya and Brendon. Especially when he first came home. Maya wanted to cart him around like a living baby doll...which would be sweet if she carried them nicely. Most of her dolls had scuffs all over their plastic heads from where she'd clobbered them against door jams and furniture as she ran through the house while swinging them around by a random limb.

"Her mother is a strong-willed powerhouse. I know Bella has struggled since the last baby came with postpartum, but I never thought she'd give in to the woman. She's always been steadfast about her marriage and being her best with her husband," Marcy continued.

"Then what happened?"

"Like I said over Vinny's orgasmic cake, I've seen this plenty of times. A trusted family member or friend gets to them when they are down and convinces them to leave. I know for a fact her mother has been sliding jabs in for years over Javier leaving her too much, and not being a stable husband and father. She's done it while he was home hosting barbeques, although I think she thought she was being clever and making it into a passive aggressive joke of some kind," Marcy huffed. "I don't think it's a coincidence she came for a visit last week in the least." Carys felt every drop of distain dripping from Marcy's tone course through her.

"Is Mike going to tell her husband?"

"He's not down range with them. This isn't something he would want to say over traced government email. So no, I don't think Mike is the guy to tell Javi he's coming home to an airbed and some odds and ends."

"Marcy," Carys breathed. "Someone needs to tell him."

"I agree."

"Will he be able to come back early and handle it before the truck pulls out?"

"Doubtful. If they gave every guy whose wife bailed that treatment, they'd have a shit show. Plus, there is always someone willing to take advantage so they can go home early. There is an old saying, 'if the military wanted you to have a wife, they would issue you one.' They like to say times have changed, but reality is this. The mission comes first. Always."

Carys stewed on her words while she worried her bottom lip. "Marcy, will you send me some pictures? Mike is right it should come from someone Javi trusts. I'll send the pictures to Eric, and he can approach Javier."

Marcy blew out a heavy sigh. "Yeah. At least then he's got a heads up."

Three days later, Marcy broke Carys's heart all over again when she reported back what Bella had told her at the mailboxes. Bella was pregnant again and could hardly keep up with the two they already had. Instead of telling Javier after she found out, she'd asked her mother for advice. Bella's mother had convinced her to move home where she insisted Bella would have support all the time.

Javier had called her soon as Eric had sat him down with the facts. She didn't *want* to leave him, but she didn't feel like she could stay here alone, either. He'd done all he could to try to change Bella's mind, but she felt as guilty to change her mind and stay as she felt for giving in to her mother to begin with.

"Except her bully of a mother is here now, *in her face.* It's easier to tell someone over the phone you're sorry than to tell a hellcat two feet in front of you you've changed your mind," Marcy fumed. "I did convince her to stop loading all their shit up and just go home with her mother until Javi gets back and they can sort it together."

"And?"

"Oh, her mother is *pissed* at me," she boasted. "I was more than happy to go over there and turn the tables on the manipulative bitch. I don't see how someone as kind as Bella came from a woman like that."

Carys felt relief flood her body. She didn't know Bella

and Javi well, but she really liked them. Hopefully Marcy's tenaciousness bought them enough time to salvage their marriage—especially with a third baby on the way.

"Does Javi know about the baby?"

"Yeah. Bella said they had agreed to two, and she freaked after he left when her period didn't come. He went so far as to promise to get a vasectomy when he gets back, so it's no longer something she has to worry about. It doesn't change she's already pregnant again and completely overwhelmed between the two they have and her pernicious mother, but at least they got it all out in the open. If she had told me, I would have helped her," Marcy added.

"We all would have," Carys agreed. "When she comes back, we need to make a point to include her."

"Agreed. I can host a few more things here, so she doesn't have to go far. I'm sure if I ask Javi if she can come instead of inviting Bella directly, he can convince her better than I could alone. She's not the type to go looking for her tribe. I think that's her downfall. She keeps listening to her mother because she's afraid to ask anyone who is actually in the life."

"I can relate to that. It took me over three years, and I'm well aware we could all get orders in the next six months and never be close again," Carys lamented.

"Not a chance in hell," Marcy insisted. "When we say *family*, we mean it. No matter what or where, we are forever family. It's time we teach Bella what that means."

———

TO: **ByAnyOtherName@Eden.com**
  From: CrayonLover@mailwarrior.net
  Re: Almost there
  You keep sending me pictures with your glazed over fuck

me eyes and I'll be coming home stiff as baseball bat, sweetheart. Fuck. You know I love when you steal my clothing, but in this case, I would have been fine if you'd skipped my pants and shown me exactly what your hand was doing below the waist band. I hope you are ready, Carys.

I'm going to devour you when I get home.

To: CrayonLover@mailwarrior.net
From: ByAnyOtherName@Eden.com
Re: Almost there
Is that a promise? *Please*...

Chapter Forty-Four

ERIC

"What the fuck is going on?" Eric growled out. He'd had about enough of this texting bullshit.

"What's up, man?" Ruben asked beside him. They were in the chow hall, shoveling down breakfast so they could get there day underway.

"Another of those random sexts. This one says, 'It won't be long now. I can make you feel so much better than she can'," he read aloud.

"Who the fuck is trying to get between you and Carys?" Ruben said angrily. "That is *bullshit.*"

"I don't know. They keep coming from randomly assigned numbers. They aren't traceable, and as soon as I block one, the same shit comes through from a different number. I asked if there is anything I can do, but since there haven't been any threats or talk of criminal activity, there are no legal grounds to have any of the numbers traced back to whoever registered them." Eric shoved a forkful of stale something slathered in gravy in his mouth and swallowed. The longer they were gone the more he missed his wife's cooking. Even the days he was stuck with cereal was better than this shit. "I don't want this getting back to Carys. She's finally acting like herself again."

"Then tell her," Ruben said with a shrug. "Send her the screenshots so she sees you aren't replying, and make sure she knows how pissed you are. Whoever it is obviously knows you are gone right now and returning home soon. No way this isn't going to follow you, Slow."

Eric clenched and unclenched his jaw several times before replying, "You're right. It's better she hears it from me. I don't want this to set us back."

"I'd lose my shit if someone gave my wife the impression I was unfaithful," Ruben continued. "Not cool."

For the millionth time, Eric bit back his strong belief it would absolutely be the other way around, and it wouldn't be a lie. With what little Vinny told him when they touched base with each other over things they didn't want Carys stressing over, he got a solid impression Carla was not keeping good company. At least, not for a married woman.

"I'll tell her about it after my shift ends tonight. No point dumping it on her when I'm not even able to answer her questions."

"And the queen of Oceanside will demand answers," Ruben said with a grin.

"That she will. In this case, she deserves every answer I can assure her with."

"How is Javi doing?" Ruben asked as they stood to bus their trays.

"Better, now he knows why Bella has been extra cagy. Her mother better watch out, though. By the time she came clean with him, he needed two hours at the gym to clear his aggression. I've never seen him abuse his body so hard before," Eric said.

"Bella's sweet, but I remember her mom. The woman is conniving."

"From what Carys heard from Marcy, conniving is an understatement. They and their clique are determined to protect Bella and help her figure out what *she* wants moving forward, and not her mother," Eric said with pride.

He'd hoped for so long Carys would find her way with the other spouses, and she finally had. One of the good things about military life, people move constantly. The people who make situations difficult will eventually move on and be replaced by others. It's a revolving door, each revolution exposing you to a new group of people. She'd found what she needed this go around and decided to stay.

And true to who she was as a person, she'd adopted friends who were as loyal and fierce as she was. They had already added Bella into their group chat, so even from her mother's house, she was still included. Carys had told him it was Hailey's idea, and Marcy was going to give her updates on her home in the chat too. The goal was to make her see she didn't need her mother to have support when Javier was gone.

"I'd say I'm surprised, but I'm not. She's always been inclusive. Sometimes I wish Carla was more…inviting."

"Inviting? She's constantly bragging about her parties and girls' weekends," Eric said with a shake of his head. They were on their way back to their bunkhouse to change for work. "That's not the same as taking people in who need it. She's usually with the same crowd. I think the word you are looking for is *nurturing.* Carla isn't one to go out of her way unless she can see what she will get out of it for herself."

"That's not right either," Ruben said snappishly. "She likes to have a tight bond with a few people is all. Quality over quantity."

"How many people were at your wedding again? And how many did *you* invite?" Eric reminded him gently. He wasn't trying to make a dig on the way Carla had pushed Carys out knowing Eric wouldn't attend without her. It was basic math.

Ruben sighed before admitting, "Around five hundred. I maybe knew a hundred of them, and most of those through her, unless they were my military brothers."

"I'm not trying to be an asshole, Ruben. This is my observation of her over the years. There is room for all types of people in the world and I don't care how Carla chooses her friends. It's how she treats those she decides are beneath her I have a hard time with; especially since it feels weaponized and divisive. You're like a brother to me, military or not— black, white, or polka dot." He gives Ruben a playful elbow jab.

"Funny, Slow. That joke gets better every time someone tells it. Fucking polka dot…" he mutters. "Only the princess gets to reference my 'dots.'"

"My point is *you* don't treat people the same as she does. It's hard for me to understand why you would tolerate that trait in a partner. But she's your wife, and I'm not going to be a dick about it." *Even though I had to skip your wedding and we are lucky to see you at all when she isn't on one of her damn trips she never takes you on.*

"I wish they got along, but I can't make Carla change her mind. She follows her first impressions, you know?"

"Yeah," Eric said, forcing himself not to react. "You can't tell someone not to trust their gut instincts."

The only thing Carla's gut assessed was whether or not a newcomer would pander to her or outshine her. But again, Eric wasn't going to be a dick and push away his friend in the process. He hadn't ever liked Carla. She felt the same way about him. It wasn't a shocker Carla's dislike immediately spread to his wife and children.

But damn, did he hate it.

The only time things had been truly easy and carefree with Ruben had been when they weren't together. He missed the easygoing side of Ruben and wondered if he saw the difference in himself.

"All I know is, I'm over this fucking sand box," Ruben said as they approached their quarters. "I'm using all my reintegration leave to hole up with my woman."

"Amen, brother."

It was about time Eric toyed with Carys again. He was jonesing for another video of her falling apart after he played with her from afar. The thought made him thicken in his pants. No matter how many times he watched the video, it never got old. She was a masterpiece. *My masterpiece.*

And to think he'd shied away from this experience before.

———

Carys

She stomped across the back yard, pacing around like a lioness assessing how to best protect her territory. Some floozy was trying to take *her* man. First Greer made passes at Carys, now Eric was getting unsolicited texts from someone. Her hackles were up.

The sound of Vinny's car coming up the long drive to the rear garage made Carys feel a tiny bit better. She watched as her best friend backed her baby into the garage with careful precision. It looked like she'd waxed it again. When the engine cut off, Carys clomped over and waited for her to emerge.

"I know that look," Vinny said as she closed her car door. "Who's fucking with you?"

"No idea!" she seethed.

Vinny glanced over Carys's shoulder toward the fence line before saying, "Let's go up to my place. I'll turn on the monitors so we can hear the kids while they nap."

Without hesitation, Carys followed Vinny up the back stairs in her garage. Vinny hit the button to close the garage door on their way to the upper landing, then unlocked her back entrance and waved Carys through to her living room at the front. They collapsed on the couch in the same way they had as kids, preparing to vent all their woes.

"Let's hear it," Vinny said after she had made sure both monitors were on.

"Someone is sending dirty messages to Eric!"

Vinny's jaw dropped. "Someone he's deployed with?"

She shook he head. "The messages keep alluding to him coming home soon, so I think it's someone here." She thrust out her unlocked phone, the first of Eric's screen shots open. "Just swipe through. They started over a month ago, and they are getting more aggressive. He was hoping he wouldn't have to say anything and it would go away on its own, but I think he's worried about our safety at this point."

Vinny's face pulled tight, her cheeks flushing with anger. She handed back Carys's phone with fire in her eyes. "He doesn't have to worry about our safety. Nobody is touching any of us. I'll talk to him about it, but this is still not acceptable."

"I don't want all this shit, Vin! *What is wrong with people?* When did marriage stop being sacred?" She let out a growl of frustration and collapsed back into the corner of Vinny's new sofa. "I like this couch better."

Vinny rolled her eyes. "Easily distracted. Look, whatever

or whoever is out there, we're a team. Nothing is going to happen because I'm here, and I'm not going to let anything happen. You know I'm always watching out."

"Yeah, what's with that? Not that I'm not grateful to know the neighbor is shacking up with Eric's old boss on the sly. Or when Carla has visitors at odd hours—I don't even know how to approach poor Ruben about that. You have been very busy around here."

"I take my role as your bestie and the kids' godmother seriously. You are finally getting your glow back, Carys. Nobody is fucking it up on my watch." The venom with which Vinny spat out her pledge sent goosebumps over Carys's skin.

"I love you, Vin."

"Same. Will you forward those texts to me?"

"Why?"

"See if I can find the source."

"Eric asked. They aren't dangerous, so there isn't anything they can legally do."

Vinny smirked. "That doesn't mean it can't be done."

"Legally, right?" she asked suspiciously.

"I promise you; I won't do anything stupid that could land my ass in jail and ruin the weekend of reunifying sex that is your due soon as Eric's boots hit the California sands."

"That's not really the same thing, but whatever. He's not happy about this any more than I am, so I'm not asking for additional clarification," Carys said as she selected all and hit forward. "There you go. Have at it."

"Thanks. Hey, don't forget I'm going to open mic night tonight. I'll be home late, so don't worry."

"Right, I forgot. Thanks for reminding me. What's on your list for tonight?"

"I made nice with the manager. He's going to let me do a

couple I had in mind and record them. I'm going to use the best ones on my ArtBeat account to help promote a big event they have coming up. Tyler is giving me a special code to offer my subscribers if they purchase their tickets through a specific link you can only get through my lists," she said smugly.

"Oh?"

"I get a cut of the ticket sales I generate, and he gets free advertising. If it goes well, we are both hoping to partner again in the future."

"Sounds like you are putting down some serious roots, Vin. I thought once Eric got back you'd be itching for a tour."

"Eh. I don't know. I love the road, but right now it doesn't feel right. Dad is looking into another short-term thing in Nashville I might join him on, but that's way out. I only agreed to go if it didn't ruin the vacation I'm going to make Eric take you on."

Carys laughed, the anger and hurt she'd felt twenty minutes ago melting with Vinny's antics. "I don't have to leave Oceanside to get laid."

"No, but you can both get laid and sleep if you leave. Trust me, you need *both.*"

"Yeah, yeah. Thanks for listening, Vinny. I don't know why this made me so angry. I know Eric isn't a cheater."

"It doesn't matter. A threat to your marriage is still a threat. Frankly, I think you should have told him about Greer."

Carys shook her head. "Maybe when he gets home. I'm not out and about enough for it to become an issue, and he wouldn't dare show up at the house. Eric doesn't need the extra worry distracting him from staying safe and coming home in one piece."

"Pot, kettle," Vinny deadpanned, holding up her phone.

The forwarded sexts were on her screen. "I know you want to believe it's different, but it's not. You should be the one to tell him, Carys. If joining your friend circle has taught me anything, rumors run wild through this community."

They did, and Carys wouldn't argue otherwise. Still, she wasn't keen on ruining Eric's opinion of a man he respected. It was a lame excuse—Greer obviously didn't deserve his respect—but she clung to it anyway. She had almost spilled the tea when he told her about the random messages, but something deep down told her to bite her tongue.

She had a nagging impression she was missing something. Until she figured it out, Carys would keep her mouth shut to anyone outside her friend group.

"I'll think on it. Now if you'll excuse me, I'm going on an egg hunt."

"A what now?" Vinny looked at her with amusement as she crossed the room to the front exit.

"To find the misleading pineapple hidden in front of my house. *Something* is giving greedy assholes the idea I'm the type who shares their husband!"

Chapter Forty-Five

CARYS

After she got home from therapy, Carys collapsed on her bed. Today's session had been heavy and intense, but she knew it was also necessary. She didn't want to be on antidepressants forever and had finally brought it up in session. After a lot of debate, they agreed to wait until she'd been on it a full six months before backing off. It would get her through Eric's reintegration.

There was so much to talk to Eric about when he got home too. Now she could see through all the turmoil the accident had thrust her into, Carys was ready to make plans. Maybe not the same ones she'd been holding in her breast pocket since they wed, but a fresh iteration including their new reality.

It still stung her heart sometimes, watching Alexis rub her baby bump while they were all together. Marcy and Hailey were talking a lot about whether to have another or not as well. Surprisingly, that wasn't as hard.

Bella's mess came up as well. Carys didn't know her very well, but she now worried maybe Eric would think she could walk away from *him*. Marcy's words had rung in her mind as loud and clear as a school dismissal bell. It was the ones you never expected who would suddenly bolt.

Does Eric wonder if he'll come home to an empty home? Even though Vinny is here to help most of the time now, the accident changed so much… But I'm getting back to being me *again. I know he sees that. I can't even breathe thinking what life would be like without him.*

She was startled out of her nap by Eric's ring tone.

"Hey," she said groggily. "I miss you."

"Hey. You sound like I woke you up. Are you feeling okay?"

The concern in his voice squeezed her heart deliciously. So much love in such a simple question. "Yeah, I accidentally drifted off after my appointment. The phone woke me."

"Ah. How was it?"

"Good. We talked about a lot of big things today and made a game plan."

"That's great. I'm so proud of you, sweetheart." There was a long pause, and while she was sorting what she needed to say, Eric tuned in as usual and helped her along. "What is it, Carys? You can ask me anything—tell me anything."

She sighed, her breath coming out a gentle hum at the end. "I know. I have been thinking a lot the past few weeks, and I think I'm ready to talk about it."

"Okay," he said encouragingly. "Shoot. I'm all ears."

"Have you ever worried I would Dear John you?"

"No."

"No? Not ever? Not for a single second?"

"Not for a nanosecond, Carys. The accident scared the shit out of me, but not because I thought you would leave. I was afraid you were already gone," he answered.

"What do you mean?"

"You weren't yourself. The love was still there on both

sides, I assure you. It was felt. But our connection was so different, I thought maybe the *you* I fell in love with was permanently altered. I worried the new version wouldn't want me the same way. I knew you wouldn't leave, but worried we'd grow apart and become strangers," he confessed.

"Oh, Eric." Carys choked back a sob. "No, honey. I'm so sorry you felt that way. I was confused after the accident about a lot of things."

"I know," he reassured. "You and Brendon could have died. When you woke up and realized he wasn't inside you anymore, it fucking shattered me. The anguish and desperation in your eyes would have dropped me to my knees if I hadn't been sitting."

"And then you had to tell me there would be no more babies," she murmured. "We had plans, and they were literally cut out of me."

"I only cared that *you* made it. It was a relief Brendon was alive, and you hadn't bled out so bad we'd lost him, but going home without a baby would have been easier than telling Maya her mother was never coming home." The weight of his hypothetical grief—even now, months later—was so heavy in his words, Carys shuddered. "The only thing taking you from me is death, Carys. I've known it since the first morning in Mexico, before I even had the privilege of experiencing your body. It was agony, leaving you there in the bar. I know what life without you is like. If you hadn't been waiting for me after all I went through to get back to you, I don't know what I would have done."

"Eric," she croaked around the ball lodged in her throat. "I'm lost without you."

"Same, sweetheart," he said gently. "So no, I have never worried you wouldn't be waiting for me. You waited in *Mexico* for me before you even knew my last name. I figure if you want to leave, you have the gumption to look me in the eye and say so before you walk out the door."

Carys laughed, one of those messy half sobs that forces the air back into your lungs with the happiness swelling in your heart. She grabbed a tissue off her nightstand and wiped away the tears and snot that had materialized with her emotions. "Yeah, I wouldn't be shy."

"My last name could have been something really atrocious, you know. You were still set to marry me before you knew what it was," he teased.

"It wouldn't have mattered what it was. So long as I got to tell the world I'm yours." She let out a relieved sigh. "I'm glad you know I wouldn't leave you."

"It's easy to believe the truth," he said. "What else is on your mind?"

"Do you still want to grow our family?" she asked timidly.

Eric was silent for a moment. "You mean adopt?"

"Yes," she said. "What do you think?"

"I think I'm a lucky SOB to have a wife with a heart as generous as yours. You're more than I ever hoped for in my life, sweetheart. Maya and Brendon too. I don't care where the kids come from, no. If you want to adopt, let's do it." His words were firm and confident.

"What if we adopt older kids? Not babies. I love babies, but Brendon's latest sleep regression has me thinking we could maybe take in kids from the foster system?"

Eric laughed. "I wouldn't want to go too much older than Maya, but sure. We can look into it as soon as I get back…in two weeks."

Carys froze.

"Two weeks?"

"By some miracle, we get to come home a little early. It's a done deal."

"Did hell freeze over?" She laughed with disbelief. *Home a week early. It's a deployment miracle.*

"As I am sitting in hell right now, I can assure you it is still hot as Satan's ass crack," he said flatly. "And smells like it."

"I'm too happy to ask how you know what Satan's ass smells like," she mused. "Do you have a for sure date?"

"Not yet, but I will soon. I can't wait to curl up around you in a hotel room. You better be ready to teach me."

"Teach you what?"

"All about your body, now you have different needs."

"You want me to show you how I touch myself when you are gone?" Carys's face flushed at the thought. *It's one thing to experiment alone, but show him what I like? He can't be serious.*

"Show. Tell. Whatever you need me to know, Carys. I love you."

"I love you too," she said.

"And sweetheart? Wear your special panties when I come home."

Oh, shit. It's going to be a long ride down the coastline to the resort I've been looking at. I'm going to erupt like Vesuvius once he gets me naked…

"Mmm. Okay. Eric?"

"Yeah?"

"We don't need to reinvent the wheel. Sometimes I do need more sensory, but I don't think I need it all the time. Now the depression has lifted, looking back, I think I was numb to a lot of things and putting too much weight in sex being the same. Even if I hadn't had the hysterectomy, my head wasn't right. Nothing *could* be the same."

"Okay."

"I'm only saying so because you are generous and always aim to please me. Don't overthink it. I'll bring whatever you want, but I still need you to make love to me like we used to."

"Good to know. I don't mind switching it up a bit, but I have to admit…as boring as it sounds, holding you close against me and moving slow and deep is one of my favorite pass times," he murmured.

"Mine too."

———

Eric

Hearing her say all the things she had gave new life to Eric. She was okay. *They* were okay. He wasn't going to return home to the same crisis he had been forced to leave in the middle of. Carys was healing, and Eric was confident he'd played a part in her emotional recovery even from afar.

His biggest fear had been coming home to even more of a shell than he'd left. Carys was full of life and love. She dreamed big, loved big, and planned big. Hearing her plan *anything* brought him immense joy and peace. It was the most revealing conversation they'd had since before the accident, and he'd missed his wife in all her glory.

We are going to be okay.

Ruben dropped onto the bench beside him. Eric had gone out to the common area where the Wi-Fi was better, sitting off to the side for a bit of privacy while he took advantage of the signal. He sucked in a heavy lungful and pushed out the last of his concerns, breathing in assurance and anticipation in his homecoming.

"You look like you are ten years younger from before that call," Ruben said.

"I *feel* a decade younger."

"She's doing well then?"

"Better than well. I can't believe how far she's come. I owe Vinny big time for making sure she had the time to work through her trauma," Eric said humbly.

"Doesn't free rent cover it?" Ruben quipped.

Eric looked sideways curiously. "She *doesn't* have free rent. Vinny wouldn't hear of it. She's helping with the kids and keeping Carys sane, but she's helping in other ways too. And she made it clear babysitting wasn't how she was paying for her part of the power bill."

"Right," he clipped out.

"Fuck, Ruben. *What happened when you met her?* I cannot for the life of me understand the bad blood between you two."

"Doesn't matter, man. We don't get along, and that's all there is to it. It's not like we run into each other much, anyway. It took *years* to meet her at all," he said pointedly. "Just drop it, Slow."

He held up his hands in surrender before dropping them back into his lap. "You still going to Georgia on the way home?"

"Yeah. I managed to get a leave en route approved, so once we hit US soil, I'll be breaking off from the group."

"You want me to be bring the heavy shit back with me?"

"Nah, I got it. Thanks, though. I just need to get home to my dad."

"How is Abe doing?"

"No fucking clue. He keeps going on with his 'I'm the parent, son' bullshit. He was spacing out his heart medicine at first, but I think he's completely out now, and they still haven't fixed his medical shit. If nothing else, I'm hoping I can at least get him a supply and put my credit card on file. Maybe get the prescription transferred to an online pharmacy so its delivered and he can't do fuck all about it," Ruben bit out. "I can't lose my dad. Mom went too soon for no fucking reason, and I can't let the system fail him too."

Ruben stopped talking beside him, obviously over-whelmed by the helplessness he felt right now. Eric could relate. After the accident, he felt like there was nothing he could do to help Carys before she opened up enough on her own to give him a bone to chew on. Abner Holt was as proud as they came, and Eric knew the only way for Ruben to get the job done was to show up and push until his father cracked.

"You need anything at all, you tell me. I mean it."

"Thanks. I have it set to be in Georgia five days, then fly back to Oceanside. I'll still be a few days earlier than they originally said getting home, so I'm looking forward to surprising Carla. She mentioned seeing her dad about the time you get back anyway, so I'll let her have a moment with him while I take care of *my* dad, and then I'll be able to give her what she deserves."

"Sounds like a solid plan," Eric said with a nod. "I can't fucking wait to get out of this hellhole."

"No kidding." Ruben snickered. "This shit is getting old. I'm due to PCS. There is an opening across the hall from you. Think I'll pull a Slow and apply for it. Try to PCS in place like you did and stick around a few more years in a non-deployable roll."

Eric patted Ruben on the shoulder before he stood. "I have shit to do. Apply for the position, Ruben. Sometimes the grass *is* greener on the other side."

With that, Eric strode away.

"What are you doing up there?" she shouted up from the bottom of the ladder. Above her, Vinny was up on the roof doing…something.

"Just checking on a few things," she called back cryptically.

My ass. "Such as?"

Vinny's pale hair bobbed along the roofline; her body blocked from view since she was on the other side of the ridgeline. "I'm almost done. Don't worry, I won't be stomping around during naptime."

"That wasn't my worry," Carys muttered to herself. *What is going on up there? She's got skills, but she isn't a damn roofer!* She was still standing by the ladder with her arms crossed and a scowl fitted tightly across her features when Vinny finally came down.

"Woo! Time for a shower and change so I can finish making this batch of content!" Vinny said breathlessly, ignoring Carys's glare as she collapsed the ladder and prepared to haul it back to the garage.

"Lavender."

"Carys."

"What were you doing on my roof? That's the third time you've been up there since you moved in."

Vinny shrugged. "I set up some cameras. The angle wasn't working for me, so I was adjusting them."

"Cameras?"

"*Discrete* cameras. You can't even tell they are there unless you are actively looking for them. I didn't want anyone thinking they were shadowy hidden pineapples."

Carys snorted, her expression softening with the joke. "Should I be worried you have cameras on my house?"

"Nope. I'm being cautious."

"Fine," she said, dropping it. In truth, Carys liked knowing the cameras were there. It was a security blanket of sorts, but after all she'd been through in the last eight months, she was still feeling prickly. At least now she knew if a new serial killer came to her house, Vinny's cameras would help the feds catch the perp.

I need to stop listening to so many true crimes podcasts while I clean. Jesus.

"Still have an appointment every Wednesday afternoon?" Carys asked.

"Yeah, why? I can cancel it this week if you really need me. It's no trouble," Vinny offered.

Carys shook her head and said, "No, that's okay. I just heard back from Eric. He gave me his arrival dates, so I'm going to go overbook the resort I was looking at."

"Overbook?"

"Eh, probably not the right way to describe it. Shit happens, so I'm booking buffer days."

"Ah. Well, if he makes it when he's supposed to, I think you should stay the whole booking. Consider those 'buffer' days bonus time with him."

"I don't think so," Carys said. "He's going to want to see the kids, Vin."

She shrugged. "I've got them. If they are doing well, you may as well stay. Why don't you see what Eric feels like doing when he gets back."

"I guess," she said with uncertainty.

"If I get really desperate, I can grab Ruben from across the street," Vinny said sourly.

Not this again. "He won't be here. Eric said he's going home to Georgia first. Something about his dad not doing well. Ruben wants to be sure things are being handled correctly before he comes home. Peace of mind."

"Oh." It was spoken flatly, as if Vinny was surprised Ruben had it in him to care enough to go out of his way when it mattered. "Well, good for his dad, I guess."

"Anyway," Carys pressed on, ignoring Vinny's attitude, "I was wanting to budget my time well. If I call to book, they will give me a special discount since he's returning from deployment. But I can't really do that with Maya blasting Moana in the background."

"Probably not," Vinny agreed. "I'll go shower then. When I get out, I'll sit with the kids so you can go upstairs and get things handled."

Carys smiled, relief washing over her. The resort only held so many rooms for these things, and she didn't want to miss out. "I appreciate it."

Vinny nodded, then grabbed the ladder and strode off around the house to put it away. It made Carys curious when her best friend had grown so *cautious*. Not that Vinny had ever been necessarily reckless—and given she was a professional musician, that was saying something—but this was… different. She'd seen it here and there over the months, but it was now glaringly obvious Vinny had changed.

She wished she understood the catalyst. When Vinny had left on her last tour, she'd been the same as she ever was, but now she was more determined, less carefree. Not *less* of who she was, but perhaps more *careful* with herself. Maybe it was whatever had happened with her ex—she'd said over cake with the girls she'd hoped at one time he might be the one to have a family with—or Carys's own crisis, but Vinny was slowly changing how she prioritized. They were almost twenty-nine. Was Vinny worried she'd float into her thirties with nothing to show for it?

It didn't feel like her, though. Vinny was still a free spirit. When she was around the house, she was as steadfast and fun as ever. When Carys wasn't in need of her help, she'd get in her car and drive off for days. How could she be the same, and yet different?

Carys stopped staring at where Vinny had disappeared around the corner and went inside to pull out the information she needed to make the reservation. It wasn't any of her business, but she hoped Vinny would eventually confide in her.

Not that anything was wrong.

She just wanted to know her friend was in a good place.

The fact she was putting down some serious roots in Oceanside and second-guessing gigs and travel with her dad was the most curious change of all. And while Carys was always happiest when Vinny was near, would it make *Vinny* happy?

"Oh, Lavender," Carys sighed out as she shut the back door. "Why do I feel like you are dead heading your life in preparation for the most stunning spring bloom you've yet to achieve?"

———

TWO MORE DAYS.

Carys nervously paced her bedroom. It was almost midnight.

Should I pack some of the things I haven't opened yet? No, he wants me to show *him what I do with my favorites. Why is this so hard?*

She picked up her Taco Tickler. Begrudgingly, she'd finally admitted to herself Vinny had been right about this little beauty. It got the job done quickly with some all over tingly down to her toes type of sensations. Success with this particular toy had given her the courage to keep opening new items to try over the past couple months.

Everything was freshly charged.

I had to get down the bigger bag so there is room for all the toys he asked for. When did I become a dirty housewife? Not that this is dirty…*I'm a damn adult. He's my husband. Gah!*

She put the toy back in her duffle and zipped it up. Fretting wouldn't change anything. They would either like including toys, or they wouldn't. And if she spent the rest of her life giving herself bigger O's in the shower than Eric could in the bedroom…well, she'd fucking cry, but she'd put on her vibrating big girl panties and enjoy her own damn body anyway.

So there.

She moved to the second bag. A backpack, really. It had a few outfits for Eric and all the athlete's foot stuff he kept around for after deployments. Even wearing flip flops, he'd had the worst case she'd ever seen when he returned last time. They had thrown out his shower shoes, replaced all his work socks, and he'd been outside with his feet in the sunshine as much as possible. Eric insisted the California sun helped it heal. She was pretty sure that was the way to cure ringworm, but after months of wearing heavy boots in the blistering heat, she couldn't blame him for wanting to feel the breeze on his tootsies while he relaxed.

Vinny: Turn off all your lights and peek out your bathroom window. Look directly below you into the Brown's side yard.

Okay...that was weird. Maybe my true crimes worries are valid after all. Carys did as she was told, going into her bathroom and closing the door so the bedroom light didn't shine through. Using the flashlight on her phone, she made her way to the window and slowly edged the blinds up after extinguishing the light.

Carys: Okay, what am I looking for, exactly?

Vinny: Look. Straight. Down.

Vinny: You might need to press your face to the glass to see it.

Carys did as she was told, again. Her eyes about fell out of their sockets when she saw what Vinny must be referring to.

Carys: IS THAT WHAT I THINK IT IS?????!!!!!!!!!!!!

Vinny: Yup.

Carys: LAVENDER.

Vinny: Don't get edgy with me, I can't help if they are LITERALLY fucking against the side of the house! The repetitive movements set off one of the cameras. *smirk emoji*

Carys: I can't believe he thought we would do that with him. Eeew.

Vinny: Think he needs Viagra? How old is he, anyway?

Carys: Stahhhp!

She was trying so hard not to laugh out loud and give herself away, Carys could barely breathe. As startling as it was to look down and see Perez and Greer fucking against the side of the Brown's house and not burst into surprised giggles, it would be mortifying to have them catch her.

When she got herself under control, she peeked back down, curiosity trumping all her morals. They'd changed positions. Perez had her hands against the wall now, Greer pounding in from behind her. Another shadow slipped into their midst, fusing into their coupling. Delicate hands ran up Perez's legs—a woman's form, clearly—tapping her legs a little wider and leaning forward from beneath. Perez's back arched further, her head flying back. Even in the dark, Carys could see her mouth open in an O, the pure bliss painted all over her face as she succumbed to the pleasure being provided.

Vinny: Are you seeing this?

Carys: Yeah.

Vinny: Some other woman is eating her out.

Carys: I have eyes, Vin.

Vinny: And I thought all the fun stuff would end when I stopped touring…

Vinny: guess not!

Carys ignored her, unable to pry her eyes off the scene below. When they shifted again, she snapped out of her voyeuristic moment and slowly lowered the blinds back down. A fire kindled in her core. Eric was coming home. In forty-eight hours, it was going to be her turn. She closed her eyes and thought about the feel of his large body pressed against hers.

Please let us connect. I can't stand the thought we'll never connect the way we did before the accident.

Her nervous anticipation was brought to heel by her persistent fear she wasn't enough for Eric anymore. If her body refused to react to him the way she longed for—the way he'd always managed to pull from her depths—how long before he became his own variation of Greer, fucking any willing partner with zero respect for the vows he'd made to his wife? It worked for some couples, but Carys knew it wouldn't work for her. She hoped the same was still true for Eric, and always would be.

Stop it. We've proved over and over our love is stronger than anything this lifestyle can throw at us. Deployments, emergencies, unexpected pregnancy, even the voluntary loss of my last living family member...it means nothing without each other.

She pulled up the text chain he'd sent her before being forced to power off his phone for the first stretch in his journey back to her, taking comfort in his words. Eric didn't talk about how he couldn't wait to rail her. He told her he couldn't wait to feel her pressed against him and the smell of her hair while he held her tight the moment she was within reach. Of being near her as much as possible, to fill up on her goodness.

They'd sent dirtier texts this deployment than any trip away before, but when it mattered, his words were affirmations of his devotion and need for *her,* not just her body. Carys had spoken at length with her counselor yesterday over this. She knew it was irrational. She knew her husband would do anything for her.

And in forty-eight agonizing hours, he would put every one of these insecurities to bed with the hug she so desperately needed.

Carys suspected Eric needed it too.

Chapter Forty-Seven

ERIC

The worst turbulence of his flying experience had shaken the aircraft so hard on their way back stateside, Eric began to nervously sweat only an hour into the flight. He wasn't one to panic, but it felt like this tin can was about to plummet into the Atlantic. Needless to say, few of them had gotten a wink of shut eye on the long flight. They'd landed on the east coast with a collective sigh of relief—even the pilot looked pale, if not a little green around the gills.

The second he made it into his hotel room, Eric had scrubbed down in the hottest water he could stand before collapsing on the bed in a dead sleep. His alarm went off way too soon, startling him back to reality and another—thankfully *shorter*—flight back to California. It was the exact opposite of their transatlantic length. He took advantage and slept through most of it.

Jet lag was a bitch.

By the time they landed, all he could think about was Carys. She seemed okay when they talked and texted, and those tempting little photos and videos she tortured him with the second half of his time down range certainly showed her improved mental state and confidence. But would his wife run *to* him, or *away* from him? Would she stand frozen on the tarmac when she saw him coming, fear undulating off her in waves?

Fuck. Get ahold of yourself.

Being away during her recovery had been hell. Eric should have been at his wife's side, reassuring her she was irreplaceable every day, in person. He hadn't even been meant to go on this damn deployment, and he'd cursed the guy he'd been forced to replace every second he was away from his family. As much as Eric loved being a Marine, he no longer felt the need and fulfillment he used to get from his time down range.

Now he was like the other lovesick schmucks, counting down the days until they could be with their families again.

Brendon was crawling all over and had started forming basic words. Eric had experienced it through a fucking screen. He wanted to be the person who caught his son when he took his first shaky steps. He wanted to start planning for the upcoming Daddy Daughter dance too. And he wanted to hold his wife in his arms every night, breathing in the rightness of *them* as she slept sprawled across his body.

It was why he'd left Greer's unit to begin with, and he'd *still* been pulled away at the worst possible moment. About a month after they'd landed, he'd found out there was another guy they could have pulled for the job instead. A single guy without a care in the world, still itching for the mission because he'd yet to find his reason to stay home as much as possible. Eric had been *livid.* It was something he meant to bring up with Greer.

Right now, none of that mattered.

He needed to find—

Carys.

She was standing off to the side in a dress he didn't recognize. The soft breeze fluttered the indigo skirt that fell just below her knees, occasionally lifting it enough to give him a view of her tan thighs. The bodice was a cream color, embellished with simple lace. The necklace he'd given her last Christmas was perfectly displayed against her skin, the pendant laying a hair's width above her ample cleavage.

When she caught sight of him, her face lit up like Time Square, all her emotions prominently on display. She took off running in his direction. Eric dropped his bags in time to sweep her up.

"Eric!"

"I missed you, sweetheart." He squeezed her tight, giving her a little spin before putting her back on her feet. But he didn't let go.

He *couldn't* let go.

Carys trembled against him. He knew she was holding back a sob and didn't want him to see or know. So, he held her. When she was ready to pull back, he relaxed his arms.

"I missed you too," she said, her voice trembling and eyes brimmed with those unshed tears. "God are you really here?" she choked out, placing her hands on either side of his face and staring up at him.

He placed his forehead against hers and locked her eyes with his. "I'm afraid if I take my eyes off you, I'll wake up back in that hell hole," he murmured.

They stood there a long time; he wasn't sure how long exactly. The crowd had thinned substantially by the time he reluctantly forced himself to let her go and grab his gear. Once he'd gathered it all up, he kept his eyes on her all the way back to her SUV.

"Do you want to drive?" Carys asked. "I can if you are tired. I know you like to drive."

He thought about it for a minute as he watched her chew on her lower lip nervously—back to the way she'd gone down on him while they drove to the vineyard the weekend they found out they were pregnant again. Eric decided it was his turn to drive *her* wild while she attempted to keep her focus on the road.

Please let there be light traffic.

"You drive," he said, a slow smile pulling up the side of his mouth. "It's illegal to use my phone while driving."

Carys blushed crimson. She'd done as he asked, then. She was wearing her special panties.

"Ohhhhhhh," she moaned as they came out of a curve. Halfway through, Eric had turned the vibrator on again, loving the way her body jumped in her seat before she threw her head back against the headrest and shuddered with pleasure. "Eric."

"Yes, sweetheart."

"You play dirty."

"Dirty? You mean like the videos you sent me while I was away? Hmmm?"

"Didn't you like them?" she asked hesitantly.

Shit.

"They were fucking torture, and you know it. I'm surprised my tablet screen didn't burn out from the way I played them over and over again," he admitted, happy to see his words change her flush from one of uncertainty and embarrassment back to satisfaction.

Good. I don't want her ashamed of sharing herself with me.

Without taking his eyes off her, he tapped his phone again, initiating a sequence of sensations against her clit he'd pre-programmed. While Carys tried to keep her cool—and failed—he got hard watching her pant and squirm beside him. Eric noticed she was circling her hips, grinding against the device in her panties as she let out another soft moan.

"You like that?" He knew she did. He wanted to hear the arousal in her voice.

"Yes."

Her voice came out as pure desire. Eric's pants became painfully tight as his erection throbbed against the fly. He glanced at the GPS. They still had thirty-eight minutes until they reached their destination.

"Eriiiiic," she moaned loudly. "I'm so sorry for every second I ever tortured you with sex!"

"Liar," he said, laughing as she jumped in reaction to the toy and drifted over the rumble strip for a few seconds. The smile fell off his face at the sound of a police siren pulsing behind them a few times, the lights flashing into the interior of the SUV.

Ooops.

"Eric," Carys said frantically as she pulled over onto the shoulder. *"Eric, turn it off."*

He didn't.

"Oh, God!" She shuddered with relief as the sequence dropped to the lowest continuous pulse. "Better, but not *off,"* she clipped out as she reached for her registration, which he had already pulled from the glove box and was holding out for her.

By the time the officer made his way to her window, she had her license out of her wallet and her window down, anxiously twisting her hands on the steering wheel. "Relax, sweetheart. Being sexy isn't something he can arrest you for."

Carys shot him a glare before turning back to her window as the cop came to a stop.

"Ma'am."

"C-can I help you, officer?"

"Are you aware you were swerving as you came out of the last turn?"

"Oh. Well…"

"It's my fault," Eric said, leaning forward. "I thought I saw an animal on the road and startled her."

She glanced over at him, eyes wide at his coolly delivered lie.

"I hate hitting animals," she mumbled into her lap.

"I understand," the state patrolmen said. "But if it's between you and Chip and Dale, I'd rather it be the chipmunk taken out. You didn't swerve into the oncoming lane, but it is a concern you were swerving on a curve, where you couldn't see oncoming traffic."

He was checking her paperwork as he lectured her, so he didn't see Carys's face turn near purple with embarrassment. Eric was having a hell of a time fighting his grin, but he was managing. The officer turned back with Carys's ID and papers, and Eric caught a glimpse of his nametag.

"You wouldn't happen to be the Officer Fuentes I hear Enzo Ramirez talk about, are you?" he asked.

The officer leaned down a little farther, taking Eric in fully. "Ramirez is a good guy. Damn fine paramedic."

"I knew it! His cousin and I got back today from the same sand box."

"Nice. That means there will be a cookout soon," Fuentes said, relaxing a bit.

"Zeke and Enzo love their cookouts," Eric confirmed with a nod.

"All right, I'm going to give you a warning. Drive safe and slow down instead of swerving next time. I don't want to have to tell Ramirez he needs to come scrape a friend off the pavement."

"Yes, sir," Carys said. "Thank you."

As soon as he was back in his car, Carys turned to Eric and sucker punched him in the shoulder. *"You!"*

"It's on low, sweetheart," he said, throwing his hands up in innocent surrender.

Carys scowled at him, but he could see the humor and relief she was trying to hide behind it. "You're going to hell for that. You just *perjured* yourself!"

"You want me to walk back there and tell him you actually swerved because you were fighting off an orgasm?"

"No!"

He shrugged, his face beginning to hurt from how hard he was smiling. "Better get back on the road, sweetheart. You got about ninety seconds before the sequence changes again. Might want to put some distance between us and Fuentes back there."

"I can't believe you used an *acquaintance* like that, either!" she huffed, but she was already heeding his advice to get back on the road. "You barely know Enzo."

The rest of the drive was smooth sailing…for Eric. Okay, it was uncomfortable, given the steel bar straining in his pants, but completely worth it to watch Carys's eyes dilate until her irises nearly disappeared as she fought the sensations he ruthlessly inflicted on her.

"Five more minutes, sweetheart," he crooned. "Then I'll put you out of your misery."

He'd have to update his review on this product. It had been nearly two hours, and the battery was still going strong.

Twelve out of ten.

Every now and then, he'd pause it and give her a break. It never lasted long, and the way her moans filled the SUV the second he turned it back on was heavenly torment. When they arrived, he watched as she used her phone to check in, her hands shaking. As amusing as it had been watching her not lose it when they'd been pulled over, Carys was about to explode now, and he didn't want it happening in front of the desk staff.

She parked, and Eric grabbed the bags before coming around and helping her out of the driver seat on shaky legs. He'd turned off the vibrator as she'd pulled into the parking lot, but he knew she was likely still pulsing hard without it on, not to mention she still had the pressure of it against her sex. Wordlessly, she held up her phone so he could see their room number.

"Let's get you up to the suite," he said roughly, his voice as colored with arousal as her entire aura was right now.

They met blessedly few people along their way. Carys waved her phone in front of their door as a digital key, and they were in. He dropped the bags and picked her up, carrying her bridal style to the bed.

He set her down on the edge, kneeling before her. He flipped up her dress, groaning at the sight and smell of her drenched panties and slick thighs. "Lift," he commanded softly, pulling down her panties soon as she did.

"Eric," she whimpered.

"You're so perfect, Carys," he said, looking up into her flushed face. "How do you want to come?"

"Wh-what do you want?"

"I want to watch you come undone, and then I want to fuck you senseless."

With her eyes still locked on his, she reached down with one hand and stroked herself once, twice, three times…he watched as she fell apart in front of him. She was the most beautifully erotic homecoming gift.

Chapter Forty-Eight

CARYS

They'd taken Vinny up on her offer after all. Not only did Eric have jet lag to contend with, neither was ready to let the other go. As he readjusted to the Pacific time zone, they settled back into their marriage.

Eric worshipped Carys every moment he wasn't sleeping or eating. He kissed all the scars across her body while telling her how beautiful she was to him, and always would be. Sometimes they used the toys he'd asked her to pack, but more often than not, they did as they had gravitated toward from the beginning.

It was still different. Without her depression front and center, Carys felt connected and fulfilled by her husband's touch again, and if she needed a little something more on occasion, they would get more creative. Eric seemed to take it as a new challenge he was hell bent on winning, instead of seeing Carys as defective.

She knew better than to doubt the caliber of man she'd fallen for, and that he'd never find her lacking. Until she was in his arms again, her legs wrapped around him while he made love to her, she honestly hadn't realized how deeply the fear he'd reject her now had taken root.

On the second day, he'd asked her to show him what she'd learned about adoption and foster parenting. With nervous anticipation, Carys had pulled out her laptop and opened all the tabs she'd saved covering the process for both in the state of California. It would take time and money, but they had both. His current position would keep them in Oceanside another three years, and they were excellent savers.

By the time they snuck up on the kids at home, all Carys's doubts had melted away. Eric had pampered her for four days and nights. They had both desperately needed the time together. Now, they needed to be with their children.

"Loving the hitch in your walk," Vinny whispered loudly to Carys as Eric spun Maya around.

"You did say *one of us* ought to get laid," she retorted with a smirk. Vinny wiggled her eyebrows in response, a huge smile overtaking her face. "Thank you, for everything. Moving in, sticking around. Giving us extra time to sort ourselves…"

"It was never a matter of *not* being here. You know that. I love you guys."

"All the same. Thanks, Vin."

When Maya and Brendon finally went to bed that night after completely wearing out Eric, the three adults collapsed onto the couch.

"Are the blinds closed?" Vinny asked sleepily.

"I closed them at sundown, why?" Eric asked.

"Pineapples," the girls whispered in tandem before bursting into giggles.

"Oh, for fucks sake," Eric grumbled, but Carys could feel

his body quietly shaking with laughter beside her. "Are you still on about that, sweetheart?"

"There were some pineapple-y things happening all over while you were gone. Now that I know about it, I can't unsee it… But Vinny can give you the replay," she said, sending them both into hysterical giggles—tears streaming down their cheeks—while Eric sat between them on the couch absolutely clueless to the joke.

"I missed this," he admitted, pulling both of them closer, an arm around each of them. "We should have a celebratory cookout soon. Vinny missed the last one."

"I'll miss this one if Ruben is coming," she muttered.

Here we go again. Carys shared a knowing smirk with Eric but kept silent.

"I have an idea. Let's make it tropical themed. We can put up tiki torches and pass out leis. Grass skirts and coconut shells not required but encouraged. And we can have a recipe competition! All recipes have to include pineapple!" Carys chortled.

"This theme wouldn't have anything to do with what you said to Zeke the last time we had a homecoming cookout, would it?" Eric mused. "He'll come without the display."

"Pineapples *everywhere.*"

Eric silenced her loud whisper with a kiss. "You're a menace sometimes."

"Hey!" Vinny cried, elbowing him.

"Owe! Easy. You're a menace *most* of the time. I didn't forget you," he quipped.

They fell into lazy banter before retiring for bed early.

———

"HOW IS HE?" Carys asked as she set Eric's coffee before him at the table. She pulled out the chair beside him and settled in with her own mug.

Eric set down his phone and let out a heavy breath. "He's okay, but his dad is giving him a hard time."

"From what you've said, that's par for the course with Abe."

"It is, but aside from Ruben, there is nobody else there to take care of Abe. Ruben did say he strong armed him into finally drawing up an advanced directive, and they are on their way to the notary now with a durable power of attorney."

"Wow. That's a surprising amount of control for him to give Ruben."

"Abe is not one who would want extraordinary measures taken to prolong his life if it's going to be hell. He's smart enough to know Ruben will never allow it, but with an entire country between them, the medical system will give him all the bells and whistles regardless of what he wants without an advanced directive. The POA *is* a surprise, but it will give Ruben the legal ability to bully people for him when called for." Eric's explanation fell right in line with the image of Ruben's father Carys conjured in her mind when they spoke of him.

"Doesn't he come home tomorrow?"

"Yeah."

"Close call."

"Oh, if I know Abner Holt at all, I'm willing to bet he waited until the last second just to rile Ruben up." Eric's slow smile pulled up as he shook his head.

"Why would he do that?"

"If I had to guess, as punishment."

"For what?" she asked. Eric took a swallow of coffee,

groaning in appreciation. *I missed these moments over coffee,* she thought to herself. Mornings were so much better with him around.

Life was so much better.

"Ruben hasn't been home as much as Abe would prefer. And since Abe doesn't like Carla—"

"Let me guess, the feeling is mutual?"

"Extremely. Because of it, Ruben hasn't been home because Abe likes to go on and on about what makes a great marriage and the dichotomy of real love. Eventually, he takes a hard left down Memory Lane, and Ruben doesn't handle a whole lot of talk about his mother."

"Oh. That's sad."

"Yes and no," Eric said, his tone laced with amusement. "It didn't use to bother him as much."

"Then what changed?"

"He got married. Abner has doubled down since. He and Ruben's mom were one of those opposites attract perfect storm loves—Abe's words. Even when we were in college, he'd go on and on about how what looked good on the surface didn't necessarily work in the real world. *'Your mother and I didn't work at all on paper, boy. But anyone who saw us together realized the paper was wrong. Real love is gritty and full of compromise. There is no room for pride.'* Or something like that." Eric grinned, obviously proud of his impersonation of Abe's deeply Southern drawl.

Carys smiled back at him over the rim of her mug. "It doesn't sound like Ruben got the memo."

"He did, but he misconstrued it until it was so bastardized, he thought he had found it."

"That doesn't sound like the Ruben I know."

"You've only met his confident side," Eric said, sadness flashing through his expression. "I have a theory."

"Go on."

"Ruben saw the way his father fell apart with the loss of his mother. It messed him up pretty bad. I think Ruben is *afraid* to find a love like they had, because he doesn't think he could survive if it ended. To make matters worse, whatever illness took his mother was treatable. There was no reason for her to die so young—which is part of his motivation to be in Georgia right now squaring things away for his father. I'm not sure he fully grieved his mother's passing, and he damn well won't lose his dad if he can prevent it."

Carys's heart swelled painfully. *That actually does sound like Ruben.* "I suppose his insistence to be called *Funcle* makes more sense in that light. There is nothing purer than the love of a child; and Maya adores Ruben."

"Yeah. It's the coward's way into experiencing pure love. But it isn't the same as being *in* love," Eric said softly, cupping Carys's cheek in his warm palm. "And more than anything, I wish he would let himself feel what I have every moment since I laid eyes on you."

Carys turned into his palm, kissing it reverently. "Come on," she said, rising from her seat.

"Where are we going?" He was already on his feet, ready to follow her.

"The shower. A speech like that deserves a reward."

"A reward, huh?"

"Mmhmm. I think you've earned butt things."

Eric laughed huskily behind her as she pulled him toward the stairs. "Who am I to argue…"

"What a loooong shower." Vinny smirked as Eric and Carys came into the kitchen an hour later.

"We couldn't seem to stay clean," Carys said innocently,

giving her best friend doe eyes and a casual shrug. "What brings you down from your tower?"

"Har. I'm not cutting my hair, no matter how many Rapunzel jokes you make.

"I'll have you know; I left the monitors on completely by accident," Vinny continued, taking on the same innocent act Carys had. "Just as I was forced to accept I'm out of coffee, my favorite little prince started giggling. It was kismet, wasn't it, Brendon?" She leaned down and kissed the baby on top of his soft down, though he was too busy slapping his cereal onto the floor instead of eating it to care.

"Ni-nee!" he said, his soft baby voice breaking into distinct syllables as he forced his new skill to fruition. He'd started with what sounded like a chant a few weeks ago, but only recently had gotten his point across succinctly enough for them to realize it was his first word.

"Oh, hell," Eric muttered. "She's too old for you, buddy."

Vinny pealed with laughter. "That's my sweet prince! That's right, I'm your Ni-nee!"

"You're certainly acting like a *ninny,*" Carys mused.

"Spoil sport." Vinny threw Carys a playful scowl before turning back to Brendon, all smiles. "Vs are hard, buddy. You are doing a great job! Mama is just jealous."

Truth.

"It's better than Maya's *'Fuck Uben'* phase," Eric said beside her. "That got us some dirty looks in public."

Carys threw her head back and laughed. "It's a lot funnier in hindsight."

Chapter Forty-Nine

CARYS

"Sweetheart, come here!"

Eric's command had Carys padding in from the kitchen to the front window where he stood without hesitation. She still had the creamer in her hand, though she'd left her mug of coffee on the counter in her haste.

"What's wrong?"

"Look," he said, gesturing out the window. "Do you know whose truck is in Ruben's driveway?"

Carys looked up through the sheers, taking in the scene across the street. A perfectly shiny, jacked up black truck was parked *in the driveway*—not even on the street—like the owner was comfortable enough being there to stake a claim off the curb. Even from across the street, the black beast screamed Road Princess and Little Penis Syndrome.

"No. I've never seen it before."

"Oh, shit." Eric's voice pitched low, an ominous foreteller of what was to come.

"Ohhh…" Carys peeked farther down the street, her eyes going wide, as an Uber pulled up and Ruben climb out of the backseat. She was suddenly glad it was a Thursday morning, because whatever was about to happen would likely be embarrassing. Most of the neighbors had left for work some time ago given it was a little after eight in the morning.

"What are you going to do?" she asked soberly.

"Nothing. Whatever is happening in his home, Ruben has to face it."

He was right, but Carys didn't have to like it. Ruben was family to them, and it felt wrong to stand here watching. "But—"

"If it gets ugly, I'll step in," he reassured her. "But I'm not getting in the middle of whatever this is."

They watched as Ruben hitched up all his deployment gear and strode toward his front door with determined strides. He disappeared inside, the closing of the front door creating unease within Carys. *What did he find inside? That's not exactly an HVAC service van…*

The front door flew open, an exceptionally average man with Carrot Top orange hair flying out completely naked. From behind him, Ruben barreled forth, throwing the man's belongings at him. Jeans, shoes, cell phone, car keys—they all flew with precision directly at the stranger's backside, the last catching him in the temple when he stupidly turned back toward the house as he stumbled.

"Good aim." Eric snickered. "Guess all those years of baseball *did* stay with him."

Ruben was saying something and pointing to the truck, his murderous gaze locked on the stranger, whose pasty white skin visibly peaked scarlet from their vantage. Carrot awkwardly picked up his belongings off the front walk, comically fumbling his keys several times before managing to unlock the gawdy monstrosity, and then peeled out of the driveway as fast as he could.

Ruben paced the walkway with his phone in hand for a

minute, tapping away at the screen before sliding it into his back pocket. He stood with his hands on his hips and his eyes closed, jaw ticking away. Carys imagined he was counting down from ten before he went back inside, a thought he confirmed when he did just that.

They stood at the window, staring at Ruben's open front door, feet frozen to the floor same as their eyes were locked onto the dark opening. She didn't know how much time passed in tense stillness before Ruben reemerged with a small suitcase in hand and Carla by her wrist. He was dragging her along, her feet backpedaling uselessly. She was no match for his physical strength, much less the calm rage bunching every muscle in Ruben's body.

Carla was dressed in a thin lace teddy, leaving very little to the imagination, a satin kimono over the top flapping in the breeze. On her feet she wore heeled slippers ala Erica Kane from an old soap opera Carys remembered her mother obsessing over when she was a girl.

Fitting, given she's starring in a soap opera in real time.

They could faintly hear the sound of Ruben and Carla's raised voices through the window, causing Carys to momentarily regret the window upgrade they'd done last spring. *What are they saying? It's too muffled to make out.*

Whatever was happening, Carys suspected it was the most passion to have ever existed between the two. Ruben waved his arms around, his body coiled to strike, while Carla did her best to look innocent and demure. The morning sun glinted off the wet streaks flowing down her face. She leaned forward to take a knee, but Ruben yanked her back up before she managed to crease the tops of her ridiculous slippers with the action.

"Well played," Eric said beside her. "Don't let her get on her knees like she's obviously been doing for other men."

It hit Carys then, the weight of what was *truly* happening. Eric had known Carla as long as Ruben had. If he suggested she was a cheating piece of trash, she was. While it wasn't a new thought to come out of her husband's mouth, seeing the evidence before her—the consequence of Carla's deceit coming to fruition before them—was so much more than secondhand suspicions.

Poor Ruben.

Carla continued to beg and blubber, throwing herself at Ruben more than once. He kept her at arm's length best he could, touching her as little as possible in the process. Eventually Carla's pleading turned to anger. Ruben stood stiff as a statue, arms crossed stubbornly over his chest, while she screamed insults at him, her body language wailing as much as the hateful glare she gave him while she bounced around in her slippers like an annoying, yippy little designer dog.

The kind with a little bow on its head, trying to disguise what a waste of oxygen and space it was with frills. That was Carla. A complete waste.

"Holy shit!" Carys stared slack jawed as a blur of platinum hair and dirty denim flew across the street. "What is Vinny *doing?"*

"About the only thing she dislikes more than Ruben is Carla," Eric pointed out. "And they *are* being loud."

"But why would she care? She's dressed like she was working in the garage."

If hatred had poured off Carla while she spewed her venom at an unyielding Ruben, she stared at Vinny with a pure abhorrence pulled straight from her hell bound soul.

And Vinny didn't flinch.

In fact, Vinny was in Carla's face.

Ruben's rage had been replaced with shock and disbelief; his lips parted as he stared at a wild haired, grease-streaked

Lavender while she gave Carla the long overdue verbal lashing everyone else who was Team Ruben had longed to deliver. Except everyone else would have been *expected*. Vinny on the other hand—she claimed to loathe Ruben. Yet here she was, meticulously shutting down Carla every time she tried to open her mouth.

A car pulled up—another Uber, answering the query *what was Ruben doing on his phone before he went back inside*—and Ruben broke away from where Vinny was now in a frosty staring contest with Carla to talk to the driver and load her small suitcase into the trunk. He waved his wife over, breaking the standoff. Vinny turned, arms crossed and spine erect, mean mugging Carla as she silently got into the car and allowed it to convey her to wherever Ruben had ordered her away to.

No sooner had the car disappeared down the block, Vinny was up in Ruben's face, poking her finger into his chest as she fumed. He began to argue back, and she shut him down as quickly as she had Carla minutes before. Ruben took a step back in silent acquiescence, his lips moving slowly.

Vinny barked a response, spun on her heel, and disappeared back across the street and down her driveway. Ruben stood there watching, his eyes locked ahead on who knew what. Eventually he turned and slowly walked back into his house, shutting the door behind him.

Carys and Eric continued to stare blankly ahead, processing what they'd witnessed.

Obviously, Carla was gone.

But what was with Vinny? Why would she care? She'd had nothing but contempt toward either of them, yet she'd run out there like her ass was on fire and verbally napalmed Carla into submission. Until she'd turned on Ruben, Carys had felt a soap bubble of hope rise in her chest that maybe she didn't dislike him so vehemently after all.

Carys had seen the look on Vinny's face when she recrossed the road and disappeared again. That was not Vinny's *no trouble, happy to help a friend* look. It was more her *cross me and I'll take you out without blinking* look.

"Wow," Eric said behind her, breaking Carys out of her contemplation.

"Yeah." She looked down into her hand at the bottle of coffee creamer. "Guess I should have brought popcorn out instead."

———

Eric

"He didn't say *anything?* It's been over a week," Carys said, her voice heavily saturated with concern.

"The second you bring her up, Ruben shuts down. He won't talk to anyone about it."

Not for lack of trying. Eric had taken every opportunity he could the past ten days to reassure Ruben he wasn't alone, and Eric had his six. The more he tried, the more Ruben clammed up.

Today had been their cookout, and despite all her muttering and sarcasm, Vinny *had* attended—though she'd managed to ensure there were at least twenty feet between her and Ruben the entire party. She'd been pleasant enough, socializing with Marcy and Hailey mostly. Lexi hadn't been able to attend, but to everyone's surprise, Bella showed up with Javier and the kids.

Thankfully Eric and Ruben had been able to finish the new play structure in the back yard during their reintegration leave this week, or they would have had a mutiny of bored tots on their hands. Ruben had mostly been his usual self. Eric knew him well enough to notice he'd been carefully clocking Vinny's whereabouts the entire time in his own effort to maintain a safe distance.

"I still don't know how two people who are normally so relaxed and fun could learn to hate each other so rapidly without just cause," he said.

"Well, there *is* a cause," Carys mused. "We just don't know it. Vinny doesn't hate easily. Still waters tend to run the deepest."

"Are you suggesting Vinny is *still?*"

"Her emotions are. You only see them because you wowed her from the beginning. Most people take a long time to earn the kind of affection you've always had from her. The music industry taught her to be cautious from a young age."

"I adore Vinny. She's like a sister to me; more so than my *actual* sisters."

"Not everyone feels that way."

"I don't see why not."

"Again, most people have to work hard to earn her love and openness. Vin saw the way you loved me, and because *she* loves me, you were in." Carys shrugged. "I can't explain it better. If you'd been less than doting when we reunited, or been a prick about Maya, she would have loathed you for all eternity. It goes both ways."

Carys's face drew in with thought, her lower lip getting a gnashing between her teeth as she stewed. After a minute, Eric couldn't take it anymore.

"What is it? I lost you there."

"Hmm? Oh." She smiled at him sweetly. "Nothing really. Just a thought—a hypothesis."

"Care to share?"

"Nope. But if I'm right, it will be an interesting process to watch unfold."

Eric stripped down and pulled back the covers on their bed, holding it up for Carys to join him. When she was cuddled up against him, he sunk into the peace she brought with her.

"I love you, sweetheart."

"I love you too."

"I mean it, Carys. You're everything to me. I will never take for granted the tenacity it's taken you to overcome so much. Our life together is still fresh in many ways, but through all the blows, I've never once had to worry I'd lose you."

Her hand slid across his abdomen, causing his muscles to involuntarily flex.

"I can't say the feeling is mutual. Every time you walk out the door, I worry you won't come back. Especially when they send you to places I'm not allowed to know of. But I've never doubted for a second this isn't worth it."

He rolled into her, gripping her hip and pulling her into his arousal. Eric's voice came out heavy with lust. "How shall I reward you for staying, sweetheart?"

She bit her lip playfully, glancing up at him through her thick lashes, the moonlight streaming in from the open window revealing her perfection.

"Slowly. *Please.*"

Three months later…

"Finally!" Vinny squealed as Bella came in with Marcy. "Can't start the blender without you! And don't worry, Bella. We didn't put tequila in everything."

"Yeah, this chonk doesn't need it," Lexi quipped, looking down at the baby she was nursing. Juan had finally gotten his boy, and the little guy was as stubborn as Maya had been. "No pumping and dumping for me. Rico refuses to take a bottle." She said it with a mixture of love and sarcasm.

Bella smiled. "That's great. We can both remember how weird everyone else gets together." She was getting close to her due date, and Carys was glad she'd stuck it out with her husband. You'd never guess she'd almost walked away now with how far they had come.

With the help of their group, they had kept Bella involved via text during the last deployment, and once Javier got back, they had immediately entered marriage counseling. Bella admitted she'd let her mother get to her but had never liked the idea of leaving Javi. The pregnancy had messed with her head, and her mother had taken advantage of Bella at her weakest. They hadn't planned for more than two kids, but Bella and Javi were ready now.

Likewise, Eric and Carys had finished all the paperwork to adopt out of the foster system. Marcy had confessed earlier in the week she and Mike were considering another baby too. Good things obviously came in threes, given all but Hailey and Sam were working on a third kiddo. With Vinny leaving for Nashville soon, it was perfect timing to gather the group for an evening in to celebrate.

Deployment had been hard. Reintegration had been harder. Tonight was about coming out the other end with intact families. It came as no shock to Carys they had all adopted Vinny, though she suspected her bestie was secretly surprised on the inside. She wasn't a military wife or girl-friend and had made it clear more than once she believed a traveling musician and a service member was a recipe for disaster.

Since Vinny had made her sinful Better Than Sex Cake again, nobody bothered pointing out they all saw the signs of inevitability between Vinny and a certain Marine across the street, who was currently hosting all the fathers and children so the women could relax with ease. Vinny could swear she hated Ruben all she wanted. The way they tried to hide from each other while also stealing glances anytime they were in proximity of each other said otherwise.

Carys and Eric had made a bet, who would crack first. The end result would please them both, so it was more about *how* they came together than *if.* It probably seemed presump-tuous from the outside, but Carys didn't think so. She knew Vinny, and Eric knew Ruben. Now if the two of them would get over their stupid hurdles and get to know each other, the Blackwoods would be most appreciative.

They were spread out in Carys's living room tonight,

snacks all over the place. She'd purchased a giant container of rainbow gold fish for the party mix she'd made and didn't feel the least bit guilty about keeping it from the kids. Vinny's custom playlist for the evening was on in the background. The blenders were singing a merry little mostly tequila laced tune in the kitchen.

Life was good.

Once they cut into the cake, things turned quickly.

"Holy shit," Bella moaned. "I think this baby just became a twin. This cake is the most orgasmic thing I've put in my mouth."

The rest of them tittered around mouthfuls of decadence. "Vinny popped Bella's cake cherry," Hailey mused. "Welcome to the den of desires, lady."

"I'll say," she replied, stuffing another bite in her mouth.

"We need a game!" Vinny announced.

"I'm not playing any more cards," Carys cut in. "Ruben is killing me." Literally. He was the master of Spades, and while Carys didn't consider herself a sore loser, an occasional win was good for morale.

Vinny wrinkled her nose. "Eeew. No. We need a *drinking* game. Motherhood made you boring, you know that?"

"According to you, I was never that fun to begin with," she retorted playfully. "We can't all be the wild child. Who would you look wild next to if I wasn't there dragging my heels? You're welcome."

Marcy laughed. "Jeez. No more doubling the tequila, Carys. You're getting bold, and it's early yet."

Probably wise, Carys thought. *I don't need a hangover tomorrow.*

"Okay, a drinking game! We'll let our resident *wild child* decide. Vinny?" Hailey said.

She put a finger over her lips in mock contemplation.

"Something to honor what we are celebrating," she said slowly. "How about a rousing game of *Things People Say To Military Spouses,*" she chirped.

"Here, here!" Marcy said with a raise of her glass. Everyone else lifted their glasses in chorus. "Rules?"

"We take turns saying something stupid, things we've seen or heard, and if someone else has heard it, they drink. Same sort of idea as *Never Have I Ever,* but all in the affirmative. Dish, ladies! Carys is hosting, so she has to go first!"

"Gee, thanks," she said dryly. "Let me think. Oh! When Maya was in the NICU with RSV, I heard one of the cleaning staff mutter the classic*, 'you knew what you signed up for.'"*

An echo of groans filled the room before everyone took a sip. Carys elbowed Hailey to her left.

"Oh, in a circle? Okay. How about, *'A post deployment baby? Are you sure you didn't cheat?'"*

Marcy nearly growled before taking her sip. It was her turn next. "Yeah, yours goes well with, *'all military members cheat on deployment. It's just a fact,'"* she said with syrupy sweet sarcasm.

"You're making me wish I had tequila with that one," Bella said. "It's one of my mother's favorites."

Carys wasn't surprised they all took a drink on that one, including Vinny. She'd overheard it while some old bitty was running her mouth at Carys in the grocer one day when Maya was still a baby.

"My turn," Vinny said. *"'You have it easy,'* comes to mind." Everyone took a drink. "Man, people are assholes," she added with a snort.

"That they are," Marcy added.

"I'm rather fond of, *'I know just how you feel! My husband had a two week business trip last year.'* In what world is two weeks a few states away the same as months in an undisclosed location where a war is actively happening?" Lexi said with a hint of malice. It sounded like she'd heard that one a few times, if Carys was to guess.

"*'Don't you think it's selfish having kids with a man who is gone too much to be a real father?'* That one stings the most for me," Bella said. "Javi is an amazing father. I can't imagine raising a family with anyone else."

"Is that another bullet from your mother's arsenal?" Hailey asked.

Bella bobbed her head around. "Yes and no. My whole family likes that one. Especially now," she said, placing her hand on her burgeoning belly. "We finally gave in, by the way. It's a girl."

They all hooted and cheered.

"The opposite of us," Lexi said. "We have two girls and a boy; you have two boys and now a girl."

"We're so excited. Javi picked three different coming home outfits after we finally opened the gender envelope. He said even *little* ladies need options," Bella said, rolling her eyes. "So much for a secret gender. He wore me down."

"Do you have any names in mind?" Vinny asked.

I can't believe she thinks she won't be a mother these days. Carys knew Vinny loved kids and had always wanted a family. The look on her face as she asked Bella her question said it all.

"We do, but neither of the boys were set in stone until they came. It's between us until she arrives," Bella said.

"That's wise," Marcy said. "When we picked Mason's name, half Mike's family were beyond shitty about it. *'Isn't that way too common?' 'Last names as first names are confusing.' 'Don't you think you should get away from M names?'*" she mimicked. "I thought Mike would blow a head gasket. We didn't say anything when we had Miles. And it's not like we all have M names on purpose. Some things just are."

"What is with that, anyway?" Vinny piped up. "It's like the second Carys was pregnant, everyone had an opinion on her diet and sleep habits and what she *had* to have to be a good mom. Even after she and Eric married, people would stop her it the store to touch her and ask questions or give unsolicited advice."

"Yeah, and when you were there I had to drag you off while apologizing profusely," Carys said with a laugh.

"Well," Vinny said, crossing her arms defiantly. "They were being *rude.*"

"They were," Carys agreed. "Before I graduated was the worst. Everyone had those pity eyes out, like the worst possible thing that could happen to me was being a single mother."

"How many of them kept in touch?" Hailey asked.

"None of them. I was excited about getting married, and nobody so much as wished me well. I would have known they were full of shit and thought my marriage was one of convenience, but it would have been *something,*" Carys said. "People who had been so supportive of my education disappeared the second I finished my degree. It was disappointing, but better than a bunch of fake friends."

"I'll drink to that!" Marcy cheered, holding her glass out to clink. "To *real* friendship."

"To real friendship!" they echoed.

They refilled their glasses before continuing with their game.

"You have such great health benefits! And housing!"

"It must be nice to move and travel so often."

"You're so strong! I couldn't do it."

"I bet you save a *ton* with military discounts."

After a few more rounds, they had degraded to drunkenly shouting out the worst of the worst while laughing. Even sober, Bella and Lexi were wheezing through their laughter with the others.

"Oh, man. What do you think the guys are doing?" Hailey asked somewhere around midnight.

"Playing Spades," Carys and Vinny deadpanned together.

"Assuming they haven't hogtied Ruben and stuffed him in the pantry by now," Carys added. "Who knows, they may have moved on to action films and flex."

Vinny snorted. "Aren't they sober?"

"That doesn't mean they aren't being juvenile fools," Marcy countered.

"I bet Juan passed out early with the girls," Lexi said. "He's the reason we need a king sized bed. They come in all the time asking to cuddle in the middle of the night. He's lucky we had enough privacy to *make* Enrico." She glanced over to the corner where baby Rico was sleeping in a portable basinet Carys had pulled out for him.

Carys stood unsteadily, holding the table until she found her land legs. *Woah. Yeah. We did not need to double the tequila.* "Let's find out," she said, walking unsteadily toward the window. She parted the curtains and looked out across the street. The other's joined her.

"It's completely dark over there," Hailey murmured, as if she'd wake the neighborhood if she spoke up.

"Yeah. Bunch of suckers," Vinny teased.

"No," Bella said softly. "A bunch of amazing fathers."

"And one godfather," Carys tacked on, thinking of Ruben. He was probably curled up with Maya. That girl adored him.

"Okay," Vinny conceded. "Last toast, and then we move on to passing out over chick flicks."

They all progressed back to their places in the living room, taking up their glasses.

"To the loyal men who brought us all together. May they stay safe and always make it home," she said.

"May they see their children have children," Bella added.

"And find support and understanding with each other, the way we have," Marcy said, smiling around their circle with glassy eyes.

"To standing firm in their dedication," Hailey offered.

"And with their wives, who will always have *their* six," Lexi said fiercely.

Carys thought for a moment. "For believing our families are strong enough without them, even when *we* know our strength comes from their love."

"To the men!"

They tossed back the dredges of their cups before Vinny called out, "Right! Enough of that. Let's watch *How To Lose a Guy in 10 Days!*"

Best girl's night ever.

————

Thank you for reading one of my stories. Find out what happens next in the Devoted Brothers series! Ruben and Vinny's story is up next, in *Ruben.* If you liked *Eric,* please consider writing a review on Amazon, or wherever you like to review. Even a few short words help small authors find our way to more readers.

Keep in touch! You can find me online, or send an email to sian@sianuptonbooks.com.

Facebook: Siân Upton *and* Siân Upton Reader Group
Facebook Page: Siân Upton Books
Instagram & Threads: @sianuptonauthor
Pinterest: @sianuptonbooks
Bookbub: Siân Upton

You can also join my newsletter and receive a **FREE** bonus novella by going to my website:
https://www.sianuptonbooks.com/
Or scan the QR code below!

Also by Siân Upton

Taste of Love **series**

Salty

Bitter

Sweet

Sour

There Was Only You (A Salty Prequel Novella)

Devoted Brothers **series**

Eric

Ruben

Zeke

Acknowledgments

Here we are, the end of another book. I think I'll say simply, write what you know…and I know enough to brave a military series because of my military family. Some of you are blood. Others, adopted along the way.

You shaped this story and the series to come. Every shared laugh, tear, crisis, redemption. They add up. The outrageous things posted on spouse and community pages. The evenings around a coffee table full of snacks where we checked in with one another and let out our situationally unique frustrations.

All the times we settled for a video call because Covid made it impossible to connect in person.

Eric, and the entire Devoted Brothers series, was inspired by the amazing people I have met as a spouse, and the misadventures we bonded over, often inspiring some of the best adventures of my life. Some of us are lucky enough to have family who can or will drop everything when we need them. I have found that is not the case for most of us, which makes our forged bonds all the more precious.

We thrive together or we fail together.

What a privilege it has been to do both with you.

Thank you for inspiring me. I hope my spin on a sometimes wild but always heartfelt tale about what it means to be a military family brings you joy and laughter, and perhaps a bit of validation.